DELL SHANNON
author of *The Scalpel and the Sword*

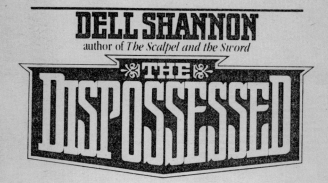

A Critic's Choice paperback
from Lorevan Publishing, Inc.
New York, New York

Reprinted by arrangement with William Morrow & Company, Inc.

ISBN: 1-55547-293-1

First Critic's Choice edition: 1989

From LOREVAN PUBLISHING, INC.

Critic's Choice Paperbacks
31 E. 28th St.
New York, New York 10016

Manufactured in the United States of America

*History is past politics; and politics is
present history.*

—E. A. FREEMAN
Methods of Historical Study

The four provinces of Ireland

ULSTER
Connacht
Leinster
Munster

Tory I.
Donegal (Tyrconnell)
Londonderry
Antrim
Tyrone
Fermanagh
Armagh
Down
Donegal Bay
Monaghan
Sligo
Leitrim
Clew Bay
MAYO
Ros-common
Cavan
Louth
Longford
Connemara
GALWAY
West-meath
Meath
Dublin
Galway
Kings
Kildare
Queens
Aran I.
CLARE
Wicklow
Shannon
Tipperary
Wexford
Limerick
Waterford
Scariff I.
KERRY
CORK

Map showing area of Ireland allotted to the "Transplanters." The county of Sligo, in original area granted and within Connacht, was later reclaimed. The remainder of Ireland theoretically divided into areas reserved only for (A) soldiers, (B) adventurers, and (C) government-retained land. This map shows original settlement area, circa 1653.

Part
One

"Necessity is the last and strongest weapon."
—PROVERB

1

IN THE DARK lifted only a little by the star-reflection of a moonless night, the Atlantic looked very cold and very black and lonely. And here on the narrow strip of rough beach, they felt very lonely themselves, two desperate men alone in the dark.

Roy Donlevy put a hand to his kilt-buckle. "Damn, it's cold," he muttered. "A sea kicking up, Fergal. Will we make it, five miles of it?"

Fergal O'Breslin was stripping off his clothes for the third time tonight. "You might live another week if you wait nice and dry for the garrison to fall and the Parliament men to find you. Get on, Roy."

"Little choice," agreed Donlevy. They had dressed again after their second swim, and their cautious haste across the little isle of Inisheer had set the blood flowing again, wet as they were; with the icy March wind on them, here on an exposed Atlantic coast, it set the teeth chattering even to think of the water waiting.

Not many folk lived on these west isles of Aran, best times. They were not big islands where a man might lose himself; and this night they held too many English Parliament soldiers for comfort, reinforcements at last come up to take the garrison at Kilronan on Inishmore, that held one of the last handfuls of Federation men holding out, even after the treaty signed last summer. They had

had no news in four months; they might be the last garrison to. hold out in Ireland. And they would not hold long now. They'd been supplied by the fisherfolk to now, but that could not last, with the size of the occupying English force as it must be through Ireland.

"In fact, I'm surprised," said Donlevy, rolling his clothes in a bundle, "we're not leading a procession in last-minute escape."

"And so we likely are, an hour or a day behind us. Hold your loose tongue and come along." Fergal had no taste for badinage at the moment—not with his uncle back there in the garrison and likely dead by tomorrow or next week, and the long road before him, and God knew what at the end of it. He stepped down to the water and the cold of it hit him like a blow; he suppressed a gasp. "Roy," he said, "do you feel you can make it? You're not as strong a swimmer as myself."

"I am still with you." They had slid away off Inishmore seven hours ago, by first dusk, and swum round the island, and made the mile swim in the dark to the middle island of Inishmaan; got safe across that island, and swum a harder, longer mile and a half on to Inisheer, past the dark rocks jutting up out of the sea, and they had walked across the rough, rocky, barren land to here. Out there across five, maybe six miles of deep, surging, fast-running channel sea, there lay the mainland coast of Clare—and a chance for life.

"If either of us weakens," said Fergal, "the other must go on. No sense dying for nothing together when one could get off. There's time—it can't be much past midnight—and the tide is running. If you weaken, turn and float for a bit to rest. If we're separated, which is likely, don't hang about the shore hunting."

"I've some sense," said Donlevy mildly. "Where could we arrange to meet?"

"We'll need to give Galway city a wide berth, but no sense going north straight up through Roscommon and Leitrim. They're less likely, please God, to have patrols out in wilder territory along the coast. And, please God, the tide will take us above the Parliament camp opposite us here. Get round Galway and go west, by way of Mayo and Sligo. Listen, boy. If we're separated, make up the River Clare to bypass Tuam. There's one place there they wouldn't be, nor any Irishman either, maybe to take note and suspect—one place we could lie and wait a day or two. Knock-magh."

"Knockmagh—Christ, then," said Donlevy, only half-humorous. "What to choose between the hordes of the Danaan-Sidhe and Parliament men? Do I believe in the Sidhe, these powerful fairy-folk?—of course not, no sensible Christian man does—but all the same, there are places I'd rather spend a night than on top of the hill belonging to the King of the Sidhe."

"For Christ's love!" said Fergal. "That is the place. Give our-selves a week to get there—call it sixty miles, roundabout as we'll need to go. If we separate, I'll meet you on Knockmagh a week today. Don't wait above a full day there."

"Agreed," said Donlevy. "If we don't meet, Fergal, you will carry my love to Shevaun and look to our boy."

"I will do that. And if I drop out by the way, you will carry the news to the family, that the clan will need to elect a new chief."

"I daresay we are making excuses to put off getting to it," remarked Donlevy.

"Very likely." Fergal slung his bundle of clothes round his shoulders by his belt, and stepped out to the strong cold surge of water round his thighs. "I'll see you on shore or at Knockmagh in a week, and God's luck with you, Roy." He scarcely heard Don-levy's wish for luck; the tide pulled at him, and the surf on rocks was loud. He let himself down to deep water and began to swim steadily, not trying for speed, only keeping his direction as best he could. The coast of Clare lay almost due east, but he did not care within reason where he came ashore, so it wasn't right up in Galway Bay. There was a Parliament camp somewhere on the shore over there, waiting cat at mousehole for the defenders to give up the Arans and run. The tide ran like a race in this narrow channel, a roar and a white thunder, running strong northeast, and he knew he might be carried north from the islands. That did not matter, it was all to the good, so he could make headway east across the tide toward land.

He had been nervous about this swim, but now he was at it—and afterward—it was a curious interval of peace between times of stress and fear and danger. His responsibility was simple; his arms and legs moved automatically, without conscious direction; and his mind was quite free, for the first and last time in a long while. Time slipped away from him too. For an unspecified time he heard Donlevy nearby, and then the tide separated them. It was either eternity or a few heartbeats he had been in the cold water, swimming cross-tide; he did not know or care.

He had time for some queer, dreamlike thoughts as he swam. One of them was that if there had not been a queen named Elizabeth on England's throne up to half a century ago, likely this Fergal O'Breslin would not be here at all, out in deep water on the nighttide—for another Fergal O'Breslin would not, probably, have been a swimmer—or for that matter an O'Breslin. For Fergal O'Breslin's great-grandsire had been one Rory McGuinness of Antrim, not an unimportant man either, once personal guard to the great prince Shane O'Neill, and given the Antrim land for service. But with Hugh Gavelock O'Neill and the O'Donnells broken at Kinsale, fifty years ago, and fled to Spain, and the power of the Scot MacDonnells broken in Antrim, Elizabeth's English came into Ulster—east and west of the Bann they came, confiscating land and driving out the legal owners or holding them as tenant-farmers. The sons of McGuinness left alive went into exile with the chiefs of Ulster, but his youngest daughter Etain was wed to one of the O'Donnells of Tyrconnell; and her daughter Ethne was wed later to an O'Breslin of the chief's line. So Fergal O'Breslin did not grow up inland, in fertile Antrim or Tyrone, but along the Bay of Donegal, to be familiar with the fishers and their boats and the cold deep North Atlantic.

The house by Lough Eask, and his mother's anxious eyes, and the clatter of horses in the courtyard—that morning they rode away—three and a half years ago . . . The sun so bright on blue water.

And he had time, there, drifting and swimming, to worry. They had defended their retreat west, last April to November, before Henry Cromwell's Parliament men, even as the few weak leaders left to the Irish Royalists—after the O'Neills were gone, Eoghan Ruadh by death and that younger Hugh by defeat and flight—were making surrender-treaty. Under McGeraghty and O'Connor they had held the garrisons of Clare, and been driven back and back, to end in siege on the Arans—a siege that could have only one end, and it soon to come. McGeraghty had seen that clear—a hard man of common sense, that old chief.

It passed through Fergal's mind slow and sharp again, the old chief speaking straight to the point, almost emotionless. "We cannot last much longer, and there is less than sense in not making a gamble for freedom—whatever freedom may be left outside, for native Irish. But there is another thing to think of too—"

And Cathal O'Breslin saying, "How many of us could get off, boats or no? If that message got through from O'Fallon was right, the war ended nine months back, official, and only remote forts are holding out, like ourselves. The Parliament will have troops to spare to send after us—these reinforcements coming in now—"

"I am ahead of you, Cathal," McGeraghty had said. "Maybe it is the death-premonition on me that makes me see clear. It comes to me that for what has happened this hundred years, and what might come in the next hundred years, we cannot any of us think for ourselves as individual men—we will need to think for our race and our nation, to preserve them alive as we can. Remember what they did at Drogheda and Wicklow and Wexford, at New Ross and through Meath, a hundred other places. The bloodlust is on them, and they would kill us to a man."

"To women and infants!" put in O'Connor with soft venom. "I was at Drogheda. I know it. And we know what they have done since."

McGeraghty said tiredly, "We cannot know what destruction they will make after this surrender, what punishments they will invent. They have killed enough of us as it is, but they will not be satisfied. We must above all think and act for our country and people as a unit, not like savages man for man. And one importance, it is the young men. We must keep the young men alive to carry on the breed and the fight. I do not know how they may get out, from the rest of us here—but those are my orders. The young men are all free to go, as they may, in honor—and the rest of us must hold the garrison until they are away, if possible."

It was like a miniature painting, seen in the mind's eye: that gray old badger of the chief McGeraghty, the men about him talking sharp and quick there in the council-room of the fortress—O'Connor, and O'Brien, and Rijordan, and Cathal O'Breslin—with his nephew behind him maybe only because he happened to be chief of the clan, if not as experienced in war at only twenty-three. And O'Brien with his vulpine face twisted in a sneer, saying, "Fine talk, fine talk! And the rest of us caught here to be taken and hanged in a row off the cliff maybe! I say, every man for himself is the only way—"

"To sue for peace and surrender now?" said O'Connor. "Is that what you say, man? Then none will get out alive."

Cathal O'Breslin turned a contemptuous grin. "Oh, well, then," he said, "we all know O'Briens, do we not? They are famous—for this and that. There have been poets made verses about it in the past." And he quoted, still smiling:

> "The race of the O'Brien of Banbha under Murrough,
> Their covenant is with the King of England.
> They have turned their backs, and sad is the deed
> To the inheritance of their fathers.
> Alas for the foreign gray gun!
> Alas for the yellow chains!"

O'Brien turned on him savagely. "Hell's name, waste time mouthing the silly scribblings of some bard dead these two centuries! There is a black sheep here and there in every family—"

"Enough!" said McGeraghty. "It is the last folly to quarrel among ourselves. I have said how it will be—all of us with grown sons will stay, the young men are free to try escape however they want."

And how many ways to escape off an island? Fergal had not considered a boat at all. There was an enemy camp on Inishmore, with reinforcements expected, and boats were the first thing an enemy would look for. . . . It had been a long swim even in shallow water, from the seaward wall of the fort round Inishmore to the shore facing the middle island—but it had seemed to him the best way, and to Donlevy too. And they had come this far at least. He wondered if many others had tried a plan of escape, or were trying it tonight or tomorrow—or if most would rely on hope of honorable quarter. From English!

Now he began to be aware of deadly weariness, the intolerable ache in his shoulder-muscles and thighs, and the numbness possessing his whole body for the terrible ice-chill of the March sea. He had no idea how long he had been in the water, how far he might have come. He strained to hear surf on shore or rock, but the wind was high. Three hours or three minutes since he had last been conscious of Donlevy near him somewhere? He could not swim farther; he turned and let the tide take him, resting. The tide bore him, presently, a heavy blow against something—rock —one of the many standing up out of this channel. He clung to it and rested a moment, gasping, as lapping waves flung spray off it into his eyes. He never remembered being so dead tired or so cold—not even after the fight at Athlone—God grant he was not far off now—

The nightmare conviction seized him, as he half-lay there clutching the rough granite, the strength draining out of him, that he had lost all direction, been carried back round Inisheer and out to open sea. Nothing to guide him—no light on land—and his vision of the stars was blurred by wet and exhaustion. Rocks all round these islands, seaward as well as landward . . . And then the wind died, and for just a breath he heard it—he thought he heard it—the blessed sound of surf on a beach, not breaking on cliff or rock. He drew a long breath, kicked the rock for momentum, and began to swim again in that direction.

But he tired more quickly now, even after the little rest, and awhile later he was thinking he must turn and float with the tide again, to recover a little strength, when he pitched headlong with bottom under him, a sudden shelf with white surf slapping it. Thank God, thank God—he had made it—had he? Was this the mainland? He staggered to his feet in knee-deep water, almost fell, and pulled himself up from the surf. Once he was out of the water he began to shake violently with the cold. He went on walking straight ahead, slowly, knowing he must not let himself stop and lie down, or he'd die of the cold. There would be cliffs here, if it was the main-land—a very narrow strip of beach—yes—the ground rose sharp under him, and he found himself fighting his way up a steep slope, up and up, gasping for breath, not daring to stop or he'd fall— When he got to solid level ground, at what he prayed was the cliff-top, he had to fling himself down exhausted, and regain breath.

The way the tide ran, it might have taken him fifteen miles north for the five miles he'd made east, and that would put him some-where around Black Head, where the coast turned east to border Galway Bay. No villages he remembered near the headland, all wild there. But there might be army camps anywhere, these days. He ran into a tree in the dark, sidestepped it; the next minute the darkness suddenly turned even darker and he felt that he had come into a wood. Good!— He blundered about, going down on hands and knees to feel the ground, and eventually as he'd hoped felt good thick dry bracken. With trees the size of these, growing close, the dead undergrowth was kept fairly dry even in winter, and there was a deal of it. Fergal unslung the bundle of clothes from his back, separated kilt, tunic, cloak, and sandals, and burrowed as deep as he could under the bracken, carrying the clothes with him and spreading them out on his body, pulling bracken up over him, heaping it on each side. When he had squirmed about and felt a little warmth begin to generate in him, he lay quiet, keeping a good hold on his belt-dagger, willing his body to stop shaking.

Dawn couldn't be far off. Scout round as soon as light showed, find more or less where he was, with luck pick up some food somehow, and make east to circle Galway town that was in English hands. Maybe only forty miles up to Knockmagh, straight, but likely almost double that the way he'd need to go, roundabout.

He wondered if Donlevy had got to shore somewhere, and spared an already-sleepy prayer for him. Break his sister Shevaun's heart it would if Roy did not come home. . . . But was Shevaun safe herself?—and their mother, and the boy—the baby neither Roy nor he had ever seen? He stirred uneasily in the bracken. No telling what had gone on since the official surrender.

He wondered how long it would take him to get home—with or without Roy. A week up to Knockmagh, and then another sixty, seventy miles up to Donegal and the house by Lough Eask . . . In the nine months since surrender, what had Oliver Cromwell's army done in Ireland?

A Federation, well, it had been less than that. Ormonde the duke, that Anglo-Irish Butler who hated Catholicism as hard as any Puritan, gathering a Royalist force here to support the Stuarts against Parliament. No Gael of the old blood, the men who had kept to the old laws and ways and dress, had joined those Anglo-Irish lords in federation out of love for the first Charles Stuart or the one now in exile. No; in these last fifty years, the religious discrimination making new laws bore hard on Catholics here, and Charles Stuart had been son of a French Catholic mother. Only one thing to be said of the present Stuart; he was King of England but he was not an Englishman. If he could be put in power, and partly by Irish Catholic support, the chance was good that he would see the laws relaxed and greater justice done.

And that was the only reason those old war-hounds Eoghan Ruadh and Hugh O'Neill, and all the Gael-Irish chiefs in the north and west, had joined the Royalists against Parliament, back in '44, in support of the first Charles. Strange bedfellows; those Norman-Irish lords and landholders looking down their noses at the Gaels, and the compliment returned with interest. Which was not to condemn all Norman-Irish; there were Fitzmaurices, Fitzgeralds, Burkes and Joyces and Lynches, truer Irish patriots than others wearing originally Gaelic names.

But it wasn't only an English army they fought; some of the men with the Federation Royalists were Englishmen. It was Oliver Cromwell's Puritan army, that iron general who had won Parliament's war against the Crown, and every man in it with the bloodlust raised in him by lies told and fervent sermons preached against the blood-thirsty Catholic Irish. . . . Lies told mostly about the patriots' rising of 1641, that abortive little war that in the end had got inextricably mixed—in principle—with the Civil War in England . . . Two counts, there were, about their bloodlust: and maybe the historians would say the religious difference was the stronger issue. But there wasn't much to choose between—Protestant distrust and Puritan hatred of Papism, and the perennial English race-arrogance, all other men naturally inferior and all Irish doubly so.

Well, it had been a fight; and, thought Fergal savagely, the Gael-Irish had done most of the fighting: the Royalist English and Anglo-Irish forces were small and ill-equipped. Had it not been a fight, against that inhuman New Model army of the iron general who had killed a king! The numbers, the guns, the horse, the supply, all had been on the Parliament side—and Providence favored numbers; but, by Christ, they knew they had been in a fight—that they did!

And now—and now? A treaty had been signed; and the O'Neills were dead or escaped to exile; the last rebellion in the name of the Stuart was put down—unless those vacillating Scots should decide to fight; and Cromwell's party in unchallenged power. And what would that mean to Ireland? Or for that matter, to England?

Fergal O'Breslin was new young chief of a minor Tyrconnell clan when he went out with his uncle Cathal and his brother Aidan three and a half years ago. He was guardian and trustee, as chief, of fifteen thousand acres of O'Breslin land in south Tyrconnell, and owner of a house on Lough Eask and a thousand acres in his own name, of his private holding. His brother and heir was dead at New Ross, at nineteen; the two hundred troopmen he had led into the fight were dead or scattered; his uncle and prospective heir— since he was the only surviving son of his father—was trapped on Inishmore and likely would be dead soon; and he lay alone here, a man on the run, with his clothes and his belt-knife, not even a hand-gun. A hundred miles off was his last responsibility, his lady-mother, widowed five years, and his sister Shevaun and her son —also the responsibility of her husband, Roy Donlevy, but what guarantee that Roy was still alive?

That was a strong tide and deep water between Inisheer and Clare, and Fergal knew he was lucky to be on land—and lucky twice not to have run into a Parliament camp on shore.

At the first hint of light in the sky, he crawled out of the bracken, stiff and still cold and desperately hungry. He donned the stiff-dried clothes, and went northeast through the wood. Now in this winter season the dawn came silent and dispirited, no outburst of birdsong to herald the light; and he knew it was only because it was winter, but unreasonably it seemed that a chill lay over the whole land, a silent agony of expectancy, for final defeat.

He came to the edge of the wood; a strip of barren land went down to sloping rocky cliff and a great expanse of water. Galway Bay, by the sun. He turned due east and walked on through the wood-edge. There was a ship near shore out there, tacking lazy northeast up toward Galway harbor, and she was a big English forty-gunner, a troop-carrier very likely. Fergal watched her awhile, moving cautious in shelter of trees.

He smelled the army-camp before he heard it, and a little horrid nausea came up in him, of hunger doubled for the smell of cooking—something anonymous, emergency-rations likely, only flavored with jerked meat, but something edible. A minute later he heard men talking, and the sounds of utensils clattering; he went from tree to tree, wary as if he stalked game—only here he was the game—and past thin growth, into a clearing, a couple of hundred feet on, he caught a glimpse of men.

A Parliament camp. The sanitary trenches wouldn't be far off —somewhere beyond the cooks' domain. He dropped flat on the ground, inching up behind a great thornbush, and lay quiet, listening. Easy enough to circle the camp, but Christ knew he was hungered, and he'd make better time with a full stomach.

A man was singing robustly to himself not far away. Fergal knew the tune, an English tune and for all that a good one. "The London Apprentice," it was.

"When I was apprenticed in London, I went to see my dear—
The candles were all burning, the moon shone bright and
    clear!
I knocked upon her window, to ease her of her pain—
She rose to let me in, then she barred the door again.

"I like your well behavior, and thus I always say—
I cannot rest contented whilst you are far away!
The roads they are so muddy, we cannot gang about—
So roll me in your arms, love, and blow the candles out!"

What a devil of a fellow it was, singing love songs at the crack of dawn! Fergal grinned tightly to himself under the thornbush. Another man came up and said something about fifteen minutes' grace afore the men formed line. The cook had a bad temper like all good cooks, and swore.

"At least 'tisn't raining agen. 'Ere, what you got for us there, Gideon?—do smell almighty good!" Fergal's nose twitched in agreement. He reared up quietly and peered through the thorn branches.

The cooks' fires were started on beds of piled stones, in a row, ten feet off; there were eight or ten cauldrons simmering, and fifteen, twenty men standing about—cooks and their helpers. A smallish camp then, up the slope beyond, invisible from here—say five hundred men. Well, it didn't look very practicable, but by God he'd do his damndest to sample what was in that nearest cauldron!

"'Ere, Gideon, for God's love lemme 'ave a taste now! I'm that empty you can 'ear me rumble arf-a-mile orf. I got me bowl, see. 'Tisn't fi' minnits aforehand, friend—"

"Ger orf, greedy-guts! 'Nother ten pound on ye 'n' ye 'on't keep up on slow march! Ah, t' get rid o' ye—" The cook ladled out, ungracious. "'N' don't I know you'll go orf private 'n' gollop that dahn, 'n' come back t' end o' line for 'nother dish from some'un else! Ye're a damned hog, Jase Bone!" Fergal held a branch aside with infinite caution: big stout fellow, clutching a bowl, already turning from the fire, deigning no answer to the cook but scuttling in this direction, true to the prophecy.

Fergal watched him pass, five feet off, and crawled after him until he dared stand up. The greedy one hadn't gone far; he sat on a raised knoll under a spreading oak, and he hadn't lifted his spoon before Fergal was on him. It was a damned foolhardy thing to do maybe, with that camp of soldiers so near. He came on him from behind, and took due care not to upset the bowl—got an arm crooked about the fat man's throat, groped for the bowl and set it aside out of harm's way, and slid the dagger-blade in nice and easy. The man gave a loud gasp and went limp.

Fergal took the bowl and spoon on another hundred yards, starting to circle the camp, before he sat to eat. There were only a couple of lumps of dried beef in the stuff, but it put new heart in him. Damned foolhardy, yes: likely the man would be found before long, dead or wounded—he hadn't stopped to see—but at that, any straying Englishman was apt to get knifed in an Irish wood, they wouldn't be too astonished or alarmed at that. . . . And anyway he had his breakfast, be damned to what might come!

All along the way he'd looked for Roy, but there'd been no sign. Damn, had he ever got to shore? No way he could know; all he could do was go on, and wait next week at Knockmagh.

And he wondered if that forty-gunner in the bay had maybe picked up other men trying for escape off Inishmore, last night.

He got round the English camp by late morning, careful in wood, crawling in open, maybe ten miles' circle. There was a village near here, he remembered that—a place called Ballyvaughan: all too likely there were more troops quartered there, and he'd need to circle it, going out of his way south.

At the moment he thought that, he was at the edge of the wood, with now and again a glimpse of the bay on his left, a mile away; the wood got deeper south of him, to his right, and he thought he'd be wise to turn, for if his memory was accurate that village couldn't be far off. And then he froze, listening, a hand reaching to his knife.

Crashing of footsteps ahead, through brush. *Ahead*. Then, not after him—or were they? Men's voices shouting in English—*This way! There they go—after 'em!*

A man burst out past thornbushes ahead of Fergal, cannoned blindly into a tree, changed direction and blundered on. A second man came after, a stout man gasping and red and winded. Men in brown robes, awkward for running. Fergal dodged behind a tree; the pursuit sounded close.

The first man was running in circles, blind, in panic. He made enough noise for four men, and here he came again, straight for Fergal like a target, and ran into him, and opened his mouth to yell. Fergal took him by the throat with one hand and laid the other across his mouth.

"My pardon, brother," he whispered, "but no noise! Get up the tree with you now—"

The man in the brown robe stared up at him dazed, gibbering, stone-white with terror. "What say you?—an Irishman you are— the tree—"

"For the love of God!" said Fergal. "Get up! Men don't look above their heads, usual way." He set foot in the crotch and got a handhold, pulled the man after him. The robed man was clutching a great cloth-wrapped bundle, and would not let go of it; he muttered incoherently to himself. He was not a very young man, and likely he'd never climbed a tree since a faraway boyhood, and he clung to his bundle obstinate, only one hand free; Fergal hauled him upward grimly, thanking Christ it was an easy oak with spreading branches. Bare now, too, but the trees grew close here; if they were utterly still, the pursuit would run by and never look up.

"Quiet!" he said fiercely. "Quiet for your life, man!"

"They must not—I must save it—my life, yes, nought at all— if I can but preserve it—"

"Quiet!" said Fergal, and steadied them both in the narrow crotch thirty feet up in the old oak.

2

THE BROWN-ROBED MAN had the wider place, a division of trunk and branch like a saddle; he scarce needed Fergal's firm hand pressing him down, but subsided astride it, hunching over his unwieldy cloth parcel, hiding his face against the rough tree trunk. Fergal balanced still on the next branch, looking down.

Here came the other man, a much older man and stout, doubling back, gasp and crash through underbrush, torn robe flying and catching. He was done, they had him, he could run no more, and he sank against the bole of a tree part behind a bush and tried to make himself small. And here they came after, five, six, seven English soldiers: and a mounted officer, head down and arm up to shield his face, riding through untracked forest. Musketeers they were, common infantry—one of the London or Home County regiments, red coats, blue knee-trousers flapping, no armor—the long-barreled matchlock guns at the ready, and all of them giving tongue like hound-puppies.

"There 'e is! Aht o' that, ye silly Irish—no funny business nah, there's a gun on ye—"

"What's 'e got? Watch 'im, Adam—'e might go for to jump us—they all carry daggers, the bastards—"

"Not no monks don't, ijjit! 'S all ri', sir, we got one o' 'em 'ere—"

"Keep him covered!" The officer, dismounting, swaggering up to the cowering prisoner. He could not help swaggering, for the wide-topped boots English army-men wore, forcing them to walk straddle-legged.

"Ar, sure-lie! Whate'er 'e's got, cap'n take lion's share! On'y nat'ral that be! You look 'ere, Cap'n Brawl, 'twasn't six month back you was rubbin' shoulders wi' rest of us as corpril—if you think we stand by 'n' see you take double plunder—"

"Shut your damn' mouth, Will Greene, or I'll shut it for ye an' take pleasure!" snapped the officer. They were all crowded round the silent, shaking, helpless figure of the fat man in his torn robe. He hugged his bundle to him; he watched them; he was deadly afraid, but there was a kind of pathetic dignity in him there, his round red face going paler now, the sweat shining on his bald head.

"Sirs—gentlemen," he said in English, in a low trembling voice. "If you please—only to believe—I will come with you, I know you must take me—by law—but I have nought you would want, believe me—not gold or silver or jewels—"

" 'Ark at 'im! No gold 'r silver—out o' one o' these 'ere secret monasteries a-packed wi' riches! It'll be gold orf one of they statues—"

"Aye, t' way them two run! An' share 'n' share alike—like as allus—cap'n, sir, no need go tellin' t' colonel abaht t' prisoner a-carryin' aught, eh?—give it up, ye silly owd fool—"

They were pushing and prodding around the man, like children bullying a playmate—no really bad humor in them, no hate or bloodlust. Yes, Fergal had seen it before, he knew them. . . . They were like mastiff-pups at play in the kennel—clumsy blow and snap, and all at once temper roused over nothing, and the teeth closing in deadly earnest.

"Please you, gentlemen—it is not—"

And the officer snatched the bundle, and its cloth wrapping fell away to show a small coffer, brassbound. Oh, yes, impatient children—they never thought to search him for the key—they were on it with excited yelps, taking a ramrod to it, then the butt of a musket—gabbling about gold and silver and jewels. And the prisoner might have run, all their attention off him now, but he stood and watched with sick eyes. The lock smashed in, and the lid thrown back—and they let out a concerted roar of disbelief and disappointment. They scrabbled about in the box, tossing out its contents for what might lie underneath.

"Nought but *papers*—there's got to be summat more—"

"All they places rich as t' Pope—must be—"

"Nought but *paper*! 'Ere, what you done wi' t' rest o' what you brung orf?"

Yes, turned ugly now, turning on him deadly now—the man who cheated them of loot. They ripped and tore at the parchment pages, all the coffer contained, in their thwarted anger, and flung the pieces away in disgust. The prisoner tried to speak in protest, he was saying again, Nothing else, gentlemen, please, gentlemen— They never gave him a chance, the officer too angered at missing plunder. And the prisoner saw what was in their eyes, and sick terror came into his face, and he broke with astonishing suddenness and was through the pushing circle of men, and running. They were after him with a roar, the officer with his handgun out—damned awkward little things to prime and cock, but quicker than a matchlock—and the gun spoke loud, and the fat man fell and crawled a few paces and lay still.

"Cheated us, t' bastards 'ave—musta hid stuff when they run from t' monastery—"

"Must be some'eres, what they brung orf—*papers*—my muckin' Christ!—gold 'n' jools—"

"T'other 'un—"

"All right, all right!" The officer, in a roar. "T'other fella can't've got far—after that 'un, ye fools! We can pick up this 'un on way back, for t' bounty at least! Ger-*on*! He went orf that way—" Swinging up to the saddle, reining the horse contemptuous and careless over the pile of torn tossed-away parchment. They followed, profane; they scattered, by sound, in the wood beyond, hunting and quartering.

In five minutes their noise had passed and they were gone. A watery sun was trying to break through a low pewter sky, and an early dispirited-sounding bird somewhere raised a tentative call; and then silence fell again, but for the wind making secretive whispers in the bushes. Gently it lifted the brown robe and flirted a finger among the scattered parchments.

After another slow minute had passed, Fergal drew a longer breath. They'd be coming back for the body; there had been mention of a bounty. Yes, the standard bounties posted for priest, monk, nun. He put a hand on the man with him. "Move!" he said. "Down with you—we'll need to get away before they return!" He saw the man clear for the first time. A thin man perhaps in the early thirties, tonsured; and he read recent history in the face, fear, desperate flight, hunger.

A monk. A Franciscan, by his robe. And the worst companion a man could choose on the run—an impractical, unworldly monk, without experience at all of fighting or running. Oh, the luck of the world Fergal O'Breslin had, forced to join forces with a lay-brother! He shook the man, rough. "For Christ's love, go down! We must get clear as far as we can—"

The monk stared at him, and at the ground below. "Oh, Our Lady have mercy—Christ have mercy—all torn and spoiled—Colum—"

"Get *down*!" snarled Fergal. He did not know what the parchments might be, but any man's life was more important than parchments. "Move!" The monk, looking terrified as well as soul-wounded, started slow and fearful down the tree. But on the ground he went first to the body, and Fergal landed light and came after him. "He's dead, never mind, nought to be done for him. For God's sake come—" But by then the monk was distractedly gathering up the torn parchment, muttering snatches of prayer.

"I beg you—if you would help me—an Irishman you are—"

"For Christ's sake!" said Fergal. He accepted an armful of crumpled parchment, and hustled the monk out of the little clearing. He dragged the man along bodily—damn the luck, saddling him with the fellow!—every nerve alert for sound of the soldiers, for a place they might go to ground safe—through underbrush and dry bracken, and the damned monk making a noise like a cavalry-troop—

"Mercy, have mercy—only if I may preserve my trust—"

"Quiet! There they are back again!" Fergal shoved him down behind a clump of young willows and rowan, at the entrance to a little copse, and fell half on him, and held his breath. There was the mounted officer, swearing, and the men after, talking loud with grievance of the men on the run from them, one clear away and one dead, and only the standard bounty to collect on the corpse, three pounds for a monk robed.

He lay sprawled, monk and rough growth under him, and heard them pass. Maybe two hundred yards to the body. He listened. He heard them, faint, stop and argue—likely over who was to carry the corpse. Oh, yes, that was English: everything done in order, by rules and regulations, all written out: they'd need to fetch in the body to claim the bounty, and likely there was some solemn regulation about that too, so many shillings deductible, allowed for the grave dug—one prisoner (shot while attempting to escape), Irish, monk, Franciscan, reported this day of—in this territory of—. . .

They were gone.

He was aware of his heartbeat, slow and heavy, and the rustle of parchment crushed between him and the monk, as he moved. He sat up on his heels.

The monk rose, stiff, from prone position, and looked at him. "They're away, brother," said Fergal. "I'm sorry was I rough, but you'll not be used to running from soldiers, and I needed to be. They're away back to their headquarters—likely in Ballyvaughan, I'd think—and we can go on to circle the village in safety, with luck. Unless they come back—and English are perseverant."

The monk stared at him dazedly. "But they shot him—like as if he were—a wild beast. Brother Colum—as never did harm to any. Commended he was, personal, by the Prior—for excellence in manuscript work—a scholar he was, and a man of peace. I ask your pardon, my friend—I should by now—adjust myself to how it stands with us, in our country now—but it is hard, it is bad to know. Not used—to running from soldiers, you say. Ah, but it is five days we've been on the run from them—since they came and fired on us at Clonmacnoise—Colum and I thought we were away safe, this far west—and then that patrol only half an hour ago— oh, Christ have pity on us! Friend, might I ask your name?"

"I am the chief O'Breslin out of Tyrconnell."

"And God's mercy—I fall into the guidance and aid of a chief, an honorable man," said the monk. He leaned and laid a hand that shook on Fergal's arm. "O'Breslin, of your love of country and your pride of race—I ask your help. It is our copy of the Annals of the Four Masters, O'Breslin—the great treasure of Clonmacnoise— the only manuscript, the only book of the whole history of our race, the only history ever written down in full—there may be only three or four other copies elsewhere—the Prior himself entrusted it—for our race it must be preserved—"

"My brother," said Fergal, "I have pride of race to call on, yes. I will help you to carry the manuscript, and God grant we get it to a place of safety—but in an emergency a book of history is dead weight. It is men's lives are important, to take the race on to the new generations—not history books. Come up, we'd best make some time away from here before the English take a notion to come back." He hauled the monk up to his feet.

"I should introduce myself, my pardon—I am Brother Hugh, of the Franciscan order— Oh, you are wrong, O'Breslin! They would destroy us entirely, I know—and all record of us—our greatness as a nation, and as a people. Are you wrong, then?—God help me, I don't know—men's lives—and the record of ourselves as a nation—I do not know! I have lived at peace for eighteen years at Clonmacnoise—and they came and turned their guns on us, the monastery is in ruins and the Prior dead, and I do not know—"

While he was talking Fergal crammed the bits of parchment he held into the coffer Hugh held out, open, and slammed down the lid and put the box under his left arm. "Yes, brother. Come on now, we'll do best to go right south—they've quartered there —and as fast as we can travel. We'll talk later—questions I have to ask you, God knows—I've been shut up on the Arans, and we had news of the treaty but not its provisions, or what has been happening since. But now we must make speed away from here."

"I will follow you, O'Breslin," said Hugh, hasty, humble. "I am coming. I ask pardon—and oh, Christ's mercy, none to say a word over Brother Colum—Our Lady have mercy—it is God's truth I'm unversed in such things as fleeing from enemies, I put myself under your guidance—"

"Then shut your mouth, man," said Fergal tartly, "and try to step soft, for Christ's sake!"

Brother Hugh stumbled and clutched at his arm for balance. "My pardon, O'Breslin. I will try. Mercy of Christ on us indeed, not the first—my poor Colum—the Prior and Brother Eochaidh and our good Brother Mael-Iosa—shot down like wild animals— and Clonmacnoise that the blessed St. Columcille himself founded—all brought down in ruins— My pardon, O'Breslin. I thank you from my heart, I ask God's blessing on you that you burden yourself with me—for myself it does not matter, but the manuscript, the Annals of the Masters—"

Fergal stopped and took hold of him and shook him once, hard. "Now, quiet! God knows who might be in earshot! We'll find a safe place to go to ground, and I'll listen to you then, for I want to know the military law in effect and where danger lies as we go. But until then, hold your loose tongue!"

Hugh blinked up at him, and a faint smile lifted his mouth, a little tremulous, to bely the anxiety in his eyes. "Oh, it is a chief," he murmured. "I ask pardon. Yes, O'Breslin. A chief it is, this ugly long-nosed black one with the black brows and the week's uncouth black beard on him, a soldier and a strong man—and a man with experience of running from the English, doubtless—"

"And what the devil do you mean by that?" But Fergal grinned, brief and reluctant. "Right you are there. For my sins, that I am."

"I am—forgive me my stupidity and slowness, O'Breslin—I am a man of Tyrconnell myself—a McFadden I am. I'll keep up to you, O'Breslin, I hear you—my tongue I'll hold—don't let me be a burden to you." He was panting, breathless, but a game one, following noisy through the wood.

"Well, damn," said Fergal with another grin. "Are you, then? Good man—you'll do to take along, my brother. Only for Christ's love, try to move quiet, will you?"

Fergal stared at the lay-brother and tried the phrase on his tongue. "An Act for the Settlement of Ireland. Are you telling me they have put such a thing through their Parliament, to be law, already? Not just military provisions, for the surrender, then? But there are a few garrisons still holding, men who never agreed to that surrender the Anglo-Irish signed—"

"Oh, yes, we had heard that," said Hugh McFadden. He gave a long sigh and relaxed more against the boulder at his back. By this midafternoon Fergal had found shelter for them, in rocky hills northwest, in this hidden spot where a great shelf of rock above made almost a cave here, and the land fell off sharp ten feet away, down to green moor and the quiet narrow shimmer of the River Clare in the distance. "God's mercy, O'Breslin, my stomach is empty. The food we brought with us was finished yesterday—"

"Yes, in a while we'll scout round and try to find something. Not much game this season, and I've only my knife anyway, but with luck maybe we can raid a farm-barnyard."

"I don't suppose we would find anything in such, O'Breslin. There's been famine—and plague—for a year and more everywhere—scarcely a farmer in Ireland hasn't eaten all his stock by last Christmas."

"That bad, is it? We saw some of the famine, yes, and starved a bit ourselves, on our way across Clare—but we weren't situated to hear news of the rest of the country, you understand, shut up in Kilronan since the first of December—living mostly on fish, the sea's still full of those! The last definite news we had was in April last year, the talk of surrender-treaty. What have they done since? This Act—"

"It is an infamous thing I must tell you, O'Breslin, and I hardly know where to begin it." Hugh sat up, hugging his knees; it was cold, and the threat of rain in the air; he fixed a brooding look on his little coffer. "Peace, I said, at Clonmacnoise," he whispered. "It seems so now, to look back! My grandsire remembered a time in Ireland when priests walked abroad in the daylight—and there were public churches, where the Mass was celebrated open. No younger man remembers such a time. But until now, when they found us—priest or lay-brother or sister of God—they fined us or prisoned us or banished us abroad. Now they will kill us outright and have done. . . . And isn't it a terrible ironic thing, O'Breslin, when you think about it? Clonmacnoise, the oldest monastery in Ireland, founded by Saint Columcille himself, the missionizer who carried the word to England—and found the Britons running wild in the woods, a people without law or any learning or civilized arts at all, savages—when already here we had old national law and a great literature and a history of scholarship and freedom for all men! He who made Christians of the English—"

"That is not a thing at all possible to do," said Fergal. "Let us say, the good saint tried."

"Oh, as you say, O'Breslin! But ironic is the word. They came and turned their guns on the monastery he built. Oh, we lived secret there, yes—as all church-folk live secret this half-century —but it's not much settled about, poor land it is, and we weren't troubled—the countryfolk were sympathetic and helpful. Nevertheless, I—and others—felt bitter for being forced to creep round corners, employ agents to sell our produce and cut down the profit—and— How peaceful it all sounds now, before five days ago!"

"Yes, brother," said Fergal patiently. "I daresay. I am waiting to hear what they've done, what's decided about new law for the end of the war. If they've hurried an act through Parliament, not to make it just military provision—"

Hugh raised his head and met Fergal's eyes. "O'Breslin," he said, "it is in their minds to see us all dead, every man of Irish blood, so they may have the land for their own. They do not say it in this solemn legal language, in the new law, but that is what they mean and why they have made the law. You know at Clonmacnoise we were known for our historical manuscript-books, and we went out of the way to get hold of documents, write down details of events important to history. Not that there was any difficulty getting hold of this—no. The official order is posted up in every place in Ireland now. I have it written down somewhere, I copied—no matter, it is all in my head—this terrible thing. Yes, I'm getting to it, I'll tell." He passed a hand across his brow, unsteady, and went on in a low voice.

"It began like so. One hundred and five men named as rebel-leaders, and condemned to death when taken. I've heard it said all but a dozen of those men were already fled abroad—Hugh O'Neill was one. Doesn't it sound merciful, O'Breslin?—only one hundred and five out of sixty thousand rebel soldiers! Then it goes on, all official, to name the new classes of all Irish folk by law. The rebel-leaders not so important, not named, they're to be heavy-fined, and all their estates confiscated. And—"

"What? Their entire holdings? But there'll be thirty, forty clan-chiefs among those, like me—land nominally in our names, but clan-land, we're only guardians—"

"The English law doesn't recognize clan rule, O'Breslin, you know as well as I. Land is land. All those men will have their whole estates taken away, and the Parliament will assign them new land—not as much, needless to say, but land—in Connacht."

"In—but—"

"And then, every man who has served against the Parliament in any capacity will have one third of all his possessions confiscated. In those laws, they cared nothing for religious difference—a good many of the men coming under those proscriptions will be Protestant, you know. But then it goes on—to the third class of Irish folk, all the native Irish who are Catholic. Not the war so much it is, the challenge against this Puritan Parliament in the name of

Charles Stuart—that makes an excuse for them—they put it on grounds of religion, but that too is only an excuse. It is—that they are English, greedy for land and possessions and never caring how or where they take it, no vestige of honesty in them. Except, it is curious about the English—the Teutonic blood in them it will be—always they need to see it written down all solemn and official, to have laws and regulations setting out the legalities of theft and murder. . . . Yes, I am telling you. The Act goes on thus. All native Irish who are Catholic, they must prove their innocency—that is the word in the law—toward Parliament. It says, any Catholic who can do so, who can prove he never aided or sympathized with the Royalists and Federation men, he'll be let alone where he is. Doesn't it sound fair, O'Breslin! But not one man out of ten thousand can do that, by the way the law reads. You know, for one matter, there's scarce a place in the country where the Federation troops didn't camp, or pass through, or hold for a little while—and any who lives in such a place, even if he never saw a Federation soldier near to, he's presumed to be a traitor to Parliament. And all sorts of other little provisions—to prove existence of treachery—are written into the law, see you. It's not one man in ten thousand, in twenty thousand, can show evidence of innocence before the Commissions to rule on all cases, the way they've defined it."

"The kind of thing they do, yes. And what punishment is visited?"

"That is the core of the law, O'Breslin. All hid in the middle of their legal language. All Catholic Irish, it says—and that will be nine tenths of all Irish folk. It is the land they want, it is a canny, cunning scheme of this Puritan general. An English proverb I have heard, about killing two birds with one stone—that is what it amounts to, only it is three birds, here. I don't know is it so, but I wouldn't doubt it, one thing we have heard—that they're hard-pressed for cash money, for gold, on account of the war expense. And this Parliament army in Ireland, its pay is long in arrears—these men are owed a million and a half pounds. So General Cromwell has a wonderful notion how to get round it—how to kill his birds at one blow. The soldiers will be paid an equivalent in land—that is how this Act continues. In our land, O'Breslin—the land stolen all legal with words on paper. For so this Act of Set-

tlement says—all native Irish Catholics who cannot prove innocency, they must go west of the Shannon into Connacht—just that
province is set apart for native Irish—one seventh of the arable
land in Ireland kindly given us!—and they must all be west of the
river by the first of September this year. Since last November there
are these Commissions here, busy in every place, deciding on each
individual man and family, innocent or no—and of course none
are found innocent. And other Commissions to allot the land—
parceling it out with official deeds to any Englishman they find
entitled to a claim. And Commissions over the border of Connacht,
government offices set up temporary, to allot little pieces of land
here to the transplanted Irish. Enough? Of course there is not
enough land there for all those! How could there be indeed?" Hugh
made an abrupt angry gesture. "A man, say, out of Wicklow—the
barren north all strange to him—a man, maybe a chief, a wealthy
man who had a thousand acres at home, they drive him up here
with all his kith and kin, and they give him a paper saying he's
entitled to ten acres of land somewhere in Connacht. Ten acres of
Connacht land that wouldn't support five cattle or feed one family
decent! And after that date set out in law, after next September,
any native Irish Catholic found east of the Shannon, he'll be hanged
without trial as a renegade."

Fergal stared at him and heard himself swear in a whisper.
"But—dear God in heaven! That will be—ninety-nine Irishmen
out of every hundred—more, if the law reads so! Connacht—the
barrenest land in Ireland—never as thick a population there, for
that the land can't support it—and they will drive a million people
and more, all those left alive after all the killing, into this little
territory, that won't give a living to twenty-five thousand—they've
writ it in *law*?"

"Yes, O'Breslin. Like as I say, they don't write, we will see
every human of Irish blood dead—but that is what it comes to.
They want the land, the good rich land for planting and livestock,
in Munster and Leinster—Meath, south in Waterford and Wexford, Wicklow and Kerry and Cork—and the fine Ulster pastures
for horse and cattle, and the Antrim plains, and even our Tyrconnell
that might be mostly mountain and lake, but the flat land there is
rich too. Oh, and I must tell you too—the Act makes a gift to the

London trade-guilds, it gives them exclusive ownership of the cities of Derry and Coleraine, to take all revenue for themselves. They have changed the name—it is London-Derry now, in law—"

"For the love of Christ! This insolence—"

"And you see, O'Breslin, the second and third birds this Cromwell is aiming at? They do this to us by law, and it is a death-warrant—you know as well as I. Almighty God, how many of us have died these three years!—half of all the Irish in Ireland—the English bloodlust, they killing babies, children, women, speak nothing of the men they have killed! And the fever plague thrice over the country—and crops stolen or spoiled, or never planted —the herds stolen off to England or thieved to feed English soldiers here, so there has been famine in some degree these two years, and people dead of hunger by the thousands. Oh, I know how the case stands through Ireland now—there is, there was, secret news among the priories and monasteries, you know. The wealth of the land, as it stood, is gone, O'Breslin. The farmlands have been despoiled and the herds are decimated—the farmer who had a hundred cattle four years back has none today, and his children going hungry. All we had left was the land, to build up a prosperous country again—and that they are taking permanent from us by law."

"But I can't believe—this wholesale—even English! This bare-faced—"

"Well, it is the money, O'Breslin," said Hugh with a twisted smile. "The cash they haven't got in hand, to pay the soldiers. And another little item Cromwell had to think about too. A young man you are, you won't remember much of that uprising ten years back?"

"No—my father went out under O'Neill then—and took a bad wound that never healed, in '43 that was, and he died of it four years later—"

"Yes. Well, you'll know how they took it, as a religious rising, and told many wicked lies about the bloodthirsty Catholics making atrocities on innocent people. Ah, it's not in me to be a fanatic, O'Breslin! I don't know, there are good and bad men everywhere, you can't tell a good man from bad by the label he wears, of Catholic or Protestant—Jew or Christian—Irish or English or French or Spanish, or any other label a man has, the groupings men make among themselves. No, it means nothing. I don't know, O'Breslin. Maybe there were wicked men ten years back, did bad things in the name of our church and our patriotism. But there were many lies told, that I know, making it sound to an English Protestant that we are all murderers and rapists and thieves. But, however that is, the time that was done, there was a great number of English merchants and other men—they called themselves a Company of Adventurers—got together a large sum of money to lend the Parliament, to prosecute the war against the Catholic Irish rebels—"

"I never heard that," said Fergal numbly.

"I daresay you'd not hear. It's only lately, in this infamous Act of Settlement, it comes out," said Hugh heavily. "Well, they didn't arrange for repayment in cash and interest, but the loan was made to be repaid in land—land in Ireland. A man who put up two hundred pounds ten years back, he's entitled now to a thousand acres of land in Ulster. A man who found four hundred fifty pounds, that's good for a thousand acres of richer Munster land. And so on, like that. Oh, all writ out legal—that is English for you. And so there are those men to satisfy too, you see? This way and that way, O'Breslin, and all official by law of England, they grant themselves the right to our land. And by the wording of the law, I must tell you too, the only land to be numbered in acres and allotted, it is arable land—bogs and mountains and moor they don't count in, but throw it all in with the counted acreage of the estates it may border on. So an Englishman who has a claim to maybe two thousand acres of land, he gets it all in good workable land and another thousand along with it in lake and hill and moor. And that is the third bird they aim at, do you see it? They'll clear out all the folk of Irish blood, never caring a halfpenny what becomes of us—and settle all the land, six sevenths of Ireland, with reliable English landholders and tenants—do you see?"

"I see safe enough," said Fergal grimly.

"Secret and private they will be thinking it themselves—with any luck, in ten years there'll not be an Irishman left alive in Ireland. The land all held and populated by good, solid, reliable English folk." Suddenly Hugh smacked one hand down on his knee in violent gesture. "Ah, a man of peace I am, O'Breslin, and I count myself a good Christian, but I'm also an Irishman. I tell you,

God forgive me, my right hand I feel itching for a weapon, to think of it—to think of it! There are a hundred little proscriptions written into the Act I haven't quoted you—what it comes to, they give with one hand, take away with the other—concessions they grant us, mercy in defeat, that means nothing in fact. They put it into the law, for instance, that any Irishman who desires to take foreign mercenary service abroad, he's free to go—but he can't take along wife, family, or possessions. So, how many will go? Decent men cannot abandon such responsibilities, and how many young men haven't some such responsibility on them? Those that haven't, yes, I think they'll leave—and at that, you know, I think that is a little mistake Cromwell makes, yes. To scatter mercenary soldiers through Europe, men with a just grievance on England . . . English Protestants are forbid to marry Irishwomen, and forbid to hire Irish laborers or rent to Irish tenants—ah, never mind the list of such laws—the sum is, they will drive us into a trap, into the one barren province, with in effect a high fence around to prevent escape— and in end effect, as it were, cut off our right hands from any chance to earn a decent living—to do aught but starve to death."

"My God in heaven," said Fergal softly. "I can't take it in, brother—death-warrant for the nation it is." He rested his head in his hands. After a long moment he said to himself, "The clan-land—they will force me, and every chief, to betray honorable trust—to all the people under me. Christ! And my own land too —my mother, Shevaun, the boy—maybe I should be thanking God I'm not wed myself, another responsibility—" And then they kept a long, dragging silence between them. Fergal raised his head and looked at Hugh.

"Brother," he said, "though you don't know what I speak of, I see the chief McGeraghty was wrong. It is every man for himself with a vengeance, after this. . . . You and your precious manuscript of history."

"The fear is in me," said Hugh low, "that a hundred years from now, O'Breslin, if this manuscript is preserved at all, it will con-stitute the history of a race extinct. Once there was a race of Gaels, it will tell—a people strong to civilization, renowned for their scholars—and renowned for their fighters and leaders, for a just national law protecting the right of the lowest man—and they all died, there are none of that people left in the world—for that the

English wanted more land, and counted no other nationality human except themselves."

"But don't say it, Hugh McFadden," said Fergal, "for it's a black lie. We won't die as a race to oblige the English, by God! Ah, God in heaven, I can't know what to do, how to plan—must get home—find what's come to them—" He drew a breath, and found just enough sardonic humor left in him to cock an eyebrow. "And it appears your days as a monk are ended. I'm a poor risk as patron, friend—chieftain, an empty rank henceforth by what you say. If you want my advice, you'll do well to go to a city, and seek out some English official, tell him the long tale, and use your talent with the pen at earning a living as clerk."

"You jest at me, O'Breslin," said Hugh tiredly. "Not but what—I wouldn't say—you're right. But men dedicated to God are notoriously impractical. If you do not mind, I—I think I will go on a bit in your company—wherever you're making for. I—to speak the truth, O'Breslin, I really do not know what else to do."

And Fergal said almost indifferently, almost absently, "You're welcome, brother. We will all need—time indeed, to think for what to do."

Bone-tired as he was, he could not sleep that night where they huddled, cold and hungry, under bracken deep in another wood. Beside him Hugh slept uneasily, his precious coffer clutched close, and Fergal thought with detached bitterness, the history books—the long record of all the years, copied at leisure by the peaceful scholars—what matter against men's lives? Yet, when one thought about it longer, that was perhaps of some supreme importance, and Hugh was right: that the record be preserved, that men coming later should know what had happened in a time no living man might remember.

He wondered remotely whether in this century or another there would yet be scholars to write down the history of what had happened this hundred years and more, and whether those who wrote would put down plain fact or perpetuate the lies, tell only the partisan view of this or that. If the only men left to write, or allowed to write, were those of only one persuasion, truth would yet be buried, past recalling straight under the weight of years. That would be in the hand of God.

And did it not all return to the ideas men had about God, entirely—and a very damned senseless thing that was, he thought tiredly. A man's notion of God was personal and private, and could it matter to God at all in what ways men believed and worshiped? No man, fallible and frail as men were, had the right to dictate to another man about that. To bring man's written laws into it.

Ironic, Hugh had said: yes. That old English king Henry Tudor had not broken with Rome over a matter of conscience: a good orthodox Catholic he had been, only engaged in a private quarrel with the Pope over that matter of a divorce so he might wed the Boleyn woman. But it had come to a break with Rome, and the establishment of the English Protestant church. Everything had followed from that, natural as day to night to day again. His only heir a weakling, manipulated by venal and ambitious men in power; and then Mary Tudor the Catholic venting vengeance on the Protestants, only to create more hatred and resentment—human people being human people. But when her sister, the Boleyn woman's daughter Elizabeth, came to the throne, it had been life and death to her that England stay Protestant, for by Catholic law she was a bastard and could not occupy the throne. From that time on Catholics in England had been persecuted and harried relentlessly. Men's ideas about God!—but those ideas had got intertwined with politics, inevitable and disastrous.

The effect in Ireland had been only a little delayed. England had laid claim to all of Ireland, by the Pope's dispensation—the only English Pope ever to rule in Rome—for four hundred and seventy years now, but up to the religious schism had not meddled overmuch with Irish law. Land stolen, parceled out by the Crown to favored men, and taxes imposed, but the only area the English controlled physically had been the Pale, the area immediately about Dublin, the largest city. Up to forty years back, few of the English who had been given Irish land had come to live here, only employed agents to collect the taxes and profits. Up to forty years back, when as punishment for the strong and successful rebellions by the Ulster chiefs England moved to occupy that province, banishing all the landholders to remove wherever they might, the whole province given over to English occupiers. That was done under the provision of the new Penal Laws against Catholics, for by those no Catholic might legally own land.

As day followed night to be followed by day—for a hundred years the men in England who had plotted to put Mary of Scotland on Elizabeth's throne, and then this or that possible claimant, with Mary dead under the ax, had joined forces with the Anglo-Irish Catholics, and England began to pay more notice to Ireland, that hotbed of sedition. But with the Stuart line back on the throne, England had had enough trouble at home. The fanatic Protestant sects in political ascendancy then, fomenting suspicion of the first Charles, married to a French Catholic wife, as suspectable secret Catholic: and that exploding into the civil wars in England nine years back. That first Parliament army had been commanded by reasonable, fairly just men, or so rumor had had it; but the one strong general emerging out of the civil wars was the fanatic Puritan Cromwell, the iron general. He was, again by rumor, worshiped as hero by the common men of England, and he was well on the way to controlling England politically. He had been the prime mover in seeing Charles Stuart dead under the ax, and England was without a king, with Cromwell in control of its Parliament. But the king had left a son, and when the Scots—with no aid from the stiff-necked Calvinist Lowlanders—proclaimed for Charles the Second as king, to be joined by the Catholic Royalists fled to Ireland, there was more work for the iron general to make, to end sedition in Ireland once for all.

He had made it, he had made a terrible end—or a beginning. Drogheda—Drogheda . . . Fergal stared up at remote indifferent starlight, in the blind silent night, and thought of Drogheda. No, he had not been there, at Drogheda north of Dublin that day eighteen months ago, but he had talked with men who had been there. The day that English army had fallen on unsuspecting, unprepared Drogheda. It was a Puritan army, and to those men any Catholic was less than human; there was no mercy in those men, only the bloodlust. The people, so many women and children, locked into the churches—Anglican churches but to those fanatics nearly as bad as Catholic—and the churches set alight to burn them. The babies snatched from mothers' arms to be brained on the nearest wall, with the excited loud jeers—"Another bloody Papist gone to meet his master the devil!"

And in the eighteen months since Drogheda, half the population of Ireland had been massacred indiscriminately, in the name of their Puritan God: all Papists servants of the devil, deserving destruction, and destruction the English had made, savage and bloody. Between engagements with the Royalist forces they had roved the countryside in an orgy of killing, every Irish soul in reach of their swords and guns. They had left behind them the towns, the countryside, empty of all but the bloody corpses. There was little military force left to stand against them, and those harried west and north relentlessly. So it had come, not much later, to this place and time, when it was not possible to stand against them at all.

And now this Act of Settlement written into law, a final killing thrust. He thought almost detachedly how very typical of English that was—the English always so logical, so methodical. In the forty-odd years since the Penal Laws had been instituted, that one prohibiting Catholics from owning land had been put into effect in England; in consequence many of them had fled to France, to Spain, other places, to escape persecution, and now since the civil wars more had joined them, being late supporters of the Stuart king. But the Catholics remaining in England were English. Ireland posed a very different problem, and was not the solution they found a logical one!

Ireland was a foreign nation to England, a nation England claimed to own but its people a different people racially, speaking a different tongue, following different traditions and ideas of law, with a very different history behind them. To the perennial English race arrogance, an inferior people. England had been busy at home these last years, and since the confiscation of Ulster forty-odd years ago had not made a wholesale attempt to implement that law against Catholic landownership in Ireland. And if that was brought about now, what a deadly devil's brood England would create for herself here!—all those dispossessed natives loose in the country! England did not want an Ireland filled with Irish natives, to own and administer, but a richly fertile Ireland empty of population, to fill with tractable orderly English, with no threat from potential rebels.

So that one of the Penal Laws would be temporarily ignored, for only the one area of the country, all the dispossessed natives would be herded into the one most barren province, and undoubtedly kept there by a strong border guard. The English could confidently hope and expect that within a few years the most of those natives would be killed off by starvation and continued plagues; and then they could claim the last province of Ireland along with the rest, as a fiefdom of England, to fill with a new population of English. It was a logical solution indeed: they would be thinking, a final solution.

Hugh stirred and muttered beside him, and with convulsive movement clutched the little coffer closer to his breast. Fergal thought, the scholar and his book of history: and perhaps Hugh had the right of it. And McGeraghty too. Some men must be saved, out of all the bloody holocaust, who would remember and tell the truth about the live present history men were living through now.

3

THE LAND HERE was barren and flat, so the great hill of Knockmagh
stood out to be easy marked ten, twenty miles away: not a high
hill, but long and regular, looking almost as if it was made by men,
and some said it had been, very long ago. It would look bare from
a distance, but there was low growth on it, and many piled big
boulders for shelter. That was where they lay now, Fergal and the
erstwhile monk who did not look much like a monk now. They had
been waiting here for twenty hours, and the fear was rising in
Fergal's mind that Roy Donlevy would never come, could not
come.

He propped himself on his elbow and looked at Hugh, and for
something to say, to take his mind off the worry about Roy, he
said that: "Not much like a Franciscan brother you look, Hugh.
Give it six months, if you live that long, you'll make an upstanding
fellow and not unhandsome at all, with a good head of hair grown."
The robe, the tonsure, dangerous markings, were gone. Luck they'd
had so far; he'd caught a lone Parliament deserter, damned fool
wandering about, four days back, and there'd been a razor in his
pack, and he'd been wearing civilian English clothes—dun-colored
breeches of the common current style, cut straight and loose just
below the knee, and a sleeveless doublet to match, a white linen
shirt full-sleeved, and a wool cloak; there'd even been an extra pair
of boots and a change of linen underwear. All that Hugh had taken;
Fergal had taken the uniform in the pack. Safer to go in English
clothes, and without the scarlet uniform-jacket, the dull-blue breeches
and white shirt were anonymous, with the shabby brown leather

boots. And there'd been a handgun, and a few rounds of ammunition for it. The tall-crowned civilian hat he gave to Hugh, to hide his shaven head. It would be half a year before the tonsure-patch was covered with hair, and all that time revealing itself for what it was; Fergal had shaved Hugh's entire head, all the plentiful brown hair straggling over his collar. "You may look damned queer, but none can challenge that. You can always say you had an infestation of lice and shaved your hair to be rid of them!"

Hugh was feeling his stubbled naked scalp now, ruefully. "Well, I no longer feel quite like a lay-brother, true, O'Breslin. . . . You are worried for your friend. I pray God he is safe, and will soon meet us here."

Fergal rolled over and reached for the bundle of food. Oh, luck they'd had: he'd taken chances, creeping into villages at night, hunting out the inns after hours, or houses where English were billeted, and raiding the larders. And once again catching a stray soldier alone, who had emergency rations in his pack. They weren't badly supplied; the new clothes, their own as spares in one of the stolen military packs, two dozen hard military biscuits, each the size of a quartern loaf, and a half-loaf of bread, and a pound or so of dried salted beef, and most of a bottle of brandy out of an inn-kitchen at Shrule. Fergal wouldn't say it would be his choice if there was decent whiskey to be had, but there was a little comforting fire in the stuff. He broke a corner off one of the biscuits.

"Yes, I pray so. . . . Stories they tell about this place, don't they? Knockmagh, the Hill of the Plain, and on top of it old Finvarra, the King of the Sidhe, holding his fairy court. There's a great cairn up there, it can't be far from us here—we should climb up and have a look at it—the oldest thing in Ireland, they say. That it's the grave-cairn piled over the great female chieftainess Ceasair, who ruled here long ago—the legend says she died just forty days before Noah's Flood."

Hugh smiled. "Oh, there's a deal of fine things said in legend. Myself, I think some of them are pretty tales made up to amuse children, and some are half-remembered stories of things that happened before we had written language, and that would be very long ago indeed, so in the long time before they were set down, they came to be changed in men's mouths, the heroes all giants and the villains all with magic powers—"

"And all the maidens more beautiful than men's dreams. I daresay. There's an old proverb about that—*Never let a good tale be spoiled for want of a small lie*. But they are good tales. Not five miles off there—out on the headland looking to Lough Corrib—they say the first great battle was fought by Irish against invaders. The prehistoric men, the little Firbolgs, and the tall strangers from over the sea, the Tuatha de Danaan. Five days it went on, and the Firbolg ruler, King Eochaid, he was killed and lies under a cairn out there, at a place called Ballymagibbon. Not so?"

"So the pagan legend runs. And the tall strangers won, and they divided Ireland between them, north and south. And so forever the southron men, they'll be little and quick and wiry and tough and red-haired, like their old forebears the Firbolgs—and the men of the north, they will be tall and lean and black and with the iron in their hearts, like the Danaan. You bear out the legend, O'Breslin," said Hugh with a forced smile. "And so do I in a way, maybe, if I've not quite your height or the same weight of iron in me."

"Yes, it's a fine story," said Fergal. "The first of so many invasions on Ireland." For the hundredth time he pushed away the little gnawing worry about Roy. "A dozen different races of strangers from over the sea, coming to conquer and steal land. For as long as there've been Irishmen in Ireland."

"And the thought comes to me, O'Breslin, that maybe there is a core of truth in the legends after all. For all of those invaders who came, with time passed they became Irishmen. The Danaan, and the Hiberni, and the Milesians, and the Fomorians that legend says were giants—in a generation after their coming, they were all one, all Irish. In our own time we've seen it, too, in the time of written history. The Vikings came and built cities, and held all southeast Ireland—and a generation later, there was a man calling himself King of the Danes whose name was O'Connor—and in the end, all those Norsemen tied in blood to the Gaels, and the Norse tongue and ways and rule all forgotten. And the Normans came, and they too became Irish, their own language and ways could not prevail—all absorbed into the Gaelic culture."

Fergal did not speak for a while; and then he said, "That's so, Hugh. But those, they have never tried to destroy us entire as a people, ever before—any of them. Not until now—not before the English . . . Quiet! Listen!" And he gripped Hugh's arm.

There were men climbing the hill, round to the east below. More than one, for the wind carried low voices. Shod feet on the rough pebbly track that was more a loose scree of stones. A man swore, and even at that distance Fergal thought he knew the voice. . . . Grown up together, he and Roy Donlevy had, Roy orphaned and the charge of his uncle who had married a half-sister of Fergal's own father, and living on the next estate up Lough Eask. . . . He listened again, and then stood up among the boulders and looked down. Two men climbing up, a hundred feet below, and one of them was a big heavy-shouldered man with a crest of flame-red hair.

"You're getting old and soft, Roy Donlevy," he called down. "I can hear you wheezing for breath from here, on a little slope like that!"

Donlevy looked up, and grinned, and lifted a hand. In a moment he was near enough to speak without straining for volume; he panted, "If this is—a gentle slope, Lough Eask is—a pond in a garden. Good to see you, man—I was feared you'd not made it to shore."

"And I for you." Fergal reached a hand and pulled him up the last six feet, to a rough embrace of welcome. "Well, for God's love, where did you pick up that black thief Kevin McCann?"—he reached a hand to the second man.

"And what did I ever rob from you, O'Breslin?"

"You stole a willing pretty inn-girl right from under my nose, the night before the fight at Athlone—and don't say you've forgot it!"

McCann collapsed on the level shelf of rock and grinned at him. "Never forget a woman, I don't, though it taxes my memory, the way so many of them will be forever throwing themselves at me." He wasn't telling so big a lie either; he was a slim, middle-sized young man of great handsomeness and easy charm, for all that he was a good man to have alongside in a fight. His home was over by Ardara village, ten miles from Lough Eask, and he was an old acquaintance.

"I fell in with Kevin four days back, away south of Galway town—well, I see you've picked up a comrade too?"

Fergal introduced Hugh hastily. "Go on, tell—you met many English?"

"Oh, a few. The worst trouble we've had was picking up enough to eat along the way! Kevin took the easy way off Kilronan—he—"

"I had to, I never learned to swim," said McCann. "Used my head I did, not like you vulgar men of action, all impulse and brawn. I lay in wait by the sanitary trench away from the siege-camp, and netted a sergeant of horse—the uniform was a tolerable fit too. It was like tricking children—never a word any said to me when I strode down to the wharf and demanded a boat on special messenger-service for the commandant. I got myself rowed over to Clare in style, by a pair of English privates."

"Now why did not I think of that? Well, here's three of us off anyway, if it's out of the fisherman's creel into the pan over his fire! Have you heard—"

"We've heard." Donlevy sat down beside Hugh and accepted the bottle Fergal offered. "Don't tell me you found some whiskey somewhere?—oh, French brandy is it—well, at least it's wet." He drank and passed the bottle to McCann. "Oh, we've heard, Fergal. That notice posted up in the first village I came to." He laughed shortly. "A little joke it is. They set soldiers to read those notices out, like as they'd need to do in England, where the most people can't read at all. A surprise it was to them that the common farmers and laborers here know their letters, mostly. And calling us a nation of savages . . . What are you thinking to do, Fergal?"

"What am I going to do?" Fergal turned on him quick and angry—Roy always the placid, amiable one of the pair they'd made since boyhood, seldom out of temper, thinking long on everything, dead serious when he did lose temper, and holding a grudge forever: and Fergal losing temper a dozen times a day, and restless, volatile as the wind. "Before God, what can any of us do? The first thing is to get home, find what this—this unspeakable settlement has already done there. Do? What can we do, but live day to day as best we can? We can count ourselves lucky, Roy, if we find Shevaun and the boy and my mother still alive! Likely enough by now—from what Hugh says, these Commissions have been busy for several months—some Englishman's been given title to my land and the clan-land too, and I'll present myself all humble to them and be granted, what, ten acres of barren rock in Connacht! So—so? We bring the family into Connacht to avoid being hanged, and likely all the house-retainers and every other soul I'm responsible for as chief, and then we can settle down quiet to starve to death."

"Isn't he anxious to keep the letter of English law!" said McCann. "Roy and I have a couple of different notions." He laughed. "I don't know my own countrymen if nine of ten of them will settle down meek and mild to starve under this settlement scheme! I'm not the only man will be thinking about—this," and he pulled his hand-pistol from his belt and sighted it. "There are fine hiding-places in the hills convenient to the Connacht border, and also convenient to these prosperous new English settlers."

Fergal raised his brows. "Robbers' roost in the woods, and living hand to mouth on the plunder you frighten out of English?"

"Likely a better living than any man would dig out of Connacht rock—and a merrier life!"

"A deal of use and comfort you'd be to your wife, living wild in the hills with a ragtag crew of highwaymen. Oh, I can see Maire McCann cooking over an open fire and housekeeping in a cave!" For McCann's lady-wife had been an O'Donnell, daughter of the chief's line, and had likely never lifted a hand to sew a button or turn a spit.

McCann shrugged and turned a shoulder with an angry laugh. "Oh, go and starve on the Connacht rock the kind English will give you, then!"

Hugh McFadden said softly, "And that is another thing about it. We have been a people known in the past for our just law and our respect for law, as well as for our scholarship. Now, when we live so long a time under law that is a mockery of law, no man with any manhood in him can lie quiet and easy without striking a blow for freedom. There will be more, as there have been many in the past, turn outlaw against the mockery—and in the end we may be a people known for our lawlessness."

Roy Donlevy rubbed his nose and said mildly, "Well, I reckon myself a sensible man. It seems to me there's a hole in the settlement law a man could walk through—and that's the provision that lets any Irishman go to take up foreign service as a mercenary soldier."

"But, man, you've seen how it reads—any man with wife, family, any responsibility, must abandon them if he—"

"Well, now, I will want to discuss it with you—and with Shevaun too, Fergal—but it's just been in my mind, that if as her brother you'd accept responsibility, say for a year, it might be I could line my pockets enough, as a paid soldier in France or Spain or Austria, that I could get all of you out abroad. You see? I've experience as an officer to claim. It just came to my mind, as maybe a good plan." He raised his blue friendly eyes to Fergal's.

After a minute Fergal said slowly, "Now, Roy, one thing I can tell you—Shevaun wouldn't like it. Not at all." Meeting Roy's eyes, he felt a little premonitory chill. That look he knew: Roy got something fixed in his mind, and not God or Satan could change him. Not quarrelsome he'd be, he wouldn't go shouting and swearing: he'd just go on and do what he'd decided, and to hell with what anyone else thought or did about it. Even someone like Shevaun, whom he loved.

"Oh, well, talk," Fergal said hastily, lightly. "None of us needs decide all in a minute, about this or that. The first thing is, get home and find how it stands there with our people."

It was the last Saturday in March, late afternoon and a thin drizzle of rain falling, when the four of them came up the last rough five miles from Ballinala village on Donegal Bay to the O'Breslin house on the south shore of Lough Eask. They came, as they had come along the seventy-odd miles from Knockmagh, much more open and careless than they'd gone that first few days. As they had drawn away from the sparse-populated coast and up through Galway, the truth had come home to them that they were no longer men on the run from enemy soldiers; that war was done; they were defeated natives moving through conquered enemy-occupied country.

A dozen times they'd been stopped by English patrols, with questions and demands for identifying papers issued by the Commission for Transplantation. "No papers yet, you haven't? Where are your homes if you have any?—ah, yes, the county of Donegal—you're going straight there? Your Commission office will be in the town of Donegal, and you must report there without delay to be classified. And just to be sure o' that, and that you're not vagrants, these names'll be reported at that office, mind."

And at the tail-end of every patrol, a collection of wrist-bound prisoners taken up as vagrants, folk without official residence who would be shipped overseas as life-indentured servants, or even possibly (if England was as short of money as rumor had it) sold outright as slaves in any nation about the Mediterranean or the West Indian islands, where slavery was still lawful, under Spanish rule.

When they got to the coast-village of Laghy, that Friday, they met a fisher-captain Fergal knew, one Cassidy. "You'll be for Lough Eask, O'Breslin," he said, with a sidewise look. "And folk there happy to see you, thinking you are dead long since. You won't want to go through Donegal town, for one visit you'll need to make there and one is enough, it full of English." He spat aside. "I'll take you across to Ballinala, and welcome."

And so they came at last (McCann's home ten miles on, and Roy Donlevy without a home at all since his aunt had remarried and conferred house and land on her new husband), to the house by the lake which Fergal O'Breslin no longer would own in law.

It was a big solid square house of gray stone, facing the water, the courtyard paved—and full of English soldiers at the moment. An officer's horse tethered, half a dozen uniformed men idling about. Fergal said under his breath, "Didn't I say it? Granted away to some English already—"

"You forget their passion for order, O'Breslin," said Hugh. "You are legal owner, they'd want you—ah—classified, as they call it, or presumed dead in law, all proper, or the new title would not be clear."

Fergal said a short rude word about English law and order and thrust open the oaken gate. Home he was after three and a half years of war and defeat, and the nostalgia for old happy times here, his love and anxiety for his people, was a hard lump in his throat. But it was Roy got to the great oak housedoor first, shouldering past the soldiers in the yard, calling his wife's name.

The door gave on the square fore-passage, the doorway to the communal hall at the left, and backed against that shut door were three women, with an English captain of foot, hands on thighs, before them.

"Offer, or I can call in my men to search 'n' take whate'er they find," the officer was saying in an exasperated tone. "You know 'tis due, why be so damnation stubborn, eh?"

"There is nothing left in the house!" one of the two young women flung at him defiantly in English. "Will you take the clothes from our backs?"

"Now that's not at all a bad idea, spitfire," grinned the officer.

"You unspeakable lout—" And then she saw the newcomers, past the captain's shoulder, and reverting to their own tongue she cried, "*Roy!* Oh, my darling love—Roy—" She ran to him.

Fergal was already holding his mother's slight body close, feeling her tears on his cheek and the deep trembling all through her. "Now, woman," he whispered, "is it a welcome for a hero, tears and weakness? And in front of an Englishman, too—"

Ethne O'Breslin drew away a little, gripping his shoulders strongly; her dark blue eyes met his almost level, for she was a tall woman, deep-bosomed and erect of slender figure, still a handsome woman at only forty years. She had given her first son the same smoky-blue eyes and black hair, her cream-matt fair skin and spare height. And perhaps, he thought, some of her courage too. "Don't make a spectacle of yourself, woman," he said, smiling into the eyes so like his own; and her grasp tightened on his arms and then relaxed.

"True enough," she said in her deep firm voice, "only the good die young. But I—I forgot that, boy—so many I've lost."

And then Shevaun was hugging him wildly, laughing and crying—pretty, quick, dark little Shevaun they'd all somewhat spoiled all her life— "Fergal, Fergal, we were sure you were dead—and Roy—oh, thank you to bring Roy back to me—"

"Here, didn't I have anything to do with it?" demanded Donlevy, outraged. "He thinks high enough of himself as it is, girl, if you must make a hero of one of us, let it be me!"

The third woman there was a stranger to Fergal, and she stood against the door quietly, only watching them all with interested eyes. Curiosity stirred in him for her; and he was aware of the English officer saying something sharp, a demand for their names and papers. He swung around.

"I am the chief O'Breslin and owner of this house. And you?"

"Well, you won't be owning it much longer," said the officer.

He was a young man, stocky and blond, and there was no deliberate insolence in his tone, only the abruptness of the soldier. "Papers?"

"I have none, I understand that I must present myself before the English Commission, but I've not done so yet—I'm only just home from the army, I've been under siege in the Kilronan garrison," said Fergal bluntly. The officer looked him up and down.

"Then you'll certain-sure be a-leaving 'ere soon, my master. You'll attend on the Commission in Donegal town, to report yourself, the nearest hour you can get there, so I order you. And these with you? I'll need to take names and particulars, to know are they vagrants or maybe on the list of wanted men."

McCann sauntered forward, hands in pockets, smiling the little cold smile he used for contempt. "Kevin McCann, landholder and recent out of the Federation army—*sir*," and the word was subtle insult. "My land's ten miles northwest. I've not been before your Commission either. I hear the order, *sir*, I will report myself there presently—my wife's slept alone these three years, at least I trust she has, and I daresay she can bear another couple of nights, if I see the Commission first."

Donlevy stared at the officer underbrowed, and his voice was quiet. "I am brother-in-law to the chief here, Roy Donlevy and also late of the army. Not a landholder, but it is understood I too must go before your Commission—"

"To be officially classified, yes," snapped the officer.

Fergal said hastily, a hand on Hugh's shoulder, "This is a man in my service, Hugh McFadden, also late of the army and in peace my private retainer. Not a landholder."

"And he too must report. I'll be here again a week today, and I'll expect to see your official papers—and unless you've proved your innocency afore the Commission"—and the captain grinned to show that was a joke—"I'll see you off the property and on your way—to Connacht or hell." His glance slid back over the women. "Meanwhile, there are the taxes due. What have you to pay?"

"Taxes—" said Fergal.

Shevaun said, sharp and cold, "You must forgive my brother, he's new to Ireland at peace, Captain, and doesn't know that every Saturday is a little Day of Judgment for Irish householders! Have you any coin on you, Fergal? What a pity, they like cash money, but they will take anything else instead. I'd not like to offer my blanket, we gave up the only spare one last week, and it's that or the tableware, and I can't say I'd like to start eating with my fingers either."

"Open the pack," ordered the officer with a peremptory gesture. Fergal gave him a look and unfastened the strap, threw back the lid. Hugh was unobtrusively trying to hide his precious coffer under his cloak. The captain upended the pack with the butt of his musket, scattering everything out on the stone-flagged floor. By the grace of God—it just passed through Fergal's mind—the stolen uniform-jacket was in the other pack Roy had carried. The captain pounced on the half-bottle of whiskey left, that they'd bought dear in Kinlough two days back, for three stolen bread-loaves and McCann's extra belt-knife. "This'll do fine, I like your national drink, I do! God's mercy, nought else worth picking up—" A quartern loaf, a handful of preserved beef. He shrugged. "Not much out o' this house the last month or so. Just as well your men come home, to get all o' you classified and turned out, eh? Well, I'll be round to examine your Commission papers—see you 'ave 'em to show!" He gave them a mocking, careless salute, and his spurred stride was loud as he went out. They heard barked orders, the men in the yard falling into line, the tramp of feet away.

Fergal said again, "*Taxes!* Now what—"

"They have stripped the house." His mother leaned on his arm as if suddenly the shock of his arrival had reached her, turned her faint; he put a supporting arm about her. "They'd have—written you down officially dead, Fergal, long ago, if it wasn't for that ruling. They'll wait to do that in law, about every man who won't come home, until September when all of us must be in Connacht—because of the taxes, they call it. The law says—every house must contribute taxes to support the English military, you see—and they take it in anything. Every Saturday they're around—to collect. It's right what he said, there's little enough left to give them, they've had everything—one way and another. Clothes, and bed-linen, and all the service of pewter plates and cups, all the weapons in the house—all the horses left, and your father's gold seal-ring the captain found in a drawer once—my jewels and Shevaun's—"

"I see. It's a thing English would do, force us to pay for the privilege of keeping them here. Where are the servants, Mother?"

She drew a long breath. "They've all been faithful and good,

Fergal—the ones left. A year back, the English took some of the younger maids, Deirdre and Eileen and—I think for camp-followers—I tried—and when they took all the crops last harvest too, some of the home-farm people couldn't live, they've gone off—I don't know where. Oh, Tadgh will be so glad to see you, Fergal—"

And affection he'd not remembered as so deep rose in him at the name of their old chief house-servant, with his father so long. "And Ailsa?" he asked with a quirked smile. "Did she run off with the soldiers too?"

"Oh, no—" She cocked her head at him. "You'll maybe be relieved to know," she added dryly, "that she miscarried the child, so you've not that added responsibility, at least."

He laughed shortly. "No odds. It's any man's woman for a night—but I'd have acknowledged it, needless to say."

It was all a confusion of cross-talk, Shevaun meanwhile calling excitedly for the servants, for Brighid to bring the boy at once— "And you never saw him as a baby, Roy, such a sweet one—but so well-grown now, and your very image, the way I wrote you—" McCann was muttering invective to himself over losing the whiskey; and then the strange girl was coming closer, saying, "I had best introduce myself, O'Breslin."

"Oh, Nessa, my dear, forgive me. Walking in like this, Fergal, you've taken my wits away—" His mother's eyes on him were anxious now, holding apology and a warning. "It is Nessa O'Rafferty. She has been with us six months nearly—her father asked —I wrote to you at Longford, the time you were garrisoned there and wrote home. But so many letters went astray, likely you never had it? Nessa—"

Fergal bit back involuntary exclamation. Nessa O'Rafferty. Her name and her presence told him all his mother need not say. This girl was daughter to an old friend of his father's; and four years back, his brother Aidan eighteen and the girl roundabout the same age, formal betrothal had been made between them. The wedding was to have been that fall. . . . But instead they had rid out to war, all in a hurry at the alarm, and four months later Aidan lay dead at New Ross.

Nessa O'Rafferty, living here like a daughter-in-law of the house. Fergal remembered vaguely that her mother had been dead at the time of the betrothal. Neither he nor Aidan had known the girl or her brothers at all, Domnall O'Rafferty had lived at his chief's house away north in Inishowen; it had been an arranged betrothal between the families. So, apparently, O'Rafferty had no blood relative to leave as guardian to his daughter—*her father asked*, his mother said. After the surrender it would have been, that was the story: the brothers dead, and O'Rafferty on his way to death and turning to the only people who could be presumed to bear responsibility, the family of her betrothed husband. Death did not cancel that responsibility: a legal betrothal was marriage in all but fact, though it had been by proxy and Aidan had never laid eyes on the girl.

He said several bitter things to himself, while he inclined to her stiffly, politely. Responsibility! By Gael law and custom, the girl was as much his charge as if she were true widow of his brother. And how in hell's name did it come about that O'Rafferty hadn't a cousin or someone to assume it instead? No matter—all dead at English hands, likely. He said noncommittally, "A pleasure to meet you, lady—" the conventional formula.

She smiled slowly at him. The thought just flitted across his mind that Aidan might have missed something by dying. Nessa O'Rafferty was not very tall or generous-rounded—and Fergal liked somewhat to take hold of in a woman—but for all her lack of stature, she had a neat little figure, as the shabby mended blue linen gown revealed, and a fine matt-white skin looking whiter against rich dark-auburn hair, and a fine pair of smoke-gray eyes with black lashes, if her mouth was a trifle large for strict beauty.

At the moment the gray eyes held an ironic small smile, and she said in her agreeable low-pitched voice, "Yes, I know it's awkward for you, O'Breslin! You never expected to have me left on your hands, did you? You'll have to blame it on the English, along with—other things. But I've tried to help your mother and Shevaun as I can."

Fergal accepted the hand she held to him, a small hard capable-feeling hand. "I'm sure of that, lady," he said. It wasn't that he disliked the girl; but, he thought savagely and ruefully, he'd sufficient responsibility on his back in this situation, for an unwed man of twenty-three, without this one in addition! Her cool glance told him that she read his mind accurately, and he was annoyed.

4

SHEVAUN WAS DEAD-WHITE and shaking, and her voice went high with fury. "Understand—understand? No, I don't understand and I don't want to, Roy Donlevy! So it's in your mind to go off to France or Spain or somewhere, for God knows how long—and away from me three years already!—and you've the—the damned gall to say it's for our own good! For Roy Donlevy's own good!—like the other men have turned their backs on wives and families that way! I never would have thought you—my Roy!—could conceive—"

"Now look, Shevaun," said Fergal, a wary eye on Roy's lowering frown. "You know Roy better than to think he's a man to shirk responsibility. He just thought—"

"Oh, *I* know what he thinks—and you too, all too likely!" She turned on him. "A fine life out there in foreign parts, swaggering about and taking war-loot in mercenary service!—oh, yes, much better than starving here under the English occupation! And not burdened with wife and family to look to, either—likely taking up with every inn-girl and wanton he lays eyes on—likely he already has, these three years!—and after a night with his own wife again he decides she's maybe not so satisfactory as some others he's— How you have the barefaced gall to say it, Roy Donlevy—for our own good!"

Donlevy just stood watching her, a big bull patient and stolid; but Fergal knew he was seething inwardly. "Shevaun, be quiet and use sense!" he ordered his sister sharply. "I don't say I'm for the plan, but Roy never thought that way at all, it's the money in his mind. I don't say it's good, to be away from you another year or two, but you can't miscall Roy like this—"

"Oh, can't I then! You men forever supporting each other! I do say it, I say he sees a fine chance for money and a merry life—and as a single man again!—and off he'll go—" Shevaun stopped abruptly and turned to face the dead hearth. Kevin McCann had appeared in the doorway of the hall with his hostess; and Shevaun was in a red fury, but the remnants of a decent upbringing held —one did not air family quarrels before outsiders.

McCann was aware of tension among them; his sardonic dark eyes slid over the girl's rigid pose, the set of Donlevy's mouth. He came to offer his hand to Fergal. "I'm just off, and thanks for the bed. God knows when we'll meet again, but luck with all of you."

"And with you, Kevin. Likely," said Fergal bitterly, "we'll be seeing each other over the border of Connacht."

"*Just* over the border," smiled McCann, touching the pistol in his belt.

"You'll take our good wishes to your wife," said Ethne O'Breslin politely, looking with worried eyes from her daughter to the other two men.

"Indeed." McCann inclined to the women and turned. Fergal accompanied him to the housedoor as courtesy demanded, and saw him out with reiterated wishes for luck. McCann's eyes said he could make a guess about the scene he'd interrupted; he made no comment, but went off quickly on his ten-mile walk home. When Fergal came back to the hall, Shevaun was railing at Roy again, saying it all over.

"If you don't care what becomes of me, I'd think as a man honorably raised you'd take some thought for little Sean!—a helpless three-year-old babe—and your legitimate heir! Plan, you say! Oh, all the fine promises you'd make about coming back with money, I'm sure—and that the last I'd ever see you the rest of my life—"

"Shevaun, we can't think that of Roy and in your right mind you know it," said her mother sharply. "I don't like the idea either, but—"

Donlevy turned his steady eyes, that had gone colder and colder the while Shevaun talked, to Fergal. "Now I'll say it just once to all of you, and that'll be that," he said in a hard tone. "By the law, we'll be destitute, and no chance here to better ourselves honest. Abroad I can earn money, and there'd be a chance at legitimate plunder too. I'll not pretend to you that I like army life, and God knows I don't look forward to being a soldier in foreign service, in the way of getting myself killed or maimed trying to fill my pockets. But it's the only chance I see to acquire any money."

"There at least you've said something," agreed Fergal.

Roy's eyes moved to Shevaun. "And you, my girl—you're a selfish child to take it like this. Nor I'm thinking you don't know me or love me the way you say at all, when right off you jump to the notion I'd turn my back on my duty. Thinking just for yourself you are. Are you thinking I want to go away from you—that I've not longed for you every hour these long years I've been away— that I'll not go on missing and wanting you all the while I'm overseas at a paid job—a job I've no inclination for?" He lifted a big hand in violent gesture, checked himself. "Maybe it's more fool I, for going on loving a woman without any generosity or understanding or trust for me at all—"

"Now, Roy," began Fergal cautiously. Donlevy went on unheeding.

"For that you haven't, to think such of me. But it's no matter how you think, Shevaun—your husband I am and it's for me to say, however you take it. My mind's decided—being a sensible man, I see it's the only way to make some sort of decent future for us and the boy. If—"

"I can't pretend to like it, Roy," said Ethne O'Breslin quietly, "but you are a man of sense, and Shevaun's husband. If you think it's the best plan, well, it's your deciding. Shevaun, you're talking wild as the spoiled youngster maybe you are, and an apology you owe your man for saying such things."

"Oh, connive at it with them because they are men, the great arrogant strong creatures riding roughshod over us! Take whatever ill-treatment they hand out, so meek and mild—well, I won't! Apologize! Every word I've said is God's truth and Roy knows it—"

Donlevy paid her no notice at all, but looked at Fergal. "The ordinary ways of life we can't live by anymore, Fergal. The woman and child are my responsibility, and you know I'm not running away from it. But, money to be had abroad or no, it won't be possible that I get money back to you—trust the English to have thought of that and have a law against it. I don't know how it might go—I hear that half a dozen foreign rulers have recruiting-agents in every Irish town, to sign up mercenaries under this law, but how long a man has to sign for, or the rate of pay, I don't know. I'll find out in Donegal today. And I'll need to ask you to take responsibility for the woman and boy while I'm away. I would think it'd be possible to send letters, and we'll keep in touch. And when I'm able, I'll come myself or make arrangements that Shevaun and the boy be got away from Ireland to join me."

"Well," said Fergal, "as Mother says, it's your decision, boy. I take your point. You know you can leave them to me meanwhile."

Donlevy gave an abrupt nod. "My thanks." Oh, mercy of God, thought Fergal wryly, didn't he know Roy Donlevy! Obstinate as the big red bull he was, he could be: try to cross him, it just turned him all the more stubborn. And if he had a fault—maybe away back somewhere in his ancestry there'd been some stolid long-headed Lowland Scot—it was that his mind worked purely in logical ways, on the basis of cold fact only, and nothing so enraged him as the emotional approach to a problem. That deliberate logical mind had examined this problem from all angles, and moved to a logical conclusion; and a deal of his anger at Shevaun was on account of her wild accusations, but half of it too because she had, womanlike, ignored the logic of his argument.

"I *won't* be left!" she cried now. "I'll—I'll—find some rich English officer to take me as mistress, if you go off from me—I swear I will—I'll—"

"Shevaun, for shame," said her mother.

"We'll find out more of the details," said Donlevy heavily, "in town today, Fergal, and make definite arrangements. Shevaun, as my wife you owe me some attention to my wishes. I've no rights over you in our law—and there are times I think maybe the barbarous English law might be convenient, giving a husband absolute control over a wife—but you will listen to me anyway. I want you to stay under Fergal's protection the while I'm away, do you hear? And when I'm able to send for you, you and the boy will come to me." He looked back at Fergal. "It may be by then you will want to get out of Ireland yourself, and will come away too."

Fergal shrugged. "Who can say? It will be as you ask, Roy, I'll look to Shevaun."

"You'll go—you're bound to go? Roy, I beg you—" It was a wail now. "Please, Roy—I'll never cross you again, if only—"

"You've heard what I said, Shevaun," and he gave her a dark steady look.

Her color flamed and she flung up her head. "Then I take back all my vows to you, Roy Donlevy—I'm no longer wife of yours, when you desert me so! I n-never want to lay eyes on you again! Go, then—get off to any foreign land you please, and I wish you a merry life of it—with however many doxies you can find to amuse you—and be damned to your fine promises!" She whirled and ran out of the hall, a hand to her face; and Donlevy made never a move to stop her or go after her.

"Oh, this spoiled child," murmured her mother. "Dear Roy, I'm so sorry for how she takes it—you know I don't feel so for you." She kissed his cheek. "I'd best try to make her see sense," and she hurried after Shevaun.

Fergal sat down at the table by the hearth and took up the decanter on it. Only about a tenth the normal yearly amount of home-manufactured *uisgebaugh* any estate had now: the grain was wanted for food: and likely in time to come there'd be none at all. He considered that Roy needed a longer drink than himself, measured it out accordingly in the two wooden cups out of the servants' hall, and handed one over. "Here, man."

Donlevy hadn't moved; he stood head lowered, looking at the floor, and took the cup and tossed off its contents without a word. "She's always had her own way," said Fergal. "It's because we're a small family, just the one daughter. A pity, but there it is. And being the youngest too—only natural she's been indulged. She'll come round, Roy, there's good stuff in Shevaun and a certain amount of common sense, when she's not in a temper."

Donlevy said briefly, "Let's hope so. I'll go up and fetch my cloak, and we'd best start for Donegal at once—a five-mile walk, and there's no telling how long the English Commission keeps men waiting, or what catechism we'll be put through." He went out.

Fergal poured himself another dram of whiskey; it was a chill morning and there was no fuel for house-fires. He drank half of it and turned at a step; Nessa O'Rafferty was coming up the hall. She wore the same shabby gown, but it became her for all its age and mended places, and her auburn hair was shining-neat in its twisted knot, and her gray eyes cool and placid on him.

"I gather that Shevaun's bent on making things more difficult than they might be," she said, pausing beside him.

"Say it twice," said Fergal with a short laugh. "Did you hear all that?"

"How could I help it?"

"God knows Roy Donlevy has faults, as all of us have, but he's not irresponsible—or a womanizer either, oddly enough."

"That's to be seen," said Nessa with a cool little nod. "Not the kind of man *I* happen to like, but I think Shevaun's a fool for all that, you know. He'll be a good husband to her, a reliable man, I'd say."

"He's a man you could trust to hell and back," said Fergal, "but I don't deny he's stubborn, and he doesn't speak out his real feelings easy."

"Yes, I see that. I'm sorry for him, Shevaun acting so. You know, O'Breslin, sometimes a girl will listen to one of her own age, when she won't to what her mother says. Would it be a help if I talked to her, do you think?"

He was a little surprised, and grateful; Nessa seemed to him to hold herself aloof, a bit, here. "It might help, yes, and thanks. I don't like to see Roy hurt so—not but what it's too late to mend that. . . . So you don't like reliable men?"

Nessa laughed, and she had a pretty low laugh, showing small white teeth. "Oh, well, I wouldn't go so far to say that, O'Breslin! Only, any sensible woman wants a man as husband who knows a little something about women—at least it seems only sense to me—not one of these innocents who've never sown wild oats, the way the English proverb runs. There's another proverb says that unpracticed musicians give no pleasure to listeners." And then she blushed faint, for unladylike openness.

He grinned up at her mechanically. "Very true, very sensible, lady." . . . No, the maidservant Ailsa hadn't run off or been carried off to serve English troops as a camp-follower, and she was still the somewhat slatternly willing girl he remembered: after long without a woman, she'd been a pleasure eagerly enjoyed last night

. . . but his mind wasn't running on that pleasure or any other now. He was thinking, wondering about this Commission for Transplantation office in Donegal. . . .

"The fool of the world I was," he said softly and savagely to Roy, "speaking out to that captain yesterday, so frank! Why for God's sake didn't you shut me up?—it was only temper. I might have told some long tale to repeat to these commissioners—never lifted a hand against a Parliament man, I didn't—" He shrugged, seeing how Hugh McFadden at Roy's other side smiled. "Well, I expect you're right—it won't matter much what we do or say, they won't be passing out any legally innocent, to retain land."

"That's foregone," said Donlevy laconically. "I'm only anxious to have this damned formality past now." He stared down at his clasped hands. "Not a word of French I have, needless to say—but there were a dozen just from roundabout signing themselves on with me. The Frenchman said, enough already signed, through the country, that they'll be forming an Irish Brigade as a separate regiment. And he said in any case, if and when an Irishman has their tongue, they like us for officers over their other mercenaries. But no knowing what rank I'll get until I'm there—troopmen only offered thirty crowns a year, I'll hope they give me some rank over that. But it seems there are thousands of us going—France, Spain, Austria—there's even agents taking men for the Russian Czar and Poland. There'll be a scramble for officer-rank."

"So many as that, fleeing from their families?" Hugh looked shocked.

Donlevy shook his head slowly. "You forget how many have died, brother. There must be many men went off three years back, leaving parents, wives, children—and coming home to find they're all dead. But I wouldn't doubt that some men are only—running away."

"Roy," said Fergal suddenly, "you're not happy about it, I know. Go back and say you've changed your mind. We'll make do somehow."

"Too late," said Donlevy with a mirthless laugh. "I've taken the French king's gold louis, man. I never was happy for it, but it seems to me the only plan. And do you ask me, Fergal, even in a foreign land and alone, and Shevaun feeling the way she does for me, and all—I think I'll be better off than you. From what we've seen, Ireland won't be a good place to live from now on."

Fergal stared down at the warped old wooden floor of the town council-hall, which this Commission had taken for its office here. He knew what was in Donlevy's mind, as in all their minds: any man who had traveled any distance in Ireland recently. One thing it had been to hear Hugh talk of it, that day: another to see it: and every man in the army had seen it before, on the way west ahead of the English forces. They hadn't spoken of it much on their way north—maybe, for all their ugly experience of war and death, he and Roy and McCann had been shocked too deep—and Hugh more so, of inexperience. . . . The empty farm-cabins, in country which had been thick-populated and prosperous: four out of five empty they passed, and who to say where the folk had gone?—dead of plague or famine, the most killed by English soldiers. It was a small marvel to see a farm-cottage with smoke from its chimney. And in the remote glens and valleys, you'd often enough find the unburied corpses, the last to die, in cottage or ditch or field. The land was ravaged: it was desolate and frighteningly silent with death. No herds in the fields, and the fields lying fallow, unplanted, for all the men dead who would have planted them.

He was a landowner, but he had never put hand to plowshare or scythe. Despite the English domination for four hundred and seventy years, that domination growing over more territory each generation, it had been possible for Irish in the north and west to keep to their own law and way, for all practical matters. There, the clan law still held as the highest rule: and it was based on different ideas than English law. Now, under this Act, the clans would be broken, and some confusion would ensue for the living under English law, in addition to all else. . . . According to tradition, Fergal O'Breslin had been elected chief of his clan; the rank was not hereditary, as rank from the old High King down had never been, in Ireland. True, only those of a chief's line had candidacy, and in the minor clans the title passed down regular enough, as it had to him; still, the rank and the election meant something—or it had until now. He grinned wryly to himself, thinking of what Roy had said about the English marriage-law. In Irish law, most of the strict tradition was put on chiefs and nobles, the higher the rank the more laws were set about such men to keep them honest:

likely because the canny fellows who made the law eighteen hundred years back knew human nature, that power corrupts. . . . This Fergal O'Breslin had learned to read in books and write a legible hand, to judge a horse, to administer tenant-land, to handle a sword and handgun, to draw a covey for stag, and this and that beside of what a chief and gentleman was expected to know. It didn't seem to him that any of it would prove useful now, in this situation; contrariwise, his rank put additional burdens on him.

Many dead, but there were still too many people who naturally looked to him to take the responsibility. The house-servants, and those of the tenant-farmers left. He thought of old Tadgh, rising seventy and half-crippled with rheumatism: of a dozen old, incapable folk on the home-farms; and always of his mother and Shevaun. It was a thing a chief, a landowner, had never needed to think about—mere living, shelter, and food. But every soul in Ireland would need to think about it now, whatever his rank.

Donlevy moved restlessly at his side. "How long will they keep us kicking our heels here, for Christ's sake?" An hour or more they'd been waiting now, since giving their names to the clerk at the door.

"It can scarcely be press of business," said Fergal, essaying a laugh; they were the only men waiting in this musty little anteroom. Most of those living roundabout would have been—what was the English word?—processed before now. "Government officials, Roy—naturally they're disinclined to work. And we must be impressed with our lowly status as conquered men." He turned to Hugh. "Remember what I told you, now—you'll say you're my retainer, late of the army. Don't get flustered, likely they'll not question you long, as you're not a landholder."

"No reason you should take responsibility for me, O'Breslin."

"I don't, man, I can't! But it's a convenient story for you to tell, to get banished in peace, as it were. You—" He shut his mouth as the inner office-door opened.

The English clerk repeated his name expressionlessly, and he got up at the peremptory gesture. In the larger office, a civilian Englishman sat at a table, in the one chair. He had a stack of account-books before him, others piled on shelves behind. Fergal went up to the table and waited.

When the Englishman judged he'd waited long enough, to have

his inferior position emphasized, he condescended to look up. He repeated Fergal's name in a bored voice. "Oh, yes. Does not claim innocency, I believe. Reported to Cap'n Wilson of the Sixth Troop, had recently left enemy military service. Well?" He glanced up sharply.

Fergal said evenly in English, "That's so."

"Landholder. I've a record of it, as one of the larger estates— if not near s' big as some." Pale eyes flickered rapidly over him. "Sixteen—thousand—acres. Here 'tis. Will you just read the official description if you can read English, an' agree to it."

Fergal glanced over the paper handed him. Rage and confusion mingled in him, foolishly, for this—a little thing—his home, symbol of all he was, set down in precise descriptive English (oh, trust the English to get all the legalities down on paper!)—this boundary, that boundary, so many outbuildings on so many tenant-farms, so many rooms to the main house, so much natural water and uncut wood. . . . He heard his voice shake as he said, "It is correct." *Wasting breath it would be to try to explain—but most of it not my land, in trust for the clan, lived on and administered by clansmen.*

"Very well. Not all's arable land, of course. . . . D'you claim any form of innocency under the law?" The man was playing with his quill, twiddling it in his fingers.

"You've just reminded me I cannot, when I admit to having been in the Federation army."

The Englishman slid a sly glance up swiftly, and down again. A glance impatient, a man forced to deal with stupidity. "If you 'ave anything to discuss *with*, I mean abaht, Master Hammond's the man to see—my superior—I could pass you in to 'im."

Enlightenment came to Fergal, and a peculiar cold rage . . . which was a damned unreasonable way to feel, maybe. *Under the conquest and occupation of a nation that could not even carry out legal-arranged theft without trickery among the administrators!* He leaned down across the table, forcing the fellow to meet his eyes. "You're saying that if I had gold to offer—for you and your superior and likely his superior to split, to satisfy all of you who've aught to do with the record-keeping—you'd overlook my position in law and confirm me in my land-title."

The clerk smiled uneasily. "No need talk s' crude. There's always the chance, Irish."

Fergal laughed. "It must be the hell of a long one, that any Irishman would have aught left to bribe with! Just as a matter of curiosity, have you come across many able to oblige you?"

"Not one in ten thousand," said the Englishman with a contemptuous grin. "But no 'arm to keep on askin', eh? You never know. It's the Commission for Allotment offices where the real pickings are, if you want t' know."

Of course, they would be. Quite expectable, thought Fergal. All those Englishmen with legal claim to so many acres of arable land, and a good many of them with cash in hand for bribes: the officers, the adventurers. Gold changing hands secret, and fertile land officially written down as barren so it could be thrown in free with this estate or that. Conspiracy among the high commissioners to share out among themselves the administration of government-retained land. And, as anyone could predict, clever men getting at the common soldiers—simple, ignorant men homesick for their own places—and buying up their land-claims for half a dozen drinks and a little persuasion. Oh, yes, there must be fine easy profits for good businessmen in Ireland these days!

"Of course, you'd ask," he said to the clerk. "First question for any landholder, that one—you don't want to miss out any chance, however long! But you must all be damned tired of asking us, always getting the same answer!" For what indeed had any Irishman to bribe with now? Their wealth had been in herds, in horses, in crops, and whatever their houses had held of value besides, the soldiers had looted long since.

"You speak civil to your superiors, Irish," snapped the clerk.

Fergal held down his fury with difficulty. This little sly middle-class rabbit of an English accountant! "Be sure if I'd anything to offer, I'd bargain with you and damned glad to! As it is, I can't take advantage of your—kindness."

"Orl right then, an' why not say so t' begin with? And I said you'll speak civil! Papist, are you?" The man drew a blank form-paper to him and dipped his quill. "Rank in Federation army? . . . Full name and age . . . You go dahn in class number two, native Irish, Papist, officer enemy army late ree-bellion, all land an' possessions to be confiscated an' vacated immediate. I've the list of those in that 'ouse 'ere—nine females, all Irish Papist, three males ditto, one male child. I take it those'll be all be goin' with you into Connacht? Any others, an' if so 'ow many?"

"I don't know. Yes, one other man—he's waiting to see you, to be classified, Hugh McFadden. Others—I'm not sure." The tenant-people left—well, they would all be banished too, as individuals. "My immediate household, just those fourteen people, yes."

"Very well. 'Ere's your paper." It was a poor-quality sheet, the ink sunk in unevenly. "Mind you don't lose it or you'll be an official vagrant an' subject to arrest. It's good for yourself an' those fourteen persons only, an' you must travel in group, there'll be patrols along all roads to check. You've twenty-four hours to vacate the property an' get on your way. Strict forbidden to remove anything from the 'ouse—there's been an inventory, so don't try. . . . What can you take? Clothes on your backs, a blanket apiece if you 'ave 'em, food. No weapons allowed." The clerk was filling out another form. " 'Ere's your land-grant papers." He pushed it across the table. "You'll present this to an office of the Commission for Transplantation across the Connacht border."

Fergal looked at it. "The transplantation law reads that men whose land is confiscated shall receive land to one third the value in Connacht. This is a claim on twelve acres."

"Even the English Parliament can't make the province o' Connacht no bigger than God did," said the clerk. "An' what's writ in law an' what's done, it's two different things, times. That's what you get, Irish—be grateful. I might o' made it fifteen but for your tone o' voice. Orl right, you're classified an' done, you can get out."

With shaking hands Fergal folded the papers away in his pocket and got to the door while he still held his temper in check.

5

"I'M SORRY TO be such a trouble to you, O'Breslin," murmured the old man faintly.

"Well, speak of trouble," said Fergal brusquely, helping Tadgh lie down and wishing he'd something to put over him, "I seem to recall Aidan and I caused you some in our time, Tadgh. Coming in over your clean floors all wet and muddy from hunting, and getting you to cover up for us to Father when we'd some devilment in hand . . . Is it better you feel now?"

Tadgh managed a smile and nod, but Fergal didn't like the look of him, so blue around the mouth. An old man, Tadgh McFergus; he'd been of a home-farm family, Fergal remembered hearing, but for fifty years a servant at the O'Breslin house.

He looked up in relief as Hugh came to sit beside them at the edge of the road. He'd have said he was a tolerably good judge of men, but some surprises he'd had this eleven days, the way people would act under such hardship. . . . It seemed much longer than four or five weeks ago that he'd first laid eyes on Hugh McFadden, running in panic from English, an impractical lay-brother with no knowledge of the world. Hugh was one of the surprises: the only one of them always cheerful, never complaining, astonishingly competent. He was smiling now at the old servant, taking off his cloak to cover him. "Take your time to rest, man. It's no matter when we get to Connacht—a long while to September and danger at being this side the border."

"But we must—by planting time." Old anxious eyes on Fergal. "To get the fields sown—best we can, to have food for next winter."

Fergal did not ask him where he thought they'd get seed for sowing, even with the little cash in hand they had to spend. He was worrying for a nearer time than next winter—for three or four days from now, when the food they carried would be gone.

He let Hugh reassure Tadgh; he looked back down the road to where the rest of them came straggling up, and not for the first time utter incredulity filled his mind. Like those dreams you dimly knew were dreams, so you weren't panic-stricken for fearful danger or much embarrassed at the ridiculous things happening. Stepped into this nightmare he had when he walked out of that Commission office twelve days ago; nothing had felt like real life since. It was nothing that could be happening (so said the private compass inside a man that had nought to do with hard facts), that he was sitting here at a muddy roadside somewhere in Leitrim, hungry and tired and afoot, watching his mother and sister come toward him looking like that.

And the damned odd thing was, he'd seen it all in a picture before—where? Unwilling boy at lessons with that prosy old tutor, a book in Latin, stories from Scripture, and a drawing of the Israelites fleeing Egypt, yes.

They came up to him and stopped. His mother's face drawn and tired under the hood of her cloak pulled up against the mist. Shevaun white and sullen-quiet, way she'd been since Roy had left; and the little boy Sean a sleeping dead weight across her shoulder, his red mat of curls tangled with her black. Nessa O'Rafferty, black shabby cloak with hood up, head down, carrying the two military packs. And behind them the rest: erstwhile maid-servant Ailsa McFergus, Tadgh's granddaughter, brown slattern wench—the other five servant-women, two young, two middle-aged, and Tadgh's wife, Eily, sturdy stout old woman shuffling along tireless. Three menservants, Art McTally who'd been head-groom when there were horses in the stable, and Tadgh's great-nephew Larr, and young Liam Fagan, just taken on as stableboy three years ago, bare sixteen now. A beggarly bunch of ragged gypsies, they looked—a chief's household!

Eily laid down her bundle and went to sit beside Tadgh; she talked inconsequentials in a comfortable voice, and the anxiety faded from his look. Shevaun sat down, graceless; the boy woke and began to fret, and she patted him in silence, soothing. "Would you like a drink, Mother?" asked Fergal dully. "I'll fetch it." He found the wooden mug in Hugh's pack, got up and started for the riverbank a hundred feet off the road. Nessa followed him and caught up where the thin trees began.

"We'll all do with a drink; I'll help you carry it." She had the pewter decanter they'd smuggled out. "The poor old man, it's hard on him, all this way. And I don't know but what—God forgive me to say it—he'd be better dead and out of it."

"No man's better dead," said Fergal hardly. "One less mouth to feed, were you thinking?"

She gave him a level look. "No, I wasn't, O'Breslin. But I might, easy—and so might you—easier, as head of the household." They came to the stream and knelt to drink and fill the poor containers.

"You and Roy Donlevy out of the same cloth," said Fergal. "The logical mind. Unnatural in a woman."

She drank, and rinsed the container, and held it to fill again. "Is it? Maybe."

The aimless anger in him, against everything in sum, suddenly needing a target to aim at, he said low and bitter, "You always so aloof and cool, whatever any says to you! As well my brother died, to miss a coldhearted wife!"

Nessa stood up, holding the filled decanter. Her smoke-gray eyes were hard on him. "And maybe that's so too, O'Breslin. We will all be living close, and likely losing our tempers now and then in consequence—if we live at all—and I expect it's only right you should know something of me, as you haven't asked, have you? Otherwise I'd not go chattering about how I feel to a stranger, even one who—even you. So you think I'm cold and hard, O'Breslin? You knew little enough about me when that betrothal was made, my stepfather's word your father took—and, no, you've not asked since you've—in this last while, have you? Of course you thought he was dead, didn't you, calling on an antiquated little legality to ensure a roof for me?—family of my betrothed—when none of you'd ever laid eyes on me!" Her voice shook; she steadied it. "And maybe it's a surprise to you he's not my own father?"

"I—did not recall, if I knew, no."

"Well, he's not—my blood-uncle, brother of my father. He's not dead, you know. Any would have told you, if you'd asked. He wanted to be free to take foreign service—just like Shevaun's husband—only he pays just lip service to duty, you see. He's in the service of the King of Spain—and he might have money by now, to help me somehow—but he won't, I know. It was an easy way to be rid of me, that was all. He never liked me much; he held it against me that my mother had no children by him, no heir. I know I'm an added burden on you, and whatever the law says it's not a rightful one. If there was anything else I could do, I'd not be here—but as it is, I am doing what I can, and I will. That's the matter, O'Breslin, and—and I'm sorry that you find me—aloof and hard—but maybe I've reason—and I don't feel so to your mother and Shevaun, anyway."

"Well, I'm sorry, Nessa," he said, looking at the overflowing wooden cup. "I'm sorry I snapped at you."

"No matter, I know you're worried to death about what will come—you were only taking it out on the nearest thing to hand." But she was still breathing quickly. "I've seen you thinking I was proud and cold, and maybe I am a bit—but I'm not taking it for granted as my right, that you or anyone else is responsible for— I'd *never* have come to your house, when he—but there wasn't anywhere else—"

"All right, you needn't go on feeling guilty for his doing."

"How can I help it? Another mouth to feed—you said it yourself!—pushing me off on you to be rid of me—"

"Well, damn, it's done and here we all are," said Fergal with a shrug. "I see how you feel, Nessa, but there's no sense brooding on it. Though I must say I'm surprised he didn't just marry you off somewhere."

She laughed sharply. "Not so easy, O'Breslin! I've no dowry at all now, and with everything in this state, men worried about the future and hesitant to take on more responsibility—"

"Yes, I see. Well, here you are, and if you're another mouth you're also another pair of hands. I'm sorry I—thought wrong about you." And he added, wanting to clear the bitterness from her eyes and not knowing how, "You know my mother's fond of you, and Shevaun too."

And as he turned back to the road, he heard her murmur, "Poor Shevaun. Yes. I've a great right to complain, for such little things, when Shevaun—even if it is part her own fault."

Tadgh was sitting up, looking better, and accepted a drink

gratefully. "We'll go on in a minute," and Ethne O'Breslin summoned a smile for Fergal. "It's not been a bad day, and we can't be far off now."

Not far off the border town of Carrick-on-Shannon, one of the places where a transplantation-office was, to allot land-claims. But where would he be allotted land?—Mayo or Connemara maybe, and another eighty miles to walk? He sat between his mother and Shevaun, and helplessly he found his mind enumerating all the horses he'd ever had. . . . Even an ass, or an ox-yoke like the old-fashioned farmers used . . . Even one horse, even that little nasty-tempered brown English gelding he'd taken off the enemy at the fight near Trim. All the troop-horses they'd killed for food last year, running and starving across Tipperary and Clare . . .

Only by God's grace he'd hung on to his temper that morning they left the house, that arrogant bastard of an English captain and his troop there to check them out and off, demanding the papers, counting heads, saying by rights he should have their bundles searched for weapons and valuables. Fergal had the handgun he'd taken from the deserter in the pocket of his shirt, buttoned under his doublet; if he'd had it to hand, or his belt-knife with it, he'd have used it. That Englishman, watching them off, out of the house built by Fergal's great-grandsire, marshaling them onto the road as he'd drive a herd of cattle.

On foot they had come, and meeting and passing many along the way—old and young, alone or in straggling groups; and passing, now and then, the dead and dying too, the sick lying at the roadside tended or untended, the men grave-digging for the lucky ones who had folk to bury them. Seventy-odd miles on foot, down the muddy wet spring roads, laden with what they were let to take, and a few things smuggled out illegal—the few things of value left in what had been a moderately wealthy house. The men in laborers' clothes, warmer and more practical, tight woolen trews, doublet and shirt—and they, like the women, wearing one set over another to carry as much as possible; a blanket apiece, and rolled in them the bone or wood-handled knives and spoons, cups, a stray dish or two, and extra pairs of shoes or sandals, and food—all they'd managed to collect for the journey. Beside the pistol and dagger hidden, Fergal had a small hoard of gold his father had hid away years ago, that the English hadn't found—ten pounds equivalent, in Spanish and English coin; he had his own gold seal-ring, and his mother and Shevaun had preserved their gold wedding-rings from the soldiers. That was what remained of an old and proud house.

And the day they came to Dromahair, the sixth day, they had news from a former troopman of McGeraghty's, chance-met: the fort at Kilronan taken three days after Fergal and Roy had got away, and only a handful left alive—Cathal O'Breslin dead, O'Connor and O'Brien and McGeraghty. And Fergal had had affection for his bluff good-hearted uncle, but it seemed just one more thing.

When he came to think of it, cold and sane, he wondered that they'd got so far, old folk among them, and so little food, and the gentlewomen not used to physical effort—without illness or death. The spring so damp and chill, the roads bad, and they'd slept out in field and wood, on the ground. Eleven days they'd taken to here, what with the women and the child and old Tadgh.

"Tadgh's feeling better, Fergal, and we'd best get on." His mother's hand on his arm. He roused himself and got up with an effort. The boy was crying tiredly, thinly, and Shevaun stooped to lift him—a sturdy three-year-old surprisingly heavy, as Fergal knew.

"I'll take him awhile—" But Hugh was already there.

"Give him to me, lady, I'll carry him a bit. There, lad, quiet now, tired you are but you can sleep on my shoulder."

"He's not so much tired as hungry," said Shevaun. All the way, all the while since Roy had left her that day, she had been silent, withdrawn, a stranger to the old laughing, careless, easy Shevaun they had known. She hadn't complained overmuch along the road, she did her part and tended the child, but listlessly. Now her voice sounded rusty with disuse. "Thank you, Hugh."

And there came a thud of horses round the curve of the road ahead, and another patrol. Fergal had stopped noting how many times they'd been halted and questioned. Any Englishman, on official patrol or not, had the right to stop and examine transplanting Irish, and they took pleasure doing so. This was official patrol, mounted captain, a dozen mounted men. Fergal eyed the horses with numb, furious envy, good round-barreled troop-horses and, by God, all Irish-bred too, by their size and weight—hunter-bred for boggy, hilly country, not light and rangy like the English troop-mounts. He groped for his official papers, worn and dirty from many fingerings.

"Transplanters," said the officer. "Papers? . . . Fifteen, that is right, nine females, five male adults, one child. You can go on." He looked down at Fergal, easy in the saddle, carelessly encouraging. "With luck you can make the border by nightfall—you're four miles from Carrick, the nearest border-station."

"That's good news," said Hugh almost genially.

Fergal fell into step beside him as they moved on. "You needn't speak up so friendly to them," he remarked sourly.

Hugh's tone was tranquil. "It's only sense to see the brightest side of the coin, O'Breslin. We're in God's hands; I take what He sends us and will make of it the best I can. Don't worry at things, friend—it's no good. You can't help it, I know, for the responsibility you feel. Myself, I have kept my faith to all my extent, and I'm at peace to trust in God."

But it was different for Hugh, thought Fergal. Hugh who reckoned his life less important than his precious history-manuscript entrusted to him. Since he'd done what he could to preserve it safe, it was a secret and a worry off his mind, and he seemed in a queer state of peace as he'd said. As if now it was up to God, to save it or not if He chose.

The coffer was wrapped in thick cloth, buried at the cost of a night's hard toil, upon stone, under the hearthstone of the hall in the O'Breslin house at Lough Eask.

They came into the border-station at Carrick just after dusk. It had been a large village; it was swollen tenfold in population now—transient English population: peddlers. Those thronged the few muddy streets, alert at placing transplanting Irish; they urged their wares ceaselessly. Most of the formerly wealthy men, gentry-landowners, would have kept a few valuables, a handful of cash money; they wouldn't keep those long, and they'd not be passing over this border again—legally. This might be their last chance to acquire many little things they'd be needing and wanting, and a number of enterprising Englishmen had realized that. Hot bargaining was going on all over town.

Fergal found a money-changer and converted one of the Spanish eight-pieces into small English coin, not letting the man see he had more. "To hell with it," he said to his mother's protest, "I won't see you sleep open in a town street. But I'd not put it past them to question how we've the coin to pay for lodging!" He should have known better, of the English: they liked money too well; the local commission-officers and military were operating the inns and vacated town-houses at a nice profit, and he hired two rooms for the women, another for the men, at a shilling apiece, an exorbitant rate.

The Commission office was shut for the day. He was feeling reckless and moody, and he went off alone to look for a drink, if there was any to be had. At the first place he asked, he ran into McCann. "You made better time down, I see, but you'll not have so many with you. Have they any whiskey here?"

"No, but I know a man has some," said McCann. "Come along." He led Fergal down several dark streets—trust Kevin McCann to nose out the nearest whiskey!—to rap at a darkened house; a little ferret-faced fellow let them in, greeting them in Irish.

"Well, and what's an Irishman doing still in business?" wondered Fergal.

"Convenient to the border, he's four months to cross," McCann grinned. "He likely does some favors for the English on the side." Over whiskey they brought each other up to date. "No, I've only Maire with me—the servants and tenants all dead, or wandered off, or kidnapped by English. We came down easy, I stole a horse out of a troop-stable halfway down, at Dromahair, and kept to the back ways to avoid patrols. I've not been to the office yet to make my claim, I had an idea there'd be secret dealing of this and that sort already established, and I wanted to investigate possibilities. . . . Hell's own luck I had to turn the horse loose before we came into town, but I'll pick up another. I'll go to the office in the morning, find about my allotment."

"If mine's in the same direction we may as well travel together."

McCann looked at him consideringly. "Look, boy," and he leaned closer, "you're a man I trust, and a good man in a fight. I'd not be sorry to have you alongside me. Are you thinking to settle down uncomplaining to dig and toil on Connacht rock and starve to death slow—or would you take a risk for something better?"

"That's a damn' senseless question," said Fergal. "Say on."

"That's just what I can't do, this side the border. A good deal depends on where we find ourselves settled. But I said men wouldn't lie down so meek to be measured for burial, and they don't. From what I hear, even in the five months since transplantation began, there's secret traders and secret raiders got busy, and loot for more to take. Not exactly as I'd visualized it, but opportunity nonetheless, for men with the boldness to reach for it."

"Mhm, yes," said Fergal. "Bands of highwaymen swooping down on lone English travelers, not much they'd get for their pains that was useful. Cash money, but jewelry and so on, nowhere to convert it. For the moment at least—or some time to come—no merchant the other side the border has much to sell, and this side we'd not be let to spend it. . . . It'll be raiding and trading on everything else, that money means—the stray heifers and horses, tools and weapons and cut timber and cloth—"

"For awhile," said McCann. "But mark it, Fergal, in time there'll be trade built up, with cash changing hands, in the big towns. Those canny Galway merchants, you don't think they'll give up their centuries-old trade with Spain for a little English law?—and the half of them with Spanish in-laws! And there are merchants other places—Roscommon town, Castlereagh, Castlebar, Ballinasloe, Ennis. And in this direction, always three out of five Englishmen who'll turn a blind eye to law to make cash profit."

"As you say." Fergal slid a hand up his jaw thoughtfully. "If we're anywhere near to the border—with fast horses—eight or ten good men—"

"You're seeing it the way I do." They leaned close, heads together over the table in this corner of the smoky little place, talking low. "And we wouldn't be leading the only raiders, like as I say—there's bands crossing the border now, coming down on the farms already settled by English, three nights a week, to pick up what they can. There'll be men eager to join us for a chance at loot, but we'd want to be careful about who we took in."

"I've three trusty men," said Fergal. "I tell you, Kevin, a bit different I'm seeing this than when you said it that day on Knockmagh. But one other thing I see, and that is, it couldn't be a matter of a band of professional robbers, with a permanent camp hidden up some glen or in hills. A damn' silly melodramatic way to go about it, and besides it'd mean leaving the women alone, and my old servants—"

"Am I a fool? Of course I see that." McCann shrugged, and the amused thought just crossed Fergal's mind that Kevin would prefer it to be like that—the bold robber-chief in his mountain fastness. A flamboyant rakehell of a fellow McCann had always been, but a man of ideas and a good man to fight alongside. "Innocent peaceful farmers, boy, if the English come asking about stolen goods—as they will!—living quiet on our allotted land, and ignorant entirely of these wild thieves who go raiding."

"Well, damn, Kevin, I'm with you all the way, but we're counting the hell of a lot of fish before we cut a pole or string a net. For any business like that, we'd need to be in a night's ride of the border."

"And I think there's a chance we will be," said McCann. He laughed, finishing his drink. "Like I told you, there's dealing already going on. I expect you found out in Donegal that most of the Commission men'd take bribes, if we had aught to offer. All these peddlers here and at every border-station—I heard from the fellow who keeps this inn, as if I couldn't have guessed it for myself—most of their wares have been bought with cash advanced by the commissioners and military officers, for a fat percentage of the profits. And among other things, the Commission offices find it convenient to hire Irish clerks for the routine account-work—at a lower wage than they'd pay English, and the Irish eager to make anything in coin, see—and likely the difference sticks to authorities' fingers here and there. But the point is, those clerks have acquired some information that way. I met one of them in here yesterday, and he told me something that sounds damned encouraging. Let's have another drink. . . . Oh, Christ's love, man, forget the money! —with any luck, we can afford to be reckless!"

"Well, what did the clerk say?" prompted Fergal as McCann came back with more whiskey.

"You know how damned methodical English are. They started out, last November, to allot transplanters' land from the west coast inland—see?—the first presenting claims were sent out to coastal areas, and when the coast strip was all allotted, the next claims were granted a bit inland—to make all the settlement in order, gradually fill up the land inwards toward the border. Well, there's four months left to the date when the settlement's supposed to be accomplished, but at this station they've already used up the land they're authorized to grant in Mayo and Sligo and Connemara and

Galway, and since last month they've had only their slice of Roscommon left to allot. Other border-stations are maybe in the same situation, I don't know, but this one is anyway."

"I'll be damned. Useful to know, yes. That makes it sound a deal more practicable, if we're bound to get land in Roscommon. At its widest part, over by Castlereagh, it can't be over forty miles to the border, and most of it's nearer twenty. With luck, we'll be in raiding distance—"

"My very thought. We'll see how it goes tomorrow, but I've a feeling we'll be lucky. And another thing, the orderly way they work it, men who present claims at the same time, they get acreages adjoining."

Fergal swallowed the rest of his whiskey. "Nine in the morning?"

"Nine it is—I'll meet you at the Commission office," agreed McCann.

Fergal's shabby retinue was waiting patiently in the communal room at the inn where they'd spent the night, when he and McCann came back from the Commission office at midday. Most of them were sitting in a row on one of the long side-benches, Maire McCann between Shevaun and Nessa; anxiety and privation on the journey had changed her a bit from the elegant, reserved lady Fergal had met a few times, but she was still a lovely woman—if not quite the sort of wife he'd have conceived for McCann, conventional opposite to his exuberance. They all looked up as the men came in, and the same question was in all their eyes.

As they crossed the room toward the company, McCann murmured, "That's a handsome girl you got wished on you." Fergal shot him a side-glance only half-humorous. The last thing that troubled McCann was his marriage-vow.

"More important things to talk of," he returned easily, and came up to the bench. "You look like a class of children waiting a tutor's instructions," and he laughed. "I'll not keep you in suspense. We've only twelve-fifteen miles to go."

"Praise God," said his mother dryly. "And what at the end of it?"

"Twelve acres of land and a farm-cottage on it, so the grant says. McCann has the ten acres adjoining. We're not far off a village called Elphin, ten miles direct from Lough Boderg on the Shannon and the border."

"That's good news about the cottage," said Hugh, but he looked between Fergal and McCann speculatively, for the high spirits neither could hide.

Maire McCann rose. "You'll want to be starting at once then, Kevin?" Her eyes held some odd expression on him, some feeling Fergal couldn't identify: but she was the same cool, formal, gracious lady he remembered, and there was the same empty politeness in her tone as she turned to Ethne O'Breslin: "We'll make company for each other on the road, will we not?"

But he wasn't interested in Maire, and he had a good many other things to think about, tentative plans. . . . The women and the servants went off to collect their bundles, and McCann said, "I'll buy you a drink for the road."

"Done." They had both forgot Hugh, still there. He shook his head, smiling, at the belated offer.

"We'd never enough money for such extravagances and I'm not used to it. . . . Something's happened, O'Breslin, to put you in good spirits overnight," he added as McCann went off. "If I had to make a guess, I'd say that you and McCann have your heads together over some scheme, and likely an unlawful one."

"And you might be right. Would it trouble your tender conscience to profit from theft on the English? Scripture says something about an eye for an eye, I think."

"A question for a theologian," said Hugh gravely. "You haven't asked how I spent the coin you trusted to me. I think I struck some bargains, inexperienced though I am at haggling. I've a good sackful of potato-tubers, all with live eyes for taking root—enough to plant one field—and a sack of rye-seed, and three spades and two pitchforks—I didn't dare buy more, for they're an added burden, and we've enough to carry as it is. I hesitated over the scythe, but it's a necessary thing, and I got the man down to three shillings."

"Yes, that's good," said Fergal absently. "You did well, Hugh."

Hugh said softly, "An unwordly lay-brother I may have been for most of my life, O'Breslin, but I've some native intelligence. I don't in truth need to ask you about the idea in your mind. Don't take offense, my friend—but McCann is a man mishonest by nature, and a selfish man. Any scheming of his—"

Fergal laughed sharply. "I've shared army-camps with Kevin McCann often enough to know him! I don't say I'd trust him with a woman I had any rights over, or a store of liquor! But he knows me too, and how far he can go." He grinned at Hugh. "And as to that, brother, you needn't imply me such a fainthearted weakling, that I'd need McCann to coax me into the enterprise! I'd not have been long making the scheme and putting it into operation myself, once I saw where I was situated! I'm not a fool either, or I trust a coward, to turn the other cheek to an enemy while I've strength in my right arm."

"And what then," asked Hugh, "when you are lying dead in a ditch with an English bullet in you, a robber caught up to?"

"They've been aiming at me for three years and more, and never hit me anywhere vital yet! If that happens, I'll just need to leave my responsibility in God's hands."

"Which is where we all are anyway," said Hugh.

Part
Two

"The fire in the flint shows not until it is struck."
—Proverb

6

NESSA O'RAFFERTY stopped to regain her breath when she came to the top of the climb through the wood, up from the McCanns' house that lay higher still over this little cleft, and where the trees ended she sat on a leveled tree-stump and looked down the hill to Fergal O'Breslin's house. She wasn't really being lazy; there wasn't a deal to do, now the small harvest was in. . . . Queer, life was. A time, not so long ago either, harvest had been just a word to her.

She wondered if Fergal was home yet from the latest raid. Likely she'd have met Art or Liam coming up the hill with the horses, to the hidden pasture, if so. Just as well she'd not met Art up here, alone. But that would come out open, to be dealt with somehow, soon or late; it just went through her mind as fleeting annoyance. She went on looking down the long slope of the hill, absent and dreamy, to the patches of fields and the house. A deal different it looked from the cottage they'd come to, six months gone. A long involuntary shudder went through her. So silly: long past and done, and—and just nature, like as Hugh said; but until the day she died, she thought, that would be an ugly-sharp memory in her mind.

Coming across the open muddy field from the road, end of the journey at last, and the women anyway eager to see the cottage, how big it was and all. Fergal wrestling with the rusty door-latch, and that stench drifting out, sharp and cloying; and Fergal stepping back quick from the open door, ordering the women away . . . but not before she'd seen. A dead man there propped against the wall, staring out ghastly—long dead, but not long enough. Someone crept into the place to die, a month or two back—or maybe the former owner.

They'd made a fire in the field away from the cottage, and stayed in the open that night, while the men—did what must be done, and cleaned the place, and next day they gathered green rowan off the hill and set it smoldering on the hearth, to fumigate. But Nessa thought all the other women shared her own feeling about that room. She was glad she slept in one of the new rooms with Shevaun now. Altogether the men had built four new rooms onto the original two, with sawn timber Fergal had got in exchange for things taken on raids. It was still just a cottage, not a real house —all of wood, and the rooms small. But with Larr McFergus gone, living up the hills with some of the other men who made up the raiding-company—and Hugh McFadden not here permanent, traveling about as he did, the house held them all in reasonable comfort—as comfort went these days, this place. Better off than many, they were.

She wondered about that place up in the wooded hills beyond McCann's house. What with all the military patrols since there was so much raiding across the border, they'd found that hidden spot to bring the plunder temporary, to keep the horses. . . . And it was all the plunder taken, of course, that had built the new rooms and put things in them—enough tableware and plates to go round, and cooking utensils, and extra blankets, and so on—even, now, six bottles of French wine sitting on the makeshift cupboard in the main room; and wasn't that men for you, thought Nessa in exasperation. Not to say it wasn't bold—and useful—of them to go raiding on the English, but it made some inconveniences too, in the nature of things. French wine, when they hadn't enough chairs to sit on or anything but rude pallet-beds. But of course you couldn't fetch big furniture over the river on horseback, and workmen and materials were scarce here.

More to the point, with the able-bodied men all out four nights a week, at a hard thirty-mile ride over and back, they weren't inclined to work in the fields daytimes, and couldn't be expected. Nessa didn't have to look at her hands, she knew how rough and calloused they were now. Nessa O'Rafferty, born into gentry, her worst task a little genteel mending, up to six months ago! Well, the backbreaking work was there to be done, all hands needed for it; at least none of them, herself or Shevaun or Ethne O'Breslin, had held themselves too good to help, and left it all to the servants with them—as some transplanted gentry did. Only, they were stupid at it at first, and the others who were more knowledgeable so patient with them—she smiled, remembering—except Ailsa, of course. Ailsa, scornful and supercilious— "I'd think anyone of sense'd know *that*, lady!"

Think of something else, quick, anything but Ailsa. . . . Shameless, insolently provocative, flaunting herself at him—a wanton—and he going out after her, casual, likely to find a convenient copse somewhere. No matter: she meant nothing to him in herself, only a girl convenient to hand, and he was a man, wasn't he, only another natural thing, and no affair of Nessa O'Rafferty's.

Only it was annoying, that girl giving herself airs—wise laughing knowledge in her eyes on Nessa. Damn Ailsa McFergus. But the equally shameless whisper in Nessa's mind added to that, I could give him more pleasure—and oh, God, eager to—if only he knew and asked.

There came Shevaun, round the new shed for the cow. A cow, it had been like king's largesse when he brought her a month ago, the beautiful red-and-white cow with her gentle eyes. (How many fields of cattle had she passed in the old days, twenty, thirty beasts—and never glanced at them?) Old Eily sniffed and said, "Half Hereford bred, do I know aught—the size o' the creature, she'll eat twice as much as a good little Irish cow." But it was a blessing—the milk, and a little butter. Shevaun would be going out to milk now, to where the cow was at field beyond the shed. She was calling little Sean, and her voice carried sharp up the hill—and so did the boy's, answering, as he ran out of the shed.

"Here I am, Mother! Oh, Mother, going to milk Etain you are, can I go, Mother? I want—"

"You want too much, nuisance— I told you not to run away from Eily again, hunting for you she's been. No, get in the house now, you can't come."

Oh, Shevaun, thought Nessa sadly, but no need to take it out on the little boy. Queer about people. Fergal now, he'd explode in four directions, and swear and shout, but when he cooled down he didn't hold spite; if it was over something important, he mightn't forget it, but nine of ten times he'd be sorry, and do something to make up. Shevaun nursed a grievance along. She'd never in this world admit it, but she was bitter-sorry she'd quarreled with her husband, to let him go off like that with her anger on him; but she couldn't show it, open, how she missed him and wanted him so hard. Nessa would hear her stirring restless at night, and didn't she know how Shevaun felt—something of the same desperate longing shaking her own body. . . . Oh, these careless unseeing men, roving off on their own ways with never a thought . . .

Sean had left the door of the shed open, and she could see part of the pile of grain there. Proud of it she was, a little gleaning hard-earned. Yes, the women had done most of the work in the fields, except the plowing to start. The company of raiders under Fergal and McCann fetched in a deal of valuables, to sell and exchange, but even across the border foodstuff was all too scarce, the new English settlers not all coming onto granted land in time to start crops, and another plague over the country this summer. Thank God, not so rife here, only old Tadgh down with it in their household, and a miracle he hadn't died. However much of value you had to offer, food scarce and dear, so the little harvest they'd managed to reap was precious. The best part of a field of potatoes, and three fields of rye. Fergal had got a heifer-calf across the border for Phelim Burke who'd started the mill over by the village, to pay for grinding.

Never look at a field of rye or wheat again, she wouldn't, or the pretty waving fronds of potato-leaves, that she wouldn't feel the ache in her back and the blisters broken on her hands, for the planting and digging and gathering. . . . Nessa O'Rafferty, living empty days as an unconsidered young lady in the great house her stepfather shared, coming down listless to meals, toying with food because she was unhappy and lonely!

She started as her name was spoken behind her, and turned. "Oh, Nessa," said Maire McCann in relief. "I'm glad I caught you halfway. After you'd left, I thought, I meant to ask if you could give me the loan of the needle this week."

"Oh, yes, I'm sure. Shevaun's just finished a shirt for little Sean, and I think the mending's caught up. One of us will bring it over tomorrow."

"I—just thought I might make myself a new gown, of some of

that dyed linen Kevin brought last week. Did you see any of it? Pretty stuff—and a good even color—I just thought I'd try. Likely I'll make an ill job. He didn't want to cut the bolt, I must take care—"

"It'll become you, and you'll do better than you think," said Nessa, smiling at her. She'd heard a priest say once that adversity was good for the soul, and she thought now maybe that was so anyway half the time. Some mean, carping little thoughts adversity had put in her mind at times, but others as well, new thoughts about trying to understand the inwardnesses of people. She'd tried to be more charitable to Shevaun, but she hadn't to try anymore with Maire. She'd thought her overproud at first, always saying the conventional, empty thing, but one thing about adversity shared, it showed you what people were really like. Maybe it had been worse on Maire than any of them, for she'd been of a very great and wealthy house, and unlike the rest of them, gentlewomen though they were, she'd always had servants even to do her mending and buckle her slippers and put up her hair. But it hadn't made her haughty and helpless as you might expect; she'd taken things well and not complained.

She was rather avoiding Nessa's eye now, and said something vaguely polite and turned away down the track to her own house. Nessa knew why; she thought likely she was the only one Maire had ever confided in, ever shown her true feelings, and that was just chance, Nessa being there when she couldn't keep it inside any longer. . . . Taking the message over the hill that day last month, that Fergal said McCann wouldn't be back a few days— selling-business over Castlereagh way. And Maire saying, Oh, yes, another easy excuse—and suddenly letting out all that bitter, wistful talk.

Well, she'd never go gossiping about it, she hoped Maire knew; but knowing about Maire now, she felt again, a great right Nessa O'Rafferty had to feel sorry for herself. A profitable contract between fathers, Maire's marriage had been, some question of McCann land given up in exchange for the great dowry she brought with her. She was three years older than Kevin McCann, twenty-four when they were wed, left unmarried that long because of all the vying for her dowry, her father unable to decide on a suitor. And McCann was the sort of handsome, bold charmer most women took to, and Nessa thought Maire had been deep in love with him—maybe still was, still trying to catch and hold his love. But he'd never cared a halfpenny for her in herself, Maire so darkly pretty, too; but forever going with other women— "He can't leave them alone, nor they him, and little enough pretense he makes about it anymore!" Maire had said. And in the five years they were wed, he'd wasted most of the dowry in gaming and extravagance, even before the English settlement-act stripping them both of all that remained.

Shevaun had her boy, and Nessa could hug a secret hope to her, about Fergal, but Maire had nothing.

And there came Shevaun back, down there, plodding along with the pail of milk. Hard enough it was to keep up one's self-respect, Nessa reflected, all the water needing to be fetched a hundred yards; they'd each of them a comb, but all too few clothes and none really fine, no ornament at all, and the few modest cosmetics they'd kept among them all but gone now. . . . She must remind Ethne to try to remember that recipe for complexion-lotion you could make from steeped rowan leaves and rainwater. . . . But Shevaun didn't seem to care or try, half the time. Her hair twisted up anyhow, and that blue gown had a couple of buttons missing at the neck—she was shuffling along like an old woman. But it did no good to say anything, encourage her; she just turned all the more sullen.

Nessa got up with a sigh and started down the hill. Dreamed here long enough she had. But for all that had passed through her mind, she had another queer thought, as she went down. It had seemed almost like the end of the world, sudden frightening devastation and destruction—everything changed, gone, all the things happening new and strange; and, maybe as people always would in a time of such emergency, they'd all behaved well and found unsuspected strength to call on. A time it had been when none of them was sure they'd be alive tomorrow—their whole world shattered around them, and danger on all sides—and they'd somehow done the needful things, however impossible it looked—then or now. But now—

Well, the immediate danger was past, and they'd found they were going to live awhile anyhow. Narrow and hard as they lived here, it wasn't the kind of danger calling for the minute's courage—it was grinding day-to-day withstanding of work and not quite enough dull food, and living too near together, tempers rubbing, and all the little nuisances of routine to be done.

They'd settled down to life again—life a deal nearer the bone than any of them had ever lived; and now, just as in life anywhere, all the interweaving strands of personality, love and hate and envy and malice, desire and greed and selfishness, charity and hope, were linking obscurely to make forever-changing patterns of people's lives. And not only among these people, but everywhere— among all these folk, half of them brought down overnight to a caste lower than their own servants had been—finding, after all the destruction and death and danger, they would live—and must learn new ways to live.

She had a vague moment's vision in her mind, of the vigorous tentacles of life taking hold again over all of them—beginning to weave new patterns of destiny.

When she came in, Hugh McFadden was sitting in the one armed chair at the trestle table, amusing small Sean with a game of cat's cradle while Ethne and Shevaun readied the evening meal. "Oh, Hugh, how nice to see you!" exclaimed Nessa warmly. He smiled at her.

"You'll never guess the present he brought," said Ethne O'Breslin. "We'll be busy every waking hour keeping Sean from mauling the poor creature to death. Not but what she's well able to look after herself, as cats—"

"Never a *cat!*" said Nessa, awed. With famine over the whole country, this three years, most of the domestic animals like the livestock had necessarily been used for food. A cat, especially a cat as vermin hunter, a real live cat, was something to marvel at. "But how *could* you, Hugh—worth their weight in gold they are—did you *steal* it? Oh—" She had found the tiny black kitten, busily washing itself in a corner out of harm's way. "The *dear* thing— and a black one too, all the luckier. Wherever did you get her, Hugh?" She knelt to stroke the little thing, and the kitten condescended to lick her finger with a rough pink tongue.

"Well, it's not much of a cat as yet," said Hugh. "I grant you it's overpayment. It's a man the other side of Ballintober, Nessa, he has a brother-in-law who lives in Galway town, and you know the Galway merchants carry on a deal of smuggling out of Spain. He's an enterprising man, Joseph Branagan, and he invested in a pair of cats from Spain over a year back. He tells me he's made twenty pounds clear out of the kits already. But the way I came to get one, well, he's also a generous man, and maybe overappreciative of the little I do. He gave me the kit for nothing, because he's four children to study lessons from me."

"And you could sell it for a pound or more, equal value," smiled Ethne O'Breslin, a hand on his shoulder. "We're grateful, Hugh."

"Oh, well, something I owe Fergal O'Breslin and his household."

"We've been yearning for a cat," said Nessa, "the field-mice so many, and other pests too, and the birds getting wild berries up the hill we could use. Darling Hugh, I'll remember you in my prayers the next year, faithful!" She leaned to kiss his cheek, and he looked a bit embarrassed, saying again it had cost him nothing. Hugh was one of the people, she'd heard Fergal say, showing some surprising qualities in this adversity. He'd stayed to help them plow and get the crop in, though he'd never been a handworker and it was as hard for him as the women; but he felt guilty at sharing the little they had, and said surely the few talents he possessed could be employed. Self-appointed schoolmaster he was now, to all the district about, making his rounds of thirty families with children, visiting each twice or three times a week regular. The Archbishops of Roscommon and Galway—and they living as poor on a few acres, but more used to it like all churchmen this half-century—approved the idea, and were organizing other traveling tutors. Hugh said, and of course he was right, the children couldn't be let to grow up savages, without any learning at all— more important, the knowledge of their nation's history, to educate them to patriotism. Always been a tradition in Ireland, he said, that every man was entitled to education, no matter his rank. It was another thing Nessa had never thought much about, but of course that was so: any landholder's household kept a tutor for the children, and the servants' and tenants' children required to attend lessons.

Hugh felt he was serving his country and his God honorable and useful, and beyond doubt he was right; but it wasn't an easy life for him, wandering about in all weathers, a radius of twenty miles, and paid seldom and little in food, shelter, castoff clothes.

But for all that, she thought, he looked well, a world different to six months back. Not like a lay-brother he looked, in ordinary shabby trews and open shirt, and his brown hair all grown in, and his complexion healthy and ruddy. Younger than his thirty-four years he looked, and not at all unhandsome.

"I was over at the Kearneys' place four days back," he was saying now, "and I met your neighbor Donaghue there, I gathered to strike a bargain over a heifer-calf. I saw it—a good buy, well-grown and Kerry bred. But he was asking too much."

"Indeed," said Ethne noncommittally. The maidservant Dareen Coyle had just come in to lay the table. And by rights Ailsa should be here to help, but (like all wantons, thought Nessa spitefully) she was lazy, and always found an excuse—she was out fetching water, or she had to sit with Tadgh, who was bedridden now and mostly looked to by Eily, she taking over care of the child as well to free Shevaun.

"It just crossed my mind," said Hugh, "to wonder where Brian Donaghue came by the heifer. Which never belonged this side of the border originally. I ran into an English military patrol a mile down the road—the fourth I'd seen in two days. The number of raiders over the border must be—um—irritating them, I surmise."

Nessa stroked the black kitten thoughtfully. Hugh, of course, did not know that Dareen Coyle—and an honest sensible girl she was—was in the way of courting with Padraig Moran, who lived with Donaghue—brother-in-law, it was said, but neither of them had a wife. Donaghue had presumably owned land, to have a claim here, but he and Moran were both a bit rough and loutish in manners. In a way, it was a pity that those Flemings, the poor things, hadn't been better able to stand up for themselves. It was a thing often happened in the last few months of the transplantation—two or three different men given title to the same land, and sometimes it came to pitched battle. Young Fleming, though, was a timid sort, and gave way before big tough Donaghue's claim—where they'd gone, who knew?—and there were Donaghue and Moran on the land adjoining Fergal's, the other direction from McCann's.

It was all a bit complicated. Anything said open in this house, in Dareen's hearing, would likely get back to Donaghue. Neither Fergal nor McCann was just sure that mattered, but it might. Complicated—well, yes, people being human people . . . The way Fergal said, every man with any guts in him at all, living in reach of the border and the English-settled towns and farms across there—soon or late the idea occurred to him to go raiding. It was the former gentry landowners like Fergal that mostly organized the raiding—some of them banding together, to lead the men with them, former servants and such—some riding alone—and some collecting a few of the desperate starving men banished here without any means to live: Fergal had taken in five or six like that. And there wasn't a night along the east border of Connacht, marked most of its way by the Shannon, that men didn't cross the water and come down on farm and village for plunder.

After the war, not many herds left in Ireland—so as the English settled their new land, they brought over breeding-stock; and hardly a morning came now that some of them didn't go out to find a couple of heifers missing, or half a litter of piglets, or a good hackney-horse. And other things—harness and trappings, a sack of grain or seed, tools, and even tableware from the house, bolts of cloth, stored food, and small furnishing—wall-sconce, candle-branch, stool. And the fierce yard-dog with its throat cut or enticed away by a bitch, the armed watchman dead and his gun missing. Well, they were irritated, as Hugh put it; English military patrols doggedly went hunting all through the counties just west of the border, and it wasn't as easy as it had been six months ago to go for plunder and get back safe.

And there were men took two thoughts, and said, why should I take the gamble when another man will in my place? . . . So now there were other raiders, lying in wait for those coming back, and ambushing the men who'd taken the risk, getting away with the loot themselves. Fergal and McCann had run into a local band like that four times in the last two months, and lost much profit. Fergal hadn't stopped cursing for a week. . . . And Brian Donaghue had taken up his land just two and a half months ago. There might be nothing in that, and on the other hand there might. Fergal and McCann both thought there was.

"Look at the great lout!" Fergal would say. "Sitting over there not turning a hand, he and that Moran! How are they living, else?

They only planted one field of potatoes and one of barley. And I had it from Phelim Burke that Donaghue paid for grinding his meal in cash money, English coin. Why, by God, I can't prove anything, but the time I went over to call friendly and get acquainted—before I suspected what the bastard was like—he had a damned great cured ham hanging from his rafter, ten pounds if an ounce —*and* the twin of the one I got out of that farm at Mohill across the river, three nights before—that some of these Christ-damned cowardly sons-of-bitches robbed me of on the way home! Don't talk to me about Brian Donaghue!"

And that last was directed at his mother. Ethne didn't believe it. She held out that Donaghue wasn't like that; not a very polished fellow, surely—but he was a Kerryman—but an honest man and genial.

That he was, all right. And why was he forever coming here? —putting himself out to be friendly and helpful— Do you let me lift that for you, lady, can't I be fetching some water for you, lady. A great big red bear of a fellow he was, in his forties, red hair all over him, growing up over his shirt-collar and likely down to his heels if you could see, and red freckles under the hair. Yes, why come so much—evidently he hadn't work to do at home, indeed —unless he was nosing about to see when Fergal was there and when not, find out about the forays Fergal led?

"I'd only met Donaghue once or twice before," Hugh was saying. "He seems a genial enough man. A good neighbor is he?"

"Oh, yes, indeed," said Ethne placidly, patting down the oat-cakes on the long-handled pan. "Of course he's only a small holding, five acres. But there's just himself and his brother-in-law. He was septman to the chief Driscoll, well-enough bred he is but he owned a bit of Scariff Island off Kerry, and that's a wild remote place, not much society about—which accounts for his rough ways. Moran was his wife's youngest brother, the poor woman was drowned in a boat-accident ten years ago."

Nessa looked at her in surprise; if she'd found out all that, why hadn't she said so before?

"I'd hoped to find O'Breslin home," remarked Hugh. "You expect him in soon?"

"Oh, I think so," said Ethne. "Not too much to do now, as the harvest's in, you know."

Hugh caught her purposeful vagueness, and raised his brows slightly, taking the hint, changing the subject, making some cheerful remark to Shevaun to force a response from her silence. Well, it might all be imagination; but there was Dareen. Though when you came to think of it, thought Nessa, it was senseless to be so cautious; the girl wasn't a fool, and she knew well enough that when Fergal was gone for thirty-six hours or two days, he wasn't fishing over at Lough Boderg. Not when he brought back a bolt of linen, a couple of pairs of troopmen's boots, a service of tableware or a brand-new candle-mold—things you didn't catch, not out of Lough Boderg in a net.

She went on stroking the black kitten, and felt her heart contract with fear for him. No, not the safest business to be at these days, raiding over the border. Left after the meal last night he had, for the hidden camp where they kept the horses that had been the first necessary plunder taken. They'd have got over last night, and maybe had to run and lie hidden from pursuing patrols today—but he should be home tonight, even if late. . . . She knew Ethne worried too, every minute he was away. But she was better at hiding it under a serene surface than Nessa was. More practice she'd had hiding feelings, being older.

And with that, a very curious thought came into Nessa's mind, and she looked at Ethne O'Breslin there, turning the oatcakes over the fire as if nothing else was in her mind at all except oatcakes. Somehow, Nessa had never thought of Ethne—like that. Fergal's mother she was, and he a grown man long since. But she was a handsome woman, her skin still white and fine, and just a bit of silver in her smooth black hair, and her figure slim and straight. She was just forty-one or forty-two.

It's silly I am, Nessa told herself firmly. What nonsense indeed, an idea like that! Besides, Fergal would go straight up in a sheet of flame. . . . She said a small prayer to herself for his safety, wherever he was right now.

7

SOME EIGHT HOURS later, Fergal was suffering a number of annoyances, and not with much Christian patience. In the last couple of months, more and more caution and subterfuge were required not only to get hold of loot and bring it back across the border but to arrive home with it intact. He thought nostalgically of last May and June, when they had openly crossed by the bridge below Killashee, and found farm-gates unlocked, not even a dog left out. Walked over casually, he and Kevin, that night last April, and taken six horses out of the troop-stables at Carrick, as safe and easy—well, almost—as they'd ever gone into their own stables for a horse in the old days. . . . Not very long that state of affairs had lasted—the sublime English confidence that officially banishing these people was going to keep them west of the border without guards posted to back up the law.

And it was senseless to feel aggrieved, for of course they'd brought it on themselves, so many raiders making depredations and the English naturally taking preventive steps.

In the copse behind him he heard snorting and stamping, and Dillon cursing in a frightened mutter, and whispers. McCann crawled up beside him where he lay watching down the hill through thick bushes. "My Christ, Fergal, you'll have us all hanging in a row over Carrick garrison gate, with this damned beast! We might as well try to get an elephant home safe—it's a miracle we've got this far, I never thought we would. And if the English don't get us, by God, we'll likely all be savaged by the brute— listen at him!"

"And were you the damn' fool let Dillon take charge? He's a townsman, and easy frighted. For God's sake go and tell Flynn or McKenna to handle it! . . . Well, I surmise one of 'em has," as the snorting died in a long whuffle.

"God damn it," whispered McCann, "that troopman still posted." No road here, three miles from the river on the Connacht side, in gentle rolling hills partly wooded; but it was one of the fairly open, passable ways raiders on horses would need to take inland, and on general principles the English patrolled all such areas. Usually a patrol passed, all orderly in group, and you could go to ground, hearing them in time, and get away in the opposite direction afterward. This one had left a troopman on watch, for some reason, down there in a thin growth of trees where he commanded a view of all the open land about. This was a way Fergal had taken home a few times lately, a clear way through not so rough wood, and a shortcut. He'd never known an English patrol to leave a guard behind like this.

The troopman wouldn't be seen except by sharp eyes knowing he was there. He had got off his horse, and blended himself into the trees; but an occasional stir from the horse betrayed him, as did some night-bird complaining of intrusion.

What the hell has happened to Art? wondered Fergal. McCann was asking the same thing. "I thought he was overhopeful, saying he could stalk the man from behind. A hell of a lot of dry bracken under those trees, to sound warning."

"So he's taking his time," said Fergal. Their voices were mere threads, not to carry down the hill.

"Christ, if he can't hear us he can sure as death hear your bastardly beast—the damndest wild idea I ever knew even you to get! He's put us in their hands near as damn' all a dozen times already in twenty hours— I don't want to be as near death again, I tell you, as back there by the bridge!" McCann's whisper was passionate. "We'll never get him to cover; for God's sake, Fergal, turn him loose and forget it!"

"Be damned if I will!" said Fergal. "After coming this far?"

Another flurry and wild rustling behind. "Oh, Christ," breathed McCann. "If we get away with this, let's try for the Carrick commandant's pet charger next time—a damn' sight easier!"

"Don't dither at me," said Fergal coldly. "I never knew you so nervous. So he hears the creature, well, there's cattle left out at field still, how should he know it's not one of them?"

"He's a bigger ignoramus of a townsman than Dillon, if he thinks a milk-cow goes rampaging and snorting like that. And how many cattle this side the border? Look, man, we've a good load of stuff besides—all that cloth, and the tobacco, and ten pounds' worth of tools, and the matchlocks—there's a time you need to cut your losses, when it means your life—"

"We're not there yet. Yes, panic about it every step of the way, but won't you be willing to share the profits afterward! Fix your mind on that, boy." Fergal was wondering about that English guard. The cold conviction slid into his mind that the guard had been left there because the patrol knew where and approximately when to expect a party of raiders. And some food for thought there was in that. For all he knew, several other bands might occasional or often come this way—it'd be odd if none did; if there had been treachery, it probably wasn't directed at any one band. If there had been treachery, it was most likely by some local farmer who'd seen raiders pass, and earned a little coin by informing voluntarily. Or could it lie closer to home—some man running with the fox, hunting with the hounds, for doubled profit? A dangerous game—but it could be done, if such a man spied around, collected information about other parties of raiders, and took care not to let the English know when his own company would be out, and took another road. Not only reward from the English on the side, but eliminating competition . . .

The name of Brian Donaghue slid into his mind, and he whispered a curse. No, it couldn't be Donaghue. Not that he wasn't capable of it, the great red bastard, but Fergal was almost certain Donaghue belonged to the home-raiders, ambushing returning bands, and it would be spoiling his own profit to inform. . . . The English threat was a natural one, nobody could expect different than that they'd go out after raiders, but these cowardly bastards who lay in wait while other men risked their necks—worse than informers they were!

Down the hill there was a sudden subdued flurry of noise—a thrashing about in the bracken—a horse snorting and plunging. Young Liam Fagan had just crept up beside Fergal and McCann; he whispered, "That's Art. Got him, he has."

"Wait for it," said Fergal. In a minute they heard the horse move; three minutes later Art McTally, a bulky shadow in the blackness, came up to them through wood to the left, having circled the open slope. He was leading the troopman's horse.

"All right, O'Breslin. It was a job to get close enough, keeping quiet, to be sure he'd not have time enough to yell. Bled all over me the bastard has. Have you seen anything of the rest of them?"

"No, but that's not to say they're not about." McCann made back to the copse for the horses, Fergal after him. "All right, we're moving. Quick—and for God's sake, Dermot, keep that brute quiet—"

"There's a hope," said McTally derisively. "Heard him down there I did, plain, and what's more the Englishman did too—I'd not be surprised was he about ready to signal his friends. If you think that patrol went off far, I don't—why leave a guard unless to signal 'em back? And what the hell was a guard doing right there, first place?"

"I am away ahead of you there, Art," said Fergal. "Less of your tongue. Right now the main thing is to get off out of it." He swung up to the saddle. Something bulky cannoned into his horse, and blew, and snorted, and stamped.

"Make any time, with this devil-possessed creature o' Satan! Give over, you bastard!" snarled Kindellan somewhere near. "I tell you, O'Breslin, we'll never do it—"

"For Christ's sake, Fergal, yes, turn it loose—"

"Now look, fainthearts," said Fergal, cold and sharp. "I'll give you all half an hour's start and bring him on alone if you like! When we've got this distance! Give me the halter, Dan, I'll take him. My Christ, you might all be timid city-clerks like Dillon, nervous as you're acting! Gentle as a milk-cow he is, aren't you, boy?" He yanked on the halter, his horse sidestepped, and something solid, hard, and powerful butted against his thigh.

"On my mother's memory, O'Breslin," said a thin earnest whisper at his other side, "clerk maybe I was, but never a coward, you needn't miscall me. Raiding I'll go behind you, and Englishmen I'll kill with pleasure, and when have I never taken my share of the load? But at traveling with a rampaging man-eating bull I draw the line—I'd sooner the English patrol took us than be gored to death—"

"Oh, for Christ's love! Ride on the lot of you or quit your complaints! He's not a savage bone in him, he'll come quiet for me, won't you, boy? That's the boy, easy, now—only a bush that is, you needn't go snorting at it—"

It wasn't exactly whistling in the dark, he thought, as he eased the playful young bull out of the copse behind the rest of the party. The worst was over now, it'd be madness to give up here. Sure to God it had looked impossible, to bring a bull over the border—but he couldn't resist the gamble, for what it meant in profit. Cows, now, they were stupid enough creatures, once in awhile you got a cantankerous beast but mostly they were easy led or driven—and calves too. And you could bundle half a dozen weaned piglets in a stout loose-woven sack. It was a good idea to muzzle a calf with your neckkerchief tied loose, lest it go to bawling; and he'd never tried to fetch back more than one cow at once, for one alone usually wouldn't open its mouth, where two or three would get to lowing for their home-field. Besides, one cow was a bulky enough item to get across. But a bull!—upwards of a thousand pounds of hot, restless, noisy, temperamental brute-power, on a single rope halter! Four miles of English territory to get over, and then the river, and then patrols to be dodged and these other predatory gangs.

What had held him a dozen times from abandoning the attempt was, in a sense, those cows across the river. By this time a respectable number had been smuggled over, and more heifer-calves. A cow was still something only a lucky family owned, but he knew of twenty or so in ten miles of his acreage, and there'd be more. The bull represented not so much immediate profit as a steady income for years, in service-fees—and more heifer-calves and, of course, eventually more bulls.

It was a Gloucester-bred bull, imported from England, dark brown shading to black, a handsome big fellow and not above five years old. Fergal had come on him by accident, in a small pen back of the stables, and was literally unable to resist him. The bull had been intrigued by novelty into having a halter tied on him, but in the moment's urgency Fergal hadn't time to look for the bull-stick to maneuver him by his nose-ring. The man guarding the place was dead by then but a neighbor-dog was raising a fuss and a light had showed in the main house. He had trailed behind the rest as they retreated, the bull seeming quite pleased to be out on a new adventure, uttering long interested whuffles and playfully butting the horse's flank. When they were clear away for the moment and joined in the marshes toward the river, McCann went off like an overprimed matchlock at seeing what Fergal had with him—and most of the men backed him up.

But, by God, they'd got the brute this far the right side of the river, and be damned if he'd give up now. It had been a job: that you could say twice. Naturally there were English patrols along all the bridges. Just as for most of its sluggish meandering up through Ireland, the Shannon here spread out in long flat boglands on either bank, open; the river itself wasn't very deep or broad, and never swift up here, but you went knee-deep in bog to get to the water, all among tall snaky green reeds. He had pulled and driven cows and calves over, the horses not liking it any better—up above Lough Boderg, before the river began to widen—but he knew better than to try it with the bull. . . . They had nearly run foul of a patrol thirty minutes after leaving the property they'd plundered, and split and run north almost up to Carrick—Fergal with the bull and Art McTally.

Art was ripening for a good taking-down, the insolent way he'd been acting lately. . . . but on the run no time to start that. And all the rest of them arguing at Fergal to give up a harebrained notion; but in the end he'd shamed McCann into siding with him. "Is this the bold fellow tricked the English into helping him escape off Kilronan?" Fergal had taunted, and McCann had sworn at him but given in. And the trick had worked—if only just. McCann and the other seven of them two hundred yards down from the bridge, making a disturbance to call attention, and the bridge guard-patrol challenging—warning shots fired—McCann and the rest galloping off noisy and open downstream, and the whole guard, fifteen strong, after them—while Fergal hustled the bull across the bridge. And the bull, unnerved by the shots and tired of this adventure away from his own pen, planting his feet in the middle of the bridge and deciding to stop where he was. A damn' close business it had been, finally getting his high-and-mightiness onto Connacht soil thirty seconds before the returning patrol's hoofbeats drummed on the bridge—and by God's grace the bull quieted down by discovery of a patch of flavorsome grass, where Fergal waited endless minutes in earshot of the bridge, before he dared move.

A close run for the rest of them too, four miles down the wrong side of the river before they shook off the patrol and scattered to swim their horses across. It would be awhile before they quit cursing him and his stubbornness . . . but he still had the bull, and by God he'd get him home safe if it killed him, if he was a month on the way. Four English patrols they'd dodged, since the bridge, and had to go out of the way north, and lie hidden—once in thigh-deep bog, the bull raising vociferous complaint—altogether six-eight hours, and a dozen near escapes in that time.

But this far they'd got—only ten miles or so from home now, and dawn was a good five hours off, they'd be in safe by the first light, with luck.

A horse dropped back from the pack of riders ahead and the led troop-horse alongside. Liam Fagan said, "I can take the beast awhile if you're tired, O'Breslin." His voice was just deepened, and as yet uncertain: very young he sounded in the dark. Fergal smiled.

"Thanks, Liam, but we're getting on fine together now—I'll manage from here in." The bull was hungry now, twenty hours away from his own manger, and twenty-odd miles of travel behind him—not counting his added exercise when he turned skittish or stubborn on the way. He was following moodily along at the end of the halter, only venting his feelings in an occasional halfhearted snort.

They came out of the trees, and there was no moon tonight but Fergal was enough used to finding his way in the dark now that he knew where they were. Farther inland from the river, out of the low bogland now, with gentle rolling hills just outlined against the sky ahead—here was the main road west, and diagonal across it sparse growth of wood and a track of sorts that wandered up toward the place, eight-nine miles off, where they had their secret pasture, on McCann's land. He pulled up, as the rest were doing; one man dismounted and walked up to the open road, the others waiting, in the shadow of trees. Nothing stirred. The man came back—Dillon it was by the thin stooped figure—and remounted.

"No sign of aught."

As always they rode fast and in a packed group across the open space, Fergal necessarily trailing after with the bull. They came up the gradual slope across the empty road, and into the shelter of scattered oaks—leaves dropping this season, dry and noisy underfoot. The bull suddenly gave a loud, long snort and stopped dead, flinging up head and tail, and nearly pulled Fergal's arm from its socket.

"Now listen, my bold boy," whispered Fergal to him, "you black bastard, enough proof you've offered you're the hell of an arrogant male creature—come up easy now, don't go mischief-making this near home—" He tugged gently on the rope halter, and the bull snorted again.

Out of the dark ahead, moving shadow massed, coming down fast on them. A horse in the lead, McCann's or Art's, reared and neighed shrill. Four, five, six horses—near as Fergal could see—bunching round the riders ahead, men swearing, blows exchanged from the saddle, but all the cursing done by those attacked—these craven whoresons of thieves went rude-masked and never spoke, to be identified later by voice or feature. Nor they didn't stay to fight it out, all or nothing—knives were out now, slashing accurate at saddle-lashings, eager hands reaching for the laden saddlebags, as they dropped free, and as a man got one he reined off and fled at a gallop, clutching his prize.

Art McTally's voice rose in a roared obscenity, and a man screamed, short and hoarse, in sudden agony. It was just chance, Fergal forty feet behind because of the bull—and only thirty seconds motionless there, so quick and violent as it always went— and another horse reared there, forefeet lashing out, and against the star-reflection through bare branches, he saw the rider as a big burly man, top-heavy in the saddle—

Mask, voice, or damn' all, wouldn't that bastard Donaghue look so? Fergal forgot all about the bull, for the first time in twenty hours. He dropped the rein and dug heel into the horse's flank, whipping out his belt-knife.

The bull was tired, hungry, and annoyed; and all the noise and confusion made him nervous. He'd been pawing the ground irritably, and now, as the rope tightened with a jerk on him, he suddenly decided to lose his temper. He lowered his head and charged after Fergal, almost alongside, and the two of them cannoned into the bunched crowd of men and horses ahead and split them apart like exploding gunpowder.

Fergal smashed into a horse, its rider half-fell over on him, and he struck out blind with the knife, left-handed. A terrific jerk on his right shoulder, almost yanking him out of the saddle—frightened yells—his horse rearing under him, rein loose—the bull, the damned uncertain-tempered bull—for God's sake don't lose hold of the rope!—Donaghue's voice was it, cursing?— He dropped the knife and gripped the halter-rope in both hands, against that powerful wanton strength, and yelled to McCann, to Art, to get to the bull's head.

Just as suddenly as they'd come down from ambush ahead, they were gone—a wild-fleeing scattered company thundering off, lost in the dark. All the horses snorting, shying about nervous and scared, from the big bulk of the roused bull making short random rushes with head lowered. "Damn it—Art—Kevin— take my horse, for God's sake! Get up on his off side—" Fergal slid out of the saddle, landing upright more by chance than judgment, working hand over hand up the rope to the bull's head. "Easy now, quiet now, my bold boy—my good boy—calmly, now—no need for all this fuss—" Christ, the brute would have his shoulder dislocated — His hand slid over a pointed, stiff, hairy ear, and down to the nose-ring.

"I'm here, O'Breslin—" Liam Fagan's breathless voice. "I've a hold on the neck-halter—s-steady, boy, calm down now—"

"Good man—Liam," gasped Fergal. "All right—I have him— easy, boy—let's quiet down now, nought to disturb you—" He hung onto the nose-ring with every ounce of strength in him. Those horns had been blunted, but this close they could make some damage.

There was an indecisive moment when the bull was of two minds. Much put upon by men he'd been recently, taken away from good food convenient when he had an appetite—which was frequently—and led ignominious as a milk-cow this weary way; he was out of patience with new experience and the men who brought him to it. But he hadn't a really savage disposition, having been well-treated all his life, and his schooling was well-fixed in his small, hot, restless mind—a man's pressure on the nose-ring, it meant certain orders to be obeyed.

He brought up short, pawing uncertainly, snorting loud. There was a man talking in a soothing voice, and a hand on his neck. He flung his head up and down, uncertain, a couple of times; but all the noise had stopped, the horses were quiet and the men about just talking. He blew out his breath in a prolonged final *Whuff* of protest, and stood still. In a minute he dropped his head to investigate the ground, and found a patch of grass, and took an experimental mouthful.

Fergal vented his vocabulary on the late attackers. "Did they get anything?"

"One of my saddlebags," growled Art. "Some of the tobacco, I think."

"And one of mine." Dillon. "Not sure I am exactly what was in it—"

McCann said with a laugh, "But I got home to one o' the bastards with my knife—did you hear him yell?" There was grim satisfaction in his voice. "One thing I'll say, they'd likely have got off with more if it hadn't been for your damn' bull! I'll forgive the beast the trouble it's made us!"

As if he understood the praise, the bull nudged Fergal almost archly. He laughed. "True for you, Kevin! Did you get a good look at any of them?"

"Now I ask you!" said McCann. "One minute's quick fight in the dark?"

"Oh, I know, I know! But I swear to Christ I could almost be certain—ah, the hell with it, they're gone with little enough loot this time—let's get on, we'll all be damn' pleased to be home and in bed after this job!"

He came down the slope to the house, along in midmorning; he was dead-tired, but a good deal pleased with himself. Done it, they had—got the bull over safe, and temporarily secure in a hastily barricaded-off portion of the horse-field up there, where the men stayed. They'd made themselves snug enough in the little hideaway, in a small fold in the hills—nothing like real hills, this near the river-land, but the country gently rolling, the slopes high enough to hide what was over them, and good stands of trees here and there. The six of them, Larr and the five men Fergal and McCann had taken into the band over six months' time, had built themselves a practical shelter there, of expediency the way their prehistoric forebears had built. . . . You came across one of those ancient places now and then, especially in the north counties: half baked mud, wattles, some rough timber, and just half the house aboveground, steps down to a big hollowed-out space, and the chimney-hole out the top of the low roof. It would be warm even in dead winter—maybe, Fergal thought ruefully, warmer than his own cottage.

He yawned, and transferred the pack of miscellaneous articles intended for the household to his other hand. Twenty-eight hours since he'd slept, and damn' busy most of that time. Yes, not such a soft job these days—what with all the competition—and that stirring up the English even more, of course. And other developments arising, unforeseen or expectable . . . Art McTally, ugly big bruiser, trained as a groom under the late chief O'Breslin— and acting damn' insolent to the present chief O'Breslin, of late— likely reckoning that when a gentleman had lost all he had and came down to this state, his groom stood on equal social terms. And hadn't there been something else Fergal had noticed once— just a hint of expression in Art's eyes, one night, on Nessa O'Rafferty. That would be a thing now, if Art got to acting *that* insolent. Well, he was a useful man to the company, but if he went too far he'd find out that Fergal O'Breslin was still a chief, rich or poor, Tyrconnell or Connacht.

And the rest of them. Careful who we take in, McCann had said, but it hadn't worked out that way—in such a business, you didn't pick and choose—and there was also the undoubted fact that you didn't especially want docile, respectable, former upright fellows on a job like this. Chance making up the company, in the main. Little Dillon was all right, a bit of a rabbit of a former clerk from Limerick town, but honest and holding a hot hate on the English for the soldiers shooting his wife and infant son. And Dan Kindellan was all right, more brawn than brain—not enough wit to be mishonest—he'd been a tenant-farmer somewhere down Waterford way. But Flynn, and McKenna, and O'Shea—Fergal would lay a small bet none of them had ever earned an honest living before the settlement-act. Not so far as he could heft that bull would he trust any of them; they needed watching.

Another little thing there too: McCann thick as thieves with

Dermot Flynn, lately. Some of the same qualities in both, of course: the flamboyant recklessness that could turn so cold-cautious in emergency. And both of them womanizers. McCann had taken Flynn along when he went over to Castlereagh to sell some plunder, last month; Fergal wouldn't doubt that they'd found a few willing women on the way. And what the hell did it matter?— himself, he was pleased to have one convenient in his own household, no prude he'd ever been. But he'd credit himself with more taste than McCann, to whom a woman was a woman. . . . Enough you met now who'd been respectable, decent females, and sold what they had to sell for food and shelter—and McCann among other men buying it without a thought, which Fergal couldn't bring himself to do. And from another viewpoint, it didn't matter about Flynn—but there was Maire McCann. . . .

He trudged at last round the end of the potato-field and came up to the housedoor. Christ, he was tired!—and damn' dirty, with crouching in the bogs, and coping with the bull (must get a permanent shelter and stout-fenced yard built for the beast), and the long ride through rough country. A bath he needed, but sleep more.

He stepped into the main room, and there was his mother sitting by the hearth sewing, and Shevaun and Nessa just sitting, and Hugh McFadden smiling at him, and they were all welcoming him in warm voices—but the pleasure of getting in at last dropped away from Fergal, and cold exasperation took its place. For there also, sitting by God in Fergal's own chair, was Brian Donaghue— the big red bastard—grinning innocently at his returned host.

8

"It's good to see you again, O'Breslin," said Donaghue, "and looking well by the favor of God. I understand you've been over fishing on the lough—any luck had you?" He had a big warm deep voice that made his every utterance sound interested and friendly.

Fergal sat down beside Hugh on the settle, and thrust the bulging saddlebag at Shevaun. "Not bad, no."

"And a queer thing to use for a creel, a good leather saddlebag," said Donaghue as Shevaun went out with it. "But there, we all make do with what's to hand, these days. Tired you look, man, that'll be a long rough walk you've had."

"It is indeed," said Ethne, "and we'll forgive you if you want your bed instead of a meal and talk, Fergal."

He asked nothing better than to lie down and sleep the sun round, but with Donaghue sitting there bold as brass, noticing more than you'd expect with the guileless blue eyes in his round red-stubbled genial face, Fergal sat where he was. "Oh, I'll take a little something first." He'd be damned glad of a drink, and he had a bottle of whiskey too—there were a few men making a little as a sideline, when they could get the grain, and asking nine prices for it, naturally. But he wasn't going to offer Donaghue a drop of his whiskey, and he took the wooden mug of milk his mother handed him, and the plate of oatcakes. She'd sparked the milk with some of the French wine, and it went down uneasy—thin sharp stuff—damn' fool to burden a bag with it, he'd been. He wondered if Roy Donlevy over there had come to be used to it or if something better was available. Roy. A letter he'd sent five months back, by a man bound for Galway town, who swore he'd hand it to a Spanish shipman on a boat for France. A whole Spanish eight-piece he'd given the fellow, half for the sailor. But no answer at all, and no knowing if the letter had ever reached Roy.

"Mercy of God on us," said Donaghue warmly, "but you've not done your trews any good, man, have you? Fell into the lough maybe you did?—it's bad footing in the marshes, and times in gaffing a big one you need to walk out a ways."

"Isn't that so now," agreed Fergal, unsmiling. He swallowed oatcake, washed it down with milk-and-wine, and added casually, "Did you drop over to offer me somewhat for sale, by the by? Maybe a half-pound of tobacco?"

The blue eyes opened wide on him. "Now what put that notion in your head, O'Breslin? Tobacco, with any in hand I'd not sell it, the habit I contracted young, I'm sorry to say. No merchant I am, why would I be coming to see you that reason?"

"Oh, well," said Fergal, "I was in at Kearney's a couple of days ago and he was saying you'd offered him a nice young heifer but he couldn't afford it. I just thought maybe you'd put yourself in the way of a little business—with this and that, you know."

Donaghue boomed out a laugh. "And who doesn't these days? —one way and another."

Fergal finished the milk and looked thoughtfully at the empty cup. A situation here now as fluid as water. Men talked and acted different for it—one would say casual, Over the river I was last night, and picked up this or that—and another would keep it to himself and see his womenfolk didn't go chattering either. The men who were open about it were those only made the venture occasionally, alone or with a friend or two, and the enterprise ended right there, with the calf or pig penned behind the cottage, the bolt of wool cut into by the housewife making new trews, the foodstuff stored or eaten. The men who were in regular business at it needed to be more careful. For one thing, they rode in larger, organized parties: they brought back more of value and at least half of it they sold or exchanged for goods or service. And because such bands were responsible for most of what the English lost, being across the border oftener, leaders and men were more vulnerable—to danger on the job, either side of the border, from householders and patrols—to treachery here. It was merchandise business, and you had to operate it like any business. A good deal of the loot was identifiable by one means and another, and there were as many careless, silly people here as anywhere else: sell such a thing this near the border, and a patrol-captain with a list of all such seeing it and asking, and a nervous housewife or a frightened man saying, Yes, sir, I had that from— So anything like that you took west, into Galway or Mayo, where—if it was ever pounced on by the fewer military patrols there—it could have been through a dozen hands.

Safeguards: yes: and not only against the fools but the villains. Certainly, apart from the identifiable stuff, an English captain would suspect a man smoking a pipe of tobacco, a housewife laying out a full set of tableware, and ask questions. The right of search anywhere, they had. But you didn't tell a buyer where you came by the stuff, and if the captain came, you looked vague and didn't know the English too well and said, Please, sir, 'twas a fellow I met on the road, and damned if I can tell his name, sir. . . . One of the things irritating the English, of course: they knew damned well everything like that, valuable, perishable goods and commodities the transplanters couldn't have brought with them, was smuggled over—but they hadn't a clue, mostly, to trace it back to the original raiders. . . . Nor you didn't sell much to any one man. There were always a few men anywhere would be tempted by rewards posted, and pass on a name to the English if they knew a name. And aside from that, if it was openly known—So-and-So leads a regular band, they'll be going over Monday night, back on the Tuesday—an invitation for all these home-raiders to be waiting for them on the way back.

Oh, you walked careful, and watched all sides, and took every precaution you could think of. But there were dangers you couldn't guard against, in the nature of things. In this household, none of the servants but old Tadgh knew definitely of Fergal's raiding-band; but they weren't fools, and likely guessed. Art and Liam lived in the house, and the careless word dropped— They were loyal enough folk, but they might be careless too. . . . Dareen and that Moran, yes . . . And Fergal knew Ailsa too well, that nought else was important to her but Ailsa. And then there were men like

Art, and O'Shea, and McKenna—a common enough type—who might easy forget caution for the sake of the moment's boast to some girl or rival.

"Oh, well, I only wondered," he said casually to Donaghue, and met the man's eyes with a smile. "The day I was at your place, now, there was a fine ham you had in the rafter—that never came off a Connacht hog."

"That it never did," agreed Donaghue amusedly. "You'll excuse me, O'Breslin, I'll hold my tongue on where I came by it—I didn't take it myself, you see—and sure to God I don't know aught but good of you—as a charitable man I'd not suspect anyone without cause—but at the same time, well, I'd not put trouble on any either."

Why, the hypocritical son of a red Kerry bitch, thought Fergal. Implying that I—And Padraig Moran ambled into the room, with the girl Dareen after him looking a bit smug and pleased with herself. Well, a girl might, at catching him. He might be as slippery and cunning as an old king-salmon, and as nasty a fighter, but no denying he was a good-looking fellow, not over thirty, tall and lean and dark as a Spaniard, with smiling dark eyes. He greeted Fergal in his soft voice, polite. Fergal slid a hand over the dirty three days' stubble of beard on his jaw, resentfully eyeing Moran's catlike neatness and smooth chin.

Donaghue heaved himself to his feet. "Well, we'd best be getting back, then, Padraig." He bobbed a clumsy bow to Ethne. "Good day, lady—you'll not forget what I said, now—you're welcome to it anytime."

"You're very kind," smiled Ethne.

"Ah, nought," said Donaghue, embarrassed. "Good day, ladies. Good day, O'Breslin. Best you get those wet clothes off, else you'll be taking cold—you want to look after yourself."

"And just what the hell was all that about?" wondered Fergal when they were gone. He looked at his mother. "You're welcome to what?"

"To a pound of sugar," she said calmly. "He knows a man in Galway who buys from merchants trading with Spanish, and peddles this and that through north Connacht. He did some favor for the man, he says, and got a cut price on five pounds of sugar, and he wants to share with us."

"Why in the name of God should he do that? He thinks we're in need of charity maybe? You're not to—"

"Well, sugar isn't exactly in the nature of charity offered the starving," said Ethne dryly. "On the same list it is as Hugh's black kitten, and that silver porringer you brought home last week, and the French wine—an extravagant luxury these days even for many English over the border! It's kind in him, he's a kind man."

"Oh, the devil of a kind, charitable fellow is Brian Donaghue, certain! I must look after myself, lest I get down sick and not be able to go out raiding so Donaghue can take loot off me on my way home! You're not to take a halfpenny's value from him, you hear me, Mother? A kitten—have we a kitten?—from Hugh? My Christ, man, have you joined a raiding-band in your off-time?—I've been looking for a cat for months! Yes, the nerve of the bastard—coming here and offering—"

"Now, you're dead on your feet, Fergal, a run you must have had this time, so long out—you need a good sleep. In there with you and get to bed, but I'll wake you in three hours or you'll not sleep tonight. And a bath you'll want then, I'll see it's ready for you. Where are young Liam and McTally?"

"Up the hill, they stayed to—yes, by God, one devil of a run we had, and you'll never guess what I brought back"—he was interrupted by a huge yawn—"a great big black Gloucester bull, to earn more than his keep in stud-fees—they're figuring a way to build a pen up there."

"The Lord have mercy," said Ethne; and Hugh McFadden began to laugh, as at the best joke he'd heard in months.

"A bull is it—and God or Satan playing ironic jests on us, isn't it plain? Oh, doesn't the wheel come full circle! Eighteen hundred years back—one of the oldest pieces of literature writ in Gaelic—tale of the theft of the great bull of Cooley—and all our pagan forebears living by cattle-raids on each other, by the same token! Full circle the English bring the wheel, but they'd never see the point of the jest!" He sat up and wiped his eyes.

Fergal yawned again and said he was too tired to appreciate a joke himself at the moment.

His mother woke him at one o'clock, and he had a meal and a bath. Women, the queer values they had—deviling at him from the time he'd begun fetching things over, to pick up a bathtub. And the devil of an awkward thing it had been to carry, too, a big round wooden affair, thigh-deep to a man. But he would admit it was a convenience, better than going down to the stream to bathe—though he couldn't say easier, what with the trouble of fetching the water to fill it, and heating enough to take the chill off. He sympathized belatedly with the servants in the old days, toiling upstairs with cans of water. And all too likely the gentle-women under his care here carrying some of this.

Yes, and if that Dareen girl married Moran and moved off, one less servant. Also, of course, one less mouth. He hadn't liked it one damn' bit, his mother and Shevaun and Nessa working in the fields like tenant-farmers' women, but you might as well try to order the ocean-tides as females.

He shaved as smooth as he could with the old razor—must have a look about for a better one, but it was one of the things usually abovestairs on the bedroom floor of a gentry household, inaccessible. He put on his good brown trews and the doublet to match over a clean shirt, and came out of the room he shared with Art and Liam. The main room was empty but for Nessa.

"I'll take a stroll toward the village," he told her.

She looked up with a quick smile from adding a little precious dried turf* to the hearth. "I was hoping you'd come out before your mother was back. There's just one thing, Fergal, maybe you should hear. I don't know if it means anything, and—your mother wouldn't like it, my repeating it." Her smile tilted ruefully.

"Well, I thought a half-year was a length of time for all these females to live close without a fight."

"It's nothing like that at all!—you know Ethne doesn't! No, it's just that Dareen and I were talking, casual you know, over the washing day before yesterday, and she let it out without thinking —I forget how it came up, something about names—that she'd heard Donaghue say one day—he was talking to someone else, it was in the village, and he didn't know Dareen could hear, likely—"

"Heard him say what, get to it!"

"That his wife's name had been Cullen before she married him.

* turf: peat

Well, so how could her brother be a Moran? I just thought you ought to hear."

"Damn," said· Fergal thoughtfully. "Odd, indeed. And just the kind of little thing people do let slip, never thinking. Of course—"

"Yes, I know," said Nessa. "That's what your mother says, of course Moran was a half-brother. And what business of ours anyway!"

"Be damned if I know why she's partial to the bastard," said Fergal. "It's still odd. My thanks, girl, it might be useful to know." At the door he turned. "And see you get one of the servants to empty that bath."

"And I would think in six months you'd have discovered we're no longer in a position to give too many orders, all in the same state," she retorted. "Whichever of us is convenient to it does what's to be done."

"Yes, they take on airs safe enough," and he scowled, thinking of Art. "I know we can't sit by and do nothing, but while there are servants I mislike to see my womenfolk at menial work—"

"Speak to your mother and Shevaun then, I'm not one of your womenfolk!" Nessa sounded cross.

He surveyed her with a grin. "No, and that's another reason —you ought to be free to get about the neighborhood and meet what well-bred single men are available, to find yourself a husband! Dareen got ahead of you with Moran, didn't she?"

"I'd not have that one if he asked," snapped Nessa. "Why so concerned for me all on a sudden? Anxious to get me off your hands, are you? I know I've been an unasked-for burden—"

"You needn't bite my head off, damn it, I only passed a casual remark! In a way I'm responsible for seeing you respectably wed and settled, and time's not standing still—it just occurred—"

"Mercy of heaven, yes, where would you find a decent man to take an old hag of nearly twenty-two? Custom, tradition, or no, you've nothing to say for *that*, Fergal O'Breslin—not your sister I am, in law or else! And if you're going out, go, and shut the door after you—seeing how dear any fuel is, we don't try to heat this part of Roscommon as well as the house."

Fergal banged the door after him and walked off toward the village at a long stride. Females! You never knew how they'd take the lightest word. Only a bit of kind advice he'd meant, it was true enough she ought to be wed at her age, and not much choice for her now, among men of her own birth here. Likely she'd been brooding on it herself, and that the reason she flew out at him— they did that sort of thing, having illogical minds, he thought sagely. . . . God knew with classes all mixed here under one economic situation, there'd be some unequal marriages. Whatever she said, he was nominally the man responsible, if custom was followed it was up to him to make a betrothal for her. And if it came to that he'd rather see her wed to a kind decent fellow of humble birth than some well-born rakehell who'd mistreat her: good and bad men of all castes. A damn' pretty girl she was, if she had a temper: any man looking for a wife might be glad to have her. No harm to look about for someone suitable, but never a word to her of the intention—invite the man home, casual, that was all.

Feeling benevolently patriarchal for these righteous conclusions, he strolled into the village in amiable temper. It wasn't much of a village, but less desolate than six months ago. Twelve cottages, the mill just outside that Burke had taken over, and the public inn. It was more or less settled down from private war, now. Famine, plague, and the English hadn't killed off all the original inhabitants of Connacht, though it was likely comparable to other places, that way, what the transplanters had found here—nine out of twelve cottages empty and unclaimed. And some bitter fight there'd been for who was to have them, of all those coming in without land-claims. All the Connacht landholders had had ninety-five percent of their acreage confiscated and seen it parceled out to transplanters, and nationality and religion aside they didn't feel kindly toward these brothers in misfortune. But by and large they'd all settled down now to make the best of the matter.

One of the surviving original inhabitants was Edmund Kearney, who kept the inn. He hadn't much to sell now, and when he had, few could afford to buy; but it was a gathering-place, and in the evenings and the slack days for farmers in winter, there was usually a small crowd there, if just to sit and talk. As Fergal came into the single long room across the front of the house—all seven Kearneys lived in the three rooms at the back—Kearney behind his counter was speaking up passionate to a customer leaning there.

"I know it's robbery, Desmond, all I'm saying is, as hard on me as you, and you can't deny it. God's own truth I'm telling you, three pound the bottle I have to pay for it—sixty shillings, I swear to Christ, half a year's wage for a laboring man in the days before the Act—and a mean man I've never been, and even supposing I was, the devil himself couldn't get more than thirty drinks out of a bottle, and if you say decent drinks twenty-five's more like it. Where's the Irishman wants his whiskey drowned in water the barbarous way the English take it? So there you are, Desmond!" He brought his hand down flat on the counter with a little smack. He was a big shapeless man running to paunch, though lean years had taken some weight off him; he had a round pale genial countenance under a fringe of sandy hair, and pale blue eyes very honest and straightforward on whoever he talked to. "I don't live on air myself, Desmond, and I've got to make a bit of a profit, don't I? Simple figuring you can do as well as me—twenty-five into three pounds, it comes out at two shillings sixpence the drink. And you can't expect me to sell it for charity, like as I say. Sixpence profit, that's what I make, God's my witness, just sixpence, at three shillings the dram."

Owen Desmond drawled, "Yes, on every drink, and right you are, simple figuring I can do—that's fifteen shillings' profit on every bottle, clear."

"And how many bottles do I get the chance to buy?" demanded Kearney fiercely. "With the grain so sore needed for flour, who's any extra to sell for making the whiskey? I ask you, Desmond! Here's this poor man over in Ballyhaunis, with his small capital—all he could save from the English thieves—tied up in equipment to manufacture the *uisgebaugh*. Little grain he can buy anywhere, it's a quarter-sack here, a half-sack there, and the most coming smuggled in Spanish ships by way of Galway harbor—but you needn't think it's that thin foreign wheat or rye," added Kearney hastily, "but honest Irish stuff smuggled out o'Dublin first place. And not for love the smugglers are in business, either—God pity the man, he pays seventeen prices for what he gets, and that enough to make a scant dozen bottles a month. You'll appreciate, Desmond, that it's a sideline with him, he can't live on the proceeds. He comes to me—and the pitiful few others he can now and then offer a bottle wholesale—with tears in his eyes, and he says, God knows, my friend, Irishmen are needing somewhat to cheer their hearts nowadays, and had I the substance I owned before the cursed settlement-act—he says—I'd give it to you at cost, I would, to give the men chance at an hour here and there of happiness. But that I can't do, he says, little enough profit I'm taking as it is, with so few bottles to sell. Charity it is at that, three pounds wholesale— which is Christ's truth, Desmond, I'm telling you."

"Ah, your heart bleeds for the poor fellow," said Desmond, "and you a charitable Christian man!"

"God's truth it does, Desmond. And," said Kearney, well away by now, "as if all of us hadn't enough grief and trouble to cope with, here is that old hag, John Dowling's wife—and a good man he is but under the woman's thumb and it's no secret I tell for everyone knows that—coming in here this very morning railing at me, saying it's the devil's work I'm on, selling strong drink, the maker taking food from the starving to produce it, and the fires of hell waiting for us in consequence—"

"Never, the old besom!" said Desmond.

"But then, females, they're bound to have odd notions in the nature of things. All I'm saying, Desmond, is the pathetic few fellows able to acquire any whiskey, they're asking more than three shillings the dram for it."

"Well, having made some bargaining myself, I believe you. The sad thing is, I've not got three shillings coin."

Kearney did not look disappointed. "What else have you got, then?"

"You can take your choice. Here's a quarter-pound of tobacco —the habit I never acquired, or I daresay it'd be even odds be- tween that and the whiskey—and"—he fished again in his pocket—"near the full pound o' powder, and either worth a pound on the open market." He laid both cloth bags on the counter.

Fergal stepped up beside him. "Hold the bargaining, I might be interested in that powder."

"Well, if it isn't the gentleman-chief the O'Breslin," welcomed Kearney warmly. "A pleasure to see you, O'Breslin! The house is honored that you come."

Kearney was one of the few men of his class about who main- tained something more than lip service for gentlemen of rank any- more; Fergal's amiable mood expanded for Kearney's deference, and he gave the man a friendly nod. "How do I find you, Desmond?" He offered his hand.

Owen Desmond said, "Middling. Better for a couple of drinks."
He was a big man, his square heavy-shouldered frame reminding
Fergal of Roy Donlevy, but dark; with his slow drawling voice and
steady eyes, he might be like Roy other ways, a quiet man to trust.
He had a little land the other direction from the village; Fergal
had met him four or five times here, and had a notion that Desmond
was in the same business as himself. "Interested in the powder,
are you? It's regulation military stuff." He pushed the bag over,
and Fergal opened it.

"So it is. Damn, Desmond, I couldn't afford all of it—or could
I? We could use it." The winter was coming down, and one way
to add to the larder was going out after game: that was the only
thing a handgun or matchlock was useful for, too noisy for raiding.
Not as much game about as there had been six months ago—
hunting seasons and private land-rights ignored out of necessity
(and some fights about that too); and you didn't see as many hares,
or grouse, or wood-pigeons now, though some were left, and breeding up. Up in the north countries—to afford hunting-pleasure to
the damned English—stag and deer were still plentiful; down here
in land that had been closer settled, not so many left, but over in
Mayo, west, and the Sligo mountains there'd still be some to feed
transplanters there. For awhile, until hungry men killed them off.
But there was game to be had for the pot, anywhere, if it had never
been dignified by the term before. Fergal had looked suspiciously
at the first hedgehog he'd faced on the table, but it wasn't unpalatable meat, and there were wild blackcock, an occasional partridge, snipe, and rooks and blackbirds in plenty, and in marshland
wild duck, and larks. The small birds made a mouthful only, but
meat. You could lay snares for hares and hedgehogs—he'd even
heard of men digging after badgers and moles, claiming they grilled
much like hedgehog—but birds you had to bring down with a gun,
if you hadn't a net. . . .

He fingered the bag of powder. "Ten shillings for half? That's
a sum of money. Could you use an ell of good stout wool?—it's
woven of virgin stuff, and dyed brown. Or I might offer you a
brand-new flint-and-steel, if I take the whole—that's worth two

pounds easy—" And was it worth it, for the powder? With the two military matchlocks they had, you shot small birds to pieces and got nothing; the hand-pistol was all you could use on anything smaller than grouse. Cheaper and more profitable to set out bait, and wait for a flock, and drop a net—but they hadn't a net or anything to make one of. . . . A godsend it would be to have some hens, and they'd be easy got across the border too. But no English farm he'd ever visited had any fowl as yet, hens, or geese, or ducks. Chancy things to raise, they were; likely the few that had been imported wouldn't be found this far west. In time to come, with the English farmers well-started, there might be some for the taking. . . . And the imported English sheep would all be farther north, in Ulster herd lands, none to be seen here over the border, and a pity, a few sheep and goats would be useful—of course, a bigger nuisance to keep than cattle, ruinous on the available pasture. . . . "Look, man," he said, making up his mind, "the ell of wool for the half-bag, or the wool and three drinks off Kearney for the whole."

"Talking with a rich man I am, you with that much real coin to pay Kearney?" The innkeeper was following the talk avidly, head cocked.

"I never said coin," said Fergal. "I'll offer Kearney an ell and a half of the same wool for five drinks, three for you and two for myself."

"Oh, well, now," said Kearney, "I don't know, O'Breslin. Sight unseen, the wool not with you, and you with the drinks drunk."

"All right, all right, then, if you agree to the bargain, I'll put down"—Fergal rummaged in his breeches-pocket—"here, a good steel folding-knife, two blades and a horn case. The wool I'll fetch you tomorrow, same time as I finish the deal with Desmond, and reclaim the pledge. You with two grown sons and children besides, your wife'll be glad of the wool, I'd say."

"Well, I don't deny it," said Kearney. "It's a bargain, and I'd not like you to think I mistrusted you, O'Breslin—a fine gentleman and chief like yourself—but you understand these days no man of common sense gives credit. Five drinks it is." He measured them out deliberate, the bottle produced from under the counter: three drams in one wooden mug, two in the other.

Fergal took Desmond's arm. "I'd now have a word in private."

They went over to a corner away from counter or door, the twenty-odd other men in the place eyeing them with sullen envy for the whiskey, muttering low together: the five or six Connacht men sitting and standing well apart from the transplanters. Out of earshot if they talked low, Fergal looked at Desmond. "I'd be glad to know where and when you got that tobacco." One saddlebag looted, last night, and it had contained maybe ten pounds of expensive cured tobacco—Art said not English-grown either, but eastern stuff, more valuable.

Owen Desmond drank. "You'll have a particular reason for asking, O'Breslin?—it's an indiscreet question."

"And so it is." Fergal met his eyes. "Straight I'll tell you, Desmond, I'm disposed to trust you. I led a troop of horse three and a half years, and it was useful experience for judging men. You don't look like a man to go round four corners when the road's open ahead—and so I'd lay a small wager you got that tobacco at second hand—if you had it today. Did you?"

Desmond looked at him a minute longer. "It was this morning, no harm to say that much."

"Was it indeed!" said Fergal softly. "Then it might easy be the same—it's eastern-cured, is it?"

"I'm no judge, but I'd say so."

"And so I needn't tell you why I'm asking what man traded it off to you," and Fergal's tone was deliberate. "I could say it was thieved out of my house—and thieved it was, true—but it's in my mind you might speak freer if I'm open with you, and God knows it's a sign I'll trust you when I say that. Maybe you and I are in competition—in a business way—or maybe not. I'm not asking. But if we are, you've as much interest in this affair as I have. It's only sense we get together to scotch any cutting-in on our common profits."

Desmond tasted his whiskey again. "A long word you've said there, friend. And maybe I'm a fool to feel like trusting a black northman like yourself—but I think I will. I had the tobacco, just the quarter-pound sack, off Padraig Moran this morning at ten or thereabouts. I traded him twenty cast bullets for a regulation English-army hand-pistol, and another pound of powder, for it."

"Now did you indeed," said Fergal in grim satisfaction. "Padraig Moran. Very interesting that is."

"A name you expected to hear?" murmured Desmond. They looked at each other in wary friendliness.

"You might say that." Fergal grinned and laid a hand on the other man's arm. "Look, man, we'll be the rest of the day communicating, hinting at each other! Can we make it words of one syllable—somewhere less public?"

"In emergencies," said Desmond, "I'm willing to be frank. Lead on, O'Breslin."

9

FERGAL WENT UP over the hill to see McCann. "I don't say it's evidence to hang the two of them, just damn' suspicious. If it was the same tobacco, there wasn't much time for it to reach Moran by the original thief, say between one in that morning and ten."

"True," said McCann, looking thoughtful. He leaned elbows on the table across from Fergal; they talked alone in this one room of the ramshackle cabin that had been on the property when they came. Fergal had not been up here, as it happened, for months: he generally saw McCann at the hideaway, as they left on raids. At the moment his mind was on this matter of Donaghue and Moran, but he was vaguely surprised, a little shocked, at the look of the place. Not a deal less bare it seemed than when they had arrived—never as big or well-built, the way such poor farm-cottages went, as his own. There was the rough built-in settle, this little table thrown together of rude-finished timber, and stood next the settle so the two stools served as extra seating: no chairs. An open shelf above the hearth held a few plates and cups, wood and pewter, and a handful of tableware; there were two pallet-mattresses, looking to be straw or husk filled, in a corner. No clothes-chest—odds and ends, spare trews and shirts and doublets of McCann's, folded neat on one end of the settle, and on one of the pallets female things, not very many. "I can't say I'm happy you talked so free to Desmond," said McCann.

"I think he's a man to trust," said Fergal briefly. When he came in, Maire McCann had been sewing at something, sitting at the table; McCann had just jerked his head at her, and she'd gathered up the stuff and excused herself, all formal, in her expressionless voice, and gone out. And jesting Fergal would make on the subject, like any man, the impossibility of managing perverse females, but he felt a trifle uneasy at seeing this woman obey an order so quick and meek, the peremptory gesture a man might make to a well-trained hound-bitch. "Desmond talked to me too," he said. "He's got a cousin and a couple of former servants with him as company—they go out two or three nights a week. He says in two months he's lost a quarter of his profit to these bastards, and he was interested in what I had to say. He agreed it's definite cause for suspicion, and that we ought to set a secret watch on them to make sure."

"I'll go along with that," said McCann, leaning back and stretching out his legs. . . . Fergal had occupied army-camps more comfortable than this place looked to be. In this time, McCann ought to have done better for his wife, with all they'd taken. Five servant-women and three gentlewomen in Fergal's house, a crowd to support—and it might have been a bigger one, God knew. Those tenants left on his former land—in the end he'd had to disclaim responsibility, he couldn't take on fifty folk. They'd seen the point—the English had made them take his point, with such poverty created overnight. And he felt still angrily guilty at the necessity. . . . And it wasn't any luxury, God knew too, that his household had now—but more than this. One iron kettle by the hearth here, he couldn't see any other cooking utensils. Maire McCann, out of a chief's castle, servants to dress her . . . But Kevin McCann had always been careless of his wife other ways, only expectable he should be in this: except that it was his own comfort as well, wasn't it? Maybe he wasn't here much at all, preferring to spend time up there with the men—so damn' brotherly with Flynn the way he was . . . what was up there to attract him? And where else would he be going to spend time? He hadn't bothered to plant even a garden-patch, but relied on exchange of loot taken to feed them—except for game-hunting, that exercise he enjoyed.

All that slid through Fergal's mind just vaguely, and in answer to one question his knowledge of McCann told him, likely he's taken up with some woman roundabout—or a series of women. One thing to go after the casual women away from home, and another to get entangled with wife or daughter near where you lived. McCann's business—none of his. But he'd no call to keep his wife living so hard as this when he could do better by her. They paid the men fair, a quarter of the profits among them, and split the rest equal; and McCann had only himself and Maire to provide for.

"All right," McCann was saying abruptly, "how do we arrange it?"

"Desmond will have a man watching Donaghue's house Monday, Wednesday, and Saturday nights from now, ready to follow if either of them goes out. We're to provide watchers the other nights."

"Fair enough. I'll tell Dermot and he and O'Shea can split the duty between them—from, say, nine to two in the morning? It'd be then these thieves ride out to intercept returning raiders."

"Well, let's say a different man each night," said Fergal. "Just to be on the safe side, Kevin. I'd thought, Liam Fagan, and little Dillon, and Kindellan. You can put Flynn on the fourth night if you like."

"Oh?" said McCann softly. "A down you've had on Dermot Flynn, Fergal, since he joined us. Why?"

"I wouldn't say that, Kevin. Just, maybe, I've more confidence in men I know better. Are you agreeable to the plan?"

"I'll go along, like I said. In that case, why not Art McTally as the fourth?"

Fergal stood up. "McTally's been doing some forgetting lately," he said with a mirthless smile. "That he was head-groom to my father and is still under the ordering of my father's son. All right, we'll leave it at that. It'll make us a man short for Thursday's outing, but worth it if we can identify some of these whoresons."

"As you say," said McCann; his eyes were veiled of expression.

Fergal left him still sitting there and went down the little slope from the ramshackle cottage and up the steeper wooded hill leading to his own boundary. No, McCann's personal life wasn't any of his affair, but whatever he'd known mildly to McCann's discredit, he hadn't thought he'd be miserly with a wife. You could forgive a man the bold sins, but not the shabby, negative ones.

His name was called softly from the pathside, and he stopped and turned. Hugh—and Maire McCann whom he'd have met on his way up . . . And damn, he thought irrelevantly, for all she'd been through, and that she was nearing thirty, she was still a lovely woman—not a type he liked himself, a quiet, queenly woman of slow dark grace and rare smile: she was smiling now, at Hugh and then at him, turning back toward the house without a word. Hugh came over to the path.

"I was sent up to catch you. Some sort of furor has been raised, and there are English patrols all about in the last hour, and every house being searched. If you've anything on you that might be dangerous, best bury it here."

"What are they after, for God's sake?"

"Your guess as good as mine," said Hugh. "The youngest Dowling was sent on to warn your house to expect them. Your mother keeps her head in emergencies. Most of the pewter tableware is under the loose hearthstone already, and the two bolts of wool and your pistol and ammunition are hanging down the well in a sack, the kitten is buttoned inside Shevaun's bodice, and when I left, Nessa and your mother were burying that ham, and your whiskey, and a covered dish of the remaining lark-pie, under the sacks of meal in the shed. And bewailing the fact that there's no way to hide the quarter-pound of butter without dirtying it, for there's no telling what soldiers will thieve as the fancy takes them."

"Too true." Fergal broke into a jog. "I'd best be there when they come. Didn't the boy say what they seem to be after?"

"No time, his father heard from another neighbor and sent him up to your place just as a patrol arrived. Your mother put him on the way home and sent one of the maids to warn Donaghue—but if rumor's right, by what the boy did know, there are twenty patrols out, likely all over the village by now."

Well, it was no use speculating; Fergal lengthened his stride and Hugh panted to keep up with him, but even at that pace and in that moment he had breath to be irrelevant. "O'Breslin, that lady—McCann's wife—something wrong there is, there."

"McCann," said Fergal brief and impatient.

"So I—surmised. As always—with a woman. In what—way?"

"Women—his own pleasure—and he's mean with her—I was shocked for how bare the house— Never mind that now, hurry!"

When they came over the brow of the hill, he saw troopmen's horses standing before the cottage; as he went down he looked out over open land to the road a quarter-mile off, and a glimpse of

Donaghue's house one way, the Dowlings' the other, and there was a mounted company on the road, and horses standing at both cottages. "God, they're out in force safe enough—" In a minute his hand was on the door, and he went in with Hugh behind him.

Three English troopmen and a captain had the whole household lined up across the room, except for the maid Dareen, who would have gone to carry warning. Even old Tadgh hauled out, looking white and ill. "I am the householder here," said Fergal in English, trying to speak evenly after his run. "May I ask your business, Captain?"

They turned and examined both him and Hugh narrowly. "Name?—and this man?"

"A retainer—Hugh McFadden."

One of the troopmen said low, "Another 'un answers to the description! We'll be herdin' fi' hunderd back for to be looked over!"

"Don't I know it," said the captain disgustedly. "Is this all the household?"

Ethne said, "All but a maidservant, who's on an errand."

"Waste o' time to ask," grumbled the captain, "and a thankless job—expectin' truth out o' Irish! A hundred patrols couldn't search ever' square foot o' land! Well, get to it—search the house, double time, and all round the outbuildings. You"—he turned back to Fergal—"will come along of us, back to Carrick garrison."

"Why? What have I—what charge—" His mother and Nessa moving in protest, going paler than before; Shevaun just stood, head down, one hand unobtrusively clasping her bodice and the kitten.

"No charge, as yet. You conform to the description of a wanted man, and all such must be passed on by one who knows that man at sight. You—"

"For God's sake, all through Connacht? You can't—"

"Ho, yes, we can, Irish," said the captain benignly. "Jus' this territory, we know he's 'ere some'eres, see—but the hell of a job, an' if it's any comfort to you, you're not the only one conforms to the description by a long shot! What you got t' complain of? You get fed by the military meanwhile! Now, do we want you's well?" He looked at Hugh meditatively, fished out a paper from his tunic-pocket, and read it over. "Six foot or an inch over—light complected—black 'air—slim-built—twen'y-five to thirty years o' age— No, I don't reckon you'd make quite six foot, nor you're not in a few years o' that, eh?" The troopmen came back with a negative report. "Orl right, just you, whatever-your-name-is, come on."

"But when—how long will—"

"Oh, Gord, 'ow do I know? I got orders and that's all about it. You come quiet or we tie your wrists and take you."

"Fergal—" said his mother; her hands twisted together tight, and Nessa's eyes were frightened.

"If you're not the fellow they're after, you'll be home again," said the captain impatiently. "Tell your womenfolk not t' make no fuss, there's nought t' make any uproar about!"

"Whether there is or not I've evidently no choice," said Fergal angrily. "Mother, don't get yourself upset for this—if it's as they say, of course I'll be home soon—let McCann know, and—"

"Oh, you're not goin' t' China," said the captain, and shoved him out the door, the troopmen closing in. His last glimpse was of Nessa's terrified look and his mother's tight-clasped hands, and Hugh was calling reassurance, that he'd stay with them.

In the middle of the village street the military had collected nearly fifty men in a resentful group, circled by troopmen like a herd of restless cattle. They must, Fergal reckoned, have been quartering twenty miles roundabout, picking up every man who answered roughly to that description. He saw Desmond, who certainly wasn't slender-made—but the captain likely figured the fellow might have taken on weight: which marked that captain as new to a border-garrison, thought Fergal grimly. He shouldered through to reach Desmond, and was introduced to Desmond's cousin Justin— "An unfortunate family resemblance," they said in unison, and speculated like every man there as to who the English were looking for.

In the next two hours thirty men were added, and then they were lined up and started on the march, troopmen before and behind, regardless of dusk coming down; straight up to the river they went, herded close and the pace swift, and crossed below Carrick to a temporary army-camp where a prison-stockade was ready for them, a bare roped-off enclosure. It was ten of the evening by then; bowls of watery stew were passed around, but no blankets, and they slept cold and hard.

Next morning they were marched up to Carrick garrison and put into the two big compound-cells under it, and there Fergal stayed for two days, with some unlucky others. A dozen or so men were taken out now and then, and did not come back—presumably released. "And, my Christ," he said bitterly to Desmond, "if they just want some fellow to take a look at each of us—! Hasn't he the strength to look at eighty men in one day?"

"Probably an officer," said Desmond philosophically, "who attends to duty an hour a day, and then off to the gaming-tables to recruit his strength." He was taken out with the next group, his cousin with him, and Fergal settled down to more watery stew and rumination.

They'd collected a crowd, but at that they'd missed a few men who conformed to that description; they hadn't covered every foot of the territory. As, of course, they realized was impossible. They might have ranged a way up beyond McCann's house (for instance), perfunctorily, but they hadn't come on the hideaway and fenced pasture there, or they'd have seized both Art McTally and Dermot Flynn, who matched the description roughly. Likely some other places they'd missed, too: and warned in time, a man could go to ground any of a dozen hidden spots in wood. Who the hell were they looking for? A man passing under a false name, and a man who was—or might be—living permanent somewhere in that area, householder or not. A tall, dark, lean man . . .

He deduced an informer who hadn't known as much as the English would like to know. And the man informed on must be very damned important for them to take all this trouble.

Yes, there was another he knew of, that they hadn't got. Padraig Moran. So, he'd got out, warned, and hidden—and he needn't have a better reason than that he was damn' tired of English military—that didn't say he was the man they were after, any surer than a dozen others who'd escaped the net. Moran. All the same, something odd about that man. Times he acted as loutish and crude as Donaghue, and then again he was smooth in manner as a city gentleman. . . .

Along in that early afternoon, Fergal was taken with the last dozen men out to the barracks-yard, where they were lined up. An English officer, a paunchy bald man with cold authoritative eyes, passed slowly down the row; the eyes surveyed Fergal, last man in the line, with chill fury, and the officer turned to the garrison commandant deferential at his side.

"These are the last? Then we missed him, God damn the luck! He slid out of the net somehow—yes, yes, you needn't tell me 'twas a hellish difficult job, when we hadn't the name he goes by —and all these natives sticking together like glue, out to thwart us just on general principles! One informer out of a hundred natives, and he not knowing enough. Well, that's that, Colonel, we've missed him again, and I fear for the last time. He'll try to slide out of the country now, ten to one—and damned if I know why he hasn't before, God Almighty knows what he's up to."

"Very likely, sir," said the commandant. "We'll put on extra guards at the port of Galway, and along the coast—"

"Oh, by all means! But I'm not sanguine. These people can be so damned cunning. . . . And the devil of it is, as I say, there might not have been one man in the district knew Maurice O'Carroll was among them, but bent on deceiving us just on general principle, they saw he was warned with others, and of course he got away west. Well, it can't be helped now." He strode off angrily, not looking back, and the commandant nodded an order to the guard-captain and hurried after him.

The captain barked, "Orl right, you're all free to go—*hout* the gate with you, and straight dahn t' the bridge—no loitering!" A couple of troopmen shepherded them at double time, and in five minutes they were back over the border and left to their own devices.

Some disgruntled talk about it, and excited talk for the name dropped, rose at once; Fergal did not join it for a moment.

Maurice O'Carroll! Right-hand liaison officer to Hugh O'Neill, that man, in the first dozen of high-ranking Federation-army leaders. His name would have been on that list of men condemned to death, all right. But the rumor had been definite that he'd been killed when Limerick garrison fell. Apparently rumor had lied. Fergal told himself he'd be damned: Maurice O'Carroll, living quiet somewhere roundabout? Well, good luck to him, but he'd made a number of his neighbors a deal of nuisance these three days—and now they had a long, cold, hungry walk back home.

He was anxious to get in, and didn't stop on the way, making a good pace. He and a couple of those making for the same village environs had the luck to pick up a five-mile ride with a peddler, one of the few prosperous ones with a cart and an old nag. It was late dusk, all but full dark, when Fergal came across fields from the road toward the house, and past the great spreading shadow of the three oaks just down the slope from the house-yard.

As he passed, there was noise of quick movement in the dry fallen leaves there, and a breathless, outraged exclamation. "Leave me go—I'll scream if you don't—"

Nessa O'Rafferty. Fergal stopped. The wet loam underfoot had muffled his steps, inadvertent, and they hadn't heard him.

"Oh, such a fine lady it is!" And that was Art McTally, laughing. "All you high-and-mighty gentry, you'll need to forget your pride, as you're slow to admit! All right, then, my girl, needn't think I'm off to assault you—just because I was bred in servants' class! What's wrong with me aside, Lady Haughty? I'm as good a man any day as—yes, and better! You looking down your nose—"

"It's—not that, Art." Steadying her voice, trying to sound calm. "Not that at all, just that I don't—it's kind in you to want to give me a present, but it's not right I take it, unless— And it's not because I think you're below me, I—it's—"

"Oh, yes, you coming down to the road twice in an hour, see if our fine young gentleman-chief's in sight! Don't I know! And looking like you could use a dagger on Ailsa, times he take her off to lay her somewhere private! Did he ask you, you'd let him lay you willing—promise, ring, or no—but you're a deal too good to listen to a common fellow as used to be a groom, even when he offers you honest wedlock! Or even take a present from him, offered without strings to it either—"

"No, really, Art, I d-don't feel that way—about the brooch, I mean—please, I'm s-sorry, but I don't—it wouldn't be right to take it, a valuable thing it is, when I *don't*—truly, I'm sorry to hurt you, Art—"

McTally dropped his tone from accusation to soft persuasion.

"Now, you know I'm not off to hurt you either, Nessa girl, wanting you honest and open—don't go pulling away from me now, let me pin the brooch on you, I want you to have it, I kept it out special, see. You're an innocent young one with a lot o' romantic nonsense in your head, is all, and don't know as romance hasn't one damn' thing to do with real loving. I could teach you, my girl—you'd soon forget your other notions—"

"Do you think I'm a convent-bred fool, Art McTally, not to know one man differs from another?—and not on grounds of caste!" Her temper going now. "And I'm not one like Ailsa to take a gift from a man just for the offering—I said leave me go—I'll not—"

Fergal walked up under the trees and saw them as shadowy struggling outline in the deep dusk. He said cold and even, "Yes, leave her go, Art. And I'll have a look at this fine present you want to give her."

Nessa uttered a little sob of surprise and relief and welcome, and flung herself at him. "Oh, Fergal—Fergal—you're home safe—so frightened I've been—" She was warm slender weight pressed on him, holding him close, and as suddenly drawing away. And layers of half-thoughts in his mind, the way a housewife built an oven-pie, one thing over another: Nessa—*you'd let him lay you willing*—the naked love and passion in her voice just now—a brooch, *a valuable thing it is*—*I kept it out special*—contempt in Art's tone, talking of his chief and master—

She stepped back from him and said something confused, apologetic, more coherently welcoming; but he did not hear it. "All right, Art," he said hardly. "Home I am, and interested to hear of something valuable you held out special. Let's see it—hand it over!"

McTally said, "So our gentleman-chief's home again. Welcome, O'Breslin. Home to lead more raids on the English he is, and take seventy-five percent of the profit just on account he was born into a chief's line! Should I say welcome indeed, O'Breslin?"

"I startled that out of you, didn't I?" said Fergal. "Open defiance cutting your own throat, and well you know it, Art McTally! I've no obligation to answer you, but I'll challenge your figures—what about McCann?"

"Kevin McCann doesn't look down his nose at a man on account of birth, my fine chief! He—"

"Nor do I, McTally, as you ought to have sense to know, and you knowing me and my father before me!"

"And what the hell else do you call it, you and McCann splitting the lion's share, and seven others to divide a quarter of the profits? McCann himself says it's unfair, *he's* not a man to think as he's due a fine living just for being a gentleman—"

"McCann we'll leave out of this," said Fergal. "You were my father's man, and I took responsibility for you as a family retainer. But aside from that, McTally, it was—and it is—a business arrangement, like any between merchant and employer. As you were paid wage and given certain support as my head-groom at Lough Eask, you're here employed as professional raider, and the agreement as binding—everything turned into a common pool and divided. And no call I have to remind you, but I will—who spends the time and trouble converting half the loot into negotiable goods, going two days' journey west to exchange it safe?—who takes thought for the direction it's safe to raid, and organizes attack and retreat, so you and the rest of the men come back night after night without a bullet in you—or lying instead dead in a ditch over the border, or hanged by the English? I do, and McCann! And by the living God, Art McTally—fairness, profit, or any other damn' thing aside—I am still the chief O'Breslin, and insolence I don't take from any man, groom or gentry! You hear me?"

"I hear you, O'Breslin," said McTally venomously.

"Then hand over what you kept out of plunder, before I count five!"

"I'll be damned if I will, my fine gentleman! I took it myself, and mine it is by right! And don't I know half your fury is on account I had the gall to approach a gentrywoman under your care!—don't want her yourself, but hands off any who isn't a gentleman! Unheard-of impudence, indeed—a groom talking to a lady! Well, by Christ, I'll repeat it to your face—I'm a better man than you any day, Fergal O'Breslin, with a woman or a weapon or any other way—and you can—"

Fergal caught him square under the jaw with all his weight behind the blow, and knocked him backward sprawling against the tree trunk. "That I'll take you up on any day in the year, you renegade son of a bitch! Another chance I'd have given you, but that ends it! Get off my land and out of my sight, and don't come whining to be taken back or you'll get a double taste of the same medicine!"

McTally got up slowly, a hand to his jaw. "By God, you needn't expect I'd do that, O'Breslin! Damn' pleased I'll be to call myself my own man for a change! Does your gentry-charity allow that I collect my clothes from your fine gentleman's residence?"—and his tone was contemptuous.

"Twenty minutes, you disloyal whoreson, that you have. Go and fetch your belongings and get off!"

"Now isn't that a generous gentleman-chief," sneered McTally. But he went off in the dark, up toward the house, a hand still at his jaw.

"Fergal—" said Nessa breathlessly, and came closer to put a hesitant hand on his arm. "Fergal—"

He turned slowly. He could scarcely see her in the almost-full dark now: a slim light blur in shadow. He knew what Nessa looked like, yes: small, rounded female, auburn hair and smoke-gray eyes: low-pitched voice and capable hands. Nessa. *You'd let him lay you willing.* It wasn't a thing he could think of, all on a sudden, with this business of Art and the red fury on top of him.

"Fergal—"

"Get along," he said roughly, impatiently, "let's get up to the house—I want to see him off and have done, and forget this whole damn' business!"

10

ETHNE O'BRESLIN EXPENDED no emotion on his safe return, beyond a warm welcome, and with a little effort he teased her for it: "Thinking it'd make one less mouth if the English decided to keep me, were you?"

She regarded him with tranquillity. "I wasn't feared for you after the first while, Fergal. And Brian Donaghue said you'd be back safe, and every man else they'd taken."

After the upset with McTally, he fired up easily. "And Donaghue's got the second sight maybe, to know what's coming true?"

"He knew—I saw he knew," said Ethne. "Sit down, Fergal—you'll be wanting a meal."

And he said abruptly, "When Art McTally is out of my house, so I will." But McTally was already coming out to the main room, a bundle slung over one arm, and Liam Fagan emerging after him, looking startled. Neither Fergal nor McTally spoke, but only looked at one another; McTally stalked out and slammed the door.

"Was it the kind of fight you can explain about to females?" asked his mother interestedly. "I won't say I'm sorry to see Art go, at that."

"You can have it in one sentence," said Fergal. "He'd been insolent to me before, he was insolent just once too often and a word too far—and I found he'd been holding out loot on us." He sat down at the table.

"O'Breslin, thank God you're back," exclaimed Liam. "Art, is it?—I'd halfway suspected that but didn't like to say—"

And somewhat unusual, Shevaun's hand on his shoulder shook,

139

and her voice as well. "Fergal—I was so afraid you'd not come home—Fergal, what happened, what did they want? The men who've come back said—"

Fergal told them about it. "Yes, O'Carroll, if you can conceive it—mingling with us cool as be damned. The puzzle is why he didn't get out of Ireland with the rest. It's only a guess, but I'd say he was recognized by some man who didn't know what name he goes by here, and for some reason couldn't find out—all they knew, evidently, was the district to look in."

"Indeed," said his mother thoughtfully. "I see. I see."

"What do you see?" He looked up, from the plate of rook-pie —mostly flour-and-water paste and potato, with a few mouthfuls of rook added—Shevaun had just put before him. The flickering light of a couple of rush-candles and only one decent tallow taper was poor, and Ethne's expression eluded him.

"Why, just I see you're likely right, that's all. And just as we were afraid would happen, those soldiers found the butter. Also the new flint-and-steel, I'm sorry, Fergal, it was the one thing we forgot to hide."

"Oh, Christ damn the thieves—that was worth two pounds at least! How in hell's name did you come to forget that?—and save half a dish of lark-pie! Oh, well, what's done is done, I don't mean to snap at you." He had been hungry half an hour ago, but the quarrel with Art and now this—and the revelation about Nessa—set him feeling uneasy and at odds; he pushed the plate away after three mouthfuls. And then old Eily was shuffling in, exclaiming joyful that Tadgh thought he heard O'Breslin's voice.

Fergal got up and attempted a smile around at them. "I'm not so much hungry as tired, Mother, I'll just look in on Tadgh and get to bed." He went through the next room that he and Liam shared, to the little new one where Eily and Tadgh slept. The other two new rooms, only one with a real door, led off the opposite side of the main room, for the other six women. Ailsa was sitting with Tadgh, and gave Fergal her fleeting sly smile.

When he'd had a few words with the old man, assuring him all was safe now, he went back into his bedchamber and in the dark stripped off his doublet. Next generation might be bred blind as moles, he thought, used as they were getting to groping about in dark rooms, any sort of artificial light so expensive and hard to come by. The door shot a thin dim ray of rushlight at him one second, opening and shutting, and Ailsa said softly, "I'm glad you're back safe, O'Breslin."

"What, are you learning to tell one man from another?" He felt his way across to his pallet-bed, three feet from Liam's: the room scarce six feet wall to wall. Nor they weren't so elegant any more to take off many clothes, going to bed. A damned queer thing it was, when you came to think: God knew they had all suffered enough big, lifetime tragedies to moan about—for the way it was in Ireland now for Irishmen—but it was the little things brought it home to you. The lack, not of a high carven-headed bedstead with a down-filled mattress, but of one blanket thick enough to keep you reasonably warm, whatever you slept on. Lack, not of the carven clothes-chest in your bedchamber at home, the orna- mented oak table with the French glass hung over it, and the contents of the drawers—gold cloak-brooches, an old-fashioned gold armlet, the formal belt-scabbard inset with garnets and pearls—but of enough clothes to cover nakedness, and provide a change of shirt while one was washed. Lack, not of the matched pewter tableware, each piece with an agate inset in the handle, but of food to eat, tableware or fingers . . . And a gentry-chief's house, like that one, appeared to him in retrospect these days not so much as representing wealth and prestige, as simply a place with sufficient rooms in it that you need not forever be rubbing shoulders with other people, but could get away to yourself if you wanted.

He ran into the girl in the dark, and she pressed against him willing, her arms going round his neck. "It'll be some while before Liam comes to bed," she murmured.

For a breath the desire tightened his loins, and he bent and kissed her. He was aware of her generous round curves and the pungent close smell of her unwashed body and hair—a slattern she was—and his tiredness swept over him again, and revulsion, and he pushed her away almost roughly. "Not tonight, girl," he muttered. "I'm tired to death, let me sleep."

But when she'd gone off sulkily, and he lay down dressed but for his doublet and pulled the blanket over him, he could not sleep. He turned from side to side, restless.

Nessa O'Rafferty. And just lately he'd been thinking, look about for some suitable potential husband for the girl. A damn' pretty girl, certain, and well-bred, and young. *You'd let him lay you willing.* Would she? Naked revealed love in her voice on his name. Himself, he'd never thought of Nessa—that way. Wanton like Ailsa was one thing, a line down the middle there was, respectable well-bred female like Nessa the other side. Honorable man wouldn't give a thought that way to a girl like Nessa, except in the way of marriage. And marriage contracts arranged with a dozen other considerations more important than how you felt for the woman. Family. Dower. Inheritance expectations. And for the situation they were in now, all the Gaels who'd kept to the old customs, that kind of thing likely all changed. But, didn't think of a girl like Nessa that way—except, like as Art said—the promise and the ring . . .

He felt uneasily embarrassed about Nessa, he didn't know quite what to feel. He took his mind off her resolutely. Yes, all the small ordinary things, that even just ordinary people, not wealthy gentry, took for granted. If he'd been asked to list all that the settlement-act deprived him of seven months ago, they wouldn't have entered his head—the humble unconsidered conveniences —taken for granted until you had to do without them. Neckerchiefs; he had three left, nearly whole. Flint-and-steel in its little box, one in every second room at home, and even a farmer with one or two. Linen washing-cloths and towels. Stockings—he hadn't any whole left, but he wasn't alone in that; and knit-wool was all imported, and dear when you got any. Shoes—now and then in remote places you'd seen women barefoot, but nobody went so from choice; and that was an item hard to pick up on a raid. Ink, paper—not that it was often wanted now; but he'd been three days finding the wherewithal to write that letter to Roy. The dull old razor, no way to sharpen it if it would still take an edge—and, Christ, had Art taken it with him? Just like the bastard that would be; Fergal was too lax and dispirited to get up and see. A fashion for beards would be coming in, he reckoned bitterly, enough men razorless. Well, they said a beard was warm in winter. . . .

The candles, yes: even if you had a candle-mold, which was a refinement—didn't need that to make rushlights—where did you get any kind of fat or grease for making tapers? Rushlights didn't take as much, being not solid tallow all the way through but a hardened coat over the pith of the rush—but some it took for that. Nobody who had any livestock was butchering; stock was too scarce and needed for breeding. When Fergal fetched home a ham or— as he'd had the luck to do twice—a quarter of fresh-killed hog— every fraction of the fat was cut off, more precious for other things than food. . . . And if you had a few rush-tapers, lucky if you had a holder for them, for wall or table.

Little things you never thought about, until— The women wishing they had a sadiron. He ought to be able to pick one up, have a look anyway, next time. Never thought about it—servant fetching in fresh shirt clean and smoothed. And soap. Every time there was a little fat of some kind, the agonized discussion again —how much to use for rushlights, how much for soap? Didn't reach far either way, needing to be heated . . . and that brought up the problem of fuel—turf was dear—and of a container—they were lucky to have two iron kettles, enough people hadn't one.

He remembered, at home, seeing the maids busy in the washing-yard at the side of the house. Just noticing casually—the household linen being washed—and passing on. Likely that big tub in the yard hadn't cost five shillings, and likely his mother and the rest would forgo a year of life to have it here. It had a hinged bottom and a spigot—and they rubbed soap on the dirtier spots in the linen, and stacked it all inside, hung over clean poles, layer after layer—and poured lye-water through, a dozen times—and then they hung each piece on the big tenterhooks to dry, stretched with a weight at the bottom so it wouldn't need smoothing. In midsummer they had all the blankets out along with the linen, and enough extra so it wouldn't matter if they took two-three days to dry. Never a thought he'd given to such mundane things, women's things—but he knew all about them now!

Washing-lye base you could make by soaking wood-ashes and straining them. The problem there, the expense of wood to burn; there were trees on his land but he didn't want to thin out much more than he had, they might be more valuable later; and, too, the scarcity of muslin cloth to strain the ash-water. Some old-fashioned, penurious-run households used to save all the urine produced by the occupants, to dilute with water and boil and store for use as a bleach on the linens. His mother had never liked the notion, and kept bran-water instead.

But if they'd wanted, not even that they could do now; as a last indignity, in a way, even that humble object the household pisspot was not to be had. Not an item you risked your neck to get across the border—or had burdened yourself with on the long way to Connacht. And of all inconsidered trifles, that was surely the least, that little prosaic necessity; even a poor farmer's house, in the old days, had contained half a dozen. It wasn't the smallest of the niggling inconveniences—the need arising at night, for instance, having to get up and leave the house, whatever the weather. And that was a half-civilized thing too (the stark difficulty of life this near the bone turning them all a bit primitive, when you came to think), for he couldn't say he—or any of them—troubled to go so far, every time, as the sanitary trench he'd seen made in the little copse up the slope. There were trees nearer the house, and at night, when it was cold, maybe raining— There had been a soak-pit behind the cottage, but the rude closet-shelter over it had been long knocked down for timber when they came, and the pit filled and noisome anyway. They had had to sacrifice a cooking-basin to serve old Tadgh's needs, he bedridden.

He turned restlessly again on the thin pallet. One thing leading to another. Like many another man here now who had been gentry in the social scheme before the Act, he could feel bitter for the way folk of lower class talked free and sometimes insolent. *To their betters*, he could say—even while he knew, honest, you couldn't judge men wholly on caste. But if you came down to it, were he and the other gentry *betters*, in this situation? What was in his mind was Dan Kindellan, a week or two ago. Fergal had been saying they ought to build a decent regular privy close to the house; and Kindellan had told him just how to go about it. Not superior or patronizing, as some would have been, but earnest—knowing that a gentleman wouldn't have the first notion of it. It seemed you didn't just dig a good deep hole and build a shelter over it, and a bench-seat with holes; you had to bake a good fifty pounds of earth to dry powder, to line the pit, and start certain underground roots there that hastened decomposition, and there should be a small outside drain for household use, emptying slops, and a draft-vent down a slope. . . . It was men like Kindellan, who might be barely able to spell out a bit of printing but knew all these useful pieces of knowledge, who might be said to be superior, here and now. . . .

And, damn, he *would* risk his neck, next time over the border, to fetch back a couple of pisspots. Out he'd have to get now. He got up in the dark and found his cloak, barked his shins on the door as he opened it and cursed. The main room was empty and dark; outside a thin mist was falling.

Ten steps from the door he ran into Liam Fagan, out for the same purpose. They walked round the side of the house together. "It's a weight off my mind, O'Breslin, you're home safe. I know you'll be tired, but there's things—well— You going all the way up to—?"

"No," said Fergal, shivering, and stopped where he was. "All the same, Liam, we ought to get busy and build a decent house-privy, before first frost." And just where would they get the sawn lumber for it? That for the house-addition—stark necessity, you couldn't put fourteen people to live and sleep and cook in two rooms, one twelve by nine and the other eight feet square—had cost him two months' profit in plunder, equivalent; and the half of that went for the one made door, at that.

He thought it was just in the last couple of months all of them realized fully—had time to realize—the primitive conditions they lived in. Up to then they'd been too busy just existing. And let no man tell him that the life of an outlaw-criminal was chosen by lazy men! It took all his time, thought, and energy, plundering over the border, fetching the stuff back intact, going long journeys the other direction to dispose of it safe. He'd had enough to think of besides all these other little things; but—

It came to him with sudden appalling clarity, how easy it was for people to slide backward into half-civilized ways, almost overnight. When the very decencies were so much trouble to observe . . . Those men up the hill living almost like animals in caves, half underground.

"Yes, if you say," said Liam inattentively. But he'd been well brought up, and he waited politely until they'd both accomplished their business and turned back to the house. "O'Breslin, did you know Dareen's not come back at all?"

"What? You mean, since—"

"Since she went to warn Donaghue about the English soldiers coming, three days back. Your mother's been worried for it—we all have, for she's a decent girl, and—and there are tales about the military kidnapping women—and keeping secret brothels, like, in their barracks. Donaghue says she left his house safe enough—"

There was a faint note of doubt, Fergal thought, in the thin young voice. Liam might be clumsy still with overgrown youth, and not much to look at, gawky flax-haired youngster beardless and given to blushing, but he wasn't a fool. Fergal asked sharply, "You don't believe him?"

"Oh, well, I don't know—why would he lie about it? I wouldn't think he's a—a womanizer himself. It's just—and there's nothing we can do but ask around, which we have—if any's seen her. McCann came, and told about your plan for watching that house, O'Breslin. I was on last night, one of Desmond's men is to take over tonight."

Fergal grunted. "Anything stirring?"

"Nought at all—and it's d-damned cold to be lying out belly to ground under a bush, just watching—but you know John Dillon's conscientious, and Kindellan too, they wouldn't scamp the hours —I couldn't say about Flynn or Desmond's men—"

"Needn't tell me that!"

"Donaghue's been staying right close to his house, nights anyway. Dillon was in the village yesterday and met him in at Kearney's, and Donaghue told him he was nursing that Moran over a bout of fever and the flux, him down in bed with it, he's that bad."

"And that might be so, too—it's been about, I had a touch myself ten days ago. Damn. We may keep a watch on for a month and get nothing, if they've dropped onto you."

"I don't think it," said Liam diffidently. "We've all been careful, and there's a growth of rowan that gives shelter not far off the housedoor."

Fergal grunted again. "I tell you, Liam, I'll spell you, your next night on watch. I want to see for myself—not that I don't trust you, you know that." He gripped the boy's arm in reassurance, and opened the door; they went in quiet. This time, once settled under his blanket on the thin pallet, Fergal drifted to sleep.

* * *

The next morning he went into the village with the wool he'd bargained to Desmond and Kearney, to pay off his score. The innkeeper was passionately interested in the late manhunt, voluble in astonishment at the revelation about O'Carroll. Fergal, not so constituted that he could be convivial in the forenoon, was rather abrupt with the man. But he roused himself to talk to Desmond serious; and Desmond roused him further by pressing on him a dram of colorless liquid— "Just for an honest opinion, O'Breslin."

Fergal's opinion was expressed in a strangled exclamation of mixed respect and horror, at the first mouthful of the stuff. "Jesus and Mary, what have I ever done to you, to get poisoned at your hand?"

Desmond said cheerfully, "Yes, I didn't get the proportions right with this first batch, it can take more dilution—which makes it all the cheaper to produce." He looked at Fergal anxiously. "Now it's settled a bit, how do you feel?"

Fergal swallowed experimentally once or twice, still tasting the first mouthful. "Man," he said faintly, "let's take some over to the site of Tara and wake up all those old dead kings from a thousand years back." He shook his head to clear it of a dim buzzing. "I feel about as I would if I'd half a dozen hefty drinks of whiskey down me. And if I finish the dram you may have to see me home—but I will. What the hell is it?"

"Potato whiskey," said Desmond. "We've built a small still out back. This is a first experiment. I don't maintain it's got the flavor of the real stuff, but you get a greater yield out of it than grain, and it needn't set so long. And it's perfectly safe, I do assure you—nothing like wood-distilled stuff, to turn you blind or seeing monsters. I'm wondering"—he took a reflective sip—"if we flavored it with a handful of crushed rye strained in—I must try some on Kearney, he's a judge. I wager I could ask a pound a bottle for it."

"And give your customers their money's worth, if all they care about is the strength of a drink!" said Fergal. "But I didn't come to talk about whiskey." However, Desmond had nothing to add to Liam's report. Donaghue, in fact, wasn't stirring out of his house as much as usual, because of Moran's illness; and three men had spent three uncomfortable, cold vigils for nothing, that was all up to now. "Oh, well, we couldn't expect to drop on them first shot out of the barrel," said Fergal. "And, damn, Moran being down like this, we might not see them move inside a fortnight at that. But let's keep on at it, ten days anyway."

Desmond agreed absently, still brooding on how to improve his whiskey; and Fergal set out rather cautiously back toward Donaghue's. He'd had only a couple of oatcakes for breakfast, which he didn't trust to absorb Desmond's hell-brew; but aside from a pleasant glow of cheerful optimism and the consequent realization that he must watch his tongue and not talk too much, he felt reasonably normal.

Donaghue asked him in, warm and welcoming. "Good to see you back safe, O'Breslin, by God's grace. A queer turnout that was, indeed. Take Padraig's chair, the poor man's flat in his bed with this fever going about."

Fergal sat down. "So I'd heard. But you were sure enough we'd all come back safe, what my mother says. I was saying to her when I heard that, maybe Donaghue is favored with the second sight," and he smiled to show it was a jest.

Donaghue laughed, big and warm. "Oh, well, I can put two and three together to make five! After all, it was a man passing under a false name they were after, and that wouldn't be you, though of course they'd not accept any identification from any soul here. . . . I'm sorry I've no hospitality to offer you, O'Breslin, but it's a shabby way we live these days."

Fergal said it was just as well and told him about Desmond's whiskey; Donaghue was suitably amused. "A queer thing it was, as you say, Donaghue—I daresay by now you've heard it was O'Carroll they were hunting. I thought myself there'd very likely been an informer who didn't know quite as much as the English would have liked."

"The likeliest thing," nodded Donaghue, "and a good job too."

"What I can't make out is why Maurice O'Carroll should be still in Ireland, the rest of the important leaders away to Spain or France these eighteen months."

"Ah, you're right, that's the mystery," agreed Donaghue, shaking his red head. "And likely we'll never know all the ins and outs of it."

Fergal leaned back in his chair and surveyed his host thought-

fully. Donaghue—like Desmond—wasn't a type of man to whom
secrecy and cunning came natural; he'd always be a bit heavy-
handed at it; and Fergal fancied he had felt the clumsy pressure
on the rein in those few sentences. Which was very damned odd;
for he'd used the subject only as convenient current topic, to es-
tablish friendly relations. He said abruptly, "I see they didn't pick
up Moran. Or a couple of my men they might have taken, too.
Maybe others—and O'Carroll among them—if the informer was
right, and he was here."

"True that is," said Donaghue. "And they'd know they must
miss gathering in some o' the men matched the description—
though a damned good try they made, quartering everywhere like
a well-trained hound-pack! No, we heard in good time what their
errand was, see, from young Terence Lynch who came up from
the village warning every house—and Padraig says to me, I'm
damned if I'm put another catechism by English, he says—just on
account I happen to look like some fellow they're after. Nor I can't
say I blame him, O'Breslin—he was in a Cork regiment, under
Colonel Driscoll, all the way through since 1648, and taken prisoner
after the fight at Tipperary, but got away again—and of course you
never know with English, anything at all they're likely to do, and
I tell you frank, O'Breslin, not a coward Padraig is, but he's nervous
at the very thought of wrist-fetters and prison-stockades—and he
not the only one."

"Oh, isn't that the truth," said Fergal cordially. "So he slid away
to hide, did he?"

"And he'd have done better, I swear, to go along with the rest
o' you to Carrick," said Donaghue earnestly. "For see you, he lay
up in the wood over the hill most of that night, to be sure they
were gone, and that's where he came by this bad fever-flux he's
taken, the ground being so damp and all. Or at least put himself
in the state to pick it up—it's been going about like a little plague.
I hear the eldest Kearney boy's that low with it, anxious they are
about him and even at the point of sending over to Ballintober for
the nearest priest."

"Is that so, now," commented Fergal mechanically, remembering that Kearney had said something about that two hours ago,
yes. "That's bad. Maybe it'd cheer Moran if I looked in on him?"

Donaghue took that as a kind thought, and said he'd see if

Moran was awake. This cottage had two rooms as Fergal's had originally, a little bedchamber opening from the main living-room; Donaghue opened that door and went in, and came back on clumsy tiptoe, easing the door shut again. "He's got off to sleep at last, so we won't wake him. Up and down every twenty minutes he's been, this last forty-eight hours, with the bowel-flux so bad as it's been, and weak as a newborn babe, so I've been up every time to help him. Let's hope this is the turning point and it's slacking off, that he can sleep."

"Let's hope it." Fergal didn't much want to see Moran; it had been a polite gesture. And there was another thing he meant to mention to Donaghue. "This maidservant of mine—Dareen Coyle —I understand you say she left here safe? You know she's not come back, apparently no one's seen her since."

An unhappy look came into Donaghue's eyes. He felt in his pocket and brought out an ancient clay pipe and a worn tobacco-pouch. "Yes, it's a bad thing, I know. That's right—and I may say I took it very kind in your good mother to think to send warning —she wouldn't know young Lynch'd already been here. Yes, that's so, the girl left here right enough—so she did—I took it, back for your place, but I can't say for sure." He was filling the pipe with slow deliberation. "Now, where are my manners!—a pipe o' tobacco I can offer you, I was fortunate in acquiring some at an advantageous trade the other day—"

Yes, by force from one of my men! thought Fergal. "My thanks, but I never got into the habit." He got up. "You'll be tired with your nursing, and I've—this and that—to do myself. I'm sorry you can't tell me more. It's worried my mother—what with stories of how the English kidnap young women."

"And so it would worry her," said Donaghue, getting up politely, looking at his pipe, "and she a good kindhearted woman. Well, I'm sorry too, O'Breslin, and we'll just pray it isn't so, that the girl's safe somewhere. . . . Do you come again when you've time, always welcome you are—and Padraig saying the same."

Fergal started home thinking moodily that he'd wasted the morning—unless you counted Desmond's whiskey as gain.

11

THE ROWAN-BUSH PRICKED hard twig-points into Fergal's ribs even through doublet and shirt, and he cursed it silently. It was cold, this late night of October, and getting colder by the minute; a glistening rime of frost shone faint on the open ground past the bush up to Donaghue's little cabin. Must be getting on for midnight, and nought stirring at all. Couldn't see whether anyone was sitting up this late, in there; the one window was boarded up solid for the winter, like all windows now.

This was the fifteenth night they'd kept watch on Donaghue, and got nothing but cramped and cold. On the other hand, in that time both Fergal's party and Desmond's had gone out on five raids, and met no ambush on the way home. If it was Donaghue at the head of these local outlaws, now lying out of the game awhile, was it because he suspected they suspected him—and why?

Fergal shifted position cautiously. This was the third night he took watch, and if he told himself the truth it was only an excuse to get out of the house. His mother's endless worried talk about Dareen; the constraint he felt for Nessa, and she acting unnaturally polite, avoiding his eyes; Shevaun's sullenness or snapping at the child for little things. All somehow intensified for the winter season coming down, shutting them up together more.

Go out tomorrow and see if he could find some game—time to check those snares set out for hare, anyway.

He didn't start at the hand laid quiet on his ankle; he took it for Liam, come up to see how it was going and offer to take the rest of the watch. He turned on his side, to give the boy room to

151

crawl up beside him—and Brian Donaghue's low rumbling voice said, "Would it be the chief O'Breslin I'm addressing?" He sounded polite and amused.

Fergal moved quick, to get away, into less vulnerable position, groping for his knife—but the damned bush trapped him—and Donaghue said, "Now, a poor opinion of me you've got if you think I'd cut your throat and you helpless on your back. No fear, O'Breslin! I surmised it'd be you on watch again tonight, and it's time we talked together open." He sat back on his heels, dim bulk in the dark; he laughed. "There's no reason all of you need go on risking a lung-congestion, lying out here night after night. That fellow was on night before last, I thought I recognized the terrible rasp he's got in his throat—that little John Dillon, was it? Take shame, O'Breslin, sending that poor fellow out in the cold and wet, thin and frail as he is!"

Fergal had got his heels under him, ready to be up at the first move the other man made. "Somehow I had a notion you'd dropped on us, Donaghue—when we didn't meet your band of craven thieves on our way back from the river!"

Donaghue heaved a long sigh, and his breath was a silver cloud between them. "That's a side issue, but we'll talk about it," he said, and now he was serious. "Not my band, O'Breslin—I don't set myself up as a saint, but at that kind of business I'd draw the line. There's a deal to say between us, and I've something to give you—won't you come up to the house and talk in comfort? It'll be a bit warmer, anyway." He wriggled out of the bush and stood up; Fergal followed him, wary.

"And what've you got for me, Donaghue? I don't—"

"Ah, drop the bold clever talk-for-effect, boy," said Donaghue, sudden and bitter. "Some good sense you must have, being your mother's son, and it ought to tell you you can trust me. I can be open with you now, and glad to. As for what I've got for you, it's a letter from your brother-in-law. Come on up." He turned and started for the house.

"*Roy*—" said Fergal, unbelieving; and then incredulity held him dumb. He caught Donaghue up; their feet made sibilant creakings in the frost, up to the house.

Inside there was a low fire on the hearth, the two chairs drawn up to it. "Sit down," said Donaghue, and went to the table. "We'll both do with a dram of whiskey, dear as it is. Not as young as I was, and the time's gone I could stalk game—human or other—on my belly in the wet and cold, and never feel a twinge for it later." He handed Fergal a cup, sat down heavily in the opposite chair, and produced a bulky sealed letter from his inside doublet pocket. "You don't owe the carrier aught, O'Breslin—he was on another job and only brought it incidental. The French sailor he had it from in Galway was an honest man, for a wonder—he'd been paid to find a carrier here, and so he did. Our man who came today with a letter for me from Galway, he was asking if I knew your name, and I said I'd deliver it. Drink up, O'Breslin."

Fergal stared at the letter, sealed a dozen places in thick red blobs—a seal he knew, though never seeing it stamped in wax before: the entwined initials and loop-design round the edge of Roy Donlevy's seal-ring. His name and direction in Roy's heavy big script. His hand closed on it hard. "Thanks, Donaghue," he managed.

"You don't ask about my letter," said Donaghue, "being polite-raised. But I'll tell you who it was from—the man you knew as Padraig Moran."

Fergal looked up from Roy's letter. He swallowed half the whiskey and leaned closer to the low blaze; he was chilled through, but his hand shook on the cup not from cold alone. "My wits aren't working full speed," he muttered, "or haven't been. Oh, yes—of course—I see it now. Your letter was to say he's safe away in a ship for the Continent. These two weeks he's been gone from here, and you covering for him, saying he's ill in bed. Yes. Moran is Maurice O'Carroll."

Donaghue drank and began to fill his pipe. "The very devil of a time you must have had, getting that bull over the river," he said ruminatively. "You made me some unwitting help that night, but if you hadn't, I'd still be pleased for you that you got him home safe. If you're agreeable, I'd well like a look at him in daylight—a bold big rampager he sounded! For one thing, there's my heifer—I've decided to keep her—and along next April I'd be pleased to breed her." His rumbling laugh again. "I can also set your mind at rest about those English you ran into—the man they left to watch, and him not the only one if you'd known it. You thought maybe they had information about raiding-companies, didn't you? They had information—but they were waiting for me, O'Breslin. I was just as relieved your man put that one out of the way. After you'd gone by, you and your noisy big bull, I got out the other way past them. What you likely surmised was right— the rest of the patrol was lying not far off, waiting signal from the half-dozen men scattered on watch. You were lucky to miss them, but you went the opposite direction."

Fergal drank the rest of his whiskey; he needed it. "Do I carry the story further to say—then that business was the result of a first piece of informing to the English? Oh, yes—I see—you'd had some sort of meeting arranged near there, with what man? one carrying messages from over the border?—and," he laughed, "we stumbled into the middle of it! Like that, Donaghue?"

"The meeting was with the informer," said Donaghue somberly. "Only I didn't know he was that then, I needn't say. No need for details. A man who had carried messages from Galway, off Dublin-berthed ships, a common peddler earning a bit on the side. O'Carroll had been thinking it might be easier and safer to get out by way o' Dublin, see you. A heavy guard on Galway harbor, account of all the smuggling—and he can pass as an Englishman easy. I'd met the fellow to take letters—no name on any of them, but there was a password to exchange—and that one letter the week before, O'Carroll's name was in it. I figure he opened it and faked back the seals after reading. And it said a hundred pounds to him, posted by the English for a wanted man."

"Oh, yes, I see. That was all he knew?"

"Nothing in any letter had said O'Carroll was living roundabout here, but that told him I would know where O'Carroll was. And myself he'd never laid eyes on, we always met in the dark. He gambled that he might get the whole reward, handing me over to the English and they bribing or torturing the information out of me." Donaghue had his pipe filled. There were four rushlights burning in a wall-holder to the side of the hearth; he stood and bent his head to one, pipe in mouth, and got the tobacco burning to his satisfaction, and sat down again—a big, heavy-moving, spare middle-aged man—as if resting after labor, with a sigh. "I've learned to go around corners, I tell you. It doesn't come natural to me, O'Breslin. Straight fight, yes, I went out under Driscoll and joined the O'Neills, and more war than you I saw, from 1644 on. A young man I was then—thirty-five I was, and thinking the world was at an end because my Ena was dead—queer to think it is, now. Five years wed, and a grief we'd no family—but what it came to, after she was drowned that time, it didn't seem any matter what happened, for a while. But you come to life again, O'Breslin, remember that—after the very worst, you come to life—if you've the guts of living life in you at all." He drew on the pipe in silence for a minute, and sighed again. "Well. Going around corners at things, like I say—six years of war taught me that. I'd been beforehand at the meeting, and I saw the English patrol post that guard in the wood, so I read the story plain about the informer. Very opportune you were there, one of your men taking off the troopman. I hadn't a notion what band of raiders it was then—later, when I heard about your bull, I knew."

"Well met that was," said Fergal interestedly. "You're putting things right way up for me. Did you get the bastard, Donaghue?"

"I took him. Once the troopman was out of the way. If you hadn't taken him off, the informer would have signaled some way to bring him down on me. You and your bull made some convenient noise for my stalking—the informer was a bit nervous for it, likely thinking it was the English patrol to warn me off. I got him from behind with my knife—he was knocking at the gate of hell before you were half a mile off. I made straight for home to tell O'Carroll, and even on foot I was there in a couple of hours. What with this and that, we didn't cross into Connacht until after the English were guarding their horses like gold, and hadn't managed to pick one up. And O'Carroll and I were both thinking it was still safe, only all the planning to make over again, and time to do that. Like you know, we were at your place that morning, he wanting to see the girl and tell her. But late that afternoon, when the Lynch boy came to tell of all the military patrols, and men being taken, neither of us had to think half a minute before seeing what had happened. The bodies found, and the English wanted him bad, they were taking the gamble too—that he was living somewhere roundabout. It was likely—and that the way it turned out, of course—they'd sent in a hurry for some man knew O'Carroll by sight, and he couldn't have been far off, turning up in a matter of hours."

"Tongue and groove pattern." Fergal gave a short laugh. "Yes, I see how it fits in."

"O'Breslin," said Donaghue, unhappy and earnest, "the one bad thing to it, my arm I'd cut off before giving worry to your lady mother—your household—but you see there was no other way about it, and that sorry I am, and O'Carroll telling you the same, for he's a gentleman and an honorable man. Dareen—a decent good young woman, and a rare pretty one too. It was awkward—romantic as you might say, but inconvenient!—they wanting to be wed, see you."

"She went with him," said Fergal, nodding. "My mother will be relieved, true enough. Are they away?"

"He wrote me on shipboard in Galway harbor six days ago, I had the letter today like I said. They were sailing for France on the next tide. A priest in Dunmore wed them on their way west." Donaghue added doubtfully, "Gentleman and important man O'Carroll was here, and he means to join Hugh O'Neill who is with King Charles over there, but as to what they'll live on—and likely the Stuart king making another try against Parliament, and more fighting and all—an uncertain sort of marriage, you might say it is. But they were both set—" He shook his head. "God's mercy, like a madman he was—knowing he had to get away quick, and no way to come in touch with the girl. And then she came up, carrying warning. That's a good girl, you know. She took it in with a glance and a word, and never a thought for that she'd not even a cloak with her—she set off with him like as they were going a mile's visit and home again."

"And good luck to them. Talk about romance! One of my old tenant's daughters, a maidservant, wedding Maurice O'Carroll! I will be damned—I will be damned. They lay up quiet until the English were gone, I suppose, and started west by night. You're clearing up a dozen mysteries for me, all right—"

"Not for open talk, as I needn't remind you."

"Christ, hardly. Though people will speculate, and put this and that together. After a bit you put it about that this Moran's left you to go off on his own, and we saying the same about the girl. To satisfy my curiosity, Donaghue, clear up another mystery. What was O'Carroll doing still here? Why didn't he go with O'Neill?"

"There's no mystery about that. He took a bullet in the lung at Limerick, and a miracle he lived, getting himself smuggled down to Kerry. It wasn't so big a lie I told—my wife Ena, she was first cousin to him, and he knew I was safe. Besides, an island's a good place to lie hid. I'd just got home to Scariff myself, out of Dungarvan garrison. He lay up there nine months and more, between life and death—a lung-congestion coming on half a dozen times so I was ready to send for the priest. A time we had, I tell you, no surgeon in fifty miles and little but fish to keep us alive. But he's a healthy young fellow, and he began to mend at last, along last March— only not strong enough to try secret escape abroad. And by then, they'd caught up to us, see you—the English and their damned record-keeping!—and banished me off the island and house—and all the particulars they asked for their accounts, you know how it was—we were chivvied into coming across like any other two transplanters. Which sure to God I am." Donaghue bent to knock out his dead pipe in the hearth.

"You could have gone with him."

"Well—it's like the old proverb, maybe—better the devil you know than the one you don't. Even the English I need to listen close at, and I doubt I'd ever pick up the French talk, or Spanish. And—well, I didn't, and here I am. O'Breslin, I'm relieved to be open with you, it wasn't that I mistrusted you any way, but—it was important he be got away safe, and he making the planning and saying, no confidants. I knew you mistrusted me, though what put it in your head I was a man to be mixed into such a business as that outlawry—"

Fergal said slowly, "Reasons I had." He turned Roy's letter over in his hands; he was impatient to get home in privacy and read it—likely some of its bulk was a letter inside for Shevaun too—but suddenly this seemed almost as important, a last puzzle when puzzles were being explained. "I thought—a good reason. Where the hell else to look, now? That night—Kevin wounded one of them deep, the way the fellow yelled—I said then, look for that one, he couldn't hide a bad hurt—but so many excuses for it, accident, illness, and we couldn't rip off bandages to see was there a knife-mark underneath. . . . Donaghue, roundabout ten that morning—after you and O'Carroll had left my place—O'Carroll met Owen Desmond in the village and made a bargain with him, ammunition and powder for a quarter sack of tobacco, eastern-cured stuff. Where did O'Carroll get the tobacco? If it was that morning he came by it, I could swear it was some looted from my men that previous night."

"So?" said Donaghue thoughtfully. "Now that's a thing I had wondered about, I had indeed. Maybe because I'm not persuasive with my own tongue, I always look twice at a man who is—and he's a smooth talker, that one. O'Carroll got that tobacco, four pounds of it—and kind in him, that amount so expensive—he's not a smoker himself but he knows I miss it—he got it, for a new flint-and-steel, and a good double-edged belt-knife, and a silver ring he had by him, that morning—an hour before he met Desmond—off Edmund Kearney at the inn."

They looked at each other. "Kearney," said Fergal in a low grim voice. "Kearney!"

"Who," said Donaghue, "has been that worried for his eldest son, the poor lad down in bed with this fever-plague."

"You needn't remind me. Kearney . . ." Fergal stood up. "I'll get home and read my letter. Thanks, Donaghue—for the letter, and—explaining how to add three and two, simple figuring." He laughed without mirth. "You've no objection that my mother hears this—to set her mind at rest for the girl, I mean, that much—and my sister?"

"No, sure not, O'Breslin—sensible discreet women they are. I—" Donaghue hesitated, shut his mouth, and heaved himself to his feet, polite. "I'll hope we're friends, for being open with each other. Do you—do you come to see me again, and don't hold it on me that I had to deceive you a bit."

"No," said Fergal absently, "of course not. Thanks again."

And for the first time in eight months he saw the Shevaun he remembered—flushed, dark, pretty girl, her eyes bright—and acting foolish like any soft female in emotion, Fergal thought with a smile: rushing in to bring the sleepy child, dandle him on her lap— "Look, my darling, from your father, sending you his love —his own hand—"

He had recklessly kindled all six of the rush-tapers. They showed him his mother looking oddly young, hair braided down her back for the night, and Shevaun laughing and crying over her letter, Nessa with her hair out of its knot too but not braided, a thick

careless tumble of auburn light across her shoulders—all of them
with cloaks huddled over their underclothes.

"You see, Mother, what he says—oh, I'm sorry, I'm sorry, I
know I've acted horrid—all this long while—but I was so feared
—it was like those other men who just went away from wife
and child without a back glance—I *know* I was a fool, Roy
wouldn't—but—you see, Fergal—Mother, look, you see he says
—fifty gold crowns a year, what would that be in shillings I
wonder—and officer-rank he has, too. Look you, my darling, he
says a fine blue uniform with gold shoulder-knots—oh, God, and
they are at war with Spain, he will be going into battles and getting
killed or maimed—"

"Dear Roy," said her mother. "Thank God he is safe thus far,
and prospering. Yes, Shevaun, my dear, I'm listening." And the
boy, interested at the novelty of being waked, of contagious excitement, trying to say, "Fad-er?" questioningly, so that Shevaun
laughed through tears and kissed him.

"Yes, your very own *fad-er*, sending us all his love—"

"And what else does he write, Fergal? In battle he's been? Is
he—"

"He had my letter in June—had to come inland to him, at
Paris—" Fergal thrust the first sheet of his letter into her hands,
hastily skimming through the second. The devil of a time with the
language, Roy wrote—the script blunt and firm like the writer:
but the job could be worse. They were training men—French and
some mercenaries, Swiss and also Polish—a dozen other Irishmen
in his corps as officers—no prospect of actual fighting as yet, quarters not too bad and good food. And don't ask him what the quarrel
was with Spain, he'd no idea and didn't care. . . . And then serious
business: the pay wasn't all clear, but he was saving as he could.
He knew a man said he could put him in touch with an honest
ship-captain who touched at Marseilles now and then and did some
business also through Galway, a decent man who'd likely agree to
escort a lady safe. It looked chancy, and it was early to talk about
it, but next year—May, June—or maybe not until fall—if he got
promotion, if he'd saved enough and a bit extra, and arranged with
that man from this end, and let Fergal know when the ship would
touch at Galway, maybe it would be possible Shevaun came out
to him. Was there a heavy English guard in Galway harbor? If

Fergal would write how conditions were for them now—it might be, by the time Shevaun could come, they would all want to come away too. . . .

Fergal handed on the last sheet of the letter, and sank into his chair by the hearth, staring at the fire banked for the night. Out to France—to what? Easy for Roy to write. Yes, and it was only if it was possible to get out at all. Illegal to leave the country, except men signed on to mercenary service. Roy said a few Irishmen he knew and others he'd heard of, men with influential connections, had got wives and families out to them. It wasn't encouraged by the French authorities, unless a man was rich enough beyond his pay to support them—and what Irishman was, and would they be abroad in foreign service if they were? But he was signed on only for two years, and there were tales about higher pay and less restrictions in the Russian Czar's service, or that of Venice. It all depended . . . from what Fergal had written of the situation at home—

Yes, thought Fergal, it depended on the outcome of the political struggle in England. Every Irishman was saying that hopefully: sure to God the upstart Parliament men couldn't outlaw the monarchy in England permanently. And when and as Charles Stuart came to his rightful throne, on several counts he would reverse all the Parliament's actions—men who had suffered loss from fighting in his cause, he'd make reimbursement: and a stronger reason too, that he'd not see any Parliamentary laws stand, that had been made while he was exiled. And he still had Catholic ties. All the banished landowners here were saying it eternally—Fergal had said it himself a hundred times: when the King is restored this nightmare will be over, we'll all be made secure in our old holdings, and all this new law in Ireland reversed. One day we'll be looking back on this time and telling tales of it to bore our grandchildren. Looking back as our own men again, landholders in our own houses, with our good servants about us, and herds in our fields, our people safe and happy.

But, if it came—and surely it must, the King back in power—what time of nightmare would they be looking back on? Two years, five, God, maybe ten. The Parliament's strength was military strength; and what military support, to challenge that, could Stuart command, a penniless exile? There was talk of a military rising in

Scotland for him, but generally speaking, only the Catholic High-landers were Royalist. Damned good fighting men, but were there enough of them?

And in England, Oliver Cromwell was king in all but name, ruling the country through his tame Parliament. Nevertheless, it somewhat appalled Fergal to find Roy writing so earnest about plans for three, four years ahead—taking it for granted the situation would be unchanged then. . . . Go to France, and wait it out?—until the King was restored, and in turn restored Irish landholders to their rightful places.

He looked up to find his mother's steady gaze on him. "You're thinking of what Roy says, getting out of Ireland?" Her eyes were faintly troubled.

"It looks to me like six of one, half-dozen of the other," said Fergal with a twisted smile. "No place for foreigners—as Irish are—on the Continent, to earn a living. Except as mercenary sign-ers-on in the army. Living hand to mouth—oh, yes, doubtless a good deal better off, for food and ordinary conveniences!—but a foreign tongue, and foreign surroundings and ways, to balance it. I don't know, Mother. If Roy arranges this for Shevaun, a ship-captain to carry her in secret, well, it's her choice—though I can't say I'd like to see her go off alone that way, with a man we knew nothing of. For myself, I don't know. I'll say what Donaghue said to me about that—better the devil you know . . ."

And Nessa made a sudden movement and said in a low voice, "I couldn't go—if you decided that. I wouldn't. Bearing expense and trouble for me—as you never asked or expected to be burdened with—"

He said abruptly, "Well, we're not starting off tomorrow! Don't go borrowing trouble two years ahead, for God's sake—a thing women will forever do."

His mother gave a little sigh. "It's a relief to know about Dareen. I'd put this and that together, and hoped—but I'm that glad to be sure, as Brian told you. He's a good trustworthy man, Fergal—I hope you see that now."

Fergal shrugged. "Oh, so it seems. I can't say I'd ever be bosom comrade to him, but—" Yes, and that was another thing, more immediate. See McCann tomorrow, and Desmond. Kearney . . .

Their two raiding-companies weren't the only ones Kearney

and his gang would have victimized. Cowards, traitors, and thieves. Justice should be brought on them. And then he thought, justice? What law held here across the Connacht border—where the English banished them like unwanted animal-pests off civilized land? —like as if they were naked wild savages civilized folk didn't want about! And keeping them, trying to keep them, this side the line by military patrol! Among themselves, for their physical situation, for the driving together of all classes and sorts, close, from wide-separated places, no official law was in operation. No justice-officer, local, to hail Kearney up to, with formal witness and evidence.

He had thought not long ago, suddenly, how it all came home to them just lately—they so busy keeping themselves alive they'd not had time to think about it . . . the trap the English had driven them into, the different mazes inside that trap. Hugh McFadden —something he'd said, that day they lay up on Knockmagh . . . lawlessness, he had said. Among other aspects of the life the English had forced them to here, was that one: they were in effect eighteen hundred years back, before the law was written out definite; and law, here and now, was what men with strength of arm, majority numbers—or coin or goods of value—maintained it was.

Rough justice, he thought. All right; but justice!

He heard his mother absently: "That's so, even if you thought it best—awhile to decide. And I'd not go either, Fergal—unless — I—" And then a sharp sigh; she laid her hand on his arm, firm and warm. "I'll not trouble you for that tonight, to upset you— when we're all so happy to hear from Roy. Tomorrow . . ."

12

"NO—NO—NO—" Kearney was trying to scream, his voice thin and high as a woman's, and he strained away from the men around him, far as the rope let him.

Dermot Flynn repeated the string of obscenities he'd overused in the last thirty minutes: he drove his fist into the bound man's kidneys, and Kearney whimpered and tried to bend double but the rope held him. O'Shea slashed him across the face with the cut-off rope's end, and one of Desmond's men uppercut him on the jaw, forcing him upright again. *Whoreson—traitor—thief—* "The knife, Dermot, put the knife on him—"

Flash of blade in silver moonlight through the trees. Impatient rough voice— "Strip him, for God's sake—let's see what we're about—English punishment, by God, for the traitor to his own folk!—much as any informer—" He was drunk, he stumbled over the words, but the knife made certain circles in air. "Hanged—and—quartered, make it—only needn't trouble for the hanging—"

"And damn you, Dermot Flynn, give the rest of us a chance at him!—who the hell appoints you executioner? Let me—" Loud rip of tearing cloth, they were pulling the clothes off, rope unloosened—white flesh pale in unearthly light, the man was soft and unmuscled—

Fergal was still half-dazed from the vicious blow on the jaw taken five minutes back from Flynn, but he summoned every hour of experience at handling men, to put force in his voice. "Listen to me, you bastards! Hands off the prisoner! Flynn, O'Shea—stand back! Justice we'll have here, but fair and according to lawful evidence—you hear me?—Kevin, for Christ's sake—"

McCann did not hear him; Desmond did. Desmond was swearing loud and steady in a breathless mutter, holding himself where O'Shea had kicked him at his first move of protest: forcing himself up on hands and knees, suddenly fastening on Flynn's ankles and pulling him down. "Hear the order—you bastard—put up the knife! Not savages we are—"

Fergal made a rush at the tangle of bodies on the ground—clumsy, the blow had spoiled his judgment for the moment; McKenna or some other man plunged in to defend Flynn; Fergal got in one solid blow, a fist sank into his body and he grunted, and Desmond and Flynn reared up over him, swinging wild at each other. He heard McCann laughing—a carefree, happy laugh.

Couldn't let them—out of hand—damn Desmond for the whiskey— Something hard connected with his right temple, he heard the blow, he was conscious of falling. He was on the ground, and that was Flynn tall over him with the matchlock gun, swinging it by the barrel. Fergal couldn't move, but he was not unconscious for the moment, seeing and hearing what was going on— His brain telling his body, get up and stop it! Savages—

He heard a man say with a laugh, "All right, boys—the faint-hearts out o' action—get to it!" He heard Kearney scream again. Desmond it was, prodding at him, involuntary moans, can't let them—

Desmond, damn Desmond, said his mind slowly. The whiskey. Shouldn't have primed them with drink. Got out of hand—*rough justice*, oh, God, he'd thought it—thought, some of them not to be trusted, but never thought—a thing like this— "Desmond!" he gasped. "I can't—Get up and—give orders—stop them—"

Kearney screamed again; he went on screaming. Not human it sounded. Like the troop-horses wounded under gunfire—the fight at Trim. The English guns. Going on and on.

Moonlight flashing silver on the blade in Flynn's hand.

He forced himself up to his knees, scarcely aware of his own voice— "Fair—and open—trial by law, you can't—" Scarcely aware of another blow, contemptuous voice cursing him. The screaming, like a woman—mustn't let— "Kevin, for Christ's sake—" Where was Desmond?

Under him, a man—heaving, saying his name in a groan. *Stop it*—the thing, oh, God, out of savage prehistory—stop the screaming—He hauled himself up again; half under him, Desmond, making breathy moans.

Just for one flash, a last moment of consciousness, vision cleared and he saw. Kearney, he saw; but not a man anymore—not human anymore. Stop it, stop it. Moonlight on the blade. Drunken voices exultant. Kevin McCann sober and laughing, Lucifer in moonlight, mouthing *Justice—justice on the traitor!*

Fergal thought he was on his feet, shouting, moving toward that unspeakable thing roped to the tree—he was never sure about that; a black swift cloud over everything, and it was all gone, and life dissolved into one vast darkness and sharp pain.

"Oh, my God," said Desmond dully. "Oh, my God in heaven. Are you alive, O'Breslin? Justin, help me get him up—"

"All right," Fergal muttered, "I'm all right." An arm helped him to sit up. It swam back into his memory, everything. He raised his heavy aching head. "Shouldn't have—primed them with your damn' hell-brew—" *But McCann hadn't been drunk.* "Did they—what did they—" His eyes focused and he saw what they had done, hanging on the rope round the tree. He lurched up to his knees and retched onto the ground.

"The whiskey," said Desmond. "Dear God, you think it'd have been any different—whiskey or no? Savages—"

"Get up," said his cousin, "let's get away from here, love of Christ!" They got up, staggering together, supporting each other, the three men who had tried to stop savages acting like savages—got what they might expect, three against ten. By God, three against *eleven*—McCann not drunk, McCann laughing, knowing what he was doing, stirring them up—

A bit later they were at the cold-running hill-stream, and gasping for the icy water; but it cleared Fergal's head, and he sat up steadier for the last dousing. "Permanent damaged are you, Owen?"

"All right—damn' sore bruise in the guts, 's all. You?"

"Took the hell of a blow on your temple, O'Breslin," said Justin, feeling it, "same as myself. A three-day headache and we'll be our own men. Well, Owen, the whiskey didn't help matters."

"Not on those—Jesus, and where've they gone? An hour—the

moon's only an hour down—they've gone after the rest, at Kearney's place!" Fergal got up to his feet. They'd taken Kearney alone, meeting him in the village street, and now—

"Boy, if you want to commit suicide, run after them!" said Desmond hardly. "Run and order them—do it nice and neat, by law and formal trial! Running berserk like they are—" He held his head and swore. "Don't tell *me*! Raping wife and daughter, killing—unclean killing—but do you think we could stop it, any more than that back there? And it's done now, the time we've been out, likely—"

"No." Fergal sat down again, on wet loam against a tree; he pressed massaging fingers on his temple. "God, no." Hadn't he thought it once lately, men sliding back to uncivilized savagery, so easy, so nightmarishly easy! Some, not surprising, men like— but tame little Dillon, and Liam—stirred up by the rest, yes— shameful, ugly, men raised civilized, so fearfully easy, all in a minute, turned back to the primal brutishness. Turning on the outlaw to the tribe, like a cannibal wolf-pack on the lone-running wolf—pain for the savage pleasure of giving pain.

Don't think about the thing that had been Edmund Kearney, back there. "No," he heard himself say again, "It's too late—we can't stop it. But, my God—"

"I'll tell you," said Desmond, prodding himself cautiously, "we're damn' lucky to be alive, Fergal, the state they were in, and we crossing them."

"Set on Kearney and mad to get at him," said his cousin tiredly, "that was it."

"And don't say *whiskey* to me, damn it—we all had a couple of drinks too—and McCann—"

"Don't talk of McCann to me!" said Fergal violently. "Not drunk he was, no more than us on two drams—certain, the rest of them got the bottles off you, and had more, and if they needed priming that did it maybe—but Kevin knew what he was about! Never thought he could—"

"All right, all right, we were fools to bring the men into it," said Desmond. "Fair, open trial!—with evidence given, and the accused having chance to answer!" He laughed bitterly. "Better if we four had marched him out without trial and hanged him before his own door!—quicker, at least." He got up slow and painful. "I don't know what you're off to do, but I'm going home and get to bed with a heated brick to my belly. And tomorrow, damn my bruises, I'll be rid of those three brute bastards I've been master to—if they've the gall to come back to me! Your arm, Justin— where the hell are we?—long mile south o' the village, damn— Are you all right to get home, Fergal?"

"Not bad at all, barring the headache, I'll make it. Yes, they'll be let-down and hangdog-sullen tomorrow, and what the hell to do with them but get rid—but I—McCann—I swear, little Dillon and Liam, I'd have sworn they couldn't lend themselves—stirred up by the rest they were—"

"All right, if you want to make excuses," said Desmond. "Myself, I'll sort it out later. Not my place to offer advice, but after this evening's entertainment, me, I'd not like to be committed to partnership with Kevin McCann. And another thing—if you're thinking all we have to worry for is disciplining the men, you can think again. All the Connacht men who knew Kearney—resenting us to start—and every honest man else, hearing about this—"

"And the Connacht men saying, what to choose between the savagery of English and these out-of-province Irish foisted on them! Don't tell me," said Fergal bitterly. "Nothing to be done tonight. Need to wait and see what happens, for that. You know where to find me—I'll see you, Owen."

"If we don't run into that gang of berserk murderers on the way home!" said Desmond.

He wasn't bad, in fact he felt queerly strong, his mind working surely at top speed. Aside from anything else, the ugly shamefulness of it, going to be one hell of an uproar over this. Do it fair, they'd said! Talk about the English . . . A voice in his mind said clear, yes, these men who'd had an example set them—the English killing and raping their way across the country, three years of war—the packed locked churches set afire, the wounded men castrated and disemboweled in street and field, the infants brained on the doorposts. But fair was the word—don't lay blame on the English for what was inside some men at birth!

He walked fast toward home, all of it circling in his mind like a great wheel. Not just this thing with Kearney. Thrown Desmond's whiskey into him, angry then, to try taking his mind off the other—shamefulness. All gone wrong, everything turned suddenly wrong, when just last night, with Roy's letter in his hand—

Seemed much longer ago than this afternoon, that other—he'd lost his temper, shouting at her, swearing. That was shameful too—his mother, calm and pale and looking still so queerly young, just saying it over quiet, all the louder he shouted. Wed Brian Donaghue, going to wed—

Impossible, mad—middle of a nightmare he was in. But right now, all that fuzziness in his head had vanished, for the remnants of the whiskey and the fight up there and the rage and disgust— it wasn't blurred like in a nightmare, he was seeing and thinking crystal-clear, sharp, and he felt strong as God. Couldn't have been such a bad blow after all, he thought almost absently.

Hell of a row over this—think how it might go tomorrow, when folk found—and knew; those men, swaggering or belatedly ashamed—and McCann—to deal with. Sure to God, say *We never meant—they got out of hand!* His and Desmond's men, weren't they? Half his mind was cold-sharp on that, half on her and Donaghue—red thief and lout Donaghue, *stepfather*—mad she was, not to be thought of—Donaghue's clumsy hands—how she could—

He came up to the housedoor, walking quick and light, and opened it, and in the second he stepped across the threshold two separate thoughts slid through his mind, little silver fish chasing each other down a clear stream.

A lock. Never thought about it, little in any house to steal— but now, little was sometimes much to a desperate man. But with men like those living near, a lock, a bolt, was a good idea. And see the women had a weapon in the house.

And a very distant, faintly alarmed whisper said that it wasn't quite natural, this extraordinary feeling of well-being, after that blow from the butt-end of a matchlock. Something not right.

But he felt fine; and when he came into the main room and saw the one rushlight burning in the wall-holder, and the kneeling figure at the hearth, everything else went out of his mind but that— *Woman,* said his mind.

All this savage energy in him, building up like steam in a cov- ered kettle on a hot fire—for all that had gone bad wrong that he couldn't change or cure—all on a sudden, it exploded inside him into hot intolerable desire, and there was the girl. The wanton, convenient in his household. He muttered her name and plunged across to reach for her, no space in him for curiosity as to why she was there.

He heard her speak, just the second it took him across the room: "Oh, Fergal—just up to see to the fire I was, I was afraid I'd banked it too much and we'd lose it—what is it, Fergal? What—" And she caught her breath sharp as he pulled her against him, bent to find her mouth.

The Christ-damned senseless thing was, he knew it wasn't Ailsa—he knew it then. Not Ailsa's big generous breasts under his hand, not Ailsa's plump pungent-smelling body—not any practiced female body against his. With her mouth surprised and soft under his mouth, his mind and body split into two things, the one no longer controlling the other, except halfway—and a very damned odd thing that was— Couldn't put down the intolerable pressure of crude body-hunger, as brute and primal as—

And, same time, his mind diamond-clear: the other one, the virgin female this was, little round firm breasts and an ignorant slender body—take care, go slow, give her time, be easy and gentle, O'Breslin—not to hurt her, fright her—make it good for her, better for you, this slim innocence hard against—

Nessa, said the other part of his mind. *No.*

Easy, take care here. Shameful, hadn't he been thinking of somewhat else, shameful—any lout of a drunken laborer, laying a woman on a barn-floor—take her decent, private, somewhere.

And it wasn't all his own strength straining her fiercely against him now, she was saying his name on his mouth, sobbing breaths mingled with his own breath, "Fergal—Fergal—my darling, it's no matter—if you want—not shamed, Fergal my dearest—love you so, Fergal—"

Never remembered lifting her into the next room. Just there, suddenly; remnant of decency in him, bedchamber and pallet— private. Clothes—damned complicated female clothes—and his own as damn' awkward— Oh, God, take care, what are you about, O'Breslin? And a voice saying, *let him lay you willing.* Yes?

Nessa.

And then the press and demand (never mind, female body was all) took whole command, and it was a long while later his mind swam back to him through the mist of luxurious-satisfied passion, into a body drained of desire and at peace. Came back, to make him aware of her gasping breath against his shoulder, saying his name.

He was lying entwined with her, warm, at heavenly rest after savage action— One minute he was conscious, coherent thought in his mind that said *Nessa*—oh, no. He was empty of purpose, and he locked his arms around her female warmth and his mind went off into blackness and he slept deep.

Nessa held him close, feeling her heartbeat slow to peace, aware of rough beard-stubble pressed against her shoulder, of heavy slow breath on her breast. Thought he was drunken, she had, at first, calling her by Ailsa's name—and that wouldn't have made any difference either, shamed as she should be to think it; she couldn't help it. But he wasn't drunken, it was something else—not right. Ordinary way, he'd never— A drunken man not so queerly sure and intense. And he'd known who she was, he had—and he'd still wanted—

She lay quiet there, her arms around him, and for awhile she was just content, not thinking at all. And then she began to feel frightened. Not right, he wasn't breathing right, too heavy and slow, and he was too cold, even here against her warmth and the blanket pulled over them. But he couldn't be hurt some way?— when he'd been so strong, so sure—

He never moved as she felt over him, gentle. So cold he was, and that labored long breath . . . Her fright grew, and she got up from him, no need for caution, he never stirred; she found her tumbled clothes beside the pallet, shift and bodice and two petticoats, stockings and garters, and the worn-out shabby slippers, and her cloak she'd thrown on when she came out to see to the fire. Mustn't let Ethne know how he'd— She settled the blanket over him, and felt how difficult the breath lifting his chest.

Groping in the dark, aware of the warm lovely ache in her loins but not thinking of that now, only him, she felt her way through the big room to the one past where she slept—Shevaun sleeping peaceful and quiet—to where Ethne and the two older servant-women were. "Ethne, wake up—please, Ethne—"

"Nessa?" Ethne turned on the pallet and sat up. "Yes, my dear—what is it?"

"Fergal—I don't know, it's something wrong—please come and see—"

Ethne was up, pulling her cloak about her. "Now what about Fergal? And how do you happen—come in drunken, has he, Nessa? That wouldn't surprise me, angry as he was—men—"

"No, I thought at first—but it's not that, he's not breathing right somehow—I—I got up to see to the fire, I was feared I'd banked it too deep and it'd be out, and I heard him—"

And then Ethne had a rush-taper kindled from the live spark in the hearth, and they were there looking down at him. His mother said low, "Yes, hurt he is—hold the light, Nessa," and knelt to feel him, turn him. "I can't tell a wound on him, but he's not just sleeping, you're right, it's deeper— Ah," and she drew a breath, her hand on his head. "Here. A hard blow he's had, and the bad place too, where the bone's thin there. I can feel it, all soft. I've seen that before, accidents and—mostly they don't know there's any bad hurt, for awhile, you see he brought himself home all right, and got his clothes off, like as he'd have done if he was drunk. I don't think the skull's cracked—it doesn't feel the same, there was that servant-man, years ago, fell down the front stair and did that, I remember how it felt, where the bone was cracked. . . . The surgeon had some long name, I misremember—and he said, when there's not a break in the bone, they come all right again in a couple of days, usually. Fergal—" She lifted his head against her, stroking his face. "So cold he is. Where would he have had this?—out on some business with the men, he said—"

"What—what did the surgeon say, that time? We ought to—"

"I think all we can do is keep him warm and quiet. If Hugh comes in the morning, I pray so, he'll maybe know more—lay-brothers, they're often knowledgeable for medicine—" Unconsciously she was cradling him to her, and Nessa's arms ached for the burden. "Please God he'll be all right, please God. And the latest word he said to me a curse—not that I could hold it against him, any son of any mother likely feeling the same, not understanding—it's no matter. Maybe Brian would know something to do, we'll send to Brian. Nessa, I couldn't bear it, losing him too, I couldn't. The three pretty babies born dead, and the three dying in their first year—and my darling Aidan the English killed, and not even a grave to mourn at—only Shevaun and—not Fergal, my first and strongest, I couldn't bear—coming all through that war, too—"

"There must be something to do—" Nessa couldn't help herself, on her knees there, sobbing with fright. "We must—"

"Oh, I know, I know," said Ethne softly. "You loving him too, my dear. I wish Hugh was here—but Brian will help."

The sound at the door made both turn. In the flickering faint light, Liam Fagan leaned there, looking at them vaguely. "Liam," said Ethne in relief, on a hard-drawn breath. "Late you are, but thank God, home. You must go at once, quick, to Brian Donaghue, and tell him I ask him to come, Fergal is hurt—"

"O'Breslin," said Liam dully, "O'Breslin—hurt? Flynn hit him —with something, yes—I think, I remember—" He took a lurching step into the room, hand to his head, and Nessa gasped: he was dirty, clothes in tatters, a great stain of blood all down his torn shirt, but not his—no wound on him, shirt gaping apart on white hairless chest. "He tried—stop us," he muttered, looking down at Fergal. "Hurt? Yes, Flynn— And little Dillon dead there across the inn-counter, all that blood, Sean Kearney's knife in him— Only hurt, O'Breslin? Lucky that is—you don't know—the way it was. The way— Oh, God," and he put both hands to his face, "I don't know who I've been this night, what I've been—never meant—never wanted—but the devil possessing all of us—"

"Liam!" said Ethne sharply. "You hear me? I said, you're to go at once to Donaghue, ask him to come!"

"Yes, my lady. Yes. To help O'Breslin. Some other man, some devil it was—not myself, not any self I ever was, God's help, God's mercy . . . So much blood, all over the counter and floor—Dillon—but not the women, not Dillon or Kindellan or me, swear it—never meant—" He collapsed then half on his own pallet, against the wall, dull gaze fixed on Fergal motionless there.

Ethne laid Fergal's head gently on the pallet and got up in one smooth motion. "Never mind the boy," she said calmly. "Nor what this is about, for the minute. I'll go for Brian."

"No—let me, please—"

"I'll go," said Ethne. "Keep him covered, Nessa, and warm as you can—and we'll both pray."

13

DONAGHUE WAS PROSAIC about it; nothing to worry for. "Keep him lying abed a day or two, when he comes to himself, and feed him light. Where'd he come by a knock like that?" He looked at Liam, in a stupor of sleep on the other pallet. "That one hurt too?—no, evidently not—by his breath, he's had half a year's wages in whiskey—price it is now—and he'll have a head when he wakes."

"We don't know what's happened, Brian, but something bad, and bad news carries fast—we'll likely hear soon."

They knew in midmorning: a big dark young man riding up, introducing himself to Nessa who opened the door, the Desmond they'd heard Fergal mention. His steady eyes were surprised and admiring on her. "Ah, that's bad," he said, hearing about Fergal. "He seemed all right, but I ought to have guessed it, I've seen that kind o' thing before. And no other man in the house—oh, Donaghue, it's good you're here."

"And you might count myself," smiled Hugh McFadden. He'd come by only a few minutes before Desmond, and agreed with Donaghue's diagnosis. "What's this all about?"

"Not," said Desmond, "a pretty tale for females, but you'll have to hear it." He told it short and expressionless, what had happened up there in the wood—and after. "They made a night of it, that they did. Like a pack of beasts run mad; the more I think about it I know we're lucky to be alive at all, tangling with them. At the inn-house—they got the rest they were after, the two Kearney boys—and the odd-job servant-man who likely did ride with the gang. There was a fight there, though, Sean Kearney killed one of

Fergal's men and hurt another, but one against ten," and he shrugged. "Oh, they made a job at Kearney's place—the wife, the daughters, and the boys—"

"The *children?*" whispered Ethne.

"Killing-mad they were, and they picked up three bottles of whiskey there that hair-triggered them all over again. Tried to set the inn alight with the corpses inside, but it was a wet night, the wood wouldn't catch. By then, the noise they made and the women screaming and all, the whole village was out—and the men after them to hold them for murder and theft—I gather it was one unholy row. One of 'em, my guess is Flynn—he had the matchlock—shot Phelim Burke dead, and there's a dozen men knifed serious and the eldest Lynch boy dead too. But even roaring drunk they saw they were outnumbered then, and ran. I said berserk, but they'd been canny enough to fetch their horses, after that first business —they got away. As a last little gesture," drawled Desmond, "they carried off Burke's daughter with them."

"Christ have mercy," said Hugh softly. "This is a great wickedness—and I'm thinking like you that you three trying to cross them, you're lucky to have escaped. You're saying that Kevin McCann did not—"

"Maybe he was drunk," said Desmond. "I wouldn't know. Nor if he was with them after—he wasn't identified. What I came to tell you, there's going to be trouble as you can guess—"

"Violence always begets violence," said Hugh.

"As you say. I said to Fergal last night, my three men I'd be rid of—well, the village-men have looked to that for me. Those three—creatures—they came staggering into my place at dawn, and the Lynches, father and sons left, and all the Dowlings, and Burke's brother-in-law Kelleher, five minutes behind them. They were ready to take me and my cousin to hang as well, but we did a bit o' fast talking, and by God's grace Lynch and Kelleher know me, they believed the truth. But they took the men—self-appointed justices for the district, the right they had. That was forty minutes ago, and they were off to hang those three in the street before the inn."

"Without trial?" asked Hugh.

"Apportion the guilt all legal?" Desmond shrugged. "Not in the mood for any solemn legal business they were, friend—having just seen eight corpses laid out and three of them females bloody-violated before killing! And there's a party gone up to fetch in the ninth, Kearney. They'll not have wasted time over the first hanging, and they know who the others were, a dozen men identified them and little Dillon's corpse told what crowd it was too—O'Breslin's hangers-on, and McCann's. I thought Fergal ought to know they'll be up, and I came to back his story personal—fast as I could, and damn letting them see I've a horse, to mark me as a full-fledged raider."

"They don't think Fergal—" Nessa faltered; he looked at her, and away from her expression.

"I told them he wasn't in it. There's men know him, that he wouldn't be. They're set on being fair, I'll say that, on taking only just vengeance. But they want those men."

"And where are those men?" Hugh's voice was suddenly loud; he stood up. "Up the hill there in the hideaway shelter, with the drink and the woman they stole and the blood hardly dry on them from their slaughter! Desmond, I'll ask the loan of your horse—as long as you stay with these women, and Donaghue too."

Desmond stared at him, and Ethne reached to catch his arm. "To go—up there? Hugh, no, you can't—they—"

Hugh looked somehow taller and broader, Nessa thought confusedly, than he'd ever been. He disengaged Ethne's hand firmly. "All of you thinking of O'Breslin," he said. "The village men are not savages, they'll hear the truth. None of you remembering at all—there's a lone woman up there, half a mile from that place where those evil men will be now?"

"Oh—Maire," said Nessa with a gasp. "But, Hugh—McCann wouldn't let—if he's—his own wife—" She realized suddenly that she'd never seen Hugh angry before: she hadn't thought kind, gentle, pious Hugh could get angry. He wasn't shouting or blustering, he'd just gone white and in some odd way deadly.

He said sternly, "Now do you think I don't know Kevin McCann, drunk or sober? From the look in her eyes I knew him, the minute I first met her—Maire McCann. He is one of the men with the devil's mark on him, who gets pleasure of giving pain. Do you think McCann would be any guard to her up there, he mixed into that devil's work last night? I'll have your horse, Desmond, to get there quick." He opened the door.

"No—Hugh—at least take a weapon, Fergal's pistol, I'll get it—" Ethne caught at him again.

"I—" he hesitated: fumblingly, suddenly, he made to cross himself. "A man of God—I know nought of weapons—not the pistol, no good it would be to me, but I'll take a knife, yes." And silently Desmond handed him his second belt-dagger. Hugh thrust it into his own belt. "Thanks, Desmond. I'll stay with her—until it's safe, or—" He went out quickly, and they heard the horse clatter off at full speed.

They did not wait long for the village men. Eight of them there were, middle-aged and young, grim-faced, listening to Desmond; one saying briefly, "We'll see O'Breslin." Nessa pressed close with Ethne and Shevaun beside the pallet, and knew they were all ready, ladies or no, to use nails and teeth on these men if—Fergal hadn't moved; his breathing came lighter and evener now, thank God. In the little room they crowded close, looking at him, Desmond and Donaghue watchful.

"Your word we take, Desmond," said Lynch, the oldest of them. "Your cousin bears you out—not that two witnesses are worth more on numbers, depends on the witnesses. I know you, and O'Breslin less well, but from what I and the rest of us know of both, you're telling the truth. It's that gang of fellows O'Breslin and McCann acknowledge as retainers—we have identification from witnesses."

"Retainers!" said another of them, loud and contemptuous. "There's a fairy-tale for the children, and we not children to swallow it. Same like your three hirelings, Desmond—and that gang Martin Prendergast keeps, and the Reilly boys over the hill, and that arrogant bastard Concannon with his crowd o' *gentleman's servants*! Hirelings for raiding-business over the border!"

"As it's gone this far, no point denying it," said Desmond. "You're not fools. One among you, is there, hasn't sneaked across after this and that too?"

"All right, Tom Burke," said Lynch sharply as the other man made to answer violently. "That's so and we all know it. We can say, sure, it's account of such organized raidings the border-guard's been tripled and more, and thrice the number o' English patrols over here to make trouble. But it's also account of such business there's more goods of value this side the river now. Never mind the argument! Only, it looks to me, maybe men in a business where they need be ready and willing to kill for the profit, they'll go to killing for different reasons quicker than other men."

"What odds there, Terence! No man in Ireland these last years hasn't killed for honest reasons, protect his family and holding!"

"Well, Kelleher—"

"For God's love, save the talk for later! So we don't take O'Breslin, but where are the rest? There's one here—the boy—but it's Flynn and O'Shea we—"

Lynch looked at Liam Fagan, still sprawled in stupor there. "Fagan wasn't named by any witness."

"Oh, for Christ's sake!" said Burke. "He's in O'Breslin's gang, isn't he? It's the whole crowd—"

"Now just one minute, Tom. We might not have an official justice-court anymore, or town or county overlord to rule on a thing all legal after evidence given—but we'll do this in order like the honest men we are. If we go off at hair-trigger and think just about blood-vengeance, to lay out corpse for corpse, by God we're no better than the first murderers. And I say it, though I'm one due vengeance, my eldest son dead on my own doorstep. Here's Liam Fagan, sure, and of all O'Breslin's men we've seen more of him in the village. A quiet lad he always seemed and decent-behaved. We've got thirty-odd witnesses, and you've heard 'em as well as me. Among them they named names, but no one of them has said definite they recognized young Fagan or McCann. The others they named—McFergus, McKenna, O'Shea, Flynn, Kindellan, and Desmond's men. And those men, none of us saw near as often, so it's good identification."

"What the hell, Terence—it was—"

"There's no accusation of Fagan, and we can't take him. Not by honest right, on any evidence."

"I'll back you on that," said Kelleher. "If we don't try to clear this bad matter up as lawful as we may, we're of the same ilk as them. All right, we miss out the lad. But—"

"Do any of you know where those men sheltered?" Lynch looked round at the household-members, cold. "Not here? But by leave we'll take a look all the same. Somewhere on O'Breslin's land, McCann's?"

Ethne faced him firmly. "My son will tell you when he's able, for he will want to see justice done same as you. Meanwhile, none of us know, but I think it is on McCann's land, above his house."

"We'll see," said Lynch. They tramped out heavily; and Nessa, Shevaun, and Ethne went back to hovering anxiously over Fergal—and worrying in whispers about Hugh and Maire McCann.

It was late afternoon, falling to dusk, when they came by again, passing the house at a little distance, one man separating to trudge up toward the door. They had—Nessa peered down the slope— the bull they had, on a halter, and one man with an improvised bull-stick, long tree-branch. She stepped back and let Ethne meet Lynch there, Donaghue beside her: Desmond had gone home.

"You've not taken them," observed Donaghue.

"Nor like to, evidently," said Lynch. "The place we found where they've been, but by the looks they've abandoned it. They'd have known they were identified, and run—likely to turn outlaw and prey on other districts. You'll tell O'Breslin when he wakes, Donaghue"—he jerked his head down the hill—"and McCann, who's maybe with that gang or not, he was not at his house and his wife knows nothing. Say to O'Breslin, that we've taken the bull that was up there. A very valuable beast it is, I know. But under any law we've ever had, there would be a blood-fine for blood if not a hanging, and fines for the lesser degrees of guilt. They were under his ordering, those men. There is Burke's wife made widow, and his daughter stolen, and my son leaves a widow four months with child. Little recompense there can be, but it seems fair, that much—if we sell the bull, supposing we find any with that much wealth, the proceeds will be divided to those losing family. Or all of us living in the village, maybe we'll buy the bull to share in his profits, by contributing whatever of value we can to those folk. For the bull is the blood-fine due them."

"That's fair," said Donaghue, nodding. "The priest at Ballintober you'll have sent to, for a decent burial. We will all be wanting to pay respects to the dead, O'Breslin would be saying it and he able—this bad business you've our sympathy for, transplanters and Connacht men alike."

Lynch looked at him and said, "It is an English-bred bull, which is appropriate for a blood-fine—English law driving good and bad, southron and northman, across our borders, and putting us all in this condition. All right, Donaghue, all right. I take the sympathy as it's meant. But you might also say to O'Breslin, there are men roundabout who will not be so broad-minded toward them as fetched those men among us."

"They are men," said Donaghue, "who maybe approved what Edmund Kearney was at, attacking and robbing his neighbors by night?"

Lynch spat on the ground. "What is a man expected to say to that? The English law, it makes honesty to have different meanings—and double meanings—among us here. I don't set up as a justice-officer. Too many blind lanes branching off that road. Just, you will tell O'Breslin." He turned and trudged away after the others.

After a moment Ethne said distractedly, "Fergal will be angry about the bull—yes, fair, but all the same—"

"My girl," said Donaghue, "we can thank God they took the bull—and that there are men with influence here like Lynch and Kelleher, who keep some civilized regard for law and order. The way things are here now, so many different groupings with reason to quarrel among themselves—feeling runs high in desperate men. Tales I've heard of things happening, and likely you have too. That business over at Castlereagh last month—gang o' local Connacht men having a little war with transplanters, and a hundred dead, women too, and property burned, and the feud still smoldering. And over Monivea way, pitched battles between men claiming the same land, and that not the only place. And a thing we aren't seeing yet this near the border but doubtless will, as things get worse— parties o' vagrant thieves, living on the run in hill hideaways, plundering everywhere and killing as they need to, when honest men stand up to them." He looked down the slope after the village- men, and he said thoughtfully, "It's like when you take home a wild young thing, you maybe trapping the dam. A nest o' young gulls I raised once, down home—and a fox-cub too—and I've known men raised wolf-cubs and other younglings. It's like that, a damn' queer way to think maybe, but so it is. You can do it easy and sure with some—the little white hares, and the voles, and young black- birds, and the fawn-deer—and it's bad to do, for if you turn them loose after, they stay all trusting and gentle, prey for any hunter. But some things, they'll always go back to the wild very easy. And it's the things stronger and shrewder and ungentle to begin with, that are like that. . . . That's—Flynn, and O'Shea, and Kevin McCann."

"Yes—I see what you mean. The strong ones—that are hunters to start, by nature."

Donaghue nodded. "Good times, you petting them and feeding them plump—the gray wolf-cubs growing up as house-pets—no reason to be aught but friendly with you. But turn them out to fend for themselves, and right easy they go back wild—the taming was all surface on them. And turning on you if the mood takes them, no odds your kindness—for only their own hungers drive them. . . . That's what we're seeing here now. The wild ones and the tame ones thrown out together to fend for themselves." And then he shut the door and said, "I'll have another look at the boy to see how he does."

And as night came on, their worry for Hugh was open; those men not up there, or had they come back? Nine hours he'd been gone, and why?

He came in as the household sat down to the meal: two horses thudding up to the door, and Kevin McCann following him in. McCann looked subdued and worried, and Hugh tired.

"O'Breslin?" asked Hugh. "The same, is he—well, times they lie like that twenty-four hours, it's nought to worry about, really. Desmond's gone?—I'll need to take his horse and knife back to him in the morning. I waited at the house until McCann came. . . . Yes, I saw Lynch and the rest there."

"This is the hell of a business," said McCann. He said it sorrowful and sober, but Nessa looking at him there, holding his hands to the little fire, thought it was a thing he'd planned to say that way. "I'm damned sorry to hear about Fergal—I'll go in and look at him, there may be something—I've seen enough head wounds—"

"And haven't I, McCann?" said Donaghue, but in a mutter to himself. McCann went into the bedchamber, and as if in absurd fear he'd make some damage, Hugh and Donaghue crowded after him, and Ethne and Nessa after them. "He's sleeping lighter now," said Donaghue.

"Yes, I see. Lucky he is that blow didn't crack his skull—if it didn't." McCann was feeling the swelling visible now on the temple. "No. My God, those savages—who'd have thought they'd—" His voice died as he looked up and saw Liam Fagan come to the threshold: Liam still pale and dull, but reasonably himself. "So you got home, did you? And the village-men didn't take you—lucky, but why?"

Donaghue told him why. "Very fair," said McCann absently.

"I left them—at the inn," said Liam in a low voice. "I—didn't have any hand in—that there, I was—frighted to see how—I ran out the back way, before the village got roused. Where did you get to, McCann?—saw you galloping out the other direction—"

"So I did," said McCann. He was still squatting beside Fergal, looking up at them, past them all to Liam. The rush-taper light made his eyes seem to shift. "God knows I'd tried to stop them, get them under control—I was thinking awhile, maybe if I pretended to go along with them, you know, they'd see reason—but I saw then it'd gone too far, and I sure to God had no desire to be identified with them! I saw the village was roused, and knew the men would run. And maybe it was selfish in me, but I thought I'd best get home before they passed—they'd run for their own place, and Maire was alone up there, of course."

"I see," said Donaghue noncommittally. "And?"

"Oh"—McCann shrugged—"if you must have the whole sorry tale, I wasn't in time. Not fools they are even in the state they were in—I got the same treatment as Fergal and the Desmonds, on my way home. Finished the night tied to a tree up there, with them trying to decide what to do with me, and—"

"That's a damn' lie," said Fergal. His eyes were open, fixed on McCann above him; he turned to his back.

"You lie still, O'Breslin," said Hugh hastily. "A bad knock you've taken, it needs time to heal. Don't try to sit up, now—" He crowded past Donaghue to kneel beside McCann there.

Fergal took no notice of him. "You know that's a lie, Kevin," he said, his voice sounding strong. "You were urging them on with Kearney. Think I wouldn't remember, or Desmond?"

"Now, boy, you can't imagine I'd join a business like that! I thought, like I say, maybe if I humored them along—and I'd drink taken, I was slow realizing all the harm they meant. But when I did—you and the Desmonds both out then—I tried to stop it, I swear to God. It was like I said, they were craven-scared then, when they'd got away, the drink dying out of them and they knowing they'd been identified. A wonder they didn't knife me then and there, but I made the deal with them—I had to, for my life —and they've gone, they've run."

Fergal raised up on one elbow, disregarding Hugh's protest. "A deal you made. What?"

"They had me in their hands, boy. But I was only one witness against them, and that they knew. I told them what they knew— there'd be men coming to hunt them, knowing they were my men and yours and living somewhere on our land. Their only chance was to run, out of this district. I said, I'd not bear formal witness on them, and I'd persuade the men here to be satisfied they'd gone, not send out descriptions roundabout, you know—if they left us two horses, and—"

"What deal was that, Kevin? Not much benefit to them, they needing to run anyway—word-of-mouth descriptions not serving much purpose at catching criminals! But they always liked you, didn't they, you a bit freer and easier with them, and not giving so many orders to keep them up to the mark!"

"All right, boy," said McCann amiably, "so they let me go because they liked me. Myself, I think it was just fright—they forgot about me, thank God, and ran, that's all. Left me roped to a tree up there, and gagged too—I heard Lynch and the rest poking about not fifty feet away this afternoon, and damned if I could attract their notice. Very near had an apoplexy, I tell you! But I managed to get myself loose after what felt like eternity, and crawled down to the house more dead than alive." He looked over his shoulder at Hugh. "It was a brave thought on your part, come up to see Maire was all right, and you've my gratitude as I said."

"Nothing," said Hugh quietly, but he did not meet McCann's eyes.

"Always a smooth tongue you had, Kevin," said Fergal tiredly, and lay down again.

Ethne came forward and her tone was firm. "Now we'll not have such a crowd round him, he needs rest. Hungry do you feel, Fergal? I'll see you have something. McCann, you had best get home to Maire, nothing you can do here tonight and you and Fergal can sort this out later when he's himself. Brian—"

Somehow the room emptied: McCann gracefully agreeing, drifting out: Hugh and Donaghue after him again as if to see him safe away: Ethne bustling out with Shevaun, saying something about warm gruel. Nessa took the rush-taper from her and went to fix it in the wall-holder. Her hands shook; he sounded so much his ordinary self, his voice strong—he would be all right— She knelt involuntarily to look at him, touch him, and his eyes opened again to meet hers.

For a breath he just fixed her with an oddly expressionless stare. "Nessa," he said.

She touched his shoulder almost timidly, and began to say, "You're feeling—better, Fergal, you've no pain?"—but his voice cut across hers.

"Oh, yes, Nessa," he whispered harshly, "and I never meant such a thing—Christ, mad I was! But it's done, and you needn't worry for it—you've won the throw of the dice, so clever, so clever—waiting to catch me when I was in a state to be easy game! You'll have the ring and the priest, Nessa, I'll do my duty by you—you knew that of me—that I'd pay my debts of honor— seducing an innocent—"

"Fergal! But I never—" His voice so bitter and weary—she tightened her grasp on his shoulder, starting to say No, no, not like that; but he turned his head away from her and shut his eyes. And then Ethne was coming back. . . .

14

·

FULL WINTER CAME down on the day Fergal was first up, three days later; men who knew said it would be a bad winter. It was, so it was: in other ways than for the weather, unprecedented deep snows and cold.

They hadn't, Fergal reckoned, done so bad the first eight months: at least he'd had occupation enough to take his mind off the privation, the never-quite-enough dull food, the lack of everything. Admit it: the women had done much of the hard work—though you couldn't say the job of raiding, and making profitable exchange for goods taken, was a lazy man's life. Coming fresh to it from the army life near as hard, he hadn't started to feel it as the others would have. And like a good many people, they'd had this and that to carry them those first months, but now they were coming to the end of their small capital of goods, and frightening poverty catching up with them. Now, everything was turning wrong and stark hopeless, every way it could.

Nessa the least of it, in a way. He hadn't intended to saddle himself with a wife, but as things went it just reinforced responsibility for her. First going tearful on him, then angry—hadn't meant any such sly trick as he charged at all, and if he thought such of her, she'd not marry him and he the last man—wouldn't marry him anyway—

He didn't argue. "You will wed me as soon as I get a priest to do it," he told her. "Never mind the ins and outs, as to blame— I was more at fault, no denying. We've both just to make the best

185

of it, that's all—I know my duty, I trust, to preserve my honor and yours!"

"Like—like the bull they took for a blood-fine!" she exclaimed a little wildly. "Just as c-cold and logical! Oh, Fergal, please—I never meant—you didn't have anything of me I didn't give free and willing, and I don't care for your damned honor or mine—I won't be wed to you, you making a duty of it! I—"

"No more I'll hear about it," he said. He didn't hear much; opportunity was lacking for private argument.

What was more on his mind, past the bitter resentment about that, was the less defined situation—other ways. Hugh refused to let him stir from the house that day, and in truth he still felt a trifle lightheaded; but the day after that he went up to see McCann and find how they stood. He talked with McCann, weighing it all careful and cold, a number of things that he'd not have considered a few months ago. Honor, he thought: only men with full bellies, larders, and pockets could afford certain kinds of honor.

Winter, and not possible to go raiding so often or so swift: on another count too, for the border-guard was growing every day, garrisons and camps closer together—talk said the English meant to put on a guard, eventually, a mile deep nearly shoulder to shoulder along the border. To keep the savage natives in their proper places . . . The time might come when it would be impossible to cross at all. But meanwhile—Two horses they had, and for that McCann had indeed made a deal with those five men; of this sort or that. Fergal couldn't afford to enquire into it, nor he couldn't afford to say to McCann, as an honest man I'll not share dealings with you.

Three men: not a problem in mathematics it was. Three men wouldn't necessarily capture three-ninths of what nine men had. They'd have to leave alone some well-guarded places the nine men could have attempted. All right. Two horses, too: if three men went, one horse carrying double and thus not able to carry so much plunder back. But better ride to raid with three men than two. And the horse—Fergal hadn't any sheltered winter pasturage on his land, however poor: nor had Donaghue nor Desmond—and if either of them had had, he'd have to pay to share it, which he couldn't afford; nor he hadn't the capital to buy feed for the horse. Or, of course, for the cow; the milk was precious addition to the larder. McCann had the pasture, not much, but some, up the hill there. If he wanted the horse fit to carry him, Fergal had to stay on good terms with McCann. Otherwise, better butcher the horse now and put the meat down in salt—if he could acquire enough salt.

What had they? Close estimate, near sixty pounds of potatoes: by winter's end the remainder starting to go bad, and if possible (oh, wasn't he learning all the small details of a poor peasant-life!) some pieces must be kept for starting new plants next season. Six pounds odd of a ham he'd taken a fortnight ago, the first meat they'd had in a month. Five bushels of ground rye-grain. Two pounds eight shillings in coin.

Now, he had seen to notice just these few days, it had all begun to catch them up indeed. The lack of meat, chiefly. Bread, potatoes, grain-porridge, didn't keep the same strength in you as meat. Nor anything else you could get with goods-exchange, if you didn't grow them yourself—onions, leeks, turnips, parsnips, cabbage, beetroot; shallots, cowcumber—and all those done for this year, save what some folk had spared to preserve—what were they, something to fill you for the moment was all. He noticed it of himself, so the other older ones would feel it more: he tired more quickly at any job, for one thing.

He had one whole pair of boots left; the women, with their thinner shoes, weren't so lucky; none of them had even house-slippers lacking a hole in the soles. Not enough blankets: little fuel for warmth besides. That he'd have to buy somehow. Each of them had some sort of cloak; that helped.

Two less mouths; his mother would be Donaghue's responsibility, and took her old chambermaid with her to his house. Donaghue, canny man, had smuggled over a substantial weight of coin, but it wouldn't last forever and next year Donaghue'd be planting fields like all the rest. And if Donaghue owned a fortune, be damned if Fergal O'Breslin would apply to him for help, were he starving!

Seven people, a child, and himself, to feed and shelter for nine months before they could count on a new crop.

He made his peace with McCann, calculatingly, on account of the horse—which if it proved useless as burden-carrier was potential food. He went through the village, where men looked cold at him and were silent to greeting, and saw the Desmonds, to talk about that. "I'd not have you think I went on running with him of my own choice."

"Needs must when the devil drives," agreed Desmond. "We'll be hard put to it to feed our horses too. At least we've still the five. Debatable point, worth more alive or dead? I'm selling one to Donaghue, we'll keep two for going over the river when possible, and may butcher the others."

"Donaghue—are you?" said Fergal. "It's possible he may come out with us, then, if he's a horse. Or he may not care to ride with McCann."

When he left, Desmond opened the door for him polite, and then stayed him with a hand on his arm. "No offense—I'd ask if you have objection to my calling formal, after the O'Rafferty girl in your house. No man's in a position to talk terms of a marriage-contract now, and if she's no dower, I've no settlement to offer. But I'd have you both consider it."

Fergal swallowed his involuntary curse. Just lately thinking, a suitable husband for her: and wasn't Desmond that? Four days earlier— He said, "I'm sorry man, you're just too late. Nessa is betrothed to me, we're to be wed at once."

Desmond dropped his hand and his eyes. "I see," he said, quiet. "Well, I'm sorry too—but my congratulations."

Fergal thanked him without expression; at least he hoped his regret was concealed.

Donaghue came in that evening, to announce that the visiting priest come for the burial-services would come up to wed Ethne and himself next day. "*If that is agreeable to you, O'Breslin?*" Fergal finished for him with a smile and shrug. "What is it to do with me? You are both of age to wed if you want!" A kind of truce he'd called for that too: nothing else he could do. He couldn't pretend to like it, but he'd no power over them. "You'll get out of it for half what you meant to give the father, Donaghue—while he's here, he'll be wedding Nessa and myself as well." He listened to their exclamations, shooting one glance at Nessa that challenged her to start a public argument now. She was silent, and then summoned polite words for their congratulations.

"I couldn't wish anything better, Fergal," said his mother. "You've relieved my mind, for leaving you!" But her gaiety faltered at his look, and she glanced between them speculatively.

"And I shall be here to see he doesn't beat you," said Shevaun mischievously, hugging Nessa. "At least for awhile! I wonder when we can expect to hear from Roy again—and if he's had our letters. I suppose he couldn't, in this time. But—maybe spring we'll hear, you think?"

"Spring is a long way off," said Fergal heavily. He hoped Nessa would not start an argument before the priest, to bring it all open; he was of two minds which was best, get her off private before and have it out—only you never got the last word with a female—or gamble that she'd be embarrassed and shamed to make a public scene. In the end he did nothing—conscious also of Ailsa's brown sullen stare; and he lay awake in consequence, worrying for that —and everything else.

So he heard the low whispers in the night-silence, and cold as it was, after a bit got up and looked into the main room, curious. One rushlight burning, to waste itself away extravagantly at this time of night!—and after a moment he identified his mother and Nessa, sitting there wrapped in cloaks and talking as if it was midday. He said so, annoyed: and belatedly thought that Nessa was likely telling Ethne the whole damn' story. Well, his mother was a conventional well-bred woman, she'd put the nonsense out of Nessa's head—would she? But he hadn't any desire to stay here discussing the matter in whispers in the midnight chill.

Neither of them offered to. Nessa said nothing at all; his mother said blandly, "I'm sorry we disturbed you, Fergal, but now you know it's not thieves broke in, you can get back to bed." And they sat, two dim shapes there, waiting for him to go and shut the door.

He did so before he cursed to himself. A thing it was like— like the somewhat lesser responsibility he already had for her: an honorable obligation; and he wanted to have it done official, and over with.

The priest came up an hour after midday, a tired-looking elderly man, Father O'Marron. Ordinary Irish folk might be in an unenviable position here, but not as bad off as churchmen: and everything considered, while there might be only one priest for every five-six villages and surrounding countryside, it was surprising there were that many left. The church had long been outlawed under English law, and any priest identified as such was subject to arrest and immediate execution without trial—being also worth five pounds to the arresting patrol. Not many monasteries or convents had survived the last fifty years in secret since being outlawed, but those that had found it impossible to reestablish here, and among the transplanters were a certain number of men like Hugh, and former religious sisters, living as they could. More had escaped abroad to shelter and safety.

And there too you found good and bad, in a sense—people they were, after all. Most of the priests were men who had voluntarily stayed, as renegades in a life of poverty and danger, to serve the people: but you found some, and some former monks and sisters—people who would have escaped if they could—who seemed to feel they were owed a living for being dedicated to religion.

Father O'Marron wasn't that sort; he was sheltered by a landowner over by Ballintober, and worked in the fields with the family when he wasn't plying his calling, traveling about to hold services once in a month or six weeks for every district of those he served. But in consequence he was a busy man, and with absent apology for haste took little time over the business. It seemed to Fergal not five minutes before he was giving the last blessing, and in a kindly, less solemn voice wishing them happiness, and expressing thanks for the gift-payment of two shillings coin—and presently walking off on his way to a sick man ten miles distant.

And Fergal had said, the priest and the ring, but of course there was no way he could give her a ring at all.

And a little flurry of leave-taking almost at once: the women's few possessions already bundled together—Donaghue being heavily friendly—all the women a bit tearful. One moment, his mother embracing him apart, and saying low, "I needn't say to you, be kind to Nessa, Fergal. You'd always kindness in you, that I'll say, whatever other traits you were born with as well. And, boy, I can't stop being your mother for that I'm Brian's wife. You will come and see me often, all of you, and I coming too." She kissed him light and quick, with a little pat on his arm. "No need to say aught polite about wishing us joy—I know it's not in you for the moment. But try to understand—and come to see me."

"Yes," he said woodenly. And not long after they were gone, and it was done—the change in his household complete. Weddings, he thought sardonically: joyful occasion or no, what a poor pass people were brought to even for that—the feasting, the music and dancing, the long formalities, belonged to the past like everything else. . . . It was done in an hour, all the business of change in his house. It frightened him a little, how easy and quick it was accomplished.

Shevaun—the old, gay, pretty Shevaun—and Nessa trying to sound as happy, bustling about the rearrangements. Nessa, who'd said scarce a word to him all day, standing white and silent with him before the priest. "But you must have the little chest, Nessa darling, Fergal is *very* particular and neat with his things, I warn you—peculiar in a man, but he's ten times worse than any house-proud woman, and he's only that little box for everything here. Look, I can easy share the long chest with Ailsa and Brighid—"

And before it was time to think of a meal—a meal! two slices of bread and half a cup of milk each, so the child might have a full one, and unsalted unsweetened gruel, and half a slice of the ham because it was a special occasion, a wedding-feast!—before then, it was done. Liam's pallet laid in the smallest room where Ailsa had slept with Dareen, and the other young maid Morag going in with Ailsa to the next tiny cubicle which had belonged to Ethne, and old Brighid with Shevaun and the boy. And Nessa's things there in his chamber, a little chest, her pallet-bed.

"Don't cry, girl," he said uncomfortably.

"I'm not. . . . Only I don't understand—how you can m-make love to me—feeling and thinking how you do. Oh, well, then, I *do*, in a way—different for men, that!—two things separate, like —like chalk and cheese!" She had drawn away as far as pallet and blanket let her.

"Now, it's an ill wind—at least we'll both sleep warmer this winter."

"Oh, that's just as sensible a reason as your real one!"

He lay a minute in silence: women. He turned and pulled her over against him, close. "Look, woman," he said. "I told you once you have a logical mind. It was a lie. Near five years back you were betrothed to my brother Aidan—by formal proxy—and it was a thing arranged between fathers—you never set eyes on him. Suppose there'd been no war, no settlement-act, you'd have been wed to him. Tales in your head like in all women's heads, romance and true love!—but you know well as me, though most young folk know each other, and most fathers try to see there's liking between them before they're betrothed, well, marriages are legal-arranged for other considerations than romance, of all things! As a fact, romantic feeling, it's a damn' bad basis for a good marriage."

"Is it?" asked a small voice against his shoulder.

"Well, obvious. It doesn't enquire into all the important matters, birth and raising and faith and family-money and land, *nor* dowries nor settlements. Or whether they're people who'll get on together natural. Now, look, girl. Your stepfather not going off so, he'd soon or late have betrothed you elsewhere, not so?—and you might not have known that man either. And me, time to come, I'd have decided it was time I settled respectable to a wife, and looked about for an honest girl to be a good match, wouldn't I? So—"

"Not for a long while! You—"

"I'm not denying it. I didn't intend to—"

"Saddle yourself with a wife, say it!"

"All right, we'll both say it!" he said in a low angry mutter. "No, I didn't. For one damn' good reason at least, my financial state! But there it is, things happen. No, I don't think you tricked me, Nessa, any longer—it was my own state that night to blame, but it comes to the same thing. You were a respectable virgin and I wronged you, I was obligated to make you honest, that's all about it. I daresay we'll suit well enough, being much of an age and the same birth, and you can't say we don't know one another, what we've shared the last eight months! You know I'll always do my duty by you, and I'll hope you do yours by me, to be biddable and honest."

"I—it's *not* just like buying a cow at market—you sound—"

"No, more like a pig in a bag, God knows!" he said with a short laugh. "And that as true for you as me. All right, Nessa, all right —say it, it's on account you've got some silly romantic notion about me, isn't it? Art saying it that night, and you shamed I'd heard! Well, Art McTally's a bastard and a liar, but he told you one truth that night, girl, and that is that the storytellers' tales of true love, they've got damn' all to do with either marriage or just the lying-together for pleasure. That's one of the gambles in wedding—you might get a man you take pleasure with abed, or you might not—and you committed either way—"

"Yes, the woman! *You* can go with any number of loose women—"

"You're oversuspicious, like all females. Surprised you'd be how few men there are like McCann, on the whole. We're creatures of habit—if a wife's reasonably satisfactory and willing, we can't be troubled to look elsewhere. In any case, it's none of your affair, so a husband's kind and generous to you. In my case, I doubt not I'll be too busy for such, had I the energy or the money," he added bitterly. "But there's a proverb says there's more to marriage than four bare legs in bed. I'll tell you one thing, I hope to God you'll not breed easy. All we need, sure to Christ, is a couple of infants on our hands."

"Oh, I know all that, Fergal," she said, her tone suddenly as bitter as his. "I know it was all accident to you, and you're resenting it, but—being *magnanimous*—and meaning to be kind—"

"I can't make out what the hell you're fussing about," he said irritably. "It's done, we'll have to make the best of it, and what I'm saying is, if it had to be, you might say we've neither of us got a bad bargain. You're a good girl, Nessa, I'm fond of you—you've behaved well this year, and I'll say it's been a trial of character. I trust you can say the same of me. We'll get on well, I make no doubt, if you make up your mind to it and act sensible. Sure to God, if you've romantic ideas about me, you ought to be satisfied! You went through the ceremonial meek enough."

She was silent, and then she raised herself up against him, and put an arm over his chest, and he felt her peering down at him in the dark: he felt her eyes and mind searching him, oddly. "Don't you *know*, Fergal?" she whispered. "Don't you *know* how it feels?—loving—someone? Yes, I did, and it was because your mother said—she said that—too. More to marriage . . . and in time, you—maybe—understanding. But—"

"Don't!" he said harshly. "Don't say—put me in mind of—" He'd made love with her, long and violent, he'd kept talking like this afterward, mainly to keep his mind off that, the monstrous thing, Ethne and— He turned and forced her down to him, and stopped her mouth the obvious way.

Nessa put her arms round him and responded satisfactorily, but then she pulled his head down to her shoulder, quiet and warm. "But not because you mislike Brian Donaghue. Any man, you'd feel the same. . . . Not shamed I am to say it to you, Fergal—as I wasn't that night—I do love you, so much. And it's taught me some things already. She's not an old woman, my darling, no more than—than Hugh's old as a man. And Brian Donaghue not that much older than her. You can't make pretense for it, there's not that much difference in men and women that way, as men'd maybe like to think. We go on being human people, Fergal. Don't grudge Ethne happiness—just because you're jealous for—"

"For God's sake stop talking of it, stop talking nonsense!" He slid his hands down her body, pulling her violently under him; she made a little murmur of passion and pressed close, willing. But it was only to take his mind from the other, to tire him to sleep easy and deep—any woman would have served.

Overnight, everything different.

They got over the border three times that month: that was all. Seven other times they started, Liam pillion behind Fergal, and were forced to turn back for this or that reason. Hard frost, that was ice in places, slowing their pace so that when they approached the border it was too late to cross and get back safe in the dark. On ground like that, every minute nervous for the horses—break a nag's leg this far from home, impossible even to get the beast back for butchering. And the guard increased and vigilant. Everyplace along the border where the bogland was wider, lower—where the trees were thicker, and it had been easier to get over, now the guard was patrolling if not permanent stationed.

The three times they got across, it was not possible to go far beyond, for more time was needed going and coming in this season. Altogether they fetched back nine bushel-sacks of wheat-flour, a quarter-haunch of fresh-killed hog, a new scythe, three pairs of leather boots, and three fresh-cured cowhides—the last two items a windfall worth more than all the rest.

A number of valuable articles ordinarily kept in the farmhouses they couldn't pick up now, for that was more dangerous business, getting into an occupied house, and on winter ground with horses heavier laden and in poorer condition now for lack of grain, they were slower getting away if alarm should be raised. Tobacco, flint-and-steels, the little locked-away canisters of expensive spices, household knives and plates and cups, made-up clothes, sometimes coin put away in a drawer, cooking-pots, fire-tongs and pokers, a hundred things salable if they didn't want them themselves—they didn't dare try for now.

In the first week of December, after a week's snow that kept them indoors, the weather cleared to gray ice and marrow-chilling wind, and they bound the horses' hooves in scraps of grain-sacks for better footing, and set out just after dusk on the thirty-mile journey. Nearing the river and leaving the horses, crawling up in cover to test the guard-strength, they found no gap really safe—at the usual seventy-thirty odds against them—all the way up past the head of the lough, almost to Carrick. They lay in half-frozen bog, eventually, fifty yards from a new-built guard-station, and heard the officer of the watch strike the hour on the station-bell. One of the morning.

"Too late to cross if we could," muttered McCann.

"Tonight," said Fergal. "Be damned if I make a thirty-mile trip for nothing. By Christ, make it sixty miles for something! Let's go up round Lough Key and see what it looks like above Carrick. Lay up tomorrow, and tomorrow night—"

"Tomorrow night we'd be three frozen corpses for the local residents to find next spring."

"All right, go on home," said Fergal, beginning to crawl backward toward firmer ground. "By all that's holy, I'm not going back empty-handed, not this time."

They made it to the head of Lough Key, north thirteen miles, by dawn, and lay all that day in a thin stand of bare wood by the lake. In the afternoon, they spent four hours' patient effort fishing—prone over the bank, watching still and stabbing at glimpsed fish with belt-knives. They got four grayling, not very big, and cleaned and ate them raw, having no means for fire. At dusk they started east on the hungry horses, and got over the border fifteen miles on, just south of a Leitrim village.

The first farm they came to they plundered, after disposing of the yard-dog. In an outbuilding they found five bushel-sacks of rye, and picked up a few miscellaneous tools, including a good

pitchfork: nothing else. But it was something. Fergal lashed two
of the sacks to his saddle: McCann would have to carry the rest,
his horse bearing only one rider. In the dark nearby, Liam uttered
a sudden muffled yelp, and Fergal turned savagely to hush him—
but stopped in awed excitement at the other sound.

"Liam, was that—?"

"Yes, I trod on its tail, I think—I'll try to find—"

And they were all, absurdly, groping cautious on hands and
knees, calling and coaxing in whispers, "Puss, puss, puss—come,
puss, come here—" Eventually something furry brushed Fergal's
wrist, and he had it, squirming indignantly in his arms. He got to
his feet with difficulty on icy ground, clasping the precious burden.

"All right, I have it. There, my beauty, my darling creature,
no harm in the world I mean, quiet now— Kevin, can you find a
sack to tie it in? Inhuman treatment for you, thou vein of my
heart!—but the only way to carry you, independent as you all
are— God, Liam, I do believe it's a tom, the big heavy jowls on
it, and the weight—"

It was a tom, a handsome big black one with a white front and
paws, to mate with the black kitten at home, in time, and produce
kits worth two pounds each, easy.

They came home twenty-two hours later, in falling dusk, after
two days and more away, and desperately hungry; but they were
satisfied of good profit from that raid, at least.

Part Three

15

"Do you hear me, Nessa O'Breslin?" Fergal barred her way across the threshold, grimly furious. "Put the loaf back where you had it from, you hear?"

"I hear you," said Nessa calmly. "Get out of the door, Fergal, and let me pass. We are not heathens or English, to forgo a little Christian charity."

"You take food out of this house, one mouthful, over my corpse! First duty is to one's own—four loaves left among seven people, no fuel for making more out of the three sacks o' grain left—and you off to give one away to strangers! I said, lay it back!"

She faced him white and rigid, the precious loaf clasped to her breast, a cup in her left hand. "Two slices of bread you had, an hour ago," she said, "and milk, and four-five mouthfuls of hare-meat. These people, nothing they've had in three days, and not young strong folk they are either. Let me pass, Fergal. The little we have to share, we'll share, in common Christian charity."

"Be damned if we do!" he said harshly. The old man, blue-lipped, lying in the road down there, the old woman pillowing his head in her lap, the dusty shabby bundles scattered beside them. Straggling groups of people trudging past, eyeing them dully, not stopping. God, on the way down from Lough Eask last year, hadn't they passed such a scene fifty times?—you couldn't stop, you couldn't offer—nought to offer. "I'm the head of this house," he choked out at her, "and, dear God, it's myself has to put the damn' loaves in the larder, isn't it?" An old man and woman, like as it might be Tadgh and old Eily, maybe loyal servants, or maybe once owning fine house and land—an old man trying to smile up at his old wife, *All right I'll be in a minute, just—a bit tired—I am, love.* You couldn't—you shouldn't—a man's first duty to his own people. "You can't feed them all, shelter them all! An order I gave you, woman—"

"I heard you," said Nessa. "I am not intending to feed them all, only these two. And I'll remind you of something Roy Donlevy said to Shevaun—not an English husband you are, to have absolute right over a wife. In Irish law females have always had equal legal rights as men, not owned chattels like livestock the way it is with English and all other foreigners. I'm not under your ordering, Fergal O'Breslin, except abed—and you've no complaints of me that direction, I'll swear. Get out of my path."

They faced each other, taut; and Shevaun came up to the open housedoor behind Fergal, hurrying. "Oh, Nessa, good, you've the fresh loaf—they—"

"You as bad!" He turned on her and shook her hard. "I'll not hear to it, Christ, all too little we—"

Shevaun wrenched away and slapped him across the mouth—and at once clutched him contritely. "I'm sorry, Fergal, I know it's only because you *want* to help them and feel—I *know* how you feel, but we can't—" And then she stopped dead and went even paler than she was. "Nessa, you've poured a cup of milk. You can't give the milk, Nessa—the loaf, yes, but there'll not be enough left for Sean if you give a whole cup of milk—put it back, Nessa—"

"You will both get out of my road," said Nessa in a steady voice. "Shevaun, if you raise a hand to me or run after, I'll likely spill the milk and it'll do no one any good. Mind, now. I am coming past, Fergal, move aside."

Something broke inside him and he took a step into the room and turned his back. He felt himself shaking-cold with anger—guilt—furious resentment—useless, meaningless grief. He heard her go out, he knew how she'd be walking with careful short steps on the wet ground down the slope where patches of ice lay in the path. He heard Shevaun going after, desperate, *Not all that milk, Nessa, please—charitable, yes, the loaf, yes, but not all that milk, a whole cup—*

He went over to the hearth and looked down, vague, at the

dead black ashes. This was the last day of March in the new year, and the fire was lost. They had been hungry before, and damned hungry—and cold, and they'd often had very little fuel left, so the fire was banked cautious; but in all the nearly twelve months here they'd never lost the fire for complete lack of aught to put on it. He must go out soon and look, and try, find something. And take the kettle or a pan to Donaghue's, nearest, for a live flame to carry back, and start a new fire.

This was the last day of March, and for ten days they had been coming past down the road—all the people out of Sligo, over the border of that county into Roscommon. The English had taken Sligo back—it was part of the province of Connacht, but they'd claimed it back, for they needed more land to satisfy all the claims still outstanding. Not much of Connacht was really good crop- or pasture-land, but Sligo land was better than the rest—so the English had taken back Sligo. And sent all these people over the border, original inhabitants and transplanters from last year alike. Where were they going? Those coming past here, to the temporary English Commission office set up in the village, as offices were established in many villages here now. Down there, at the inn-house this one was—where the Kearneys had died and little Dillon's blood dried rusty on the counter. They'd be given claims on land here, those who had grant-papers to show. Land, here: there was no more land to give away here. All too likely, the English commissioners carelessly granting land already occupied, and more fights started over that.

His mother in Donaghue's house would have fuel: squares of dried turf, bracken gathered last fall, a few sticks of fallen branches. Donaghue's fuel, and damned if Fergal O'Breslin would ask—even offering what he could in payment. And his mother wouldn't take payment. Any man might borrow live fire from a near neighbor, that was different.

He turned to the door slowly; he'd had only two meager meals in thirty hours, and felt listless. He went through the women's two little cubicles to the third, to see how Liam did, who'd been mostly abed with a chest-congestion this week. "Feeling better, are you? Of course, what you need now is doses of strong beef-stock and some good lean meat to put heart in you."

"I'll be fine in a day or two, O'Breslin," said Liam, not looking it, but grinning up at him determinedly. "It's time we made another little trip east."

"It is and all. I'll get a new fire somehow, today, and if tomorrow's halfway clear, McCann and I'll go alone. No, you won't get up and come—you're mending, senseless it'd be to get your death of cold over again and be down another month! We'll make it alone. And, my Christ," he added, attempting a laugh, "I do think I'll be needing to risk my life and get into a house, to acquire a decent razor. Look at you now, sprouting a fine crop of whiskers—another six months and you'll have the chore of shaving regular—and with two of us using it, this damned old blade won't last much longer, its best days were past when I got it five months back."

"Well, then, it ought to be me tries to pick up another," said Liam, stroking his cheeks a little self-consciously. "I'm strong enough to ride tomorrow, O'Breslin—"

"You are not. My household's diminishing fast enough, I'd not like to lose the only other grown-up male in it, and be left surrounded by these managing women! Well, meantime I'll see what I can do about the fire."

Collecting his cloak from his own chamber, he came out to find Nessa and Shevaun back. Shevaun was sitting on the settle weeping, and the boy leaning on her knee, ready to cry too for her sobs. "Mother, don't to cry—please, Mother—"

Nessa stood looking down reflectively at the dead hearth. "All right, you needn't remind me," said Fergal abruptly. "I'm just off to do something about it."

Nessa looked up slowly, and slowly raised a hand to brush away tears on her own face. "I wasn't pointing it up to you, Fergal. I'm sorry I had to act so to you—you'll forgive me."

"It's likely you were in the right of the matter—Hugh'd say so. Laying up reward in heaven, for charity to the stranger in the gates. The only thing is, woman—at the same time you're bringing the date nearer we'll maybe be claiming that reward off Saint Peter. Never mind, he's more like to let you in than me, I know, girl. What's the trouble on Shevaun?"

"Nothing—very—much," said Nessa. "They wouldn't take the cup of milk, is all. Sean came following down to the road, and the old woman said—we must keep the milk for the child—for that they were old, and it's not much matter about them, but the child—must have a good chance for life. . . . They'd owned land in Cavan. Three sons they had dead in the war, and a widow-daughter and her three children all killed by the soldiers as they marched through toward the siege at Longford. And all that long way to walk over to Sligo last year—and working to get a field or two planted—and now driven off down here. They've gone on now, maybe not to get far, he still looked bad. Blessed us for the loaf, they did. . . . Fergal—the old man, he looked a bit like Tadgh, did you see?"

"Yes," said Fergal. "Yes." Tadgh had died in January; and an old man he'd been, but he'd have lived on to older age, and not died so long and hard, if not for that terrible journey on foot down from home last year, if not for the backbreaking toil and the lack of good strengthening food here. And Fergal and Liam had broke their hearts and snapped a shovel-handle digging a grave up the hill, in the steel-hard winter ground; but damn the shovel and the ax they'd blunted, they couldn't bury him shallow at three feet—predatory wild things about, foxes, and Donaghue had seen a wolf on his land, in Christmas week, he said. Aged old Eily it had, overnight. But that was a queer thing too: Father O'Marron had said it—at the second burial. The old folk, he said, they were the tough ones: eventually, they went, but they had more fight in them. It was the young ones gave up and slipped away easy. The young maidservant Morag, not as old as Nessa she'd been—dead in six days of the lung-congestion. Two less mouths to feed. "Yes, I saw."

"Fergal—I know it's a silly thing to say—but what did they ever do, what did any of us ever do—deserve this, all this? Not soldiers, fighting the English. People like that—like us, Shevaun and Sean and old Tadgh—I don't see why God lets—"

"What did we *do*?" said Fergal. "Why, you brainless female, that's an easy question! We got ourselves born Irish instead of honest, upright, civilized English folk!—that's the black sin we're doing penance for!" He came over and gripped her shoulder a moment. "I'm sorry I snapped at you. I'm going up the hill, see if I can find anything to burn, maybe borrow a bit from McCann against our next raid. Back in two-three hours." He went out quick, and halfway up the hill found himself wishing he'd kissed her, just for comfort, she'd looked so forlorn.

* * *

End of March, end of the worst of the winter: the season would be turning from now on, thank God, and in six weeks or so, time to begin planting, if it was an early year—eight weeks at the outside. But meanwhile, the ground was still wet and hard, and a few patches of thin hoarfrost and ice left from the last snow. Fergal plodded up the slope to the first trees, and cast about for dry branches left hanging, to pull or knock down. Not many: most had been used long ago. But he found a few sticks, and collected them in the grain-sack he'd brought. Wood was impractical fuel, burning away so quick, but this would serve as kindling.

Over the brow of the hill he stopped hunting and went on down across the little hollow to McCann's place halfway up toward thicker wood. A drift of smoke from the rude chimney-hole: a fire here, at least. Fergal rapped politely at the door, and was aware of quick, flurried movement beyond the thin partition. In a moment the door swung back.

"Well," he said in some surprise, "good to see you, but I hadn't expected to, here."

"I was—I will stop to see your house—on my way down," said Hugh McFadden. "I—" He stepped back, and Fergal entered.

"It was a message," said Maire vaguely, "that's all—nothing. How do you all, Fergal? It's been so wet and chill, I've not felt like coming out—a month it must be since I've seen Nessa and Shevaun. Your mother's well?"

Well! Again the mingled anger and embarrassment for that possessed him, for the conventional question: he hesitated and answered brusquely, "Yes, my thanks, Maire." Be damned if he'd blurt it out, the silly and disgusting thing—the two of them so pleased about it—he felt again the queer pang that had struck him, for the bright happiness in his mother's eyes. Christ, of all absurdities—and Nessa only twenty-two, strong and well, and no suspicion of conceiving in five months—and the boy Sean turned well past four, *grandson*—Ethne Donaghue, two months with child!

He said hastily, to put it from mind, "We've lost our fire, I came to ask if you'd spare us a bit of turf or somewhat, Maire, against whatever we get on the next raid. Liam's been abed with a bad cold, and not fit to ride, but I thought if it was clear tomorrow, or even if Kevin's agreeable we could get off by this dusk, alone —with luck I'll pick up enough to buy some turf off Lynch, among other things." Lynch was one of the men with an income of sorts guaranteed, owning part of a peat-bog.

"Oh, that's bad, Fergal, I'm sorry. Yes, of course I'll give you something—"

God knew it wasn't that he wanted Nessa pregnant; but so damned absurd it was, and not least of its absurdity the way they were so pleased—in times like these, looking forward to an infant!—Donaghue beaming like a twenty-year-old bridegroom, damn him! "Thanks, Maire, keep account of how much, and I'll make it up."

"Oh, it's no matter," she said. "Not turf it is, I've been burning dried horse-dung. It lasts very well, and really doesn't smell much at all, as you'd expect. And it costs nothing, so—" She straightened from half-filling his sack, from the sack by the hearth; she said carefully, "I'm sorry, Fergal, Kevin's not here, as you see. He'll be up the hill at the pasture, seeing to the horses. Won't you go up and see him?"

"Yes, why not walk up and meet him, likely on his way down," suggested Hugh genially. "If he's agreeable to your going out tonight, you might get off near at once, to save some time. I'll carry the message down to your house, and the fuel as well."

Fergal hesitated. "Oh—leave it. Look, tell him, we'll say definite tomorrow, Maire, unless it storms. I'll get back with this and start the fire." She let out a sharp little sigh; he looked at her with more attention. "*Dried horse-dung?* By all holy, I'd never thought of that! It burns well? I'll be damned. And come to think, I'm entitled to some of it, one of the two being my horse! But they can't produce enough to supply you all the while?"

"Oh, no," she said. "No, not quite. I'll tell Kevin." She had, of course, lost weight like all of them, but in some odd way, he thought suddenly, still looking at her, her beauty had—sharpened, was the word?—for privation: her fine white skin translucent, her dark hair in its coiled knot smooth and thick, her dark eyes looking larger and brighter for the thinness of her cheeks now.

"I'll be glad to carry down the fire," said Hugh, "if you'll walk up to meet McCann."

"No, I'll not bother. Get the fire started and have a hot meal of some sort, and I'll be in better state tomorrow to ride. Tell Kevin I'll be up, an hour before dusk. Walk back with me, Hugh?"

"I'll tell him," said the woman. "And say to Shevaun and Nessa, I'll try get down, see them, soon." Fergal was still looking at her, so he saw her eyes move to Hugh, some expression he couldn't name in her look. "Thank you, Hugh."

"Nothing. Yes, I'll come." And some nameless look in his eyes on her. He took up the sack and went out ahead of Fergal, who gave her another word of gratitude as she handed him the lid of the cooking-kettle with a generous live-smoldering lump of fuel on it. They started down the hill, Fergal blowing on the spark and shielding it from the wind with his free hand.

"How goes the schoolmastering, Hugh?"

"A somewhat thankless job—schoolmastering always is, O'Breslin. But I do well enough, by God's favor."

"So it appears." Fergal looked at him and suddenly laughed. "Almost I'm tempted to say, It's an ill wind— All that time ago, there you were a terrified fellow running from English, I hauling you up that tree—skin-and-bones you felt, and I confess it, I was cursing to be saddled with an unworldly lay-brother! Man, have you turned ghoul, or sold your soul to the devil, or what? Ten years younger you look—"

"Don't say such, even in jest!" Hugh's tone was sharp; and then he laughed. "Well, an odd thing it is at that, I grant you. But you see, I'm visiting a number of households, thirty at least, and offered a little food in most of them— I daresay it's true I get more meals than most folk. And I expect it's all the exercise I get traveling about, that—" He gestured vaguely. It was true enough: he looked a different man from that one who had babbled fearfully to Fergal in the wood that day. He walked erect, head up, and he'd filled out, chest and shoulders broad, and looked a vital strong man less than his years. Since the tonsure was covered, his once shaven head bearing thick brown hair, he looked scarce his true five-and-thirty. Someone had just trimmed his hair for him, too—Fergal felt at his own too-long straggling crop, and thought absently, Try to pick up a pair of shears as well as the razor; the Dowlings owned the only pair of shears for ten miles round, and were understandably chary of loaning them—there being no grinding-wheel for sharpening nearer than Castlereagh.

While he thought that, Hugh had gone on talking inconsequentially, and as it were half to himself. "I—just turned fifteen I was, when I went into the order. My people dead, and I'd a great-uncle—guardian—who was a priest down at Ferbane, and he—thinking it would be the best life—put me in, you know—the way he reckoned— To have a good education—I'd always a bent toward scholarship. And we weren't asked to take our final vows until we were eighteen, but—even then—it's no great age either—to have had experience, and know—what the renunciation meant—for everything."

"Yes," said Fergal inattentively. "Hugh. Whyfor did you and Maire McCann press me to go up and find Kevin in the pasture?"

"Why, did she—or I? Only a suggestion, O'Breslin—idle talk. Have you had many of these poor folk out of Sligo past today? God's mercy on them, He knows what will become of them."

"I can tell you too," said Fergal bitterly. "Those who don't starve will create more problems for the rest of us here."

"Indeed . . . These bands of outlaws—I remember Donaghue did predict it—preying on their own people, now it is difficult to prey on the enemy. Once I said to you, a theological problem—but if not that, one of principle at least. The end justifying the means—and English the enemy—but, only a short step from raiding and robbing the enemy house to pillaging the neighbor-house. Desperate, lawless men—or merely lawless to start with, and chance—or the devil—bringing their lawlessness out open . . . I have heard that fifty houses roundabout have been attacked and robbed, this last two months or so."

"That's right enough. I've fixed a makeshift bolt on the door, and I always leave the hand-pistol primed and loaded, with the women, when I'm away by night—and have taught them to use it. There'll always be a few men turn traitor or savage, in straits." He blew hard on the spark, cursing the wind.

"And maybe," said Hugh thoughtfully, "men like Edmund Kearney was, an amiable mask to their neighbors by day, ravening wolves by night."

"No, not as bad as that, these. Make haste, man, we'll never get this fire back alive! No, they're landless men living on the run, those fellows, plundering different districts every month. Places I've heard of round here, that've been attacked, ten miles' circle every direction—sure to God, fellows like that with stolen horses, but it might be a dozen different gangs making that much robbery, you know. And half of 'em by now escaped, on into Galway or Clare, to rob there. No way to come up with them, of course."

"Quite possibly so," said Hugh.

"I'll tell you why they fright me—not shamed I am to say it, I go cold to think of it, and not one Christ-damned thing any of us can do to safeguard ourselves. That English Commission office down there," and Fergal jerked a shoulder in the village-direction. "You'd think one lesson would be enough, and so it has been for most settled men! Even a kitten puts a paw on a live ember only once! But you take a few hotheads like such outlaws—what the hell do they care for the residents of a place? A little drink in them, and they coming down on a Commission office—"

"That business at Athleague, last week. Yes." At Athleague, the newly-set-up Commission office—a family-house requisitioned, the occupants dispossessed until the Commission's business was done here—had been invaded, and the seven Englishmen making up the office-crew laid out neat in a row before the door, each with his throat cut. Planning had gone into the affair: the corpses stripped before murder, for their good English clothes, and their horses vanished, and no food left in the house. For one hour it had been a heartening jest, a blow returned for a change. . . . The English were aware that there'd be no earthly use ferreting about with questions to find the guilty men: they wasted no time on that. An hour after the first English patrol came and saw the corpses, they rounded up twenty men at random, the first to hand, and lined them in the street and shot them down.

The replacement Commission men at Athleague had stayed unmolested, while the bitter talk went on in corners, in voices held low. And the killers at Athleague had likely been local residents: and no local resident anywhere, hearing that tale, would join a similar plot. But these outlaws on the move might easy get such an idea—a Commission office in one out of ten villages all through Roscommon: and the outlaws, of course, escaping easy afterward, and leaving the local men to bear the blame.

"Yes," said Hugh again. "Violence begetting violence, like as always . . . One of those bands will be those former men of yours, too." It was an obvious remark, almost inane, and Hugh McFadden was not given to inanity; but Fergal, blowing on the little spark, heard him only vaguely.

"I daresay. Thank God, we've made it, in this wind a miracle the flame wasn't lost—get the door, will you, Hugh?—Nessa, She-vaun, make haste with the fuel, I've a new fire—"

16

"FERGAL—"

"Well?" Fergal turned on his side indolently. McCann hadn't spoken for a long while; it was still and quite peaceful in the little covey. The oaks were so old and bowed that bare as they were they made a shielding bower here, and sheltered up against a slope there was even a patch of new grass for the horses. Fergal had been, futilely, all those months back in his mind: a daydream in which he'd taken another road. Should have been longer-sighted for it: disclaimed responsibility for those young, strong servants as well as the tenants, to leave just the family—and gone straight over to Galway town, struck a bargain with some foreign captain, got them all out abroad. Once there, sign on as mercenary—wasn't Roy right about that, money at least! Not the easiest or best life, but better than anything they had here. Hindsight always clearer than foresight . . . "Well?"

McCann was sitting hunched against a tree, arms round his knees. Fergal had had his fill of Kevin McCann some while back; yesterday dusk he'd had more than his fill, opinion dropping another notch; right now, and maybe for that reason, he saw the other man clearer than in some months, as if meeting him new. He saw that indefinably all McCann's surface gentry-smoothness had worn thin: he looked exactly what this year had turned him into—the bold raider-chief, raffish, more than a little crude, calculating to selfish ends. Not the four days' black beard-stubble, or overlong hair, or the black-rimmed broken nails, the mended buttonless shirt with no collar to it, or shabby faded trews and cracked boots.

No man looked much different in those respects these days. Something namelessly rakehell and beyond-law: that unpleasing combination of recklessness and cold caution somehow closer to the surface.

"What does that lay-brother of yours want, sniffing round my house?" he asked.

"Hugh McFadden—none of mine he is, Kevin, his own master—now. What d'you mean by that, any road?"

"Oh—" McCann shrugged. "I come in, and there he is. Twice every three days. God's grace, no nuisance of offspring I've got for him to be teaching their letters, and my house isn't on his way between any two places. All right, what is at my house?—my wife."

"What the hell are you talking of, man?" Fergal sat up with a jerk. "And what brings this up now?"

"You might say I've been brooding on it," said McCann, soft. They were eighteen hours out from home; they'd had good luck last night, getting across south of the lake and visiting three farms for good plunder. But they hadn't got back to the border in time to cross before light, and they were lying up here, hidden, a mile up from Killashee village, waiting for dark again. They hadn't talked much: little to say. At the second farm they'd taken the chance of entering the house, and got clean away with four loaves of bread and half a meat-pie as well as other valuables; the pie being awkward to carry, they'd finished it between them, and with full stomachs for a change had taken turns sleeping; it was barely midmorning now.

"For Christ's love!" said Fergal. "That's the damndest silliest thing I've listened to in a year. Hugh? A vowed religious he is."

"I never heard that church-authority says a monk's to be whole castrated same time he takes vows. Tales I have heard, and so have you, about vowed religiouses—and priests."

"The benefit of the doubt I'll grant you before I call you mad," said Fergal coldly, "on account you don't know Hugh as well as I do."

McCann shrugged again. "And that's so. I'm like to, meeting him so often! You don't think, then—?"

"I do not. Would that maybe be the reason," asked Fergal, "that your lady-wife was wearing a sizable black bruise on her face yesterday, Kevin?"

"What the hell, man, she told you she fell against the hearth! You take me for a—"

"Keep your voice down. I couldn't say, Kevin—not being an eyewitness. The English like to call us savages, but Hugh Mc-Fadden might remind you—he's by way of being a historian—that far as eighteen hundred years back, we had written law here—and one of them said it was a felonious crime for a man to strike a female, and if it was his wife, it was cause for her to demand divorce."

"What in Christ's name are we talking about?" demanded McCann. "All right, I imagined a piece o' nonsense. So we're even—you doing the same. Drop it, boy, you can't think I'd do such."

It was, for no discernible reason, futile soft talk to turn away wrath. Suddenly everything that had been smoldering between them—from Fergal's side anyway—for nearly half a year, flared up. Fergal sat all the way erect and regarded him, cold and curious. "The smooth side o' your tongue to me, Kevin McCann, and the hell of a lot you convince me! I've known you too long, you talking just as smooth and we both youngsters up home, before either of us had our first belt-knives. You're usually up to some devilment. Now I think, there was something I meant to mention to you, and that is the fine ivory comb that girl Ailsa has. I daresay—if it was you gave it to her—you warned her to keep it hid. You ought to know women better, man, after all your experience! They can't resist showing off possessions."

"Ailsa?" said McCann. "What have I to do with that one?"

"Very likely, what every second man she meets has to do with her. Yes, a fool I was right enough, thinking it'd be a breach of honor to disclaim every soul once dependent on me as chief—and double fool for keeping her in my household! Oh, sure to God, I was pleased enough to have her there, convenient, before I had a wife—and now I think, I was maybe damned lucky not to pick up the French sickness off her, she likely consorting with any peddler or soldier or even English, at Lough Eask before. But however that is, she's by way of being a nuisance in my house now, bone-lazy and giving herself airs. The women tell me, and this season when I've been home more I've seen it myself, she's off on some business of her own, couple of hours here, three-four hours there, and saying, oh, Down to the village I was, or Over to see Maureen Dowling, some such excuse. If I know Ailsa, she's let herself be laid by half the men in five miles' walk, for whatever they've got to give—or just because she fancies them."

"Oh, I shouldn't wonder," grinned McCann. "That one, she makes you believe the proverb, nine cocks to satisfy one hen! She can't be, what, twenty-one, and I'd reckon she's forgot who first laid her and when."

"You're wrong," said Fergal. "That was myself, seven years back, and she miscarried a child of mine too, which was a mercy."

"And you virgin at seventeen, to take her word? Man, if that one kept her maidenhead at fourteen years, I've never laid a woman!"

"Who in hell's name d'you call that slow a starter? Enough girls I'd had before, I knew. And that's a side issue, what matter is it? Well enough you know me, no prude I am to look pious at you for it, your own affair it is. I don't give a damn for your morals or for Ailsa—"

"And the girl teasing at you, for devilment, and to annoy your wife—is that it?" McCann laughed. "How many times have you said it to your wife, Fergal—*Not a damn I give for Ailsa?*"

"Which is none of your affair," said Fergal. Straight to the target that went: damn Ailsa, brushing against him, flirting slyly, hinting. The damned odd thing was, if he'd been so indecently unreticent to say it to McCann, he'd never the least impulse to lay a finger on the girl now. Just slid through his mind, quick—Nessa—*No complaints of me that direction, I'll swear.* Well, he hadn't. Gamble, he'd said, in wedding: that way, lucky he'd been. . . . "You're off the point. When you came by yesterday morning, I noted you having a few words private with her, and times before too. I don't give a damn if you lay her, Kevin, but if it was you gave her that comb, it looks as if you're holding out on me from our plunder—"

"You've gone off like a hammer-filed matchlock," said McCann easily. "So the girl's got an ivory comb—loot indeed, wherever she had it. If you're bound to have a serious answer out o' me on such a charge, two reasons I'll give you why it wasn't me gave it to her. For one, I'm not such a Christ-damned fool to give a female like that any presents—and for two," he laughed, "I'll flatter myself to say I never had to bribe a woman to lie leg-spread for me."

"And if that's a lie it's not too steep a lie. But as to your first reason, I ask you, an ivory comb! Ordinary way, valuable, yes. But here and now, an extravagance—like trying to sell French wine to starving folk. Whoever had it wouldn't sell it easy or for much— it's the sort of thing a man would give away to a girl like Ailsa, plunder there was little real value in."

"That's so," agreed McCann seriously, a hand stroking his jaw thoughtfully. "Go on a step, man, and acknowledge something else. You and I haven't entered a dwelling-house in four months, until last night—and where else would a raider pick up such a thing? And would you or I or any other man with sense trouble to take a thing like that on a raid?—as you say, not a thing there's much demand for!"

"I've got to say you're right." Moodily Fergal prodded a twig into the earth, drawing patterns in the patch of soft turf between his knees. On second thought, he couldn't see Kevin McCann giving away aught of value (whatever sort of value) where it wasn't necessary. Yes, true that no man working this way, coming across-border in secret, would take that kind of thing deliberately. . . . He said suddenly, softly, "By God, I tell you where a man would get such an article. One of these outlaw-bands—this and that side of the border they roam, I've heard, and on the English side stopping coaches as well as attacking houses, and prosperous-looking travelers both sides—peddlers and such. Yes, an ivory comb—a gentry-lady's thing—as it might have been in some Englishwoman's reticule, she traveling in a coach stopped by outlaws—" He looked up at McCann, and for one heartbeat surprised strange expression in the dark eyes, before they dropped. McCann leaned to grip his arm.

"Quiet! Someone below there—coming up this way."

They had been too engrossed in argument to hear, before. Both of them froze, listening; but the man approaching, cautious-quiet, had already come too near. Just time both Fergal and McCann had to draw knives, when he slid under the low-hanging branches and straightened to look down at them pleasedly. "Now put up the blades, my bold boys," he said. "All I'm after is a bit o' reasonable talk with you."

Half to their feet, they both stared. The Irish he spoke; he was a man of middle years, stocky and graying, with square amiable features and mild blue eyes. His shapeless brown trews bound with leg-wrappings below the knee, and collarless shirt of home-woven cloth under a short cloak, were farmers' clothes. In fact, he looked to be like any tenant-farmer or small landowner either of them had known before the settlement-act.

"What—" began Fergal stupidly. McCann gestured with his knife and maneuvered the man between them, watchful.

"Not exactly a social occasion," said the newcomer, "but I may as well introduce myself—Thomas Carmody's the name." He sat down next to Fergal and let out a long breath. "By damn, a chase I've had after you! Good and quiet you move, even if I was only five minutes behind you as you got away from my place—but I did reckon you'd not make it back to the border afore light, see, and I tracked you a bit, and for the last six hours I've been casting round all the places you might be lying up—a stubborn man I am, I grant you." He brought out a ragged kerchief and mopped his brow; he looked at Fergal solemnly and said, "You're welcome to the spade and the hayfork, and the jacket too—daresay you're in more need than me. It's the coin I want back, in the inside pocket."

"The coin. I don't—" Fergal laughed incredulously. "*Your* place—the last we—are you telling me—"

"So you heard us," said McCann, and his knife was an inch from Carmody's side as he squatted down, close. "Casting round after us—with how many English military on the hunt with you?"

"Now, no need to miscall me," said Carmody. "I'm not like some fellows, damning men like yourselves seven ways from Sunday as outlaw-thieves. You, or some o' you, hit my brother-in-law's place last week, and wasn't he in a temper over losing that new scythe-handle! I says to him, Dan, I says, what odds? You can't cut the English landlord's wheat without a scythe—even an Englishman will see that—and the factor'll be bound to supply you another, as he wants the crop reaped. Landlord's buildings robbed of landlord's goods—us only the tenants—and I says, good luck to the men of our blood with the guts to come raiding. Though I don't deny it's annoying, when you take tobacco and ground flour and such. A bit better off than you we are, this side, but not all so much better than we don't miss food and household stuff."

Fergal said, "Put up your knife, Kevin. Tenants—Carmody,

you're saying there's Irish folk this side, still—tenants!—but the Act—not one in ten thousand could prove innocence, be let to stay! I hadn't an idea—"

Carmody looked interested. "Is that so, now? Well, I'd wondered. No legal communication you have across, and sure to God the English wouldn't go discussing it with you! And those of you coming to raid, not settling down to idle conversation with the householders . . . You talk like a gentleman."

"Yes, some respect in your tone," said McCann sardonically, "for a clan-chief! And easy for you to say, no alarm you raised! A witnessed guarantee of that you've got on you?"

Carmody gave him a leisurely glance. "Constable of horse I was under Prendergast, and fought alongside the O'Neill troops from Meath to Cork. No more dealings with the English I want than needful these days. A chief, is it?—northman by your talk." He mopped his face again. "Well, I needn't say you've my sympathy. Bad enough for those of us with modest substances afore the Act —farm of my own I had, sixty acres just north o' Thurles—I'm a Tipperary man—but a deal worse for folk as were used to having servants and hunting-horses and aught they wanted any way. Look now, you being a gentleman-chief I make no doubt we can settle this with no argument, fair between us. Like I say, you're welcome to the old coat, it's the coin-piece in the pocket I want back. My lucky bit it is, see you, I always carry it on me. Priest'd say 'twas heathen superstition, but I do swear it fetched me safe out o' a hundred battles, and tell the truth, I've got now so I do feel uneasy, it not on me somewhere. You know how a man comes to feel about a thing like that. And it's not as if it's worth aught to you, you couldn't spend it, get anything for it save as a curiosity, like—it being an old Roman piece, see."

Fergal got up and went over to the horses. Hard as it was on the beasts, you didn't unsaddle, lying up like this: you might have to move in a hurry. The third place they'd plundered last night, the least they'd taken there—new spade and hayfork, and an old woolen jacket-coat he'd found hanging on a nail in the shed. He had bundled it into a saddlebag without looking at it. Now he unlashed the thongs and took it out, worn but still whole and warm—useful. He felt in the one pocket inside the breast, and brought up a thin cold round thing, and looked at it.

"Ah!" said Carmody in a relieved sigh. "There she is, sure! I always keep it by me, like I say, but what with being worried about the cow—it was her first calf, and she made a bit o' business about it, she's half Devon-bred, not as tough as ours—see you, I took off the coat and went in without thinking o' my lucky bit. Woke in the night I did, and remembered it. And Eileen says, what's off with you, turning and tossing like a sin-tempted monk, she says, and I says, I'll not rest until I've gone down for it, right uneasy I feel without it. And so I did, just in time to glimpse you two getting out the gate. And Eileen, she'll be thinking I've been kidnapped by soldiers, away this long, but I did feel as I must have it back. You do see now, it's worth nought—save to me, as my lucky bit."

"So it isn't," said Fergal. The thing was so old, it was only roughly circular; it was silver-alloy, but worn thin. There was a woman's profile in relief on one side, and letters—English-alphabet letters—which of course were Roman letters first. He turned it curiously and made out the words—*Sabina*, this side, and on the other, another profile, and a laurel-wreath part worn away, and *Hadrian*. "No, it's worth nothing to us, take it."

Carmody accepted it eagerly. "A gentleman you are indeed, and I thank you. I do know 'tis a senseless thing, but I've carried it so long, it's like part of myself, see. I had it from my uncle, I only a lad. He was tenant to the chief O'Riogan, just north o' Dublin, and that's not far off Tara where all the old High Kings lived. He turned it up with a spade one day, good thirty years back it'd be, and he showed it to O'Riogan, he told me, and O'Riogan said it is a Roman coin, fourteen hundred years old— and likely some o' the loot the Irish sea-raiders fetched back. You'll have heard that in those times, Ireland being strong and rich and England just a colony o' Rome, the High Kings and chiefs and princes did use to go raiding on the west coast. Which is the only way a Roman coin could get into Ireland, for they never got a foothold here, O'Riogan said." He fingered the coin in satisfaction.

Fergal couldn't have been less interested in dead-and-gone history. "This is something new to us, Carmody," he said, sitting down again. "How is it there are still men like you this side— tenant, you say?—to an English owner. What—"

Carmody looked up from the coin. "Yes, well, like I say, I did wonder—a-many of us did—if you over there knew it." He laughed, putting the coin away carefully in his shirt-pocket. "English owner, sure to Christ! There's no other kind o' owner in Ireland now, this side the border. Nothing you've heard of how it's gone here?" He stretched out his legs, relaxing, and looked from Fergal to McCann thoughtfully. "Yes, by the look of you, we're a bit better off, right enough. Not, I do assure you, to call ourselves well off, understand, but we eat most days—which is what life's come down to, not so? Well, I tell you how it was." He showed them his slow, wide grin. "The English acted just a bit too clever for their own good, with that settlement business. Sure to God, they writ the law so—like you say—not one Irishman in twenty thousand should be let to stay east o' the border—and all the land they granted away to new English owners. But it didn't come about just the way they reckoned it would, you see. First place, a-many of the new owners, they were the common English soldiers, and it was figured they'd settle down on their land peaceful to work it. But a good half of 'em, they were feckless enough to get rooked out of their land by smooth-tongued fellows as saw a chance to acquire land—"

"That I'd heard was happening," nodded Fergal.

"And them as did come onto the land, they were unsatisfied. A good many of 'em were city-men, see, and didn't they complain," said Carmody amusedly, "how there wasn't any beer, or easy girls in regular houses like they was used to. Ninety-nine out of a hundred of them, in the end, they sold out their grants, mostly to Englishmen who had land near. I'll tell you what it came to, a year and five months after that Act. They granted land to the soldiers in little parcels—sixty acres, forty—by rank, see. But the most of those are gone home to England, and the landholders—like as it was a-many of those Adventurers, they call themselves—buying up soldiers' land, they had bigger acreage to start with. Most English landholders here now, they've got what would have been a chief's holding, legal, in the old days—a thousand, fifteen hundred, two-three thousand acres. God's mercy, for six drinks in a Dublin tavern they got hundreds o' acres—as a business-gamble, see."

"I wouldn't doubt. Yes."

"But," Carmody laughed, "just a bit too clever they were with that Act. Thinking to settle five sixths of Ireland with English— all ranks, owners, tenants, skilled men, shopkeepers—towns all cleared out well as countryside, as you know. What happened, or what didn't happen—the English just wouldn't come over. All the folk they needed to settle here, turn it into a prosperous English land. The landowners come, a few of 'em, but there weren't any tenants to rent to, to work the land—all the business in towns dead, account there weren't any shopkeepers and traders—and you couldn't get so much as a chair put together, or a pair o' breeches made, for there weren't any carpenters or tailors left. Reckoned on replacing all those with English, but the English haven't come, nor won't. And mind, the most of all these English landowners, they never meant to come, live on the land—it was a business investment with them—English merchants and gentry, living in London year-round as it might be, hiring a bailiff-factor to account to 'em for land-rents. A great nuisance it was to them," said Carmody, giving Fergal a solemn wink, "roundabout last planting season they began to realize it—they'd chased all the possible tenants over into Connacht! You might say it put those Englishmen in a quandary, nine of ten of 'em being city-folk as don't know a scythe from a spade, or a Kerry cow from a Limerick hog—or wanting to know."

"I will be damned," said Fergal. McCann, since the talk veered this way, looked uninterested, scowling down at his knife.

"The profit off our land they wanted, but they didn't want to live on it—gentry *or* farmers. And the law says they can't hire Irish tenants. But none of 'em's been paying any note to that for a year. Well, you take my own case. We were caught this side the border after the official date for transplanting—me and my wife Eileen and the four children, and my brother-in-law Dan and his woman Maura. Eileen, she was with child, and it came on unexpected at seven months, and gave her a bit o' trouble—there we were, in October, up the hills in Tipperary. Well, I says, it's a thin hope to expect reason out of English, but the best we can try is explain how it was. So we came down toward Newport, to cross the Shannon there, see, and a bit out of the village, here's a man a-horse stops us—my heart in my mouth, for don't we know English are apt to shoot first and ask explanation later, you breaking one of their rules. But he was a Lowland Scot, a gentleman's factor, and right off he says, would Dan and I take on as tenants in Longford? And thinking it over, as he explained the situation, it did seem a bit better chance. They were scouring the whole border-counties for stragglers then, to take as tenants, and fetching back the skilled townsmen too. I'd say half o' the folk as didn't start for the border afore last summer, they never crossed at all—by then the new owners were desperate in need of tenants to work the land."

"That many—"

"And a-many came in just this last fortnight, since they took Sligo back, too. And a good number of those that got over to Connacht, and were squeezed out o' their land-claims or nearly starved, being landless, they came drifting back by fall, and got places easy. . . . We're on Lord Errington's land here," said Carmody. "Two thousand acres he holds—living in London and keeping two Scot factors here and one English—and by Jesus, the three of 'em always pulling opposite ways, by what the tenants say! Six hundred-odd tenant-farms to oversee. And all of 'em occupied by Irish tenants, the only ones to take on the job, being desperate and starving."

"I will be damned. . . . So it's going like that."

McCann looked up. "How does it go for you, you do well?"

"It could be worse. I tell you, I think it will be, as the population gets built up again, see. Right now, the landholders need us, and they're walking soft—talk about the donkey atween two bales o' straw!—see, official-like, they're breaking the Penal Laws by renting to us, and same time, if they're to have any profit, they've got to. They've limited the rate o' profit tenants can earn, and it's a bitter taste in the mouths of us as once owned our own land, these factors so high and mighty for the foreign landlords of stolen ground. But they do need depend on us, and even put a little investment up, for future profits." Carmody's grin was sardonic. "Breeding-stock they've brought over, and had to give tenants credit to buy seed, and so on. No, we're none of us getting rich, nor we won't ever, but I'd say we're better off than you over there, sure."

"That's saying little," said Fergal, "but I'd agree."

"So it seems," said McCann; his tone was thoughtful, and there was brief speculation in his eyes before he dropped them again to the knife he played with absently, tossing it from hand to hand.

17

WITHOUT WORDS, AS they came to the rough track that mid-morning, they pulled up and Fergal dismounted. Whether they raided south or north, they generally came back this way, to avoid passing any farmhouse; here, where the faint track crossed, they were halfway between the hill-pasture and McCann's place. As usual, Fergal unlashed his saddlebags, slung them over his shoulder. He took the hayfork and spade off McCann's saddle; they had agreed on division of plunder as they lay hidden over the border.

"Well, I'll see you," said McCann, taking the rein of Fergal's horse.

Fergal glanced up at him. "We'll talk it over, right, I'll see you, Kevin." He turned and started down the track; McCann rode on up with the horses, to leave them at pasture.

The track sloped steep here, and Fergal jolted down it tiredly, weighted with his loot. *Loot*, he thought. Indeed. Man's first duty to his own; but it was an uneasy reflection now that for a year he'd been—call it by the right name—stealing from his own countrymen, not the enemy, and countrymen only a little better off than he. He'd argued it with McCann: mishonest. And yet, if they were to have even bare subsistence, how else to have it? Through this winter, there had been death in Connacht, hardly a house untouched by death, and some ravaged: and death not only of illness worsened by poor food and privation, but death of stark starvation and cold.

He was tired, he was disturbed in mind about that, but as he came in sight of McCann's poor cabin, with its thin drift of smoke,

other things—equally disturbing, this way and that—slid above
the thought of Thomas Carmody, tenant-farmer.

McCann. Not a damn it meant to him, who he robbed from.
McCann not so nice in his choice—any kind of choice. Yes, McCann
likely was or had been one of Ailsa's lovers, but it wouldn't have
been him gave her the comb. A man in one of those roving outlaw-
bands?—and where would she meet one like that? Well, a girl like
Ailsa—

Maire McCann, there in this house he came to. A beautiful,
quiet, forlorn lady, with a husband a good deal younger, and not
a kind husband. True, what he'd told Nessa: most men not such
rakes as women suspected. But many a husband kind and fond of
a wife, not always faithful, and no matter that was, so he kept his
duty by her otherwise. People not all made alike, a man wed to a
woman as wasn't satisfactory abed—account of how she was
made—natural it was he'd go elsewhere, but he'd no right to use
less than kindness and generosity to her only because she didn't
match him that way. . . . And that was a thing you couldn't tell
about, just on looks or acquaintance; but Maire, he wouldn't have
said she was a cold woman. But McCann wouldn't need an excuse.

Yes, Maire. Hugh. *Hugh.* Mad, sure to God Kevin was—think
such a thing. But Fergal couldn't help remembering how he'd been
surprised, three days back, to find Hugh here. Bringing a message,
they said vaguely—unwillingly he remembered—and an indefin-
able glance between them. Hugh looking so strangely young and
vital this last half year and more . . . lay-brother and scholar at
Clonmacnoise, the oldest monastery . . .

Hugh, saying aloud to himself that day, "Just turned fifteen I
was." And something above and beyond any formal teaching, any
unthinking acceptance of tradition for that or any matter, rose
strong in Fergal, to agree, Oh, yes, too young: not fair, idealistic
fifteen blind and deaf to the realities of human life that is lived in
the body.

He stopped in the path and hesitated about going aside to the
house. If he should find Hugh here— And when he met McCann
here, forty-six hours ago, the woman with that colored bruise down
her cheek, saying so quick, *I fell against the hearthstone . . .*

He was saved the decision. She had heard his step, and came

to the door—alone. The bruise had faded a little. "Oh, Fergal—I wondered if it was you. I'm happy you're back safe."

"Kevin's taken the horses up, he'll likely be home in half an hour." No, she didn't look a cold woman, that way or any other—only, he thought suddenly, an unloved woman: forlorn was the word in his mind for her.

"That's—good," she said. "I'll start a meal, then. That is kind in Kevin, to take up the horses, save you the extra way. Good luck you had?"

"Yes. He'll tell you."

Maire McCann said softly, "Will he? Yes, Fergal. You're wanting to get home, of course—Nessa will be worried until you're safe in. She doesn't show it, but worry for you she does. And Shevaun, of course. I'll be expecting Kevin then, soon or late."

And for that, and his idle wondering thought about her—tired as he was, the desire rose a little in him (Nessa, warm and hungry in the dark), and he said, "I know, Maire, I'll get on," and he turned down the track toward home.

The old woman was upset— pouncing on him as he came in, babbling desultory thanks to God he was home safe, rattling on incomprehensibly in her excitement. "My best I did by her mother, O'Breslin, but God making some that way— His own purpose, or maybe the devil—my own granddaughter!—Tadgh did use to say—but I'd not have you think I knew and didn't say—"

"All right, Eily," said Fergal, dropping the bags. "Let me take a breath! What's all this about?"

"I'll tell him, Eily," said Nessa. "Don't upset yourself, no one blames you." She exchanged a glance with Shevaun, who took the old woman's arm and coaxed her to the settle.

"Indeed, and what I say is good riddance, and you should have listened to both Nessa and me last year, Fergal. We've had enough uproar about this, and Liam up out of a sickbed thinking he'd need to save us all from murder—likely having a relapse for it now—for the love of heaven, Nessa, take him off private to hear the story!"

"I will." She gave him a little push toward their chamber, followed him in and shut the door.

"Now what in God's name has happened here?" And damn, even in the midst of his alarm and curiosity, he was conscious of the desire, facing her there so close. He untied the throat-strings of his cloak and slung it to the pallet. Thinking on the way, damn this close living in this cramped little cabin!—man couldn't take his wife off private in broad day, without the rest of the household—And here, this excuse, whatever it was, shutting them in together. He pulled her into his arms and kissed her; he muttered, "I'll listen in awhile, girl—"

She kissed him back hard, her arms tight round him. "Always give thanks when you're safe home, Fergal—" But she held him away, resisting his arms. "You'd best listen now," she told him firmly, a brief smile in her eyes. "Well, isn't it a man I have, coming in from two days' ride hot to make love!—now, mind, I said we must talk—"

"We lay up most of yesterday," he laughed into her loosened hair, "not quite all so studdish I am! Nessa—"

"Now," and she pushed him away. "Serious this is, you must know at once. Mind your manners and pay attention."

"I will—five minutes. Tell it short." He sat down on the pallet, back to the wall, and watched her pleasurably as she fumbled at her hair, resetting pins, smoothing the knot.

"Well, I don't know as I can . . . oh, *damnation*—excuse it, but we will all be looking like wild women soon, if hairpins continue so scarce! I'd only just enough left, and there is another prong broke! . . . It's Ailsa, Fergal. She's gone for good—where, I don't know."

"You don't tell me. Household in a turmoil for that?" He laughed shortly. "Good riddance indeed."

"Mhmm?" Nessa glanced at him sidewise, over hairpins held in her teeth. "You don't mind—"

"Oh, for God's sake! You know I never gave a damn— Mind having one less mouth to feed! Didn't I say it to McCann yesterday, should have been rid o' the girl long ago. The way she's acted to you and Shevaun—and bone-idle—"

"For all but the one thing! Well, it was a turmoil, how it happened. You know Shevaun and I both saw that ivory comb, and told you. It seems old Eily heard us talking of it, and asked Ailsa direct where she had it—yesterday this was. Ailsa said it was no one's affair but her own, and Eily said she'd long ago given up expecting decency of the girl for men, but a matter like this, she'd a right to know and so had you. And Ailsa said—" Nessa gave him a look half humorous, half rueful. He laughed again.

"No need for a blow-by-blow account! I can hear them. Two hound-bitches snapping."

"It was rather like that—really frightful, Fergal, the set-to it turned into—Ailsa was furious, the things Eily said, and Shevaun lost her temper and joined in with Eily, and I said this and that myself. I daresay we were heard in the village! Ailsa was quite beside herself at the last, she threw the fire-tongs at me and went for Shevaun with the poker—"

"My good Christ! She didn't—"

"No, she didn't hit me, and Liam came running out and caught her and got the poker away from her—Ailsa bit his arm—and he said this and that, you know, I'd never seen him out of temper before but he was for certain then! And Ailsa screamed out she'd stayed longer in this dull house than she'd ever wanted, Eily insisting on it, and not a minute more she'd stay now—" Nessa stopped and eyed him thoughtfully. "And ins and outs to that you know well enough."

"So I do. She's deviled me since you and I were wed, trying to coax me into lying with her even once—and I trust you know well enough, not because she was specially interested in me as a lover, but just to make trouble in the house."

Nessa laughed. "Men. Never as much they know about women as they like to think. That was some of the reason, but mostly it was to get back at me. For being a lady—for having given her orders back at Lough Eask, and here at first—for that she knew I despise her—and because she thought the same as you thought— once—that I'd tricked you into wedding me. Oh, she's sly, she knew most of what went on. . . . But all this, it was just what went before. She said she'd leave here for good, for a better life, and she went to collect her things—and both Shevaun and I with the same thought, that it'd not be beyond her to take Shevaun's things, or whatever else she could bundle away quick—you know—so we made her pack up everything under our eyes. She was—just contemptuous, then. Reckoning on being done with all of us, so she didn't care what we saw. Fergal, she had all sorts of things hidden under her clothes, besides that comb. A lady's velvet reticule, like Englishwomen carry, and a pot of French-made rouge, and half a dozen silver-gilt buttons, and some good bone hairpins, and a ring—a trumpery thing only gilt, with a French-paste emerald—and it was in a little linen case that had *four steel needles* stuck in it! Four! And—"

"Do you say," said Fergal slowly. "Yes, loot of—one sort or another, I see. Wait a bit, that says something to me." Now his impulse to passion was cold in him, and his mind was working. "Ten days, two weeks back, there was that peddler killed and robbed up near Boyle—fellow called Costello out of Galway town, he made the rounds of all Connacht with his wares twice a year or so, regular, and folk knew when to expect him. Didn't I hear you and Shevaun saying, last fall when he came by, he'd said he'd have needles for sale this spring? And you were talking of it a bit ago, expecting him along, wondering how much he'd be asking."

"Yes. We both thought of him—all his pack stripped, they said, when he was attacked. And—what is it now?"

"Nothing," said Fergal. "Go on." Nothing relevant. Faint, unfamiliar odor in the house these last few days, not really unpleasant—as Maire had said—just different: the dried cakes of horse-dung burning. A good half-sack there had been. See Lynch tomorrow, bargain for some turf.

"Well," Nessa took a breath, "we said a few more things—not able to help it, you know!—and she bundled everything up quick and started out. But like as if she had to have the last word, she just flung it back, she halfway out the door—if we were so mad to know where she came by all that, and we jealous for it, well, no law there is about giving presents, and that's what it was—presents from better men than those in this house, her cousin Larr Mc-Fergus and Art McTally! And she banged the door after her, and off she went."

"McFergus and McTally!" Fergal was motionless one moment, and then sprang up to his feet. "But—" He did not hear what else Nessa went on to say. The two names occupied his whole mind, one astonished second, and then, smooth and easy, the whole picture took shape and color and showed itself to him.

He did not hear himself swear—and it was less curse than prayer, for such a Christ-damned fool.

All the little pieces of the picture he'd had, and never put them together until now. Had the wit to put them together.

A stupid child struggling with a difficult lesson: and when it was learned, how very damned simple it looked!

"Fergal—what is it?"

He looked at her without seeing her. "Christ," he said quietly. All the little pieces.

Dried horse-dung. Lasted well, yes, but not so slow-burning that two horses would keep up any sort of supply; and he had said so; and Maire had answered with curious emphasis, not *quite*. Two! Seven, nine, how many horses?

Won't you go up the hill and meet Kevin, Fergal? The sharp little disappointed sigh when he said he'd not bother.

That's kind in Kevin to take up the horses. . . . Fallen into a habit, that had—how many months?—coming back that way, no sense both of them going all the way up to the clearing. *Where those hireling raiders had once their shelter.*

He had not been up there for five months. Met McCann at the house, by dusk—he fetching the horses down.

Ivory comb, lady's reticule, gilt buttons, gimcrack ring, French rouge. Unsalable things, whatever intrinsic value, here and now. Sort of things, taken along with more valuable loot, a man would give away careless to a girl—please her without real cost to himself. Except the needles, so valuable, and even men like that would be generous on occasion.

Hugh. As well as her—won't you go up the hill, O'Breslin? And why the hell hadn't either of them talked plain and open?

Last several months, these outlaws living on the run attacking fifty houses roundabout. And more: peddlers, that one and others. And across the border, times, for the better plunder. What Carmody said—some few English there, factors, their wives, a landowner here and there coming to see his new holding: and the tenants just a bit better off than folk here.

Kevin McCann, the bold raider-chief. The wife-beater. Look in his eyes when Carmody said that, *a bit better off*—speculation in his eyes, maybe wiser move across the border permanent, better plunder, and English patrols about the same strength either side.

"Fergal!" said Nessa. She sounded a little frightened. "What is it? You look—"

"Christ," he said again. Hugh, saying irrelevantly, Men like Edmund Kearney, amiable mask by day . . . Saying, Those former men of yours. Why the *hell* not talking plain?

"But would he dare?" he whispered to himself. "Would they dare?" And a small, nearly forgotten echo of his own thought awhile back—maybe that half-underground shelter up there warmer in winter than another kind of house. That was it, of course.

"Fergal—where are you going? What—"

He turned with his hand on the door. Absently he said, "Yes, I had better take that," and came back and opened the little chest where he kept his clothes, and found the handgun. The English pistol he'd taken off that Parliament deserter—he and Hugh coming up through Galway on way to rendezvous with Roy Donlevy at Knockmagh—a lifetime ago, a year ago last month. There was a handful of powder in a sack, and five bullets. He loaded and primed the pistol, and his hand was steady; he put the powder and remaining bullets in his pocket. He cocked the hammer; it had the hell of a hard action, it wouldn't go off by accident. No, that it would not: if that hammer snapped down, it would be for his finger on the trigger-pull, and if it wasn't Kevin McCann out front of the barrel, it would be Art McTally.

Tom Carmody, tenant-farmer, and all the rest like him over the border.

Cover, damn' useful cover—the double play!—McCann offering this and that in exchange, or for sale. Oh, well, middling common knowledge it is, McCann rides over with O'Breslin, that's where he'll have had it. Average of one raid a week the two of them making, this winter! Sure to Christ, Kevin had had leisure to spend! Kevin McCann, *a deal with them I made:* so easy and accommodating to Fergal O'Breslin (who had all but charged him with murder, that Kearney affair!) and generous over division of loot. Couldn't he afford to be!—Fergal O'Breslin his cover, and cover for the rest of those bastards!

He put the pistol in his pocket. He said to Nessa, and it came out casual and absent, "I'm going up to see McCann. There's a thing between us to settle, once for all." He went straight out, all his tiredness forgotten and everything else but this one vital, fearful matter.

He left the track almost at once and made a circle about the approach to McCann's house, going up the hill through trees. As he came above the level where the house stood, a hundred yards left, he moved more cautious, keeping as far as possible in the trees, dropping flat to crawl in cover across open spaces. He moved up the hill diagonal, taking time to it to go unheard and unseen, as patient and skillful as ever he'd stalked game in the hills of Tyrconnell—or English sentries across seven counties—or any other kind of game.

The clearing lay in a slight hollow at the top of the hill, like a dish with a rim—trees all around, and they had put up a rude fence closing in most of it northeast, apart from the sod house: makeshift rope and unsawn logs between the trees there, and in the open, posts, with rope and logs between—for the horse-pasture. Fergal went up the other side of the slope, northwest, not to let the horses hear and betray they heard. Once he scared up a hare, that scuttered before him in panicky bounds, making brief crashing in the bracken, and a jay chattered in alarm; he froze where he was, long minutes, before going on.

Twenty yards from the dish-rim of the hollow clearing, he dropped flat and crawled the rest of the way. He heard, as he inched silent over turf and through new grass, men's voices up there; he heard the excited whimper of a dog, and went cold—but he crawled on.

He heard Art McTally laugh, free and high. Art, coming just this far when ordered away, and not long after, all the rest of them having to run, after that Kearney business. Roving band of outlaws—not roving long!—coming to winter here, secret, and McCann riding with them by night as they went to plunder—and kill when necessary—anywhere and everywhere. Other Irishmen, across the border.

He lay prone, half behind the twisted trunk of an old oak, hidden by tall-grown weeds, and looked down across the clearing. A good view he had.

McTally and Dermot Flynn were playing at a wrestling-bout just down from the sod-shelter door. Stripped to trews they were, well-matched in size, only McTally showing a chestful of curly black hair and Flynn hairless, powerful-muscled fine body cleaner-lined. Looking on, calling advice, laughing, McKenna, O'Shea, Larr McFergus—and Kevin McCann, much at home with this whole bastardly crew, sure to God he would be. Women—of course, women—three anonymous slatterns, in the crowd about the wrestlers, and Ailsa, shrieking excited advice now to Art, now to Flynn. And two people sitting apart, not together. Dan Kindellan, paying no attention to the play—nearer Fergal, propped against the fence, mending a bit of harness. Serious, moody look on the work in his hands. And a woman—girl—just sitting quiet, staring into space. Fergal had seen that one before, and in a moment he placed her. Burke's daughter, stolen away with them that night.

There were twelve horses inside the fence. And alongside McKenna there, a big gray wolfhound. Stolen or found: some highbred dogs and hounds left homeless now, uncaught to be killed for food the last year. Wolfhound, kept only by gentry in the old days, wouldn't McKenna be pleased to master one? Maybe one of the trained hounds with a chief's troops, equal to a horseman in a close fight.

But at the two odd folk out, Fergal looked again, and out of the numbing-cold fury possessing him felt remote pity. The girl he could guess about. Cowed and brutal-used into dull apathy now. If you gave her the choice, come away home to your mother, or stay, she'd likely say expressionless, It's no matter either way. . . . And Kindellan he knew about. Guilt, yes, but no scale weighing it true. Kindellan the slow-witted, humble farmer, used to obedience, anxious for praise, no idea of his own ever in his head, naturally following any group of men he found himself in. It'd take him twice the time as another man to mend that bridle, but a good honest job he'd make of it. Tenant-farmer in Waterford all his days, Kindellan would never have raised a hand against any. He'd be vague-troubled about what he was into now, trying to puzzle it out—going along with them because he knew nought else to do —keeping, clumsy-shy, away from the women—misliking much the others did, but helpless to stand out, or go to fend for himself.

Fergal lay there five minutes, looking and listening, rock-still and breathing shallow. He forgot Kindellan, and thought about his own situation—and McCann. Important thing here, scotch the whole lot of them, but especially McCann. Couldn't attack them single-handed. Get out, and very damn' quick and quiet, and go down to rouse the village—collect enough men, and they with a score to pay off—thirty men—and come back to deploy round-about, in concerted attack.

He slid backward, cautious, to begin silent retreat.

McTally had the seventh fall on Flynn; they got up laughing, and the women were shrieking laughter. The wolfhound had been intent on them like the rest, but now got to its feet, and turned uneasily to scan the wood. Fergal marked the hound, and his heart sank cold. A bitch-hound, always keener to give warning—and join a fight—and she showed bare patches on flanks and neck, where she had borne the army-harness, collar and belt set with spikes sharp-filed: a war-trained hound she was.

She put her head out, sniffing, and rose up on McKenna, pawing at him. Trained not to bay, but give silent information—a stranger nearby! She was a good bitch, likely she'd served some Irish troops well, and it was sharp ache in Fergal's heart to do it; but she'd give more trouble than four men together. If these bastards were to be caught and brought to justice— He took careful aim, and he heard himself whisper, "God forgive me, good girl, but it'll be quick."

The shot was shocking noise, the very moment they took the warning and turned, stiffening, to look where she led. The bullet took her clean in the front flank; she was dead before she fell.

Fergal was on his feet and running, heedless of noise now, knowing they'd be after in full strength. He couldn't stop to reload the pistol; they were only twenty yards behind. Canny: practiced: spreading out behind him and below, to drive him northwest—over to the open track and toward McCann's place.

But McCann was with them. Too near. Fergal thought coldly, a fool I was to get up and run. The bitch out of action, I might have lain hid however close they hunted. Maybe. Too late now. He slid down a steep place, and the open track was before him. And the cabin, its back to the trees, ten yards up the other side of the track.

McTally and McCann yelping to each other, behind.

The door was open, and Maire McCann stood there, shielding her eyes from the sun, looking up the hill. And Hugh McFadden was just coming up the track.

Fergal took the open space in a dozen dodging, desperate strides, calling to her as he came. "Out o' the way—let me in, Maire—Hugh, to me, quick!—in and shut the door—" He hit the doorpost with a thud, avoiding her, turned and shoved her inside, and Hugh was on the threshold as the door swung. Fergal pulled him in and slammed the door. There was an iron bolt, and he shot it.

Outside, a pistol spoke, and the bullet smashed through the door-panel and hit the iron kettle across the room. It clanged loud, and echoed the noise lingeringly.

18

HUGH MCFADDEN MOVED quickly to pull the woman from line of the door. And that was the first time he had touched Maire. It was the new Hugh McFadden had the practical wit to do it: more and more these thirteen months, frighteningly, not feeling in himself like any Hugh McFadden he'd ever been before.

He looked at Fergal O'Breslin there, against the opposite wall, and even as he spoke another part of his mind remembered the hour they had met—oh, another Hugh indeed that was, panicked by pursuit, babbling about a precious manuscript-book of history. That man, there in the wood in Clare, he'd only just been born into the world, halfway through his life; this grown-up man had no impulse to babble. He said, "So you've found out, O'Breslin. And letting them know!" Anger in him for that, because it put the woman in danger. Young, hot-hearted O'Breslin, always action and not thought!

Fergal was recharging the handgun. "Love of God, man, did I mean to? Didn't know they had a hound to get wind o' me!—meant to get down and rouse the village." He looked up from the pistol, and uncannily took Hugh back to that other day: just the same gesture and look as when he'd shaken that frightened robed lay-brother and said *Hold your loose tongue!*—the arrogant line of jaw stained with stubble of dark beard, and the strong neck-muscle visible for open-necked shirt as he turned his head to listen, wary. "Christ," he said, "what the *hell* made me run here, into a trap? Mind not working—to think account of the woman, his wife, being here—but don't I know Kevin better than that, think it'd make a difference—and the rest of those whoresons too!"

"That you should indeed," said Hugh. "Are they all out there? They know who they're chasing?"

"McCann and McTally will have sighted me across the open. And why in Christ's name you didn't tell me—either of you—you knew, what you said the other day—"

"No, Hugh did not know," said Maire quietly. "I thought—I could be brave enough to tell you, Fergal—no matter how Kevin said he would kill me, when I found out, if I said one word to any. But I have—I have been afraid of him so long now—" She put trembling hands to her mouth. "I tried," she whispered. "I hoped you'd understand—and—bring it open, have this wickedness done—"

Hugh took one step nearer her, but he was looking at the other man. "But I did know, Maire." And that was the first time he had spoken her name. All the times here, long quiet talk between them, but impersonal—because—oh, because they both knew, and were both afraid, of themselves. "I heard him say that to you, I was at the door that day you talked of it. You must have guessed I knew—and I tried to warn O'Breslin, but I dared not be open, to have McCann believing it was you. I know him too, Maire, I know he meant that threat."

"All right, I'm a blind fool!" said Fergal.

And Kevin McCann's voice called from the other side of the door, "Fergal, boy, you can hear me?" No more shots; he sounded nearly genial.

"I can hear you, Kevin."

"And your pistol recharged!" McCann laughed. "Don't think it'll be much use to you. Maybe the game was almost played out anyway. Damn' fools, Art and Larr, to pass plunder on to that girl, but soon or late you finding out another way—if it wasn't another way than that. What brought you up, Fergal?—did Maire tell you?"

Hugh opened his mouth to answer that, desperate, but Fergal spoke first. "Three and two I put together for myself, Kevin—and should have three months back!"

"In a temper you sound," said McCann; he was close to the door. "You've too tender a conscience. So the game's done, and I can't say I'm sorry. Bored I've been getting for it of late, putting up a front of domesticity! We've been thinking of moving on, with the winter past, to find a better hunting-ground. But I'd prefer to start off in organized train! A bargain I'll offer you. . . . Put up the gun a minute, Dermot, give us a chance to settle it peaceful."

"I've made my last bargain with you, Kevin McCann."

And Flynn, near too: "Don't waste breath, Kevin, make an end to the lot, the easiest way, give ourselves time to get out!"

"I said, put up the pistol! Who's leader here? Fergal, boy. One advantage to dealing with such a stiff-necked man of honor. Give me your word you'll not set foot out o' this house, to go and send men after us, for six full hours, and we'll go peaceful, right now. No discussion—yes or no! Seven of us men, and none of us with your softness, boy. There's a woman in there with you—if you say the wrong word I'll fire the house and make a job—enough of us to see you don't get out. And down there at your place, only a new-bearded boy to put up a fight—maybe you've hinted your knowledge to your household, too—a job we'd make there as well. Except for your wife, Fergal—too pretty a woman to die young— I think we'd take her along, we're short a woman apiece."

"You heard what I said, Kevin." But Fergal's voice was uneven; his hand shook as he lifted the gun.

Hugh took another step nearer the woman. He thought confusedly, fire: flames of hell: and he inviting them maybe, oh, God, the thoughts and feelings in him. This man new-born to life. Long back, oh, yes—not new thought and feeling it was—the awful need and desire gripping his body: the Prior saying, the devil's temptation—the Prior saying, prayer and fasting . . . She stood there white and erect, like image of saint on tomb, and his body and spirit and all that was Hugh McFadden, new or old, was violent-wrenched for her beauty, her helplessness, her aloneness.

"Maire," said the voice outside softly, "unbolt the door. . . . You hear me, Maire? An order I'm giving you. You know what to expect, do you disobey my orders. Unbolt the door."

And Fergal O'Breslin was the man threatened, the man bringing this on them, but she looked at Hugh. Their eyes locked, and he knew all of Maire McCann that minute, the little left he had not known. . . . Come here he had, powerless to help himself, to this woman—telling himself lies about kindness and charity, for awhile—making excuses like that to come—fighting all the feeling in him, and abandoning his soul to the devil—and at the last, now, by God's grace he could say honest he was seeing it clear and sane. If it was the devil telling him that, he was not strong enough to fight it anymore. . . . A dubious peace at Clonmacnoise, and refuge in the books he loved; but he had not chosen that compromise, not at uncertain fifteen. Nothing else known, and a fine thing to dedicate oneself to God's service, but—but—

No, nought new, one part of this hunger in him. But the greatest part of it new, the personal part; not need-for-female, but beyond and above that primality: Maire. All that was important to any Hugh McFadden, whether he belonged to God or Satan. And a place he had come to where he could not believe a kind God looked wrathful on what He had arranged. Like so much else in life, this was made to mean sometimes good, sometimes evil. And when it was for the true loving, it was for good.

Their eyes met, and after all their formal cautious talk together, the admittal was naked and honest between them, this one last moment. *I have gone all my life unloved,* they said to one another, *and I love you beyond life or death or God.*

"Open the door, Maire!" said McCann, savage.

She said clear and loud, "If you will come in to do murder, Kevin McCann, you'll ram the door down before I open to you! I have taken my last order."

And Fergal said, sudden and desperate, "Give me a minute, Kevin—your bargain I'll consider!" He made a fierce gesture at Hugh and Maire with the pistol, motioning them to the back of the one room, far away from the door as they could go.

"Two minutes' grace!" said McCann.

Fergal pulled Hugh close to breathe into his ear, "I'll get out the window—if there's not a man on guard—try to make it down to the village. If I gain three minutes' start—hold them as long as you can!" He thrust the pistol into his pocket.

You can try, thought Hugh; but if you make it, not back in time you'd be. The one little window was not boarded shut for the winter: of course McCann had not troubled to do that much for her comfort; she had fastened a square of blanket over it, makeshift. That was pulled away easy; Fergal hoisted himself up, got one leg through. A last glimpse they had of him, wearing taut grimace for the effort of moving silent, holding himself away from scraping the house-wall as he slid down. He was gone; they heard a faint rustle in the undergrowth under the window, and then nothing. No guard there, at least.

"Hugh," she said softly, "I am so sorry to bring this on you."

"It is no matter, in the end," he said evenly. "I am glad to be here." He went to the hearth and took up the poker: an ancient one, tip burned away and twisted, but still a weight of iron, a weapon of sorts.

They stood motionless, the width of the room between them, and looked at one another, and listened. And in the silence his whisper carried: he did not know if those outside the door could hear, and he did not care. "Maire—Maire. Many a night's sleep you have cost me—and now it seems all empty as the wind. Foolish little quibbling—over what rules men have made, not God."

And she whispered in return, "I'm so sorry, Hugh. You shouldn't have come—making excuse—and I wanting you to come. They—men like you—different-seeming, but I knew—but it's all changed now, here and now—"

"Yes," he said. It was strange, how long two minutes could be: time for long thought and memory in a man's mind. In just ten seconds or so now, McCann would be challenging from beyond the door, and would know; and after that, it would be however God meant. . . . That was what the Archbishop had said, *changed.*

He had spoken a little of it to the Archbishop, his soul-searching for it. Brothers in Christ of the order of Francis were not under diocesan churchmen, but responsible only to the Holy Father in Rome; but the Archbishop was an experienced, learned churchman, a man to consult in trouble. His look had been grave and compassionate, and he had said that. "Do not think you are alone, brother, in these times. I trust I am a devout Catholic, but this I will say—in Ireland these last years, it is easy for a man to mistake his vocation to your calling." Yes; the order's rules sent its members into the world, on the Church's business, mingling with lay-folk; but here, these fifty years, men of God must live secret from the law, and so they lived away from the world of men. Since his fifteenth year he had been—the only word—away, and he had made himself find that dubious peace, and be content in it. "Not alone you are," the Archbishop had said. "Many of you thrust out—into life, as it were—who would perhaps have learned, before ever you took vows, that your call to God was not true or strong enough, had you ever known life, before. I am not able to advise you, my brother. All that is in my heart to say to you—any of you so troubled—it is that God is very merciful, and very loving, and all-understanding of humankind."

If nought else was sure in life or death, that was sure. Hugh felt the weight of the iron poker in his hand, and he smiled at her. "Maire," he said, "it is all right, we're in God's care still, and forever will be. God can be wrath, but He is always love—and that means all the kinds of love there are, Maire. Just now, I've come to understand that, and to find peace for the understanding. Life or death, Maire—no matter—any kind of loving better than not-loving. Maybe God's one secret rule of life, that is."

McCann said sharp and cold from outside, "Fergal! Your time's long up! Yes or no!"

"Don't you fear, my heart," said Hugh. "I'll not let him hurt you, this side death." He turned and went to the door; he raised his voice. "Now give O'Breslin a chance, McCann! It's no trivial thing you ask of him!"

Silence, one heartbeat; and then McCann uttered an obscenity, his tone shockingly ordinary. "The window—Dermot, McKenna!" Too old a campaigner to be tricked for two seconds. Suddenly, all exploded into noise outside: men running, heavy steps in bracken: men shouting. McCann cursing himself for a fool, his voice receding— "Kindellan! Watch the door—fire the second it opens!"

It meant curiously little to Hugh McFadden. He looked at her, as if memorizing the shape and color of her. . . . McCann would doubtless be back. Nor just this minute there was no space in him for caring if Fergal O'Breslin was safe away, to rouse justice on the evil men—and he had some regard for Fergal. All noise and confusion about: but for the first time in half a year he had found peace within himself, and peace with God.

There was shooting, down the hill. The terrier-bark of pistols, the hound-bay of matchlocks.

"Don't you fear, Maire," he said.

Her dark eyes were steady on his, and a light deep in them. "I am not afraid, Hugh."

* * *

Neither of them had moved when McCann came again, ten long minutes after. Again, men running past, the other way: angered, excited men. McCann, breathless and sharp—"All right, Dan—up with the others! We're getting out, quick!—I'll follow, five minutes." His fist smashed on the door. "Maire, let me in!—oh, Christ damn it—" And then his shoulder to the door.

The whole house poor slat-board: the bolt held, but at the third blow the partition splintered in a long gaping crack, and he reached in to draw the bolt. He flung the door inward to crash on the wall, and stood there looking at them—cold-angered, triumphant, vindictive, excited.

"And if I'd time or if it'd be any profit, I'd see you two dead as well as Fergal O'Breslin!"

Behind Hugh, she made a little sound of pity and grief. "Did you kill him, McCann?" said Hugh. "O'Breslin who was your friend in boyhood, another place and a better time?"

"Friendship a luxury I do without. People useful to me or not, and no sentiment tied to it! He'd ceased to be useful. He is dead, down the hill—and damn him to bring this on in such a hurry!" McCann was across the room, flinging clothes at random into a saddlebag. "Some man may just wonder who had the powder for all that shooting, and come up to see. And no telling if he said aught to his own household—" He straightened from lashing the bag; he laughed, and started toward the woman, smiling. "Feared I'll take you along, Maire? By God, I'll be glad to be done with you!"

"McCann," said Hugh gently, "not a hand on the woman, or by the God I have served, you are a dead man."

"You—" said McCann; he threw back his head and laughed. "Oh, by God, yes, two thoughts for that I take, haste or no! One way, I ought to be hot to kill you both—men jesting behindhand—Kevin McCann, the hell of a man he must be, his wife laying up with a monk! But second thought, you'll have longer torture than I've time to give, do I leave you to each other—these tame little farmers roundabout shunning you for sinners, and the both of you with outsize consciences to tell you the devil's got lease of your souls! My jest, that is—and I'll be laughing at it often, think of you—aren't you a match for each other!—coming to hate each other, on account I let you live. Better vengeance!"

"God pity you, Kevin McCann—there is a lease on your own soul, and I think it is a short-term lease." It was a queer impersonal pity one moment flooding Hugh: this young, handsome man in pride of strength, the bold confidence like an extra cloak slung around him, tangible. Everything—and nothing—about him to envy.

"Oh, my timid-sinning little monk! Is he any good to you at making the beast with two backs, Maire, or do you maybe take all your pleasure holding hands? A matched pair, safe enough!—you don't-touch-me, you keep-out-o'-my-bed!" He seized hold of her, pulled her up to face him close. "No use to me you were, but for the dowry—won't it be a relief to be rid of you for good! Maybe I should be thanking the fellow, to take you off my hands—if he's the guts to, open, which I doubt! And if he doesn't, you can starve for all o' me, and good riddance!"

"I warned you, McCann—not a hand on her—"

Maire did not flinch away. "There was a time I was eager-willing to be a good wife to you, Kevin. But too much you like giving pain—all the ways you can."

McCann said viciously, "Oh, take your pale little joy of each other, you two!—and is there aught true in what the priests tell, may you burn in the devil's personal cauldron for it!" He struck her backhanded across the breast, sudden and hard, and she staggered back to fall against the table and lie still. Hugh sprang at him, the poker raised to strike, and McCann stepped out lazy and contemptuous, and left-handed knocked him back to sprawl on the hearthstone, and flung the dropped poker after him.

"Still on speaking terms with your God, give thanks I've not time to see the two of you die slow—as I'd like!" He showed his wolf's white smile, and snatched up the dropped bag, and took two strides out. Ten steps away, he began to run, light and swift, up the hill.

Hugh got to his feet and wiped the blood from his mouth. He shut the door and dragged the table against it to hold it so, and came back to kneel and lift her. And affection he'd had for Fergal O'Breslin, but this moment that grief was remote in him, absorbed with her as he was. He carried her across to the pallet by the hearth, and he meant to lay her down there, but when he had, he was cold for lack of her weight against him, and he half-lifted her again in his arms.

All the long while, foolishly fighting—what was of God. His arms trembling a little for her warm weight and her nearness. "Maire, Maire," he murmured. All untried on his tongue, the words of love, all passed over unused, the long sterile years, all unpracticed his eager young-feeling body at this way to say it, *I love you.*

Her dark lovely eyes opened on him. "Hugh—Hugh—he's not hurt you?" she gasped. She lifted a hand to his cheek.

As if instinctively he turned his mouth to her palm. "Maire, my heart's dearest," and that came out of some deep instinct too, older than himself, the words easy in his mouth. "All right you are, my heart, my life?" So queer, so queer—the quiet airy chamber at the monastery of Clonmacnoise, and he copying old manuscript. The Prior: "Secular verse, part of our race's literature, and thus worthy to be written down—but dangerous and troubling to the soul of such as we, and I so advise, brother, that you say a cleansing prayer afterward." Clear in his mind the words came back now, and all to guide him, teach him, the words out of the old Gaelic literature. *Love is no painful sickness: what they say of it is false: no man was ever healthy that was not in love with a woman. . . .* "Maire, thou vein of my heart," he whispered. The little pulse beating there in the hollow of her throat, like a bird fluttering, and no conscious intention in his mind, but his mouth against it, and her arms warm and strengthening around him. *The dearest woman under the sun—I shall conceal it no longer—my love for her has left me senseless. . . .* The prayers said, he lying taut on hard pallet for the need and desire. Not only of the body, no, a lie it was: not God, Who made it to be, said so uncompromising, always sinful it is. That was false, a lie men had told. Not only, not always, of the carnal body: a thing of the spirit too, another facet of love, that was always from God. *A roaring flame has dissolved this heart of mine—*

He lifted his head a very little way, their mouths apart at last, and at last he said it, "I love you, Maire, I love you."

"Hugh," she said against his shoulder, "oh, God, don't let me go. Hugh, tell me—to be strong—put you away from me, I will try—my heart's darling—a man like you—Hugh, I love you."

"I'm not telling you," he said into the pulse in her throat. *I was in bondage to love.* . . . "Any kind of loving, my darling, it is God's—but were it not, I could not go from you—and God help me to tell you how I love you—" *Though I were to die for it* . . . The warm beautiful round breast under his hand, and her mouth again under his mouth. For the first time in all his life he felt wholly adult, he felt to be—any man—master and slave. . . . And the last conscious thought in his mind, Oh, yes, of God—from God: for, as close to heaven as any human can come, in life.

It was falling to dusk when Brian Donaghue trudged heavily up the track to that house. He was unsure what he would find there, and when he saw the broken door, he feared what he would find. Nothing he had said to the distracted women of what he thought, but there had scarce been need: Nessa had said it, they had all said it—*McCann.* And coming up, Donaghue had expected the smooth lie, the plausible disclaim of all knowledge—and he had meant to get past it to the truth, if the truth should show the wolf gone back wild, and shatter all pretense. He was not afraid of Kevin McCann; he would have taken him, and brought him down for justice.

But when he saw the door, he knew McCann was gone, and pretense gone too. Violence before and after—whatever brought it on—and maybe the woman also, and McCann fled, unable to hide guilt this time. Or gone to create a lie to back up a plausible hiding of guilt?

Donaghue went up to the door. "Maire McCann, are you there?" He did not expect a reply: dull surprise he felt to hear something pulled away from the door. Hugh McFadden it was opening to him, and the woman kindling a couple of rushlights, coming to speak his name and then Fergal's.

"Yes—you knew?—why did you not come, to tell, to—it was McCann?"

"We should have come," said Maire softly. "When they were gone, we should have, Hugh."

"What's happened here?" And even as Donaghue heard, took

in what Hugh was telling, another information showed itself to him, in the woman's lingering touch on McFadden's arm, the way they stood close, as if unconsciously leaning together, and a look he knew in a woman's eyes—the opulent peace of love fulfilled for the moment, to renew itself again. The man there, his voice incisive as Donaghue never remembered hearing it before: authority and strength in his very stance . . . A little gossip on it, that Ethne would never listen to . . . Both shock and pity rose in Donaghue's mind, but the pity stronger. He looked away from them, from their proud peace after passion. He said, "So they're gone, and McCann—in the open—as outlaw leader. A mercy he did not kill you both." And two ways that could be taken.

"I know that, Donaghue," said Hugh McFadden gravely. "It is a terrible thing, about O'Breslin. The body found, and that is why you came up—knowing it was McCann killed him. God have mercy on his soul, and for those women."

"Fergal is not dead, McFadden," said Donaghue heavily. "Not as yet. Three bullets in him, and deep, and bad places—I think one has touched his lung. I don't know if he will die. Yes, I found him—we have been working over him, trying—"

"Oh, I must go to Nessa," said Maire. "Hugh, we must go—"

"I'll come," said McFadden. "A little knowledge I have—pray God we can save him! I did not know, Donaghue, McCann said he was dead—I'd have gone—" And he caught his breath in a sigh, and in the near rushlight his eyes met Donaghue's, and read that Donaghue knew. He said quietly, sadly, "If you and all of them—would want me, would want us—to come, Donaghue."

Donaghue reached a hand to his arm, brief and awkward in friendliness. "Come, Hugh," he said.

19

NESSA WENT TO the door with Owen Desmond when he left. This soft June day, the door stood open, and a shaft of sunlight struck across the threshold; she raised a shielding hand to her temple, but not all against the bright light. "I don't know how to thank you, Owen. You know we're grateful, but it seems we've used up all the words to say it."

"Ah, what's a hare or two," said Desmond easily. "It won't be long before Fergal's out setting his own snares, now—by harvest he'll be taking his turn with the scythe."

"Yes," she said on a long sigh, "yes, he's so much better now." It was only this last few weeks she had begun to realize how much Desmond and Donaghue had done, had given: those two months before a long nightmare when time meant nothing, and nothing was really clear in her mind except all to do with Fergal: every little important change in him, good or bad, the continual care he needed, and the darker nightmare-times when they had thought he would die between one hour and the next. After he had somehow come back a little from the loss of all that blood, when the bullets were taken out with what skill Donaghue and Hugh had, there was the fever and lung-congestion coming on; and somehow nursing him past that; and then the terrible day there'd been a hemorrhage from the lung, the unhealed scar coming open in his chest—all of them certain he would die, all the blood lost again. And more fever, and the long time he lay, mending slowly but too weak to lift his head.

Since it had been sure he was recovering, she woke to realization that he would have died, and all the rest of them starved, likely, but for what Donaghue and Desmond had done—and Hugh helping as he could. Donaghue in a way might be said to have the responsibility for all he'd done—helping Liam get the crop sown, and sharing his own store of food, besides doctoring Fergal's hurts. But no call on Owen Desmond to be so generous—and sadly Nessa knew why he was. . . . Both of them bringing meat, and good bones for stock—strengthening things an ill man needed: and tending Fergal's rabbit-snares, and taking trouble to make good bargaining for the litter of weaned kittens, in Fergal's name. And not asking a share of the game they took on his land, and bringing game from theirs too.

"Good to see him looking himself again. And you, Nessa."

Nessa looked away from the love in his steady dark eyes that he could not conceal. She liked Owen Desmond, and was both sorry and embarrassed for this. She said, "I don't know how we'd have got on, without all you've done, Owen—you and the others." She saw Shevaun coming round the side of the house, and that worry caught at her. "Owen—there's been no word of that peddler expected?"

He followed her glance; before he could answer, Shevaun was up to them and asking the same question, had he heard aught, passing through the village? "No, I'm sorry, nothing." The light died from her eyes. Peddlers, wandering about and all of them getting most of their wares in the port of Galway, were always the letter-carriers. There had been no more letters from Roy Donlevy since that first one, last October, eight and a half long months ago. Fergal had written to him then, and Shevaun too; and Shevaun had written thrice since. But nothing had come in return.

"Owen's brought us two fine hares, look." And Shevaun managed a smile and thanks. Desmond said again he must be off, and started down the hill; Nessa knew he held himself from looking back as he turned into the road. She said, "Never mind, Shevaun, the peddler will be coming through soon enough, and very likely with a letter this time. Maybe Roy's been out on a campaign somewhere, no chance to write." A thing they had been saying often and hopefully.

"Yes," said Shevaun. The boy came running up from play, face alight, and she bent to hug him with unwonted hardness, so that he yelped in half-protest.

"Oh, Mother, you've not gone to milk Etain yet? May I go to watch when you milk her? May I—"

"Yes, little nuisance, of course you may—I will be going in awhile, I'll call you to come." She glanced at Nessa: "Mother's here? She said she would come today—there," to the boy, "your grandmother is within and will like to see you. But go quiet—in your uncle Fergal's chamber she is, and we mustn't disturb him, is he asleep."

"Ooh, I'll be quiet, I will—has Granddam her little baby now?—why not, Mother?—when will she have it?"

"In three months, and that is three eternities to you, youngling! And remember what I've said, don't go flinging yourself at her or climbing in her lap. In with you, now." He ran in, and Shevaun leaned on the doorpost, looking down the hill to the road. She put up a work-roughened hand to finger the frayed neck of her gown, and said softly, "Yes, Nessa, I know what you're thinking. As well, maybe, you miscarried the babe, and not so far along to make it a bad illness to you. What with us being so near the bone as we are, with Fergal—But—I know how you feel."

"*Something* it would be," murmured Nessa. Little Sean, so well-grown for five years, a handsome small one, so quick and bright and mischievous.

"Something," said Shevaun on a long indrawn breath. "Oh, God, but—! Every time I look at him, I am seeing Roy—Roy. . . ." She turned her face to the house-wall in sudden taut anguish. "Not—not everything it is, the child."

Nessa put an arm about her in futile comfort. "I know, Shevaun, I know."

After a moment Shevaun took another painful breath. "I was up the hill to see Maire and Hugh. You see . . . I don't know how God feels for it, Nessa, maybe they are both doing great sin, maybe it is a—a terrible wrong thing, like most of the village-people think, and even Mother feeling it's wrong, for all she sympathizes, in a way. I just don't know—but—to see them together, oh, Nessa, it's like to break my heart, to kill me of—wanting. . . . They're so—it's like as if you stepped inside a fairy-charmed circle, they living in it—the peace in them—"

"Oh, yes, I know," whispered Nessa, "I know." For she had been in that house up the hill too, and those two coming here; how could any of them say to Hugh and Maire, do not come?—feel that they hosted evil? Both so kind and good, coming to help, and even giving things of the little they had. Maire helping every week with the washing, and it was Hugh had finally stopped the frightening hemorrhage that day, with a certain kind of moss he knew and went hunting. Unkindness they'd had from the village-folk, most people roundabout, who said so righteous, black sin—a vowed monk, an unfaithful wife! But Nessa couldn't feel they were wicked, knowing them: nor it didn't seem that anything sinful could make such happiness and content. A fairy-circle, Shevaun said: it was like that, a circle of shining peace all round them, for their loving and being together. Quite different they both were, and yet still themselves—as if somehow they'd turned into the people they were meant to be.

A queer way to think, and likely Father O'Marron would say all wrong; but privately Nessa thought that was the truth of it. Both of them taking a wrong road, and then suddenly coming back on the right one; and it must be by God's grace, or they wouldn't be—as they were. Nobody knowing Hugh could say he was a bad man, and that was how he felt. All Maire's old stiff shyness gone, that had maybe just been fear of life itself for the hurts it had brought her . . . And you'd think that Hugh, being what he'd been, would feel guilt on him even happy as he was, but instead—he had said it once to Nessa, they talking alone—something like the peace of God had come over him. "And it's not in my heart to believe I'd feel so, were God wrathful for me or Maire. I know in my mind, all the laws for such things, they say we're wrong—but God sees into our hearts, to judge us for ourselves—and not always by men's rules, or even those men say He has made—and how do we know that is true? You don't feel Maire's wicked, for that she's unfaithful to a bad husband? Or I, because—"

"How could any of us feel that, Hugh?" And remembering his gift of the kitten, now the sleek supercilious Shena, whose litter of kits had bought an extra blanket for Fergal, and new seed for the fields, Nessa kissed his cheek. She thought but didn't say that anyway when you went over to the devil you had something for it of worldly reward, so all the tales said; and heaven knew Hugh and Maire hadn't.

She hadn't been taking notice of aught but Fergal then; it was only of late she realized that too, how it had been for them. Hugh had left off his schoolmastering, for however the Archbishop might feel, most families wouldn't welcome him in now; his few possessions he'd taken up to Maire's house, and borrowed from Donaghue to buy seed, and dug over and planted the fields that McCann had left wild. He had knocked out the timber from the sod shelter up the hill where the outlaws had lived, and patched the little house weather-tight with it, and dug a kitchen-garden that Maire took much pride in—a home they had made, however small and poor. And with however much trouble . . . Lynch, that righteous stubborn man, refusing to sell his turf to such as Hugh McFadden; and the once Donaghue had made the bargain in his own name for Hugh, Lynch finding out and refusing to deal again with Donaghue. Lucky it was that Degan, who owned the rest of the nearest peat-bog, had no such nice scruples. And those would have been hard fields to dig and plant up there, steep-sloping and rocky. And the house bare even of the few amenities they had here in this house.

Nessa knew; since Fergal was so much better, she had been up there on errands or just for a visit with Maire. Nothing they had—the few sacks of grain and potatoes McCann had left her were near all used now. Not even a proper baking-iron Maire had, only two old pot-lids that Hugh had filed smooth; they'd scarce a shift of clothes; it wouldn't be once in two months they tasted meat, for Hugh didn't like snaring the little wild creatures. Not even friends they had, but for those in this house, and Donaghue, and the Desmonds more cautious and distant: everyone else holding aloof. Worse to come, too: for Padraig Burke, who had taken over the mill after his dead brother, said open he'd grind no corn for such sinners; and come harvest, Hugh would need somehow to get his crop ten-twelve miles to the next nearest mill—and maybe that miller saying the same thing, the way gossip got round. And even did Hugh get it ground, he'd need to pay the miller with part of the crop, and what was left wouldn't carry them through the winter to come.

But they weren't worried for that, or for anything. They were just happy, that tranquil peace surrounding them; if they'd been King and Queen of Ireland, no happier. And being in that house, seeing them together, you couldn't but feel it was God's peace and content they'd found, nought sinful.

"Oh, I know," said Nessa again. "The way they are together—it's like to break your heart." Fergal, Fergal, saying so logical, daresay we'll suit well: and so their bodies did (and God knew she willing him back to full strength for that reason too, the comfort of the body), but there was more than that—there could be more than that.

"I must go in to see Mother," said Shevaun, and went.

Fergal, my darling dear, thought Nessa desolately. Ever to understand, and share—all the rest? Yes, Ethne and Brian Donaghue, something of the same strong quiet peace between them . . . Fergal had called his mother's name, in fever, five times to the once he'd muttered her own; and she was shamed of the jealousy for Ethne that put in her.

The late-afternoon breeze had a chill bite in it, for all that it was June. Nessa stepped back into the house and shut the door. In her heart was sorrow for Owen Desmond, and for Shevaun, so alone, and for herself—not for Hugh and Maire, who had all that was important. But she summoned a smile for Liam Fagan and the two old women Brighid and Eily, and said somewhat noncommittal about starting supper.

When Ethne came out of the bedchamber, shutting the door quietly, Nessa said, "Sit down a bit before you go." Secretly she was worried for the older woman's worn, tired look. This year had been hard on all of them, and the anxiety over Fergal had not helped. And she knew how Ethne felt for it—regardless, a woman couldn't help welcoming a child, for all that the times were bad and it made trouble and worry. The way women were made: like as Shevaun said, she'd grieved over miscarrying, two months along, even knowing the work a babe would make, the extra things needed and all; even so— But it had been a dozen years since Ethne had borne a child (and losing all those after her dead son Aidan, too); she wasn't as young as she'd been, and what with the poor food and hard work, she'd not been well through this pregnancy. A small relief it was to Shevaun and Nessa that she had Caitlin, her old maidservant, with her: Donaghue was good and kind, but not the same as a woman.

"Only a minute, I must be getting back. He's just drowsing, not really asleep—after all the exercise he had, I understand, up two hours and walking the length of the room." Ethne smiled. "He'll be a nuisance to look to, until he's full well, now—weak enough not to be doing for himself, and strong enough to complain! It's the worst stage of an illness."

"Oh, don't I know! But ten days back, when he roused up and swore at me for that the washing-water was too hot, I gave thanks to God for the curse!—the first time I was sure he'd live. He is near himself now, but for being weak. Ethne—is he still brooding on that business?"

"It's not so much what he says," said Ethne slowly. "He's given over talking about it, that Thomas Carmody and all he said about the tenant-people over the border. But he's still brooding on it, yes—and you knowing it too, no need ask me. I think that's in his mind more than wanting revenge on Kevin McCann."

"Yes, that's a man for you," said Nessa. She wielded the knife vindictive on one of the two little pieces of hedgehog-flank left, cutting it up into the potato-and-cabbage stew; the bigger piece must all go to Fergal, to build his strength. "Their roads crossing again, he'd take vengeance on McCann, but right now he's worried for the future, and that's part of it—while McCann's part of the past."

"Y-e-s. And feeling guilt on him, too, because— But he not the only one, Brian and the Desmonds have felt much the same."

"Yes." Nessa fitted the lid of the baking-pan over the heaped mess of stew and pushed the pan into the hearth, lifting the peat-square on each side with the poker, coaxing a third square to rest over the top. By the time Shevaun came back with the milk, the stew would be hot. She sat back on her heels and looked up at Ethne. "No middle way with men, is there? Either they've no honor at all, or they're overnice for it. I do think, that way, it's laid heavier on his mind—that all the while he was robbing from poor tenant-folk, and Irish, instead of English the way we all thought—than the trick McCann served him. And like as you say, other raiders feeling bad for it too, knowing. And some not caring a tinker's awl. What I feel about it, well, I'll be that thankful not to have him going out into such danger, anymore—for all the profit he fetched home."

"Don't I feel the same, for Brian?" Donaghue had used to go out with the Desmonds now and then. "Half the bread I'll take, with the man safe at my side! And at that, even without that profit, we'll have no less than many folk." Ethne laid a hand on her swollen body. "And we both wanting the child," she went on softly, "but times I can't help to think, Nessa—born to what and what purpose will it be? The way it is for us here— All the talk about when the King comes to England's throne again, we'll all have our rights restored, and all be as it was, for rank and wealth. But somehow, I don't feel—I'll ever again set foot in our old home at Lough Eask."

Nessa looked into the low-leaping fire to hide her concern for the other woman. "All the talk, yes. I don't know either, except —maybe that's just the reason. Something Fergal said once . . . when he and Roy and—and McCann escaped off the Arans, that the garrison-commander said, it was the young men must have the chance to get out—for that the English would see our whole race killed off, and we should think not just for ourselves, but the nation, to preserve the bloodline."

"The bloodline!" said Ethne, sharp and savage. "I of the O'Donnells, an old and proud clan—and Maire too, see what she's come to!—and my son's father a chief in his own right! His own pack of hounds he kept, and I with a gown for each day. Twenty servants in the house, and meat at every meal! And this minute I'm without a needle to mend my husband's shirt." She rose and took up her cloak, a quick angry gesture.

"So you will borrow our needle," said Nessa.

Ethne dropped her hands from the cloak-strings and leaned to kiss her. "Don't they say youth adjusts better to adversity! I'm sorry to snap—you're a good girl, Nessa. Yes, I will take the needle, and Brian will fetch it back tomorrow if I don't. It's just—now and again—I go to thinking how life was—before." She laid her hand on the door, and then, half-turned, she added in a low voice, "And I was thinking Fergal would get past it, but—he's not. He hates to look at me, like I am, Nessa—he hates the notion of the child, he won't hear talk of it."

"I know. I've tried—but he won't hear me either."

"I can't hold it against him—my firstborn—but it does hurt me. . . . But nought to be done for it, and—and I'd best be getting home, not gossiping here."

"Take care going down the hill, now," said Nessa anxiously.

Fergal heard their quiet voices clear enough through the ill-fitting door, but paid no notice to the words. He lay on his back, staring up at the rough-timber roof, and once again, for the thousandth time since his mind returned to his own use and he was mending back to himself, he was helplessly, angrily trying to add up the fearful debts he'd incurred . . . through Kevin McCann and his creatures of killers. Sometimes it came out a higher figure than other times, but however he reckoned, an appalling sum.

Oh, sure to God, they all said so easy, Put it out of your mind, boy, happy we are to help! A man couldn't take charity and keep any self-respect. And from Donaghue too, mostly. Christ, nearly three months, others supporting his household. The fields planted, and seed bought for that, and food given in charity—grain, game, God knew what. And it would have been more, if not for the cats, the blessed cats—thank God for them, the big tom with Hugh and Maire, the litter of seven kits sold for a good sum. But still, owing a debt he was. He moved restlessly on the thin pallet. Must get back to full strength soon, soon, and— Yes, how in hell's name pay off the debt? The crop barely enough to feed them through the winter. Only way to have extra profit, raid over the border—preying on Thomas Carmody and all his ilk, their own countrymen—as much outlaw as Kevin McCann!

The blanket slid half off him for his turning, and at once he was conscious of chill. In June!—this contemptible weak body, legs shaking for half a dozen steps taken, not able to dress itself without help— By God, let the damn' blanket lie, body had to be put in its place, all the sooner to toughen and come under his control again. And by the living Christ, if ever he had a rumor of Kevin McCann's whereabouts, he'd walk the length of Ireland to pay him back in his own coin, and usurers' interest atop of it!

Nessa came in with a plate, and exclaimed at the blanket, and adjusted it over him, one arm round his shoulders to help him sit propped against the wall. "When you're done with this, there's a cup of good beef stock, and a slice of sugared bread—as reward for walking so steady your first time up. There, now." She set the plate in his lap and put the spoon in his hand.

"Women!" he said. "Sorry you are I'm able to feed myself again—you all love to make infants of us! And where did you have the sugar, for God's sake?"

"From Owen Desmond, as a present, I told you before—last week."

At least, not from Donaghue. He took a mouthful of the stew, aware that it was rich with meat because she'd added more to his portion. "You needn't watch every mouthful, I won't overset the plate."

"If you did, it'd be of contrariness," said Nessa.

He looked up with a reluctant smile. "A crotchety old man I sound—excuse it." Snapping at her so, this last week, all on account he was better, quite himself again except for the little weakness—and touchy, remembering dimly how they'd all tended him like an infant, his pride smarting for it, and needing now to emphasize his recovered manhood.

"Well, they do say dead hounds don't bite," said Nessa dryly. "You can snap cross as you please, Fergal, until you're whole well again—we're pleased to hear it."

He laughed; and for the first time in a long while now he was feeling hunger for food, but he put the spoon down a minute, still looking at her. Something stirred faintly in him, something exciting and encouraging—another kind of hunger that a sick man didn't feel. Nessa. A bit thinner, a tired look in her smoke-gray eyes, but still lovely . . . Losing the child, and likely that his fault, making her worry and work. Or Kevin McCann's . . . Hadn't thought much for it then, when she told him: now, a queer double feeling he had. Lucky, one way, the situation they were in; and yet—and yet, a kind of dim regret at the back of his mind, for no reason he could conceive.

And now, unexpected and exhilarating, the body-hunger in him again, for her. Just a bit, with this weakness in him too, but tomorrow—next day—he'd be stronger, he was gaining back fast even to feel that as lazy anticipatory desire. And now he'd like her to stay, talk to him as he ate, but she was whisking out. Clatter of plates on the table, and their desultory talk—Liam coming to the door to smile and exchange a word.

The little effort of feeding himself tired him again, and he leaned against the wall and shut his eyes, resting a moment before he called to her to fetch his plate. So easy still he drifted into a half-sleep, and he thought the tapping was part of a half-formed dream, until he heard Shevaun exclaim, "Now who'll that be at mealtime?" and the sound of the door opening. A murmur of voices, one a strange man's, and then Shevaun's excited joyful cry, "A letter? Oh—"

Fergal sat up. That peddler, and a letter from Roy at last?—something going right, anyway! "Shevaun," he called, "fetch it in!" But she was already in the doorway, Nessa behind her. The color dying from her cheeks, and the letter shaking in her hand. "Roy? What—"

"It is—it is *my* letter," whispered Shevaun. "My last letter back—and—"

"Bring it to me," said Fergal. Nessa took it from Shevaun's nerveless fingers; she looked at him as she brought it, pale too, and said somewhat about not upsetting himself. He did not hear, looking at the letter. It had gone a long journey since Shevaun had written out the direction under Roy's name, the regiment and the garrison and the town in France they had from his only letter last year. It was stained and worn from being carried, but the seal was unbroken, and above her script someone had written a couple of lines in thin angular black letters: Latin, it was, blurring a little in his vision.

A long while ago, that prosy old tutor, a little Latin dinned into Fergal's head, but all forgot now. He looked up, past Shevaun's stricken expression, to Liam in the doorway. "Go up and fetch Hugh," he said quietly. But he knew, and all of them knew, what Hugh would be telling.

20

WHEN HUGH CAME in, twenty minutes later, Maire was with him. "I don't like to leave her alone, we've had folk prowling about by night of late, stone-throwing and such, and digging up part of the garden, just random mischief."

"Oh, Hugh, that's—I'm so sorry," but Nessa spoke mechanically; and Liam would have told him why he was wanted, for he too looked at Shevaun sitting dumbly there, twisting her hands together, and at Fergal, propped on the settle, a blanket around him, holding out the letter.

"Let me see," he said, and went to take it. He stood looking at it, profiled in the fire and rushlight: thinner than he had been, a sudden sputter of flame in the hearth showing his jawline sharp, unexpectedly strong. He looked up slowly, and his voice was gentle. "I am so sorry—but it was good in this man to spend trouble and coin, that you have definite knowledge. It's clerical script, likely he is a—a brother, some monastery in France, and using the Latin for that someone will know it in every country, to translate. He writes—'This man is dead of wounds and fever, at Jaca in Spain, three months. A comrade buys masses for him here, I send this whence it came that his people shall know.'" Hugh laid the letter on the mantelshelf. "I am so sorry," and he touched Shevaun's shoulder; his eyes went to the little boy unconcernedly absorbed there before the fire, with the rude-carved toy horse Donaghue had whittled for him.

Nessa and Maire went to her, but she sat erect, white-faced, not beginning to weep at once. And Fergal, with the sharp pang of loss and grief like a new wound in him, heard his voice more bitter than sorrowful: "Oh, weren't you right, Hugh—weren't you right! You saying to me, that first day we met, it is in their minds to see us all dead—every soul of Irish blood. Starve us here, banish us abroad to die in foreign quarrels—any way expedient, be rid of us!—Oh, Christ, better if he'd fallen in the name of his own land, three years back . . ."

Hugh made a helpless small gesture. "There is nothing to say to you, except—God's will."

"And don't say *that* to me," said Fergal, low and savage, "for it's a lie! God's will!—the Englishes' will!" He looked at Shevaun—the other women about her, arms and voices offering ready sympathy if no comfort, this first moment of knowing. He said, sudden and sharp and strong, "Shevaun! I've nought to say to you of comfort or sympathy—all in my heart to say to you, as you keep any pride at all, look to Roy Donlevy's son, that whatever other principle is taught him, he comes to manhood with a solid core of hatred for the English! The English—the English—devil's spawn inflicted on mankind—it's no matter, Sheevaun, if your son lies dead at five-and-twenty like his father, so he has got a son to follow him and be nurtured to manhood, by God, on nought but thin bread and hatred of the English! And *his* son—let it go on a hundred generations—sent to hell or heaven, at eternity's end every soul of us keeping that, whatever of life we've forgot else— the English, hatred of the English, and vengeance at the world's end—" And the words were dammed in him by painful obstruction in his throat, and he put shaking hands to his face.

Shevaun said in a remote, thin voice, "There's no need to say aught to me. That, or anything. What is always said—so many having so much less. Six months we had, that much. And—I— have—his—son. Yes, Fergal, I know. For that—I will think later on. There is nought anyone can say at all for it, any time." She got up to her feet, heavy and slow as an old woman, and went past all of them into the chamber off this room, and shut the door. Maire turned, blind with tears, to Hugh; he put his arm about her, but his eyes were on Fergal.

And Nessa raised a hand to brush her eyes, but came to him quickly. "Back to your bed you're going, this is not—the best thing in the world for you, as you are," she said unsteadily. He let her help him; the little surge of passion was dead in him, the grief coming instead. She settled him on the pallet, tucking the blanket round him; her hand rested light on him a moment as he turned his face to the wall. "She is right—nothing ever to say." The two old women out there, shrill, raising the traditional *caoine* for the dead.

"Go and stop that," he said wearily. "Heathen custom—tearing us all apart the more."

"And frighting the child—yes." She bent and kissed him, and went out. After a moment the high wailing died. He lay motionless in the dark, feeling the hot tears that would not fall, and thinking— Only postponed. Any hour these five years any of them might have died on the field, or of starvation here, or been randomly murdered by English, and enough had—enough had. Only added bitterness that Roy should die for a foreign king, on foreign soil.

And life left must go on, whatever man died. But just this minute it seemed too heavy a burden to take up again: he was too weary and weak to shoulder the load life allotted. He lay dumb, only existing as mindless entity, an endless time: dimly aware of hushed talk beyond the door. After awhile, his mind began moving again, and it presented him with a thousand pictures of Roy, all their lives together since boyhood. And in the end, memory lifted his sick heart toward life again.

Didn't remember which battle it was, the fight at Trim or Cogan or Banagher—so many battles—but it had been a rout, they had retreated in disorder. He saw it clear again now, the tired beaten men in ragged groups where they made cold camp, and butchered a couple of troop-horses for food—a desultory count of casualties and the little ammunition left—and some one of the other officers muttering, "Even if we can rejoin the main forces, God, the enemy at our heels now—expect us to make another stand—nothing to meet them with."

And Roy Donlevy, big solid bulk in the dark there, lifting his head to say quiet and steady, "As many stands we'll make as there are men left. There's a proverb for it, brother—*If you want fire, look for it in the ashes.*"

It was as if he had come back to say it again to Fergal, this desolate minute. Fergal drew a long breath and turned to his back, from where he had huddled against the wall. Yes, man, he thought—yes, Roy. That is to remember and hold to. By God, we will.

He thought, They can strip us of everything except our courage and our hate—and while we hold those, we hold all important.

With time passed he grew stronger, back to full health. His clothes hung loose on him, and the first time he walked down the hill he took awhile to get back, resting every third step; but by the turn of July toward August, he was himself again. And reckoning a changed state of affairs for his household. Not only for Roy being gone, Shevaun a pale slim grieving shadow of herself, and his own confirmed responsibility for her and the child. Not only for the end of raids over the river, and the profit taken. Other things, indirect, that made difficulties.

English law might list all Irish in one class, and that lower than the lowest English class: but inevitably there was some feeling here, and likely across the border, for former rank. Some humble-born men nursing resentment for gentry, secretly glad to see them brought low: some still keeping the ways of servitude. Some gentlefolk taking it as their right to stay idle, bitter against ill-bred upstarts: some with more sense. The Connacht folk still standoffish from transplanters forced on them. And all the ways all these people had gone in extremity, creating new lines and feelings. You could say, Fergal thought, that what had happened to his household in this time past was individual example of how it had gone everywhere. . . . The best and worst of every soul showing plainer, for these straits.

But the result of it for Fergal O'Breslin and his house— The village-folk had looked askance at him after the Kearney affair; some of them the sort that liked any chance to vilify a man of rank, on whatever grounds. And it was easy for them, and most others living roundabout, to think now for this latest business, A case of thieves falling out, and what to choose between? Especially as Fergal O'Breslin and his people were friendly with those sinners up the hill, lapsed monk, adulterous wife! Nine of ten people, how they would always cling to conventionalities—narrow minds without a hint of charity, for a thing like that, where they might be generous elsewhere. Yes, Lynch so just over the Kearneys' murder, so rigid-righteous about this—and he scarce the only one. Connacht-folk and transplanter alike, most people here were unfriendly now to Fergal and his house, and to Donaghue who was connected and also a friend of Hugh's and to the Desmonds.

Hugh knew it, being no fool, and said he'd not blame them to disown the friendship. "So it's just contrariness," said Fergal angrily, "and all of us cutting off the finger to spite the hand, that we let them see you're friends! What the hell is it to them who I name friend? Or for that matter, the state of your morals? Something in Scripture about casting the first stone—"

"Which is very much to the point," said Hugh dryly, fingering a bruise on his cheek. "I came to ask if you or Donaghue would see Degan for me, to contract for a little more turf, what I can afford. The last time I was in the village, there were stones thrown—some of the bigger boys. I'm not afraid of them, but if I should be hurt serious, or even killed, it would leave Maire unprotected."

Fergal said he'd see to it, and added a few words about vicious little bastards. "Don't stir up the fire hotter by talking to those folk," said Hugh. "Not only provoking more trouble, but stronger dislike on yourself. I don't know, we'd maybe be wiser to go right away, somewhere we weren't known—but there's the land here, at least. . . . Oh, it was only to be expected, people feeling so— but—a man knows the state of his own soul best, and I—we feel to have made peace with God for it, is all I can say. It is for Maire I mind."

"I know, man." And Fergal came himself, in the next weeks, to hate going down to the village, any reason: men eyeing him cold, unspeaking—Degan, the one or two others who condescended to bargain with him for exchange of goods, saying no more than needful and that in no very friendly tone. Not all on Hugh's account, no: more than half of it maybe went back to Kevin McCann, Fergal knew grimly.

And every time he or any of them left the house these days, all the rest saying, "Take care of patrols!" That was another thing. . . .

Nessa had said it to him, that first time he had felt strong enough to go out, try his strength; and he had stared, and said the English military weren't after him for aught, far as he knew. And Shevaun coming suddenly to grip his shoulders in a tight embrace, strange wild fright in her eyes. "Oh, Fergal, yes, take care—don't go down to the road alone—not—not to lose you too, like *that*—I couldn't bear—"

"What is all this? Patrols—"

"I—we're not sure," said Nessa. "I don't believe what foolish people say, but they are taking prisoners. It started a week or two after you were hurt, Fergal, we've not said anything before, for you'd have worried, any of us out. You never know when they'll come along—not the regular policing-patrols, others, more men —and they take just anyone they come on, of the sort they want. No reason—just, they seize them and fetter them and take them off across the border."

"Christ's love," said Fergal, "you're telling me—no charge, or any excuse? What sort do they take—and what's said about it that you don't believe?" He had never seen either of them look like that.

Shevaun put a hand to her mouth and turned to crouch on the settle. "I couldn't bear—"

"It's just a tale to fright children," said Nessa. "That—that they're short of food across the border. Just—"

"Oh, my God," he said. "Who do they take, Nessa—who's been taken from here?"

"Ab-bout twenty folk, thus far. The way it looks, they only want youngish folk—but not children, thank God for that. Since it started, they've taken young John Kelleher, and his wife too— three young ones left there, for his parents to care for—and both the youngest Lynch boys, the ones sixteen-seventeen, and near a dozen women—some of them wives, I think Catriona Dowling was the youngest, just fifteen. They don't take old people—"

"The tough, thin old folk," whispered Shevaun. "No. Butcher to poor advantage, they would."

"Stop saying that, it's silly," said Nessa sharply. "Even English—nobody of sense could believe it! Don't go brooding on such a fond thing, Shevaun. Of course there's some other reason, Fergal, but it's a—a frighting thing, you know. Just taking folk off, like as they gathered a herd of cows to drive . . . No, nobody's ever heard aught about any of them, since. It's not just here, the patrols are all over Connacht. There was a peddler stopped by last week, said they came down on one village in Mayo and took near everybody in it—only the folk over forty years or so, and the children, left."

"Not the old folk—Christ—"

"No, John Dowling's old mother was coming up from the village one day, and a patrol came along and seized her—she said she was like to die of fright—but when they had a look and saw she was sixty-odd years, they laughed and let her go, said she wouldn't fetch much, and something about the order saying none over forty. They had twenty or thirty guarded prisoners with them, and one of the men called out to her he was Cathal Doyle from Castlebar, and in God's name would someone send a message back to his wife to say what had happened to him—taken him out of the field they had. The Dowlings told the next peddler who came by going that way—but the poor woman deserted, bad to think of, and hundreds like that there've been, just marched off with no chance for farewell even. You see, whatever reason they have—a terrible thing, and we've all got used to watching for them. You'd best not go along the road, Fergal, until you're stronger, to run."

"Christ," he said again. "And who's to say—that *is* just a tale?"

But like Nessa he couldn't quite believe that. Since then he'd seen it for himself, and learned to watch, and take to his heels for the nearest cover, at the first noise of a mounted patrol. It might be only a regular patrol, stopping occasionally to search a native Irish for weapons, and looking for contraband—or it might be one of these others. Discretion the better part of valor: five times in the next two months Fergal lay flat in a ditch or crouched in shielding bushes, and watched English soldiers take some of his neighbors who hadn't been so swift or so lucky. Saw them reject the two children with young Maurice Kelleher's wife, while they took her—children crying and running after, she screaming, trying to get free. Saw them pass the two old women of his own household, Brighid and Eily, and seize on Sean Delaney, and he a tough active young fellow who put up a fight—two holding him, a third clapping the iron wrist-fetters on, and he added to the tally of eight or ten people well-guarded at the rear of the patrol.

It was the same two or three patrols apparently covering this district; and putting together what he and other men had seen, he deduced that those captains were not directly under orders of the officers in the guard-stations detailing the regular patrols, but sent out from across the border. Apparently too in liaison with similar patrols farther west; for all the village had seen what must have been several joined troops, a hundred men, marching in three hundred-odd prisoners, to hand them over official to a captain here, who sent them on with new guards toward the border. That was six weeks ago, the largest group coming past—kept apart, and exchange of talk punished, but a few shouted messages across the prison-lines told those were folk out of Mayo and Connemara, far west.

Those local-roving patrols used the local station-barracks: a military-policing garrison established here, since the settlement, every ten or fifteen miles, and one of them just outside this village the other way from Fergal's land. The patrol riding out from there was the one he'd oftenest seen—the captain a short stout red-faced man, past middle age, and looking bad-tempered.

Fergal was in the village the day that man died. Just passing through on his way to see Desmond, he came past the smithy to hear loud English swearing inside, and grinned to himself, glancing in. The smith, Hennessy, was a fellow like Dan Kindellan, slow of wit, and he hadn't much English. The captain, visible in there alongside the forge, was apparently of that numerous body of English convinced that if only one shouted loud enough, these stupid natives must understand.

Half a dozen men were lounging about outside, listening idly, no vestige of a smile on their faces. Degan, Lynch, the Brogan brothers, old Gorman. The Brogans hadn't been quite as unfriendly as the rest, and Fergal stepped over to them. "What's the conclave?"

"The Captain Benedict is wanting Hennessy to come up to the garrison-smithy, for a bit of work," said Con Brogan gravely, "the regiment-smith having broke his leg—likely by way of one of those bad-tempered English hacks. He came out a minute ago, the captain, to ask if any here knew the English to interpret for him— red as fire he looked." He spat thoughtfully. "A pity, none could oblige him." Fergal grinned again; every man there had more English than Hennessy, but he could imagine the bland blank looks turned on the Englishman.

"Unfortunate indeed," he agreed as gravely. The English cap-

tain stormed out of the smithy at that minute; as Brogan said, he
was purple with fury, still swearing to himself. He made for his
big gray troop-horse tethered in the road, but halfway there he
faltered, put up a hand to his chest, and half-turned with as be-
wildered a look as Hennessy wore, staring after him; his mouth
worked, and he fell in a crumpled heap.

The men stirred, but none started toward him. "Worked himself
up to an apoplexy he has," diagnosed Degan.

"Very likely," agreed Lynch, sounding mildly amused.

"Damnation on us," said Turlough Brogan soft, "if he's dead—
trouble. There being no English witnesses."

"Christ, yes," said Fergal. It went against the grain to give help
to an English, but if they took it into their heads the villagers had
attacked him, and he alone— He went over to the fallen man and
straightened him out to lie on his back. He unbuttoned the uniform
tunic and slid a hand inside to feel for the heart. The heartbeat he
could not feel, but a folded wad of paper dislodged from the pocket
there lay on the officer's chest, and Fergal pushed it aside as he
opened the tunic wider. Then he heard Lynch say, "Patrol—regular men." He heard the patrol coming up behind; and in one
motion he swept up the folded paper, thrust it inside his own
doublet, and stood up; if they saw it there, saw him putting it back
whence it fell, sharp questions and accusation.

The patrol, nine mounted men and a captain, halted; the officer
leaped from his saddle and strode over, questioning loud and suspicious, bending to examine the body. "What's happened 'ere?—
Cap'n Benedict it is—dead—" He ripped open tunic and shirt,
looking for the wound he expected to find.

A subtle change passed like a shadow over every Irishman there,
except Fergal. It was a thing they had long learned, so it came
almost instinctive as breathing now, to many men: the last weapon
of the conquered. Turn the enemy arrogance to advantage, act the
fool and clown with them, amuse them however you may, with
absurd mispronunciation of their tongue or the overemphatic deference they never recognized for contempt—make them laugh and
say to each other, *Like children, these natives, and damnation
comic, eh?* Put them in good humor—literally for your life's sake.

Con Brogan gave the captain an ingratiating smile and said in
English, "Why, sure to God, Your Honor, the poor man did get in

that terrible a temper, y' see he was tryin' talk to the smith here, a stupid one he do be an' the cap'n come out red in the face as any comb-standin' cock, beggin' your pardon—"

"And reckon as he took what they call the apple-plexy for it, your honor," Degan took up the tale. "The poor fella, dangerous a temper can be, me brother-in-law's sister's man had the selfsame thing happen—all along of her bein' such a bad cook, and he—"

"Yes, yes," the officer cut them off, shrugging, looking at them with the contempt they had angled for, the kind of contempt that said, *Harmless*, stupid natives. "You were close over him," and he looked at Fergal. "Was he alive when you touched 'im first?"

"He was," said Fergal evenly, "dead when he fell, I would think." One out of a hundred men who could never bring themselves to wear that mask before the English, and he was one of them. Call it contrariness; and it didn't go by former rank, for not all such men had been of high rank. Just, for life or soul, unable to demean themselves. He said, "There was no indication of a heartbeat or pulse. Not three minutes ago it was he fell."

Quick frown from the officer; they did not like an educated native. To be reminded there were such—not all savages. This officer was one of the middle-class Parliament men elevated from the ranks, and his accent on his own language was rougher than Fergal's. "*Sir* you say to an Englishman, Irish!"

"I beg your pardon, Captain," said Fergal. "It was natural agitation to see the poor gentleman in such sudden extremity, *sir*."

The captain stood up from the body. "Well, it do appear 'twas natural—the regimental surgeon will say." He hesitated, looking at them, deciding whether to take them in for questioning—ostentatiously ignoring Fergal; and shrugged again. "Martin, Wells, take up the body—I'll bring his horse. There'll be an inquiry, but don't reckon 'twas aught but natural."

In five minutes the patrol was riding off toward the garrison, the body slung between two saddles. Indefinably again these men here changed to their own adult selves; indefinably, for the moment, Fergal felt small relaxing of unfriendliness toward him— they had been men of one blood dealing with the enemy, just then.

Lynch said reflectively, "It's to be hoped the regimental surgeon is skilled enough not to leap to conclusions and say the bastard was poisoned or some such."

"And I'd not put that past them," agreed Degan ruefully. "It's also to be hoped," and he turned to Fergal, "that paper you took off him wasn't so important to be missed."

"By God, yes, I'd forgot it." Fergal took it out and unfolded it. "No, I wouldn't think—it's official written orders is all, every officer would have a copy, and likely none would think to look—" His voice died as he read.

"What is it?" asked Con Brogan.

Fergal looked up from the precise black lines of English script. And the ordinary way, he lost temper easy and took out violence in cursing or hitting; but for this the temper was cold in him. This was beyond any fury. It was—very nearly—beyond the tale to scare children. He said expressionlessly, "So now we know. . . . You all read English?—that's as well, for I'd not like—to translate aloud—this—this infamy." He put the thing in Brogan's hands suddenly; he felt, absurdly, a need to cleanse his hands of holding it. And he had no desire to stay here and discuss it; he said abruptly he'd be getting on, and walked away from them toward Desmond's.

But as he went, every word of that was clear in his mind, the look of the page, as if he still held it.

Official orders. Direction: Colonel thus-and-so, such-and-such regiment, garrison-number . . . to be copied and distributed to all officers of patrols-for-revenues in Ireland . . . bold black signature at the bottom, Lieutenant-of-General Commanding (acting) . . . "This trade affording such needed profit to the Commonwealth, it is to be required that effort be forthcoming to provide more salable merchandise immediately, a minimum of two thousand females between ages sixteen and forty, and fifteen hundred males between ages sixteen and thirty, so soon as they may be taken. There is great demand in the new-colonized island of Jamaica, elsewhere in the Indies, and in nations about the inland seas, for strong and healthy slaves, and it be of prime import and loyal service to the Commonwealth that a good number of such be made available while the level of price shall hold so high. To be noted, in regard to females taken: certain proportion of these are intended, by special request of the Governor of Jamaica, for service in the civil and military brothels, therefore it be urged that care is used by officers of local patrols to see young, strong, comely females be collected. This business be most vital to the present welfare of our great

Commonwealth, to the effect of which is here appended the personal directive-order I as acting Commander do receive this day of our honored Lord Lieutenant of Irish Affairs, Henry Cromwell, son to our illustrious Lord General, who do write:

" 'Concerning the young females and also the males, though we must use force taking them, yet it do be so much for the public good and advantage, I do urge that you use diligence in so dispatching patrols to gather them. So long as the Lord be pleased to keep our hearts upright before Him, we shall see our new nation flourish, but there can be no denial that revenue is needed, and these natives fetch good prices in all slave-markets. I apprehend that all must agree we can well spare much portion of the native population within Ireland, and moreover, who knows but that in the end this may be the means to turn the remainder into Christians.'

"So directed this day under my hand, that the number of such natives set as mark for each troop-patrol, by each month, minimum to be ten individuals, preferably female. Official reports of numbers to be due-filed with the commandants of border-garrisons."

No, nothing to say for that. No curse carried any weight for that. But yes, there was one thing to say, for that. It was English.

Part
Four

"The spark sleeps in the stone."
—Proverb

21

WITHIN A SPACE of four days, the whole pattern of life—even precarious as it was—shattered to ruin about Fergal.

He was over on Desmond's land that day, after game. They had made agreement to be free of one another's land for hunting; mutual advantage on the surface, but one way Fergal might repay the debt he owed, for he held more land, and he need not come onto Desmond's as often as the other way about. They were making the rounds of rabbit-snares, he and the two Desmonds, and looking desultorily for signs of hedgehog or any other small game, though it was difficult to kill these days. The English patrols were so often in earshot of a gun fired, and coming out on the run to find the man with the illegal-owned weapon, to confiscate it. There had been some reprisals attempted against the slave-taking patrols, and they were uneasier than ever for armed natives.

At the dozenth snare set Owen Desmond pounced on the third garroted hare they'd collected. "Not a bad average, one apiece." Fergal accepted it reluctantly, half minded to make excuse to take nothing more.

"By rights Justin ought to have the lion's share," he said, "being a new-married man and doubtless in need of strengthening meals." Justin was recently wed to the oldest Gorman daughter. He laughed and said Fergal underrated him.

"You can say that of me five years on, when I've a family to provide for!" And as they moved up the hill, presently by natural association of ideas he added the polite enquiry, "I hope your lady-mother's well, by the by?"

Fergal felt himself stiffen, hating the question, hating the very necessity to admit a fact. And he was ashamed of his own feeling, how he found it an effort just to look at her, as she was—gross swollen body, somehow disgusting, and he an adult man who'd once swollen that body too. He opened his mouth to formulate some conventional answer, and Owen Desmond said suddenly, "There's a patrol."

They were, here, up the slope of hill just above the road out of the village: below them was the one arable field on Desmond's land. The late-summer wild growth was thick here, under a tall stand of trees. Instinctively, at the words, they all took shelter, crouching behind the nearest oak, looking down across the ripening barley-field.

A patrol, guards behind with half a dozen people, just rounding the curve of the road toward the garrison a mile off. And a sudden flurry—a shout, and one of the prisoners breaking away desperate past the guards, running like a deer into the field, toward this slope. It was a woman, her skirt flaring—she holding it up with fettered hands, not to stumble—a young, nimble woman. One of the mounted guards fell out of line after her; she had only twenty yards' start, but the standing crop slowed the horse where she ran through easy.

Fergal heard both Desmonds curse the damage the horse made to the field. She was half up the hill now, running straight toward them; she was into the wood, and saw them—shying aside in startlement—as she passed: Roisin Kelleher it was, an only daughter, and bare sixteen, and two of her brothers taken by patrols a month ago. Panic had near lent her wings, she flashed by and ran on for the higher slope and thicker wood—and here came the trooper, crash under the trees—

It was one of the times you didn't think—for all the cold sense in them, it was instinctive as pulling burned hand out of fire. All three started forward to intercept the horse. Fergal's hand closed on the loose rein, as the horse shied off from their sudden appearance; the trooper gave an involuntary startled yell, and the horse sidestepped into a tree almost at full canter, throwing the Englishman off-saddle. He was up, swearing, reaching for his pistol—Fergal had been yanked sidewise to smash against the tree trunk, and let go the bridle, momentarily dazed—he made a rush for the soldier, and heard Justin call urgently, "The horse—God's sake, the—"

Too late: the frightened horse was off, blind through the trees, back the way it came, plunging downhill. All three of them fell on the Englishman before he got his pistol cocked. He staggered back under wild blows, and Owen Desmond followed him up first, a solid crack to the jaw, left-handed, reaching for his knife with the other hand, so swift it happened. The trooper fell back hard against the oak two feet behind; they heard his skull crack, and he slid down and lay still.

They had all seen too many men dead to mistake one.

Faintly, up the hill, that one heartbeat of time, they heard the girl still running—well away, if there was no immediate pursuit.

The patrol-captain had reckoned one mounted man would catch up a woman on foot easy: the troop had halted in the road, awaiting her return. But even half a minute not enough grace: that long ago, the riderless horse was sighted—an order barked—and now three men looked at each other across a dead man, and forty yards away eight mounted Englishmen came on at the gallop.

Fools: Christ-damned fools: afterthought! They turned and fled up, knowing the land, to the one deep cover near, a shallow copse all surrounded with tall bracken. Cover only for the time being, soon enough found with search. They lay almost on top of one another there, prone, the bracken high all round.

The girl was gone. With any luck, safe away over the top of the hill, and down the far slope to the village and her father's house.

But this side of that minute, three men on casual business— the other side, three lives forfeit.

Not safe here five minutes, eight men beating the under-growth—having found a comrade dead, and not by a girl's hand.

All three of them, lying here breathing shallow, had years of experience at war-campaign: there was no need for long words.

"Ten minutes outside before they're on us," breathed Owen Desmond.

"Yes . . . Blame it on our mothers' teaching," muttered Justin, "Courtesy and aid to females. And no dice to throw for the loser."

They looked at each other, breaths mingling for closeness: no, no need for longer words. The entire patrol into the wood all about, now—shouting, circling close. Life and death between two breaths taken. War-campaign had taught them the rule, give the hound-pack one fox to follow, they'll never suspect more in the den. One fox to lead them away.

Owen Desmond's mouth stretched to a smile. "Why, no need for dice, is there, cousin?" he murmured. "You are both married men, with responsibilities—I am not. What's the gamble?—ninety-ten odds? The odds an Irishman's used to, boys. I'll see you both later—the one place or the other, heaven or hell."

"Owen," said Fergal desperately, "no—wait, let's see how it goes—"

Desmond laughed, soundless. "It's a thing to do quick or not at all. And in Christ's name, see I don't die for nought, if I die—lie here like corpses, the both of you, until they're clear away!" He touched Fergal's shoulder, light and swift. "And then, get you home to Nessa, boy—and do you give her—my dearest love." He crawled out of the copse in one motion, and got up to his feet, and ran crouching low, dodging, through the trees, heedless of noise. The troopers were deployed to each side, beating the bushes; he'd no choice but to run straight for the open, downhill.

He made fifty yards before they brought him down—the simultaneous crack of matchlocks shocking-loud in the quiet wood. The last twenty yards he made with English bullets in him, faltering. He fell where the belt of trees ended, down the slope into his standing crop, and the chasing, yelling troopmen gathered round in a group, dismounted, talking loud, swearing.

Justin Desmond buried his face in his arms, but Fergal watched until it was done; and he had seen many men die, and other friends among them, but the hand closing on his heart, a physical-felt thing, had never been quite so cold.

They came back, two of them, and fetched the troopman's body down, and lashed it to his horse. They had given up the girl: she was safe away. But, an Englishman killed, and vengeance demanded. They had that, life for life. They argued; they swore; they hacked off the head, rough, with the captain's sword, to spike over the garrison-gate. They rode away at last, with the handful of slave-value taken in a mute sullen line between guards, and left the bloody maimed body lying there to redden wet a new patch of the grain.

* * *

When Fergal came up to his own door, the need to see her and hold her was oddly urgent in him. Nessa. Owen Desmond had loved her, romantic, and maybe that was half the reason he was dead. Nessa O'Breslin, and Fergal had wed her only to satisfy honor: a suitable enough match, but not one he'd sought: and she was young and pretty and her body eager, and he had taken pleasure in her, he was fond of Nessa: if he must be saddled with a wife, she turned out a good choice. . . . He hadn't thought or felt much for it beyond that. Now he was conscious of some other nameless emotion stirring faintly; he felt he might find a little comfort in her close warmth.

But his house was empty save for Hugh and Maire, and Liam, and the little boy. Maire came to him at once, wearing a forced smile, so that intuitive alarm seized him. "The rest of your household is all over at Donaghue's, Fergal—your mother is gone into labor, a bit early. No telling how long she'll be, and I've come to look after Sean and see you and Liam have a meal of sorts—" And even the forced smile died at his look; she said, "Fergal—what is it? You've not been at Donaghue's, it's not that she—?"

He sat down and told them, briefly. The body taken down to Desmond's cabin, Justin gone for the priest. When they had said the little there was to say, he added dully, "Did you ever play that child's game—counting down—one gone, and one gone, and one—Like that it is—" And then the significance of her swift frightened question struck him. "Mother—? Is it that they expect—it'll go bad with her, Maire? The midwife—"

"We won't borrow trouble," she said gently. "Neither Donaghue nor your mother thinks much of that woman calls herself a midwife—an ignorant old hag—they've not called her. Brighid and Eily and Caitlin, they've all birthed babes before, and aught the midwife could do so can they, and likely better. It's just that it may go a bit hard for her, her age and all—she's not been well of late."

He got up, saying tiredly, "I must go over—see—"

"Now sit down," said Hugh. "Nothing you could do, you'd only be in the way. Nessa said she or Shevaun would be back after supper, to let you know. And you're in no state to be upset any more—"

"I am the one who is all right, Hugh," said Fergal with a wry grimace.

It was not until midevening that Nessa came in, with no news but that Ethne was yet in labor. "Nothing you could do, Maire, it's just—to wait. I was a bit in the way myself, the old women can do all that's needful. Shevaun will stay, of course. It's bad on Brian, he's beside himself."

And later, she wept against Fergal's shoulder in the dark, for Owen Desmond. "His life for yours, he sent you back to me safe —but the waste of it, Fergal, just as old as you he was—"

"Waste like that in Ireland now, nothing out of the way . . . Nessa—yes, I know, the reason it was—Nessa—" New feeling, queer, in him. He wanted her body, urgent: a man who had that day come safe away from death, he needed it as affirmation. But he knew she was weary and heartsick, no passion in her; he forced down his own desire, new tenderness flooding him—and that strangely doubled for the silent gratitude he felt from her, drifting to needed sleep on his shoulder.

A night's interlude between nightmares . . . They were at Donaghue's house an hour after dawn; Ethne was still in hard labor, the twentieth hour. He had seen women in labor—camp-followers on the march, countrywomen where battle-lines were drawn— but it was different, here and now. He her firstborn, and more than half of Fergal O'Breslin was from Ethne, whatever he was as a man.

The rest of his life—and later he was deep-shamed for it—he never forgot the exquisite pain of triumph, when she called his name instead of Donaghue's. They let him go in to her, to the little chamber where she lay writhing on thin straw, and he held her hand tight, kneeling beside her, telling her he was here: all his love contending with abstract disgust for the ugly crudity of life struggling there before him—half Ethne, half impersonalized gross Female. But the pain-twisted mouth was saying his name, not *Brian, Brian.* . . . "I'm here, Mother, my darling heart—"

Blue eyes so like his own opening on him. "Fergal," she gasped. "Fergal—" And one minute her hard grasp relaxed on his hand. "Yes—kindness in you always, boy—but wanted to say to you, if you'll but open your heart—Nessa, to love her as she— But it's a thing comes or not, no reaching it by intent. Fergal—"

"Yes, I'm here, my dear."

And she twisting away in sudden agony, so that the old women sent him out—to where Donaghue sat, white-faced, silent, listening for the cries she tried to suppress: just sitting there, hands tight-clasped, waiting. And presently getting out his empty cold pipe to turn it round and round, helplessly, in his fingers. The women coming and going—looking anxious, and the first pang of fear in Fergal's heart for their expressions.

Forty hours she was in labor, before the end. Justin Desmond coming, telling somewhat about the funeral-service for Owen, seeing how it was here, going away; the time passed vague for Fergal, he was unsure when any small event of that time had happened, exact. Just the women moving about, the screams she could not keep back, and Donaghue sitting there opposite, forever turning his pipe round in his big hairy red hands.

And at last no more screams, and they came and said in hushed voices she was dead—she was gone. Explanations: women's excuses for it: child in the wrong position to come natural, not well she'd been—losing half the babes she conceived, not right-built for the bearing. A hemorrhage, and the babe dead too, born the wrong way and the cord torn before the child breathed. Women's answers.

She was dead, all that got through to him—he blundered in and saw her dead, bloody, obscene, mark of agony still on her face—and he turned away in involuntary revulsion, to face Brian Donaghue there across her twisted body.

"Murderer—murderer!" he said, high and wild. "Killed her— sure as if you drove a knife in her—you bastardly killer—"

And Donaghue, in a whisper, "Ethne, my darling—my darling heart—God's mercy on all of us—Fergal, boy, I loved her, I loved her—for Christ's sake don't say that to me—lest I believe it, oh, God, Ethne—"

"You killed her, you bastard—whoreson—killed her—just like as if you took a knife—"

"Oh, no, God, Fergal, don't say—"

"Murderer! You—"

"No—God—" Donaghue's voice queerly soft, "but you're right, Fergal, boy, Christ have mercy—killed her I have—my own darling—"

Hands on him, voices at him, soothing and protesting. *No blame*, they said, *no blame, God's will is all*. A lie, a black lie. Donaghue the killer . . .

Nessa's voice not reaching him, or Hugh's reasonable quiet words: but Shevaun he heard, hard and anguished, her hands gripping him: "Stop it, Fergal, for God's sake—making it all the worse for everyone—"

"And you ought be saying the same at him, the bastard! What the hell are you thinking of, defend him—say—" But he saw then that Donaghue was gone, stumbling out, less tragic than absurd, heavy middle-aged man weeping open as a child. And Hugh's arm leading him out too, and his own tears choking off any more curses, turning him blind and deaf.

But he heard old Brighid's murmur, "A third there will be—who? Never two without three—never two without three."

They were not even let to bury their dead decent and open here now, unless without religious service: the word of God to be said over the grave, by a priest, it must be in secret, at night, lest the English see and come to seize the priest and hang him.

Owen Desmond's headless body was buried the one evening, the day Ethne died, and her they buried the next, in the little plot outside the village where Father O'Marron had consecrated the ground. Kelleher was the one man of all their neighbors who came to Desmond's burying, and that was lip service only, for that—accident or no—Desmond had died in protecting Kelleher's daughter as well as Fergal and Justin.

No one but themselves came to Ethne's burying, and Hugh and Maire. Donaghue stood apart, motionless and silent, through the ceremony; he spoke no word to any, and Caitlin said he had not spoke at all since that hour of Ethne's death. And the bitterness was still strong in Fergal's heart, but he had come past that first wild shock of grief, and he knew Donaghue suffered too; naming Donaghue her killer was childish. One minute there in the dark, as the first clods of earth were laid gentle on her blanket-wrapped body, he felt the impulse to put down his spade, go to Donaghue and say, I was in the wrong, don't hold it on me, I spoke wild; I know you loved her too, I'm sorry, man.

But the remnant of long bitterness against Donaghue kept him from it, then—and the soul-weariness numbing him for violent emotion expended. They left the new grave and came back toward the village street, all in silence. Opposite the door of the inn they came past a little group just emerging—brief light from the open door showed Lynch, Gorman, Burke. Lynch had a little drink in him, the way he lurched into Fergal's path. "Ah, O'Breslin the fine gentleman-chief it is! God takes no account of high breeding, so you find, O'Breslin, not so?—you'll have been out this night seeing your lady-mother put underground, eh? God's judgment on you and your house, for condoning sin and forgathering with sinners! Ill luck you might've expected, and nought but ill luck to come, you keeping company with such—fornicating monk, married harlot!"

"Get out o' my road, Lynch, you're drunk," said Fergal wearily; even the anger was dull in him. And even of that Donaghue taking no notice, but trudging on ahead, not turning. Fergal shoved Lynch aside; the man snarled, and then recognizing Hugh and Maire, he bent and collected a handful of stones to fling after the little party. And the priest had held uneasily aloof from Hugh, more troubled than shocked; but he was no fanatic, and he turned back now to speak sharp in reprimand.

"No sins on your own soul, Terence Lynch, and you so certain you know God's final judgment for any soul? Think for your own!—you expecting mercy from God, show it to your fellowmen!"

Where their ways parted, Donaghue's place beyond this, he stopped in the road and spoke at last, his voice remote and hoarse. "Caitlin—will be coming back to your house, O'Breslin."

And again Fergal had impulse to speak, and did not: dully he thought, a thing to say private to him—presently.

The priest asked gently, "Would you like me to come on with you, Donaghue, perhaps some comfort—"

The big red bulk that was Donaghue stirred convulsively. "No, I thank you, Father—I'll be best—alone. But I'll hope—you will find it in your heart—to pray for me. O'Breslin—Fergal? I'll ask a thing of you. Come to my place in the morning, early, will you do that? Give me your word to come, as a man of honor?"

"I'll come," said Fergal. He would say it then to Donaghue, I'm sorry. Now he only wanted the oblivion of sleep.

"I will be waiting," said Donaghue lowly, and turned away.

Fergal plodded on with the rest, the need for sleep rising like a black tide over him. It was vague in his mind, coming in at last, at last able to lie down, and sleep that was more like a little death taking him down into the dark.

But he woke in the dawn, his mind sharp-working, and there was fearful cold knowledge in him. Single terrible knowledge—all his weariness, every other emotion, gone from him. He lay still and he said, *Oh, Christ, no,* to the thing in his mind: but he knew—he knew.

Nessa slept sound and sweet beside him. He slid from the blanket quietly, not to wake her. He found his shoes and his cloak, and went out silently to don them outside, in the sweet chill dawn. *God,* he said in his mind, *please God, no.* But all the while he knew.

Somewhere a late hardy lark began its piercing triumphant hymn of joy to the rising sun. *Oh, God, I should have said it to him when I felt it,* Fergal's mind told him bitterly. Never two without three.

He walked across his field tall with the harvest-ripe crop, and across Donaghue's field, to Donaghue's little cabin, to find what he knew he would find. Past the neat-kept kitchen garden that Donaghue had labored at, and the rowan-bush where once Fergal had lain at suspicious watch on him. The housedoor gave to his hand. He could have told accurate what was waiting inside.

A considerate, thoughtful man, Brian Donaghue. He had spread a blanket to lie on, not to make a stain on the floor, and banked the hearth-flame careful, and careful too he'd been to measure the powder, not to use so much at such short range to make a flash and maybe start a fire. And making sure beforehand that it would be Fergal who came to find him, not some of the women. And a thorough, efficient man, too: no chance he'd taken on finding the heart, but laid the pistol to his temple.

Fergal sat down beside him and laid a hand on the big hairy hand resting so calm-relaxed on the broad chest. "Brian, I'm sorry," he whispered. "Oh, God, let him hear me say it—I'm sorry. It

was a lie, Brian—not your blame, no one's blame. Brian, man."
Admit it now, past all the childish jealousy and foolish possessiveness, the grief he had caused her for it, the sorrow he had made this good man. This man who had never had a deal in life, this staunch quiet humble man who had only kept faith as he saw it, for those he loved and liked—a kinsman, a friend, a woman.

"Please God," and never any time in his life had there been so much humility in Fergal O'Breslin's voice, "let him hear me, God, let him know—Brian, forgive me . . . And God, don't hold it on him, put it on me if there's blame, I made him think it—"

But it would be a long grief in him and a heavy weight on him, that he waited too late to say the rest. *Forgive me* never said too soon.

He said it desperately to a dead man. And he thought again, desolately, *Count down! One gone, and one gone, and one—*

22

So there he was arguing with the priest, hot and bitter. "Lynch you said it to—you using the same arrogance, say you know God's justice so sure?"

"It is not what I say but the rules of the church, my son—" the priest mild. "One who takes his own life may not lie in consecrated ground."

"Church-rules—men's rules—what men are always so eager to define as God's intention! Proof you have of it? The right he has to lie by her in death—"

No use it was, of course. In his own land they laid Brian Donaghue, the priest making short ceremony. And that was the fourth night from the day Owen Desmond had died.

"My dear," said Nessa softly to him in the dark, "it's no matter, Fergal, don't think it. Just their bodies—not really themselves, you know. If God is merciful as we think, they're together—God wouldn't condemn Brian forever, for the one thing, when in all else he was so good."

"I should have—" Fergal whispered, "I should have said it to him—I knew that, Nessa, I did—only jealousy and selfishness like as you said, that I wouldn't admit it. A good man he was—if any's earned a place in hell, it's myself—"

She laid her hand across his mouth. "Don't go brooding on it, Fergal. He knows now, and—and so do you, to look past your own blind feeling, another time."

He had nothing to say for that; they lay quiet a little, some comfort in closeness and warmth. He was tired, but he knew he would not sleep. It was enough to rest here, silent in the dark, and let the heart begin to heal as it could—with a scar left.

Then, abruptly, not enough: not even that would he be allowed. Small noise at the door, the door opening. No, said his mind, not something else now, let me just rest a little. She was almost asleep beside him; she stirred as he sat up.

"O'Breslin—" It was Liam, anxious apologetic whisper. "Awake are you—O'Breslin?" He came a step in.

"Yes, what is it?" And Nessa was rousing up, to echo him drowsily.

"I'm sorry to disturb, but I was just out, and there's what looks to be a bad fire up the hill, you can see the flame—"

"Oh, God," said Fergal. He got up, fumbling for his shoes. In half a minute he was outside with Liam, and saw it, the other side of the wooded slope, a great glare in the sky and now and then glimpses of a reaching finger of flame. "Christ!" he said.

"It's been a dry summer—"

"That's not wildfire, boy," said Fergal grimly. "That's Hugh's crop burning, and some bastard set it alight deliberate!" He ran back to the house. "Nessa!" he shouted. "Shevaun! Get up—bring all the tools we've got—hurry! Fire up the hill, and the wind bringing it this way—for God's sake hurry!" He seized Liam's arm; they ran to the shed, found the two spades, and made up the slope fast as breath let them.

"My God—I never thought, O'Breslin—the wind—"

"Save your breath!" panted Fergal. Deadly fear engulfed him, damn the crop, as he toiled up the slope. Count down! Not Hugh and Maire too, only for that they loved each other—narrow men so certain-sure they knew God's laws, making rules all rigid for the what and where and when of love—and, God, yes, what to choose between?—turning on the unconforming ones as savage as those creatures of McCann's had turned on Edmund Kearney! Not Hugh and Maire, please God—any merciful God—those two gentle souls with the love shining from them together—

He came over the rim of the slope, the little narrow vale down beyond and then the steeper hill—he saw the fire. He said, *"Christ!"* A good hold it had, the strong night-wind fanning it. The tall crop of barley was half gone already, and the flames had eaten down from where the house was—the house— His breath was gone, his heart like a drum for the run uphill, but he ran again, fear and anger lending strength. He cannoned heavily into a man in the dark under trees, and his mind said with savage cold certainty, *Lynch—likeliest Lynch, though others in it with him maybe!* He gripped the man fiercely, and Hugh's voice said, "Fergal—thank God—"

"Hugh!" he gasped. "God be thanked indeed, man—Maire?"

"Yes, I'm here, Fergal, all right—but the house, oh, our little house, everything—"

"Hell with the house, as long as you're safe! If we can drown it with earth now, save some o' the field—Liam, to me—come on, man—Christ, nought to fetch water in if—"

"We can't save my field, Fergal," said Hugh almost calmly. "Let it go—madness to try. Lucky we'll be to save yours, the way the wind turns. Maire, go down to the others, I take it they're coming, and set them clearing out the growth down there, anything it might get hold on—if we can contain it for lack of fuel—"

She was gone, running. They set to work here, the three of them, tearing and digging at the wild stuff in the fire's path, but within ten minutes they saw it was hopeless—thirty men might have done it, clearing a strip round the fire to ring it in on itself, but it was too near where they started clearing: before they had done twenty feet it was roaring down on them fast, eating grain and bracken and trees impartial. "Try it farther down!" shouted Fergal; they turned and ran. "Hugh—you didn't see who—? Never believe—it was wildfire starting on its own—"

"No—likely some villagers—God's grace I woke, it was near the house."

"Bastards—" No time or breath for more of that. They ran, they came to the women, all but old Eily left with the child—the other side of the little vale, already at work with the tools they had, hayfork, scythe, the old blunt ax, hands. For what seemed eternity they worked like madmen, fighting time and the wind, clearing a pitifully narrow strip. But, God, time the flames ate to here, so fearful swift and insatiable, the twenty, thirty, forty feet they had managed to clear would never be enough—

(And as he dug and ripped frantic at tangled undergrowth, he knew that the fire was seen now by neighbors, and ordinary way men would have come out to help—no sign of that!)

It came over the slope, across the vale, God, so soon, so swift—a front of flame four times as long as the path they'd cleared. No good at all, they might as well have saved their strength— "No use! Get out—run—get down to the house, save what we can!"

Down the hill, breathless, panting, and the old woman there in the kitchen-garden, staring up—the boy's piping gleeful voice, "Oooh, look how it's different colors when it moves so funny—is it the moon fell down, Eily? Is it—"

"Eily," Fergal ordered, trying to draw new breath, "take the boy and go down across the road—well away—don't think it'll leap the road, but better go far enough on, up toward Donaghue's. Rest o' you, get the house cleared—everything we can—Liam, fetch the cart, and Nessa, better go down and open the field-gate, bring the cow—hurry—Eily, you'll take the cow with you to be safe—"

And all too little time, the way the fire swept down— The rickety hand-cart, that should have been piled with the reaped harvest next week, was loaded now with household goods, the iron kettle, the plates and cooking-pans, the food left, the pallets and blankets. Not everything—not time for everything. All too soon, greedy fingers of flame reaching out ahead of the main holocaust, touching the wild grass behind the shed, and that old dry wood, to catch and be consumed in a minute.

"Get out—run!" Fergal and Liam strained at the cart, Hugh steadying the load; they reached the road and turned onto it, over to Donaghue's land (that would be some other's now, the first who could hold it against a hundred men's greed)—the wind set the other way, and this little crop would not be burned, at least. They struggled up the gentle rise to that empty cabin, and from there, halted safe, they watched. The shed went up in a wild flare, and a minute later the cottage caught; before it was well wreathed in smoke, the fire was through the garden and chasing triumphant downhill into the barley.

An hour, two hours, the destruction of a year's labor and next winter's food.

And Fergal heard himself laugh, sounding half-hysterical. "Oh, by God, but look there!—didn't reckon on that, the bastards—the wind'll take it right down onto Dowling's place, and maybe into the village! You'll see them out now, all our good neighbors!"

They were already coming out—little black specks of running men silhouetted in flame, down there—let them fight the monster now, yes, and see their goods and gear go up in smoke! By God, let the whole village burn—serve them best, their own bitter medicine!

"The waste, the waste," said Hugh at his side sadly. "Yes—*digged a pit and fallen into it themselves*—"

And Eily agitating about the cow, wild-frightened the creature, and pulling away to run—"I couldn't to hold her, God knows where she'll be—"

Shevaun was hugging the cat to her; the other women all had arms full of miscellaneous goods. Strangely, none of them wailing over sudden disaster. Nessa's voice was nearly serene. "It might be much worse, Fergal. We're none of us hurt, and we've saved a good deal, clothes and food and household things."

"Sure to God," he said harshly, "only a little worse off than before!"

Fire no respecter of persons: their neighbors came out in strength to combat it, all the village roused. That many joined, they managed to clear a belt to contain it before it reached the village, but the wind as strong as it was, it might have carried the flames across, only for a thin drizzle of rain beginning to fall as first light showed in the sky. By a gray reluctant dawn, the fire was burnt out, leaving a great sword-shaped scar, black and reeking. All John Dowling's crop burned, as well as Fergal's and Hugh's, that house gone, and Gorman's cottage damaged where a spark leaped, both the Brogans' crops lost, and all the meadow-pasture this side the village.

It was small savage satisfaction in Fergal's heart, that; he knew certain as if he'd seen it that that fire had been set deliberate, meant to destroy Hugh's hard-won little field of grain—and he could have named the men who set it—Lynch, Burke, probably Kelleher. As pleased to see Fergal O'Breslin's crop and house destroyed too, but they hadn't reckoned on the rest. Fire, like as the proverb said, good servant, bad master!

The good milk-cow Fergal never got back. When he had searched and asked awhile along the way she'd run, it was borne in on him that he wasted time: the bland looks and innocent denials told him.

Someone had her penned secret: and if later he identified her, there'd be a dozen men to swear she was legal-owned by this man or that.

He came back to Donaghue's cabin at midday; Justin Desmond was there with a gift of bread, an offer to help—"Whatever you're thinking to do, Fergal. There's this crop here—ripe for the scythe, and I daresay you've a claim on it of sorts—"

"Of sorts," said Fergal, and smiled. "Some man will be moving up here and establishing right by possession—and to my land too, likely. Most probably the Dowlings, being adjacent. I'm not thinking to do anything more here, Justin, and if I was I'd not drag you into it, to bring their malice on you too."

"Miscall me, do you," said Justin, "saying I'd turn my back on a friend on account of majority opinion?"

"Well, you won't be called on to decide either way. I don't see anything left here for us. I can't speak for Hugh, but I'd say the same for him, and that he and Maire will do best to try what I will."

"What's in your mind, Fergal?" Nessa put down the ladle, looking up uncertainly from the hearth, from the pot of thin gruel. They were all staring at him. "Where—where could we go else? I'd thought—"

"There's a time to cut losses. Bad enough if it was but the material things. But with nine of ten of all the folk about feeling as they do, we'd not go through the winter without starving—you all see it well as I, if you'll admit it. I see just one way to get through the winter and have somewhat at the end—go over the border and take on as tenants to an English landlord."

There was a moment's silence. Hugh said heavily, "If Maire and I go, these people here might—"

"Greater chance they might not! This isn't all on your account, Hugh—it was Kevin McCann and his killers brought down dislike on me first. And even so, had we coin and goods to live on here somehow, what makes you think I'd want to stay near such neighbors?"

"There is that, true. . . . That man you met over there, he said—but no certainty of finding a tenancy at once—"

"So, as God wills, we starve—little or long, life or death. If I'm brought to starvation, maybe begging charity to feed my family, man, I'll rather be among strangers than these people here, to afford them more joy, seeing O'Breslin the chief come to that!"

Nessa's look on him was still troubled; it was Shevaun who leaned to grasp his arm hard. "Yes—yes, Fergal! We'll go—they'll not be given a chance to jeer and downlook us again! No matter what we come to—"

And Nessa touched his hand, brief and warm. "If you think best, of course we'll go."

Another little silence, and then old Eily began to cry gently. "O'Breslin, served your line I have—me and mine—fifty years—but I can't face it, O'Breslin. A hindrance I'd be to you only, now—and the long road to go—and to leave where my Tadgh lies—"

He looked down at his clasped hands. Maybe unfair to ask her, an old woman bent with rheumatism, but—starve here or there . . .

Justin Desmond looked from him to Hugh, back to the old woman. "Then there is a thing I can do," and he leaned to touch her shoulder. "Would you care to come to us, me and my wife, Eily?" He smiled at her. "Not charity, you may belittle yourself but I'm thinking you'd earn your way. Meriel will be having a child in the spring, and grateful for your help." He looked at Fergal, and his eyes said what would be unkind to say in her hearing—doubtless not too long, we will see she is looked to and content as may be.

"That's very kind in you, Justin. Eily?"

She looked up to Desmond's reassuring smile: doubtful, thawing, she considered. "A day's work in me still, I'd try—be of use, indeed. A gentleman you are. I—it's just the notion of the long road, another strange place—if it's right with O'Breslin—"

And Caitlin speaking up, a bit defiant and embarrassed, how she'd not said before, but the widower Matt Carney was after her to wed him, and she did reckon—feeling some like Eily, to pick up and go on to a strange place again—if O'Breslin would understand it . . . And Brighid was welcome, stay on with her and Carney, another pair of hands and Carney with only himself to support, they would do well enough.

"Yes," said Fergal. Count down . . . just as well. He knew these three older women had felt not so much different than their neighbors about Hugh and Maire—only saying nought for it because of their dependence on him, as his old retainers. And at that, how often coming out, deferentially smug over this or that, with: *Your father would never have—!* "It is right with me, whatever you all wish to do. We've all—just to do whatever's expedient, now."

He went over with Hugh that afternoon to poke about the ruins of the cottage, see if aught else could be salvaged. They found part of the poker buried under charred timber, and the half-melted remains of a cooking-basin. "We're told," said Hugh, looking at it thoughtfully, "that God's wrath can be terrible. But I think—God being patient and long withholding retribution, you know—that men's wrath makes a more terrible destruction, as it falls so often and so—wanton." He sat down on a fallen-in roof timber and turning the little lump of melted stuff in his hands, he added, "Yes, the sensible thing to do—we'll go over the border with you. But I'm thinking, Fergal, we'd best part there, and Maire and I go opposite way from you. Say it was halfway McCann and his cutthroats—only the start—most of it, the way they feel for us, and you befriending us."

"I might say it again, maybe only contrariness." Fergal tossed away the poker. "Damn, I'm no theologian—and come down to it, like the priest said to Lynch, no man with the right to judge another, for no man without sins of his own on him. Am I thinking crooked to say, all a man's got to judge by is what he knows of a man and feels for him, in himself? I'll tell you, Hugh—no disrespect to church-orders, but you right this minute and that man I met in a wood in Clare, it's two different men. And you here and now, I feel to be the better man—all I can say. A man I've—more respect for, and liking, as a man." He was a bit embarrassed to say it; he looked away.

"Something strange I'll tell you," said Hugh in a low tone, "and that is, I—I feel to be a better man. Yes, the Archbishop was right about that. Easy to live quiet and peaceful—if you never come to grips with naked life—shutting yourself away deliberate. Maybe even stranger it is, as I've said before, I don't feel uneasiness for it, how God will judge us. Some new thoughts I've had this half-year, and among them that—aside from any vows made to God, see you—it's a thing dependent on circumstances. No harm Maire and I make to any soul, to be loving each other. Not as if Kevin McCann wanted her or loved her, he deserting her as husband—as if we made sorrow for any human soul by it. If so, it seems to me, yes, it would be wrong. But any sin in it, I'll take it on myself, to abide by God's judgment. And," he smiled, "maybe another little sin I'll suffer for, but I'll not hesitate a minute to tell the lie, wherever we settle next—that we're man and wife. Which would keep our neighbors from feeling how these folk have—but we will still know, and you." He dropped the ruined pan to the ashes thick at his feet, a final gesture. "If you'd prefer we turn the opposite way—to find possible haven over there—say it, we will understand."

"It's the opposite I'd say, Hugh, and Nessa and Shevaun too, I know." Suddenly the little embarrassment dropped away from Fergal, and he laughed. "Why, man! If we apportion blame all so finicking, don't I share it? If I'd never run across you that day, you'd never have met Maire at all."

"If you'd never saved my life that day," amended Hugh. "Yes—like dropping a stone in a pool, and the circles widening out. A different man that was indeed. Ready to give my life to preserve a manuscript-book of history, and you said to me, dead weight, come to a choice of men's lives or history-books. Right you were, my friend."

"Well, I spent some labor helping you hide it safe, at that. I wonder if and when it'll be brought to light."

"Not by myself, at least. For that I've kept my trust as I might—the Archbishop here knows, and has sent information to Irish scholars abroad. The record of our race!" said Hugh suddenly, violently, and stood up. "Words written down! The record of any race is in the living men and women making the new generation —burn the books, you don't destroy the people, so long as the people live their history is safe. God has His own way of teaching us truths. My life for the book—that other man's life. My life now for the child in Maire's body—and whatever laws God or men make for it, not all the books at Clonmacnoise, all the books in every library in Ireland, worth the life—even the one, least life."

"Maybe God would agree with you there," said Fergal soberly. He looked at the ruined black hole that had been the hearthstone of his house—poor barren peasant-cottage, but home for eighteen months—and he thought, a child. Just as well Nessa had lost the child . . . but—but—what?—unidentifiable feeling in him, no matter. He said abruptly, "Well, so that is another reason we had best make haste to get settled where we can, and how we can."

Some argument he had with Shevaun about the cat. Things they couldn't carry, to be bargained off here as profitably as possible, preferably for coin but at least for things they could carry; it seemed to him that sleek black Shena was one of them. "You'll not sell her, Fergal! Break Sean's heart it would, and all of us as fond of her—"

"Now, look, girl, you can't carry a cat thirty-forty miles—she'd fetch three pounds—"

"Let him sell her," said Nessa dryly. "Only foolish folk say cats love their places better than people—some do, some don't. See how that tom of Hugh's went back wild, so we thought, but I've wondered if he found his road back across the river to his old home. I warrant if we sell Shena she'd get away and come after us an hour later." But the risk Shevaun refused to take; Fergal gave her best, shrugging, and with Liam took the cart into the village loaded with miscellaneous gear.

He didn't look forward to the bargaining as an easy or pleasant task, and he was not disappointed. Thinking crooked, he had said to Hugh. Every soul of them knew as well as he that that fire had been set, but for the unmeant destruction it had made they weren't blaming those who had set it; it was as if they put the blame on the victims, for being there that honest men had a reason to set the fire. They gave Fergal sullen resentful looks, or looks of secretly malicious pleasure to see him forced to barter essential goods. They offered absurdly low exchange and openly sneered at his holding out for better.

Lynch came along as Fergal argued with Degan over the price of the big iron kettle. Two groats offered: Fergal holding his temper tight, to have this whole business over, and get away. Lynch spat and said, "Fair offer, O'Breslin, for tainted gear out of a house that welcomes in folk turned from God to Satan! Take it, my fine chieftain!—and try to barter the coin for bread! Every man in this place knows what to expect from decent folk, does any oblige you!"

Liam said angrily, "You mind your tongue, how you talk up to your betters, Lynch!"

"Oh, no, Liam," said Fergal in a hard tone, "don't put it on grounds of rank! Prince, chief, commoner, the hell with rank—all plain men together here, by rule of English law, aren't we? Not a question of rank, but Christian honesty. Make me an offer yourself, Lynch! You ought to be rejoicing that you've succeeded in your intention—destroy or drive away!—we'll be ceasing to infest this Christian neighborhood, and the quicker I bargain off this gear, the sooner we'll be away."

"Is that so now?—and good riddance! Intention, you say—are you making an open charge on me, O'Breslin?" Oh, yes, so quick to pick that up, knowing himself guilty!—no more evidence Fergal needed.

He looked Lynch up and down. Last year, he'd have lashed out physically with curses; but he had learned of late that there were things struck sharper and deeper than physical blows. Plain men: couldn't judge a man by his breeding, like horse or hound: but that mattered to Lynch, or he wouldn't be so quick to suspect arrogance. Give him what he expected: Fergal put into his look all the gentry-superciliousness for bumptious peasant that he'd ever had turned on him by English. He smiled slowly, and said, "No, Lynch, I make no charge on you—little to choose there'd be, between the justice meted out by my good Irish neighbors here, and English anywhere. Not my place to remind you of a thing the priest said. And the time I'd not waste, wanting to be on my way from this place. There's a proverb for it, Lynch, maybe you've heard—*Who would have good vengeance, leave it to God.*"

He turned a contemptuous shoulder before Lynch's expression changed—to catch a strange shadow of guilt in Degan's eyes. "Speak up, Degan! Two shillings the bottom price."

Degan dropped his eyes. "Two shillings it is," he said expressionlessly.

23

FERGAL DID NOT believe what they found at the Connacht border. It was the last day of September when they came to the banks of the Shannon; he had not crossed that border since the first day of April, that final raid he'd made with McCann. For eighteen months previous to that, bent on enforcing the settlement-act, the English had been increasing the guard, and new garrison-stations had been built every month, until they stood scarce a quarter-mile apart.

Remembering that, he settled the women in a sheltered copse, that evening of the day they started the journey; he and Hugh went on, cautiously, to find a good place to get over. Forty yards along the riverbank they came on an old fellow casting for salmon, who drew in his line at sight of them and hobbled up to ask if they'd cross the river—"A boat I have, take you for small pay."

"But the guards," began Fergal.

The old man laughed and spat. "Ah, no need worry about them! Both stations up and down from here empty, they don't go to bother overmuch about the border these days, see you. Do seem's if they give it up as a bad job."

"But—" Well, what else had Carmody said, six months back? "I will be damned," said Fergal half to himself.

The old man ferried them over for a threepenny piece—extravagant, but easier on the women, with all they carried with them. Right up a passable inlet, beyond the bogland, they were landed a hundred yards down from the looming bulk of the guard-station, one of the crude-built wood-frame barracks put up hastily last year. But no patrol on watch, no regimental bell striking the hours of guard-duty. Their boatman shipped his oars careless of noise. "They do leave some on duty, here and there, but it's all one and the same, most places—you buy the captain a drink, or some such, and walk across by a bridge, no trouble."

"Now you tell me, with my coin in your pocket," said Fergal, still incredulous.

"Such a thing there be as going at a job too thorough," said the old man, and there was something venomous in his sardonic chuckle. "*Which* it's to be reckoned the English do discover! You'll have heard, take example, about those three hundred Mayo folk as an English officer marooned out there on an offshore island bare quarter-mile long, ten mile from mainland—two years back 'twas—and all but one starving, those as stayed, and drowning, those as tried get back to shore. Just a bit o' jest by that officer, he in liquor and saying it'd be a fine test for the power o' our church's saints, let us call for a miracle! Yes, men, I'm the one came off—I be—always a strong swimmer I were, but I do pride myself on that one, and I three-and-sixty turned that same month." He spat, and laughed, and unshipped oars. "Tell you, my men, English do find out twice too good a job they made at killing off Irishmen! They're needing 'em to work the land now, if they're to have any profit. I do reckon, likely, that English officer wish he'd not been so quick that time! But we do oblige 'em—so we do—" His laugh was inane. "Breeding so fast like horse-gnats in summer, make more slaves to serve English, aye, that's what we're at now-adays!" He shoved out into the inlet, still chuckling mirthlessly.

They spent the night in the empty guard-station.

It was vaguely in Fergal's mind to find Thomas Carmody, who might offer advice about factors and landlords. Somewhere over by Killashee, that farm they'd looted that night, eight or nine miles on from here. Carmody had been friendly, that time; if he was still here—They made an early start next morning, south on the road along the river, but watching for patrols: even if the slave-taking troops did not ride hunting this side the border, which was by no means certain, any regular patrol would arrest them as vagrants, and that would likely come to the same thing, sold to slavery abroad. Twice that morning they scattered off the road to hide in tall grass or trees or ditch, as an English patrol came by.

The third patrol came on them unawares, or they on it, round a bend of the road under trees: the usual nine men and a captain, but these halted for a brief rest on the march—men dismounted, men lounging sidewise in their saddles. Too late to hide or run, they'd seen Fergal's straggling little company— At his involuntary curse, Shevaun, startled, let go the string serving as leash for the cat, and dropped her bundle of clothes and household goods. The cat flashed across the road in a black streak, and the boy ran after, heedless of his mother's frantic cry, all their voices calling him.

The English captain at the patrol's head slid from his saddle and caught the child in mid-flight, and lifted him. "Now, not so fast, young one! Your pet is it, that fine black puss? No fear, you'll have her back—Kean, Curtiss, Warren, get you after the cat, fetch her here—and handle her gentle, mind!" He came down the little way to where they stood tense and waiting helplessly in the road, and he said soothing to the child, "Don't fret now, they'll bring her back to you safe. Do you know my tongue, boy?—it's all right, no harm I mean, one o' my own I have just your size. Will you tell me your name, young one?"

The boy was just five years, but of all he'd learned in a short life that was the lesson he knew best: fear and caution for English! He pulled away rigid from the arms about him, silent, lip-quivering, every muscle taut for the first chance to get away and run to safety.

The captain gave him into Shevaun's reaching arms, and he turned and clung to her, face buried in her shoulder. Humorous shouts from the troopers chasing the cat in the field alongside the road. Fergal took one involuntary step to put himself between the women and the Englishman. He met the captain's eyes and the captain met his, steady. The captain was a man of forty years or so, good-looking, the fair Saxon good looks, regular features, crisp-curling red-gold hair worn a little thin by the helm he had taken off to hang at his saddlebow; his blue eyes were grave, the smile in them for the boy fading as he looked at Fergal—and at Hugh and Liam who stepped forward too, ahead of the women. He glanced over their shabby bundles, their clothes powdered with road-dust.

He said quietly to Shevaun, "A well-grown lad he is for, what, six years?—only five? A handsome boy, mistress, credit to you. My own youngest that size, and turned six." He looked back to the men. "You're removing?" and his tone was soft.

None of them spoke, only watching and waiting. And a couple of the troopers came up grinning, with the struggling cat—one of them nursing a deep-scratched hand. "Here she be, cap'n! An' a true creature o' Satan safe enough, wouldn't you know she belonged to Papists!" The laugh good-humored, rueful. Nessa took the cat and retired quickly behind Fergal, murmuring soothing words.

"That's well," said the captain. "Saddles—we ride in a moment."

"Sir—?" The trooper with the shoulder-knot marking him corporal looked questioning from the little group to his officer.

"No, it is all right—they're not vagrants, I am satisfied of their destination," said the captain. "Saddles!" The men saluted and tramped back to the waiting horses. The captain's eyes held sober compassion, again meeting Fergal's. "You've trained the boy well indeed—have nought to do with English. . . . Bad seed we sow here, to reap a bad harvest in time to come. Don't misjudge us all as fiends incarnate, my man."

Fergal found his voice to say evenly, "Our thanks for your favor, Captain."

"An educated man you sound. Oh, a terrible harvest we prepare for England here indeed, God have mercy on us," said the captain, low-voiced, and made a little helpless gesture. "All of us must live—I too have wife and children to provide for—and captain-rank doesn't talk back contrary to headquarters-orders. I do what I can, and there are a few other men feeling so who do what they can, this place and that. Don't think us all inhuman, subscribing to inhuman laws without thought, I beg you. I'll wish you good fortune, to find near safety and rest."

It was Hugh who said, "We thank you, Captain." The Englishman bent his head, turned and walked back heavily to mount his horse. The patrol rode by in line, and Fergal let out a held breath.

"And I do wonder what deviltry lies behind that, him letting us go! Bribed by landholders' bailiffs, maybe, they in need of tenants?"

Hugh said gently, "Could you not think of him as he asks, Fergal? An honest man he sounded to be. As we can't claim all Irishmen are men of goodwill—witness some we've known—can we say every last Englishman evil?"

Fergal laughed; he looked at the women, still white and trembling for the danger, at the little boy huddled on his mother's shoulder. "Man, look you don't get into trouble one day, able to credit English with any generous motive! Take kind words from an English as meant honest, you won't live long!"

By dusk, asking direction, they came to the farm Fergal had once plundered in haste; he wondered now why he had made it an objective, but all Carmody or another man in his place could do was refuse him aid. He left the others in the road, walked up past the kitchen-plot, and tapped at the door. And only once he had met Thomas Carmody, but he knew him at once there in the doorway—the supper-hour, family at table visible inside.

"Now your face I've seen before," said Carmody, "and where was it?" He cocked his head, ruminating.

"I'll recall myself to your memory—"

And the big man laughed and swore, enlightened: "By damn, it is! The raider I followed up after my lucky piece! Over the border again, are you?"

"The first time since, Carmody."

"Well, you were the one with the honester eyes, that I'll say. That bold boy with you then I'd not trust far."

"And how right you'd be. I'd ask favor for favor, as I made you a small one that day—"

"Not so small. Turnabout fair, what is it? . . . Ah, over for good are you, to settle? . . . and family with you—man, come in— Eileen!"

"We'd not impose, and we've some food with us still—"

"Well and good," said the little plump woman come up behind Carmody, "but there's a patrol due here by dusk, and bound to take you all up as vagrants, find you in the road. I do see there's a young one down there too, and it's chill at dark. Fetch them up, not much we have but a fire at least."

And later, settled about the little hearth, the women chattering low together at one side, the two grown Carmody daughters making shy overtures to young Liam, Carmody offered what information he had. "I wouldn't doubt as Master Jason Horder"—he gave the English address contemptuous emphasis—"'ll take you on. And, damn, it'll cost me and Mulcahy a pound apiece, come to think. See, there's Forgan's place, fields ready to harvest and none to do it. Forgan and his wife both kidnapped off by revenue-patrol five days back, at their own door. And God's mercy on them, good young folk and well-liked—I'll not speak long of it, too sorrowing for Eileen, she looking on Noreen Forgan as another daughter." He shook his head. "But point is, the crop—Horder made the bargain with me and Mulcahy to reap it, and hating to pay out extra, but he couldn't expect we'd do it for nought. Reckoned to start on it day after tomorrow. Now I figure he'll give you Forgan's place, and you'll get the crop to harvest, and full profit. Not that *that* amounts to much—the mill's English-owned, natural, part o' the factor's overseeing, and the charge triple what you're used to. But there, if we're to have profit at all—" he shrugged.

"Who's the landlord here?"

"London guild," said Carmody, stretching his legs to the hearth. "Goldsmiths' Company—private bankers, see." He fetched out his Roman coin, turned it in his fingers, flipped it. "Lady uppermost. Like so, O'Breslin—toss a coin, call head or bottom-side, see— only like on this here piece o' mine, it's heads on both sides. And that's how the English law's set up, them having first call and always calling heads. Fellow as used to do clerk-accounting for Horder— and another tale *that* is, too—Waterford man he was—he told me they do figure on sixty percent yearly return on the capital investment in Irish land." He chuckled without mirth. "But it's pull devil, pull baker—hinder each other they do, in taking profit! See, the Parliament's revenue-patrols kidnapping folk to sell into slavery—and wouldn't they be getting good prices indeed, for upstanding young Irishmen and comely Irish girls—" Carmody looked at his own two there, fresh pretty ones, sixteen and eighteen, Fenella and Sheelagh; his expression mingled anger and sorrow. "Oh, yes, sure to God. And the land-bailiffs like Horder, they between the hammer and the anvil, see—patrol takes off the tenants they hire, and no complaint can they make, for they're breaking the penal law by renting to Irish tenants first place! And the owners coming down on 'em for short profits."

"I see, yes. What about this factor here? What terms?"

"Horder—well, he is an Englishman," said Carmody with a shrug, "and the terms are English. Another coin with two heads alike. They need tenants to work the land, but it runs against the grain in them to make much concession, and things being like they

are for Irish now, it's no choice we have but take their terms. Six
pound a year for Forgan's place—eight acres—if you take a cow
on lease, feed her yourself, and the factor deciding when to breed
her so you're lacking the milk, and the calf to feed six-eight months
after weaning. But at that, the terms might be worse. See, a profit
the factor's got to show, and a damn' good one. You have tools
stolen, the cow maybe, aught you need for working the farm—by
these outlaw-bands coming down on us—factor's bound to replace
it, if he wants the job done. . . . I'll tell you, O'Breslin, like I said
to you before—this reason and that, their settlement scheme's
failed, way they meant it to work. Way it's gone, most of the landownership's gone to great parcels of acreage held by gentry and
corporation, and that means men like Horder over us—and black
and white that is, sure, plain issue. And in truth, an Irishman I
am and patriotic as the next one, but I do find it in my heart to
be sorry for the few English took that settlement-act at face value,
way it was intended, and stayed on land granted. Oh, well, you'll
see—you'll find how it's gone here. . . ."

Fergal saw how it had gone, this side the border—two and a
half years after the settlement-act was law. He read some of the
tale in Jason Horder, the bailiff, that next morning. Horder, standing wide-legged, consciously arrogant, there in the courtyard of
the big stone house once home of whatever Irishman had owned
land about—not as much land as the acreage now administered
from here. Horder, thirty-five or on a bit, sandy, not within six
inches of Fergal's height, pale freckled skin, pale quick-moving
eyes: one short leg stiffened from a war-wound here or in England:
the conspicuously careless dress high English gentry used to affect,
open-throated shirt, unbuttoned doublet—and Parliament-army
cavalry-boots wide-topped—and a cavalry sword-belt with a pistol
thrust through it.

Horder, any English factor here, aware he lived among enemies, at once insolent for power over them and uneasy for there
being so many of them: his mastery not by that pistol in his belt,
but the English military stationed near and police-patrolling. He
lived in this gentry-house, so much better off on his wage than
even English officers that he kept half a dozen Irish servants: twice
as well off as he'd have been in England in the same position, and

not only for the money but social prestige: here he was a little king. It was a move in the game he had to play, come out to interview prospective tenants instead of having them in—emphasizing it, they low native peasants, he English. And his pale eyes secretly busy on Fergal's height and shoulder-breath, secretly uneasy for their unaccented English answering him.

He accepted Fergal as tenant, casual, not to let him know another tenant was needed; he glanced at Hugh and said, equally casual, in his high nasal voice, "You sound to be halfway educated, my man. By any chance d'you read and write?"

"I do—sir."

"Ah. Enough to keep accounts and such?"

"Yes, sir. I have done clerking work"—Hugh smiled faintly—"for another master, sir."

"Convenient," said Horder indolently. "I'm in need of a clerk. Six pound a year and your keep ... A wife? Well, no help, she can call herself another maidservant for her keep." *How kind I am, not so*? said his tone. "You can have a chamber in the servants' wing here. We'll see how satisfactory a clerk you are. Report to my office in the morning, eight o' the clock sharp." He gave them a curt nod and strode back into the house, spine consciously straight.

"Convenient!" said Fergal. "My God, Hugh, better off you'll be than me! Cash equivalent, I'll be lucky to see three pounds a year profit—and you sitting easy under a roof and earning double at pen-work."

Hugh was still looking after Horder. "Yes—we'll not starve this winter at least. I don't know about easy, Fergal. That Englishman will demand a deal of humble bowing-and-scraping at him. It's maybe fortunate I am—you might say—trained in humility. But I'll confess it, meekness does not come as ready to me these days as it used."

"It's not a trait comes very easy to any Irishman!—but English don't look below surfaces. We're all learning to act the humble inferior to their faces—to stay alive for the day, please God, we can show them our true opinion!"

And that was part of how it was here, necessity constraining these people closer-ruled by the conquerors to show the conquerors the fawning deference demanded—amuse them to belief in these peasants' harmlessness, by assumed crass stupidity.

How it was otherwise, he saw and heard the first few days—this place, any place, miniature example of the whole country. Halfway, and sardonically, he could share Carmody's sympathy for the four Englishmen in the neighborhood who had elected to keep and work the land allotted them as military pay. Redmond, Sutton, Daly, French. All former common soldiers of Parliament, humble-born countrymen, Redmond the oldest at three-and-thirty, each with upwards of twenty acres, modest holding. Aside from the ten or twelve bailiffs within a twenty-mile circle about, they were the only Englishmen here, except of course the military which kept to itself socially. Redmond had fetched his wife over; the others had been single men. It was against English law for Englishmen to wed native Irishwomen, but like the tenant-law that one had not been possible to enforce: lonely single men not kept so by words on parchment! Sutton, Daly, French all wed to Irish girls—who had taken them calculating, for the security of themselves and family. Only, Daly's wife alienated from her family, because she so demeaned herself—daughter to the chief Ryan she was, the other two less highborn. Sutton saddled with a family of in-laws to support, French the same.

And Carmody said, amused, females being how they were—! Those marriages made by civil English ceremony, but the women never stopped deviling the Englishmen until there'd been secret marriage-service by the priest—who lived as tenant, unknown as priest, of course. And the English husbands not daring to reveal his true identity when they knew it, for fear of vengeance. The two wives thus far with babes seeing them baptized, to be raised in the church—and at least one of the three husbands, Daly, so helpless in love with the wife that he might be persuaded to turn Catholic to please her. "If they're to have any peace at home, see you—" chuckled Carmody.

Hugh said to that, rueful, ironic, "Do you believe the prophecy now, Fergal? In less than three years! I said it to you, that day we lay up on Knockmagh. They come, the foreigners, and a little time passed, they are Irish. . . . Yes, these children bearing English surnames—but a hundred years hence, maybe thought of as Irish surnames, like as others that were once Norman."

"But not many like that, settling permanent," Fergal reminded him.

"No, not many." Fair example, here: four landholders with eighty acres among them, out of five thousand acres owned by gentry, merchant, corporation never seeing the land but hiring one like Horder to administer it. And alone the men like those four came, alone they stayed. There was an inn in Killashee village that was all part of the Goldsmiths' Company's acreage here—local tenant holding it, and that illegal too—the man who had owned it outright three years back, one Colm Devesey. And those four Englishmen coming in there of an evening, to buy a glass of the raw weak whiskey Devesey had to offer, for a little congenial men's talk—to see every other man in the room turn ostentatious aside, making private low talk in their own tongue. The English would sit awhile together, and times their talk was dispirited and times angry, resentful: and get up and go, with none calling farewell but a cold silence held until they were out the door.

Nuances: Redmond holding bitterness for the other three that they couldn't force their Irish wives to befriend his English one, she with no female friend this side Portsmouth—the only other Englishwomen about the disreputable camp-followers to military, and a few bailiffs' wives who held themselves of higher class. Rumor said Redmond would soon be selling out his holding and taking her back to England, for her discontent and his here.

And the Chalfonts, that was another part of it—and rumor saying for that, that it was a thing happening often elsewhere. A magnificent jest that was, told in secret like one too frank for mixed hearing. An English officer, Chalfont, coming with title to house and land owned by Sean O'Ronan. Maybe O'Ronan had some crafty Norman blood in him, biding a few weeks, finding out by devious ways that the Colonel Robert Edward De Montmorency Chalfont, scion of old gentry line, turned Parliament man for safety and profit, was a single man with nought but distant cousins as family . . . That haughty Englishman was rotting bone and flesh in an unmarked grave somewhere on that land, but there was a family of Chalfonts in the house, to show their legal deed—and polite hospitality—to any English official: and after such a one rode off, to comment amusedly in Irish. . . . "O'Ronan says to me," said Carmody, "what's the name? An old and proud one, O'Ronan— but if they'll hang me as O'Ronan and leave me in peace as Chalfont, by Jesus, boy, I'm Chalfont!"

And maybe—with a bad year for crops, individual ill luck, the English law tightened up—some man who knew that jest informing secret for reward, and investigation made. Or maybe not: who could say?

Another part of it, Donovan. The one Irishman in ten thousand with the money to bribe the Commission and keep his own land, Donovan. No money he had left now: he giving generous aid, shelter, food to so many homeless, at first—paying for his tenants' corn-grinding when the mill came under English ownership and the charge was tripled; and now, every indigent in the county taking it as a right to demand charity of Donovan, and his tenants resenting that he asked more than token rent—weren't they and he Irishmen together against the foreign tyrant? More patriotic he should be! Donovan disillusioned at incessant demands, having given all he had, and as resentful toward them . . . "Human nature," said Hugh with a sigh.

Two and a half years since the Act was made law, since it began to be enforced. Men still saying, when the King is restored to the throne, all these Parliamentary acts will be reversed, and everything be as it was before. Fergal wondered: even if that should happen, for the material restoration, would any of them high or low be quite the same as they had been—after existence on this level?

He had said to Hugh, Another man you were: he could say it of himself. Lough Eask before the war a thousand years away, but not much nearer that young chieftain of the clan who had swum ashore from the Arans over a year and a half ago.

It was a stout little cottage, clean and neat; and when they first entered it, Nessa looked round and sat down on the settle and began to cry. "I know it's s-silly—I'm sorry—it's just, she must have b-been—*that* good a housewife, and so f-fond of the house —and carried off like so God knows where—"

"Eileen Carmody said she was with child." Shevaun put down her bundle and gazed round, at the well-swept hearthstone, the two wooden plates and tableware set orderly on the table, three cooking-pots lined by size in a row to the side of the hearth, scrubbed wooden ladle balanced across the biggest, and on the little mantel-shelf a wooden mug holding a handful of late wildflowers—dead and drooping now, but they had doubtless made a brave bright show the day Noreen Forgan was taken away, to be sold into slavery and likely end in a military brothel. In the one tiny bedchamber, a new-filled double pallet neat with two blankets folded, and a chest: in the second, the rough-shaped pieces for the cradle Forgan had only begun work on—the framework done, painstakingly put together with hand-whittled dowels.

Their clothes in the chest—what they had not been wearing. "Oh, I *couldn't*—" Nessa, unfolding the two shabby homespun gowns, so neatly mended. "But I suppose we must be s-sensible for it, threadbare as we are ourselves—"

The kitchen-garden well-weeded, and a modest display of late onions, leeks, cabbage. A field of potatoes, two of rye, eight acres of well-kept farm. Good supply of food in the house: she had put down meat in salt, and some vegetables.

Fergal had felt bitter as any man at the slave-taking trade, and he had felt personal fear of the slave-patrols, and fear for his people. But for the first time then he felt the true inward terror, cold down his spine, for the thing itself, in implication, for the individual. He felt it, looking at Owen Forgan's extra pair of trews, worn and mended, and the two ancient shirts clean-folded ready there, a handful of odds and ends, that a poor man kept unthinking—knife with broken blade, harness-buckle, three bone buttons, pewter candle-holder with the handle missing. All that was left of Forgan, as if he were dead. And better were he—than to be shipped and sold by age and weight and strength, like horse or cow, and likely see his wife sold away elsewhere—maybe before that babe was born, the cradle in there meant for.

The Carmodys had warned them to take care: the revenue-patrols now, here, were taking children, any old enough to walk. Doubtless good investment, long-term, for the foreign slave-buyers—slaves who would remember nought but slavery, less likely to rebel or run away. Or so they might reason. . . .

He looked at small Sean there on the hearthstone, coaxing the cat to quit its fastidious prowling of a new place. He thought, no matter the age, a son of Roy Donlevy—who was also half O'Breslin—would not grow to a mindless slave content with slavery, anywhere, anyhow. He thought (fingering Forgan's mended shirts loving-washed by a good wife), Take them from the mothers' breasts, the blood was still Gael, and the memory of freedom bred into the bone—and maybe by now the instinct for rebellion. Bad slaves they would make indeed.

He put the clothes back in the chest. "Sensible," he echoed Nessa. "So we must be, use things usable. Damn, a queer thing I'll say—he was the hell of a better farmer than I'll ever be, all so thrifty-weeded and neat rows planted!—a kind of obligation on me to live up to him!"

24

HORDER CAME BY, along that next midday. Fergal was just up from the field, approving Liam's digging-over of part of the garden for winter-roots to be put in; they both looked up at the sound of the horse. It was a ramping big black English hunter, and the factor sat easy in the saddle with the deceptive slouch of the natural horseman.

"You're settled in—good." He glanced casually at Liam, no interest to the factor who or how many in a tenant's family. "When can you have this crop all in?"

"I wouldn't say—sir. Five days, six."

"Four make it," said the factor. "Your day for the mill is five days from now. I make sure you've been told the terms—" No offer to discuss those when he accepted Fergal as tenant: the terms the last thing a prospective tenant asked about, for any terms offered a better chance than the alternative—being taken up on a vagrancy charge. "You to pay the miller's fee, one shilling the ground bushel. You'll be paid two shillings the ground bushel at the mill. Your farm-rent's due the day after your corn is ground."

"Yes, sir," said Fergal, expressionless. He knew the terms from Carmody; for his situation, taking over this end of the season, he had reckoned the sum. With luck, he might realize two pounds. You could live on a pound, two pounds a year; most Irish folk did, now. You lived near the bone, and the larger a family you had to feed, the nearer the bone you lived. The kitchen-garden, the one out of three fields put down to potatoes, would feed you through the year, after a fashion, enough to keep alive, and when you could afford it you bought a little meat. What you didn't buy, or would save up coin five years to buy, were luxuries like salt, new cloth, shoes, and such.

He could keep out five ground bushels of his grain, if he wanted. Or give up ten toward the cost of grinding. No benefit to him, it would come to much the same thing: less cash profit, and more profit to the landholder, for the miller was a tenant too, hired at six or seven pounds the year's wage to run the mill, and in that time earning upwards of four hundred pounds for the owner: any grain taken as fee belonged to the landholder. Coin with head on each side, sure to God.

"I'll have the crop in by then, sir. Next Thursday that will be, for the mill?"

"Thursday, yes." The factor lifted rein to ride on, and then checked, something more personal and interested in his light eyes. "Here's a pretty wench! Your woman?"

Fergal glanced round; it was Shevaun coming down from the house a few yards away. She heard the factor's half-insolent comment, but only met his gaze brief and cool, and said to Fergal, "If there's a cabbage fit to cook, fetch it in, Fergal, will you?"

And so far had he come on the road of compromise, for safety's sake, that he answered the factor first. "My sister, sir." And, "I will, Shevaun." Looking at her, he discovered with a little surprise that Horder was right. He hadn't consciously looked at Shevaun, that he recalled, in a long while; and maybe no man ever saw his sister as a woman, as another man would. He knew she'd changed, since Roy's death: the careless, gay girl he had known changed before that, but these last months more, to seem sometimes older than any of them, in sense of maturity. She was too thin, he saw now, and too pale—oddly, the way Maire had looked six months back, the white skin translucent, the too-grave set of the mouth. And with a sudden pang, he saw their mother in her, for the little aging: the sharpened line of jaw, the steady blue eyes under slim arched brows, the same—Ethne in her as she grew older.

Horder grinned down at her, amiable, admiring, showing stained teeth. "Well, you I'll come to have another look at when I've time!" He touched heel to flank and rode on, and the set of his shoulders said he knew she looked after him.

As she did. "So that is Master Jason Horder."

"Busily getting sins recorded on him against Judgment Day. It is. His impertinence you'll have to listen to, for I daren't talk back at him," said Fergal grimly.

"No." Unexpectedly she added, "I'm sorry for that man. One of those needing all the while to remind himself, A great strong fellow I am—and saying and doing things to prove it, just to himself." She laughed with little contempt, and Fergal knew that Roy was in her mind, the quiet strong man who never boasted of strength or used it wanton, who never wasted time talking of what he'd do, but did it.

"Pity wasted on the Englishman," he said brusquely. He found an early winter-savory cabbage, and took it up careful; they went up to the house in silence.

The meal was just finished when Hugh and Maire came in, with largesse: a dozen tallow candles, a pound of fresh beef. "Nothing's lacking at the house," Maire disclaimed Nessa's astonished reluctance to accept. "The factor expects the best food and service, and he's sharp at asking accounts, they say, but so many excuses to give as reason for buying more, you know."

"Yes," said Hugh absently, seating himself at Fergal's gesture. "Easy to encourage his notion that they're feckless managers, and waste goods—and every time one of these outlaw-bands makes a raid, the servants claiming they stole thrice what was actually taken, to make excuse for replacement. And wasn't that another thing I said to you that day on Knockmagh, Fergal—turning us lawless, not feeling it as lawless, equating patriotism with mishonesty. And in a sense, isn't it at that."

Maire was answering Nessa, "Nice folk?—oh, yes, welcoming us in, and we've a comfortable chamber—so good to be in a real *house* again, Nessa, you can't think!—solid walls and doors, and good furniture— Homesick? No, not for—any other home I ever had, that wasn't real home. They're no matter really, those things—" But all the while her eyes kept straying to Hugh, troubled.

"Something on your mind," said Fergal, eyeing him too.

"I don't know—" Hugh raised one hand, let it fall in a helpless gesture. "Just a feeling I have, Fergal, that—that we're not settled here, not *to* settle—whether for all of us, or myself and Maire, I can't say. An uneasy sort of feeling—but there, premonitions usually the result of indigestion," and he smiled; but the smile faded at once. "Another thing. You haven't heard about Jason Horder, the tale Carmody said we'd hear. No—if you had, you'd still be swearing."

"What is that about?"

"How he came to be in need of a clerk. He killed the latest one," said Hugh. "A man by the name of O'Hanlon. Horder found he'd been falsifying accounts and pocketing some of the coin collected in rents and such. No challenge or charge—he shot O'Hanlon in the back in the factor-office at the house—as a lesson to the neighborhood what comes of cheating the bailiff."

"That is a thing Horder would do," said Fergal coldly. "English."

"English," said Hugh. "How they do revere the letter of the law. There was a coroner's inquest, they call it, presided over by a military judge, to make official decision for the record, was it murder, or manslaughter, or natural death, or suicide, or whatever. Last month it was."

"And the presiding judge deciding it was suicide—any Irish daring to deceive an Englishman was willfully courting sudden death?"

"Well, not quite," said Hugh. "I had this from Brady, Horder's head manservant. The judge ruled that there had been no need for any formal inquiry in the first place. He read out an official pronouncement by the military government in Dublin, which is to be taken as legal precedent henceforth in English law for the governing of Ireland. The killing of an Irish Catholic, male or female, cannot constitute murder in any degree, for such natives are not to be classified as human beings under the law, but as equivalent to livestock. Had the shooting taken place on another man's land, and O'Hanlon been tenant to another landholder, Horder would have been guilty of poaching, same as if he'd shot hare or grouse on private land. But since O'Hanlon belonged to land Horder administers, there was no case, for O'Hanlon was not a human being by law, you see."

Fergal sat up and stared at him. He said softly, "They have written it down as official law—like that? By Jesus— And what am I swearing about, to hear it? *That* resting heavy on your mind,

Hugh? After knowing the profit England takes in the slave trade, with these superfluous natives who can so well be spared from their own country?" He threw back his head and laughed, savagely. "Brother, who is astonished to discover that the sheep-stealing wolf has a full set of teeth?"

He and Liam got the crop cut in the four days allowed, if only just. And two of those four days, coming back to the cottage, Fergal found Horder there, pale eyes bold on Shevaun, following her down to the stream when she fetched water, or watching her weeding the garden.

"What's he after, the bastard?"

"What would you think, Fergal?" Shevaun smiled, scornful. "And aside from *that*, he's lonely. Laugh—he is—the English are all lonely here anyway, wouldn't they be?"

"He had best take care," said Fergal. "Lip service I'll pay, to act humble as they please, that we live—but only so far in that, if he offers active insolence to a female in my guardianship, he'll wish he had not."

Shevaun gave him a thoughtful look, silent. He couldn't identify her look, and he was oddly uneasy for it; he put some sharp private questions to Nessa that night, when they were alone. "You've not seen him touching her? If she's thinking to suffer his impertinent attention to avoid the danger from him if—"

"I couldn't say, Fergal—I don't know." She sounded troubled too. Fergal lay awake: life at low ebb in him, the bone-weariness for hard work on small meals, and their whole situation here, and now this business of Shevaun, all converging to tell him how wrong he'd been. Worse off than before: shouldn't have come . . . He shifted restlessly on Owen Forgan's pallet. Damn, he still felt an interloper here, not to say a thief, wearing Forgan's trews that were in better state than any he had, eating the loaf Forgan's wife had baked, and talking with Liam about finishing that cradle in there for Maire's babe, by next May. . . . Shouldn't have come. Across in Connacht, poorer land, and English there too, but not so close over you, not like this: tenants here a bit better off materially, but giving up more freedom and personal integrity for it. Should have stayed, damn the bad neighbors, taken Donaghue's cabin and land, made do somehow. Hugh and Maire better off here, maybe, none knowing about them; and yet, living in the same house with Horder—

Horder and Shevaun. The factor, like most unmarried factors here, took a woman from some tenant-family now and then, they respectable girls with naught to say for it, for a night or longer; he'd installed three successive doxies in the house, Fergal had heard, kept them two or four months—or until they got with child—and dismissed them. . . . Shevaun. Roy. Shouldn't have come here . . .

He sat bolt upright suddenly. Not the wind, any ordinary night sound; that was—a man walking near the house, an incautious step, a pebble rattling—

He was up, silent, and out to the main room in two strides, to where Liam had his pallet in a corner. "Someone prowling outside," he breathed as Liam sat up at the hand on his shoulder. "You go right from the door, I left." He eased the door open gently, no betraying creak of hinge, and they slipped out to the cold dark. No moon, and a foggy sky: a thin mist that was not quite rain falling.

As he turned to circle the cottage, listening, he knew what it was: damn' fool not to know at once! They preferred the former gentry-houses over here, which if occupied sheltered bailiffs, with more value to be taken; but they came down on other places at random, too: all grist to their mill. A raiding band, maybe two men, maybe ten—

He came round the back of the cottage, soundless on shoeless feet, and thought the black density of shadow there ahead was too solid for real shadow; he made a rush at it and grappled with a man. Startled grunt, whiskey-laden breath in his face, his fist connecting with rock-hard body. He heard Liam shout; he heard a stir of another man or men over by the shed, and he took a blow to the face, a blow to the body, but kept his grip on the man, this one he had at least— "Liam!" he called. "To me! I've got one o' the bastards—"

The man raised a knee into his stomach, sudden and violent, followed it up with a wild hit for the jaw that connected straight enough to stagger Fergal backward a step and break his hold. In that second the man was gone, running, careless of noise—and as he ran he shouted, just once—"Get out, boys!"

Fergal fell, off-balance, against the cottage wall. He stayed there, half-upright, breathing hard. Conscious of the cold, the chill mist, now. He heard men running, and down there in the road fifty yards away a horse snort and stamp—yes, sure, a man left to keep the horses for a quick escape—horses sidling about, fretted for riders running up, and sudden soon-faded thunder of hooves on turf galloping off.

A shadow stumbled round the other side of the cottage. "O'Breslin? I had hold of one—as they ran, but—" And the door opened again, noisily this time, and Nessa's voice called his name, frightened.

"All right," he called back. "Liam—did you hear? Not mad I am if you heard too—that man shouted out, by God, I swear it, Dermot Flynn it was, as I stand here—"

"I heard, O'Breslin—it was Flynn, I could swear too."

"Kevin McCann in twenty feet of me, maybe!" said Fergal, deadly quiet. "Christ in heaven! And what to be surprised at, come to think? We guessed they came over this way, for better loot. So we did. . . . I warrant it was Dan Kindellan left with the horses," and he laughed short and sharp. "Damn, there's a destiny in it, I'm not done with McCann yet—by Christ I'm not. One day—" And Nessa came running up in the dark, breathless, anxious questions.

"Fergal, what is it? We heard—" A light in the cottage, Shevaun calling too from the door.

"All right," he repeated. "Look in the morning, see what they got off with. Flynn, my oath I'd take it was. One day, by Christ, I'll come up with Kevin McCann, to pay him what I owe. . . ."

At the mill next morning he had the satisfaction of seeing Horder furious to hear of the loss of tools, the milking-pail, the whetstone. "Bastards!" But a shrewd stare on Fergal; if his servants told him the tale and gained thereby, at least he knew it was a trick tenants might try. "I will check against the accounts, what articles were supplied to your farm, and the value." His sinister scowl was empty threat, thought Fergal: so easy to hide this or that, for later recovery—and not always for use, but sale or exchange, safe profit.

Horder and men like him were little kings here, but likely they never suspected the second secret life these people lived under them—its devious-calculated economies, or its watchful attention for all the nuances of feeling from these men with power.

The miller was a shifting-eyed fellow who fawned on Horder; Fergal was of no mind to trust either at true count, and he and Liam spelled each other watching while the grain was ground. He left Liam there past midday, for an hour, and went to the inn, hoping to find Carmody, whose crop was in, ground and sold two days ago. Carmody was there with his neighbor Mulcahy, a taciturn little fellow half his size.

Fergal sat down with them, shook his head at Devesey—whose whiskey wasn't worth two shillings a dram, if Fergal had the coin—and asked abruptly, "What do you know about these outlaw-bands, Carmody? They must all have headquarters somewhere?"

"Thinking of going back to your old trade," grinned Carmody, "or just curiosity is it? . . . Oh, had a visit from some, did you? Well, enough of them there are roving about, God knows. They may make a bit better living than the rest of us—or a lot better— I wouldn't say for less work, but we do hear these days they don't live less comfortable by a long way. Some, anyhow. Daresay there be a few gangs still just camping here or there, week or month, living on the run as you might say, see. But not so many wild places for 'em to make their hideaways, along here in the Shannon valleys—no hills. We do hear—"

Mulcahy took his pipe out of his mouth and said, "Percentage o' the take—town merchants. Carrion-hawks, sure."

"That's it. See, no Irish supposed to live in towns, but be no tradesmen nor shopkeepers, didn't they—English wink at it—but it's English control all the merchandise supply. And everything scarce, like as you know. Same like the revenue-patrols and the farm-factors, all English but pulling opposite ways—and the factors for town property and police-patrols, see, the same. Regular business it is with most o' these bands, they with decent quarters and stables, over in Longford town, Athlone, Cavan, Carrick, Trim, any good-sized town. Covered by merchants there, taking what they rob, see. A market for everything, old or new—they make higher profit, daresay, on what they get off military-supply trains, but not so often they can ambush one o' those. Oh, sure to God the English military know about it, but add the sum yourself, O'Breslin—like as Mulcahy says, English bailiffs in with the merchants and tradesmen for the profit, see, and helping cover the thieves."

"Do you tell me," said Fergal slowly. "Yes, of course. A practical arrangement." He had thought of McCann and those men living wild, on the run; but come to think, private enterprise like that impossible over here: outlaws had to have a safe market for their wares. Longford, he thought, likeliest Longford town. Kevin McCann there, eight-nine miles away, in safe comfortable rooms behind some shop, or in some town-house, him and the other men and their women. Living one damn' lot easier and softer than himself or, God knew, any halfway honest man.

Carmody was eyeing him curiously; he'd no intention of embarking on explanation, but said abruptly he must get back to the mill.

The count was a hundred and fifty-two bushels, ground. Hugh, who had come in meanwhile to record the transaction, set down the tally in the factor-book, and Horder paid out the coin to Fergal, from the locked leather bag at his hip—fifteen pounds four shillings. A weight of coin, more than he'd seen at once in five years; and most of it never got into his pocket. He paid the miller, and that was a farce of exchange: seven pounds twelve shillings, and the miller handed the coin on to Horder as mill-earning, and back it went into the bag.

"If it's convenient to you, sir," said Fergal, "I may as well pay my rent now, a day ahead."

"Quite convenient," said the factor carelessly. "Save you the walk to my office, eh?" And back into the bag went six pounds, rent for the year. Fergal put away his remaining one pound twelve shillings, expressionless before the factor: but some random bitter thoughts went through his mind for it. Thoughtful it was, to pay in small-denomination coin; it looked more value, and would it not be paid out over the year a penny here and there!—double handful of coin, in pence, halfpence, tuppenny and thruppenny pieces, but a couple of shillings too, and the dull gleam of silver stood out. He'd thought all those Latin lessons had vanished from his head, but he made out the inscriptions on those two coins—half of memory from the last time he'd handled shillings. One from the Scottish

James's reign, and on it the pious message *Let God arise, let His enemies be scattered.* One from only a few years back, a war-made coin, oval-shaped, with Charles Stuart's initials and, below, *Whilst I live I hope.*

He thanked the factor, holding any sarcasm from his tone, and went out with Liam, toward the village street. Past the mill-office shop where a tenant could buy flour at one shilling eightpence the half-bushel (there was one-and-four profit to the landowner on every bushel, but casual profit, for who could buy much? Most of the grain went to the towns and back to England). Past the cobbler's shop, he hired like the miller, and nineteen shillings in the pound of his charge going back into the factor's bag: past the wheelwright's and the carpenter's, the same there, and the harness-maker's, and the smithy—all the same. Sixty percent yearly return they figured, London guild—what were two thousand Irish acres worth, a village thrown in?—ten thousand pounds? Six thousand pounds yearly profit—

But that was at the back of his mind. Chiefly he was thinking coldly, Kevin McCann—Longford town?

The factor came to the cottage two hours later, as they were just sitting to the table. Nessa whispered a small curse on him, whisking the basin of stew back to the hearth to keep warm. No knock at the door; he walked in, and went through the little gesture of fastidious nose-wrinkling for peasant dirt and odor. Fergal saw Nessa bristle with the need to tell him she had scrubbed down the floor that morning, and put the pallets out to air, and washed her one spare gown and shift. Remotely a part of Fergal's mind recalling cynically, Nessa O'Rafferty, lady-bred, wed to a chief—doing servant's work in her own house—house? farm-cabin of thin boards plastered with clay!

But Horder was not looking at Nessa; his eyes went first to Shevaun, standing there quiet. He said to Fergal, "I've had a look into the record o' this farm. You're credited with what you say the thieves stole. If you'll apply to my office, the clerk'll see you're issued replacement out o' supply."

"My thanks, Master Horder." Already the factor's eyes were back to Shevaun, bold, a hot gleam in them. Fergal took a step toward him. To call back attention he said, "Your pardon, sir, but the farm-cart—it's in need of a new wheel, if you'd grant—"

"Buy one," said the factor with a shrug; and then he laughed, and took hold of Shevaun's arm in a rough grasp. "Or, well, then, let the female here buy it for you, eh? Bargain for you, Irish! I know well enough, what I'm so generous give a doxy out o' tenant-cabin, she sends half back to her folk—what odds?—more fool she! How's for that, girl, eh? What's your name?—outlandish-sounding that is, like most o' your heathen names! You come stay with me awhile, and you'll not lose by it—how'd you like a new gown, say, and meat to every meal, and maybe a little coin to spend how you like—other things? A fine time I'll show you, so I promise!"

Fergal took another step toward the man, and sudden deadly fear rose in him—that he would turn coward for it, for the danger it meant to cross Horder: not danger just for himself. But before he moved again, Shevaun spoke. She was looking up at the factor, to his hot lustful eyes and excited grin, but she spoke to Fergal in their own tongue, quietly.

"Stop where you are, Fergal. I'll go with him, it is all right."

"My God, Shevaun, no—you'll not, just to protect—no—"

"Other reasons," she said. And to Horder, in English, "You'll give me two new gowns maybe—sir?—and a pound, or two pounds, or three—and give my brother a new wheel for the cart?"

Horder laughed. "All that," he said, and bent and set his mouth on hers brutal, gripping her close.

"Shevaun—" Fergal made himself put a hand out to the Englishman's shoulder, and Nessa's two small hands held him back.

"I said, be still, Fergal." Shevaun was still breathless from the kiss. "Not for saving us only, the harm he could make. A chance to have a little profit, is it not?" Her tone was hard. "My own decision."

"Shevaun," whispered Nessa, "but so shamed—to let you—"

"Why, no need. We have all made sacrifices." Shevaun smiled up at the factor, a hand on his chest; she said in English, "Sure, master, I'll oblige you, but just you let me say a word or two to my brother, sir, would you? Better he knows than to cross you, sir, and myself as well." She looked at Fergal. "It is only my body," she said gently. "A month or two, what is it, Fergal, against all our lives maybe? No matter at all. Roy is with God, and if he can know, he would say the same—nothing I can take from him, who has all my love."

"By God, Shevaun, Christ, oh, Christ, I'll not let—" And he could not make himself move: coward, coward!

"It's all right, Fergal. I've my son to think for, Roy Donlevy's son, that he has food and shelter and all needful to grow to manhood. And the rest of you—and myself as well, haven't I? It's nothing hurtful to my real self, Fergal, God knows that, and so would Roy."

"Enough talk," said Horder with a loud laugh, and pulled her toward the door.

"Oh, Christ," said Fergal numbly.

And the boy ran up to her, clutching her skirt. "Where are you going, Mother? Can I come too?—I want to come with you—please—"

"Oh, your brat, is it?" said Horder. "Damnation, now, and me thinking you were virgin—well, man can't have everything, and they do say an old oven heats quicker, eh?"

"Nessa," said Shevaun, "please look well to Sean, the while I'm gone."

"I will, Shevaun, I promise, my dear," whispered Nessa.

"My heart's vein," and Shevaun knelt to hug him, "this time you can't come, but you'll be very good and mind all Nessa says, and I'll bring you a fine present when I come back, there now." She kissed him quickly; she rose and looked at Fergal again. "Don't make it for nothing, boy—hold your hand on him, no more a coward for it than I for accepting any sacrifice you've made. Only my body it is."

"That's enough o' your heathen talk and to spare!" said Horder with an impatient laugh, and hauled her round roughly. She let him lead her out with not one backward glance.

25

NESSA HELD HIM close in silence, listening to him say it all over, bitter and self-contemptuous. "Coward, coward, I should have killed him—should have—"

And at last she laid her hand on his mouth and said, "Stop torturing yourself for it, now. We both know you're no coward, Fergal, you couldn't help but see the sense of what she said, that's all. Are you thinking any father or brother of those other women Horder's had did not say all this to themselves too? So Shevaun's a lady born, daughter and sister of a gentleman-chief! Virtue less important to any of lower birth? God knows those other men will have felt bitter as you, letting their women buy safety for them— but it's simple figuring, Fergal, four people, five, everyone in a family, against just one—and lives against virtue. You heard the Carmodys tell about the McBreens."

"I heard—about McBreen," he muttered tiredly.

"When Horder came after his daughter, McBreen knocked him down—and so Horder evicted the whole family, and they were taken up as vagrants a mile down the road and put with those to be shipped to the slave-markets."

"Yes."

"There's the child," she said, "and Liam, and Horder might count in Hugh and Maire for that they came with us, and banish them too. Six people, seven if you count Maire's babe."

"For God's sake, so calm like you counted cows in a field—! Oh, God, I know, Nessa, I know—but— Shouldn't have come

here, what the hell was I thinking of, say it was the only way?
Shouldn't have—"

"Late to think that," she said. And she sounded calm as he
said, but she didn't feel so. Oh, she knew how he felt, and worse
for a man too—shamed, to stand by not raising even a curse: and
you were taught that honor and virtue stood above life, but when
it came to other lives than yours—Strangely, she could share Shevaun's feeling: this was just one more thing—like having had to
learn about the menial work there'd been servants to do, before:
learning how to milk the cow—none of them had ever done such
a thing, but Liam had taught them; and doing without soft beds,
enough blankets for comfort, enough solid food to satisfy hunger,
enough hairpins, all such ordinary things never thought of before:
mending every garment you had until it was more mends than
whole pieces left: and now going barefoot indoors, to save the last
shabby shoes you had as long as possible. Another thing like that,
only a bit worse: that was all. . . . She heard the child whimpering
to himself in the other room, not used to being alone.

"Oh, Christ," said Fergal, "what are they bringing us to? The
King back—restoration made—what good, if we've been turned
to less than men, meanwhile! I should have killed him—"

"Fergal, I must go to comfort Sean—let me up now. I'll just
settle him off to sleep again, and be back. Do you try to get to
sleep too, my dear—no use brooding on it, round and round
again. . . ."

When Shevaun came in, three days later, Nessa was thankful
the men were out, that she could talk quiet with her a bit. A
quarter-ham Shevaun brought, and a length of new linen dyed
blue, and five shillings coin. She kissed Nessa, sitting down with
the boy on her lap, and for awhile was busy answering his questions
and soothing his fretful disappointment that she would not stay.
He settled at last to the bright-painted wooden ball she'd brought
him, and she looked up to smile at Nessa.

"But you needn't look so mournful at me," she said tranquilly.

"Was I then?" Nessa smiled too, briefly. And they could not
talk really open, because of the child there. "There's—things I'd
say, Shevaun, but you knowing them as well as I. And it's maybe
silly to say—I mean, such a thing, it's not really any difference

what man—but I'm sorry it is—one like him." For any woman who knew anything about men at all would know that about Jason Horder: he was one of those needing to hurt, to show his male power—a man like Kevin McCann.

"Yes. Likely not for long, and it might easy have been yourself he fancied—thank God it wasn't, Fergal would never have kept hands off him."

Nessa looked away. "I don't know, Shevaun." For his pride, for his honor, for the surface look of it, maybe not: it was his rigid honor had made him wed her in the first place. But to Fergal himself—? "Oh, Shevaun, a terrible thing it is, however we make ourselves look at it—I've prayed for you, and will. Fergal's right, saying we should never have come here—bad things happening before, but nothing like this—"

"Nobody can look ahead. All we can do is meet things as they come. At least," said Shevaun wryly, "I'm in no danger of being miscalled, everyone knows how it is—including Horder. And, yes, of course most men wouldn't care much for an unwilling bedmate, but that—makes it all the better for him." She checked herself, looking at the boy, dropped her voice. "I'd not think it's for long —half of it for him is the forcing of it, you see. But he can't touch me, Nessa, not in myself—I am all right, nothing he can take from me."

"I'd—not be so brave as you."

"Oh, I wouldn't have thought I could be, either, but come to the point, you find you can do—whatever's needful to do. . . . It helps to have Maire in the house, and the servants are friendly. And not the least help, what I can bring you—"

"You will hear something from Fergal about that," said Nessa.

So they did. He came in, to turn a little white at seeing her, and go to embrace her in silence. But for what she had brought, he went dead pale and his voice shook. "I'm not only to stand by and see my sister debauched, without a word or a curse on the whoreson—but share her earnings like any procurer! By God, I'll not touch—"

"I'm not asking you to," said Shevaun calmly. "The ham I brought to feed my son strengthening meals, and Nessa welcome to it too, and Liam. The cloth is for a new gown for Nessa and shirts for Sean. You need have nothing to do with that—and as for the money, it's mine, and I only ask you to keep it safe for me. Don't be a fool, Fergal. What's done is done, let us make the best of it."

"Might as well be hung for a sheep as a lamb, is that what you're saying?" he exclaimed furiously. "So much honor gone, to hell with whatever is left, too great a luxury for low native peasants! Oh, God, Shevaun—"

"You're splitting hairs," she said. "Didn't Owen Desmond say a thing to you—if a sacrifice is to be made, for God's sake see it's made *for* somewhat!"

"Oh, God, Shevaun," he said again, but in a different tone. "I know, I know. Ought never to have come—but—what are they doing to us, here?—no need sell us abroad as slaves, sure to Christ, when we're turned the same here, men only in name—to put safety above any sort of pride. Shevaun, Shevaun—and nothing I can say to you, you know all I'd say—"

And when she had gone he sat at the table not touching the meal Nessa laid out, only leaning head on hands there above his plate. Liam, embarrassed and uncertain, eyed him uneasily, ate quickly, and said he'd go over to Carmody's an hour if no objection. He was by way of opening courtship with the older girl. Nessa said inattentively, "Of course, Liam." When he had gone out she went to Fergal and laid her arms round him from behind. "My dear. I know, I know how you feel, Fergal—"

He leaned back against her suddenly, as if too tired to sit up. "If she did not look at me out of Mother's eyes," he muttered. "Her very look and way—it's as if I betrayed both of them at once. Oh, a coward—Christ-damned coward—look at it any way, I was a coward!"

And Shevaun might say, likely not for long; but Nessa knew well there were minutes could seem like hours. She found herself reckoning time, now, from the night Horder had taken Shevaun, counting off the days, thinking, another gone for her; maybe a month, maybe six weeks, he'd tire of the cat-and-mouse game, and let her come home—and after a bit go out after some other woman, God pity what one it would be.

It was nine nights after, by that reckoning, when Fergal went over to Mulcahy's after supper, to bargain for extra winter-seed. Liam was at the Carmodys' again. Nessa settled the child to sleep early, and sat in Fergal's chair at the hearth, working on the new gown. Now the tedious part was done, unraveling loose threads from the cloth-edges for the actual sewing, she could begin to see it taking shape, and feel pleasure in the color and texture of it. Tiresome that none of the sewing-threads was any length; every few stitches she must stop and rethread the needle. But she was getting on with it, she'd finish this seam tonight, at least.

She looked up as the door opened—Fergal was back early. But his name died on her lips at sight of the man there in the door, closing the door behind him, leaning on it, one hand in breeches-pocket, smiling at her. The extra candle she had lit for sewing flickered light and shadow across his face.

"Nessa, girl," he said, "just as pretty as ever you are." It was Art McTally. She didn't quite believe it, but it was Art. He came toward her, into the full light, and dazedly she saw that he was well-dressed, not like servant or poor man now, but good new-looking English clothes, linen shirt, thick brown wool trews and doublet—but a sheath-belt, incongruous, two pistols through it. "Nessa," he said again, and came right up to her chair. "Been watching I have—every night I could, since we knew O'Breslin was here. Waiting for you to be alone. Kevin saying I'm a damn' fool, but there—man takes a fancy for a girl, times, can't get her out o' his head—and a fancy I always had for you, some reason." He put his hands on the arms of her chair, leaned down over her, steadily smiling. "Turned me off you did before, and I asking you to wed all lawful—but there's been water under the bridge since that night. Maybe you'll take two thoughts for Art McTally now, seeing how he prospers! Seeing he could give you a kind o' life you're used to, Nessa, eh?—all the things you used have—lady born and bred, in a fine gentry-house! Nessa O'Rafferty—"

She tilted her head back, rigid, meeting his eyes. "But it's Nessa O'Breslin now, Art."

"Is it indeed," he said on indrawn breath; but he did not move. "Now that's a pity, girl—you'd have done better wait for me! Our fine gentleman-chief O'Breslin hasn't done so damn' well by you, look o' things here. And sure to God how would he, him such a proudful honest man!—rather lie down meek for English to walk on than show he's a man at all, and take some o' his own back from English! What—"

"Have you seen any English in this house, Art? You and the others paid a visit here one night—" Her voice was steady, but she felt her hands trembling, cold against each other. Oh, Fergal, come home early, she prayed, come now, soon!

He scowled. "Hell with that, what odds! So you're wed to him—and—I don't know but I do like it better that way, by God." He still had not moved from where he leaned over her; now suddenly he transferred his grasp to her shoulders, pulled her upright against him. The half-finished gown slid to the floor, needle still stuck in the latest stitch—she might have run the needle in him, if—oh, Fergal, please don't stay talking, come soon— "Nessa, my girl," muttered, "I can give you hell of a lot more—living fine I am now, aught you want I'll give you—"

"Let me go, Art." But she did not struggle, knowing that would only provoke him.

He laughed. "Why, girl, you think I've taken all this trouble, get you alone, to ask polite—and bow at you like a gentleman, you saying no at me, and go off all so meek? Nessa—Nessa, I'm not off to hurt you, don't think it—just, never could put you out o' my mind, for any other female, somehow—and that night, finding it was O'Breslin here—I—I did have to come back, secret, see if you too—" His hands were hard on her, and something both rough and desperate in his tone. "You come quiet with me, girl, just think how soft and good you'll be living with me! I promise you, aught you want, see? Money I've got, we're all living good now, you'll have half a dozen new gowns, and plenty to eat, and soft bed, and coin to spend in town shops—see—just think for that, silly you'd be to want to stay here instead! But so I warn you, you're coming along o' me, howsoever you come—don't want to hurt you, Nessa, but I'll take you tied if I must, and—and after, you'll be glad I did, my girl, all I'll give you—make it up to you —see? Not so haughty you'd look at me as before—when I can give you all *he* can't—"

"I never felt haughty at you, Art," she said breathlessly. And queer it was, her saying it to Shevaun, *wouldn't be so brave*, almost the same happening to her, maybe to try if she would be. A dozen thoughts flashing through her mind at once, confused. Fergal suspecting McCann and the others were living in Longford town: were they?—the nearest town of any size. If she could leave word for him, who—Queer, but not like Jason Horder: she'd never been afraid of Art McTally. And likely he didn't know it himself, but the most of his wanting her, she knew, was account of her being a lady born, and he so quick to suspect all gentry of downlooking him. Yes, he'd rather take her as Nessa O'Breslin, wife to the clan-chief he'd once served as groom.

"You'd not do that, Art," she said, trying to smile up at him. Let Fergal know somehow—

"Don't you fight me, Nessa woman," he said, tightening his grasp; and then he looked past her, with the quick awareness of the hunted, and relaxed the next second. "Ah, only the young one—"

Sean, disturbed by the voices: and now fear did catch at Nessa's heart. He was old enough to give information: did he remember Art McTally, from the long while back it would be to a child? McTally a bold, desperate man—pistols in his belt—but he couldn't, he wouldn't— She said calmly over her shoulder, "Now get back to bed, Sean, like the good boy you are."

"Oh," he was sleepily excited, "*two* pistols you've got—Uncle Fergal did use have one, but he hasn't now—" He came up to them, interested. "Could I touch one, could I? Could I hold one, just a *little* minute—I'd be careful—"

She saw the indecision in McTally's eyes. She bit her tongue hard to keep from the swift assurance, *He won't remember you, don't fear!* Say it, make him think just contrary! And for fear her wits sharpened, and she said quickly, "All right, Art, I'll come with you, I—I do see as you're right, better off and all—I'll come." A chance there must come, once out of the house in the dark, to get away and run, hide. If this first chance failed. "But look, Art," and she put a coaxing hand on his chest, "you'll let me fetch a few things along, won't you? Just a minute I'll be collecting a bundle—"

The pleased look in his eyes flickered in a second to a narrow scowl; he was quicker than she'd reckoned, to understand. "Oh, sure to God, make delay until O'Breslin comes home! Nought worth a farthing you've got here, to carry—buy you all new, didn't

I say I would, and finer than you've had before! You'll come now—"

Thank God the boy didn't speak again, at least—to remind him. A chance there must come to get away later— She let him take her out, she stumbled purposely on the sloping path from the threshold, and he swore, and jerked her up roughly. "No noise—damn, Nessa, don't make me—not off to hurt you, only—"

At the bottom of the little slope where the road came past, he turned off to the field—of course, his horse hid away somewhere, in trees— She stumbled again and gasped, "Please, Art, not so fast, I'll come, but please—" Please, Fergal, come! And like answer to her prayer, there came the sound of a man walking this way up the road, toward them. It wasn't Fergal's step, that she knew well, listening for it so many times; it was Liam Fagan coming home, the lighter, quicker step of a man smaller than Fergal. . . . Couldn't get away from the strong grasp on her arm, and Art was already flinging around to put a hand on her mouth. Nessa twisted away frantically, and frantically she called, loud as she could—"Liam, it's McTally, taking me—" And the hand clamped down on her mouth; she was half lifted, half dragged on, he was running heavily across the field. She heard Liam's startled shout, his running steps after.

She went deliberately limp, let herself fall against Art—delay, Liam was coming— He shook her hard, and she hadn't reckoned on his strength, he lifted her wholly and went on, fast, and in a minute the dark was darker and she thought, that stand of oaks at the field-corner. A horse there, blowing softly—little chink of bridle—and now she couldn't hear Liam behind at all.

The worst fear yet claimed her—couldn't be that there'd be no chance—*a chance had there been for Shevaun?* She began to struggle with him, she turned her head and set her teeth in his wrist, and fought against that iron grip, and he let go of her with the other hand so her feet found the ground— "Little vixen," he panted, "oh, my girl, don't make me—by God, I'll have you, if I need to —" He slapped her once, hard, and then he gave a queer little half-sob and hit her with his clenched fist, harder—and everything went away from her into darker night.

* * *

Fergal did not stay talking at Mulcahy's. When he came up the path he was surprised to see the door open; he took a step over the threshold, and saw the three candles flaring wildly for the night breeze from the door, the half-finished new gown dropped careless by the chair, the little boy standing there looking undecided whether to cry.

"Uncle Fergal," said the boy, half-excited, confused, "Uncle— he had *two* pistols—just like the one you used have—"

And with that, heavy running steps pounding up, Liam at the door white and breathless. "O'Breslin, thank God—thought I heard your step—it's McTally, he's taken Nessa, she called to me—much as he let her—I ran—but he'd a horse hidden, he's away—he—"

"I *said* as I'd be careful, Uncle, but he wouldn't let me hold one. He told Nessa—he told Nessa as he'd give her fine new gowns, and—and—but he looked cross, I—"

It was the strangest feeling Fergal ever remembered, feeling the wrong word; time slowed and stopped right there, so he had infinite space to think and notice and plan. No need take it in as jumbled appalling fact, leap to action the next second: all the little ramifications of it fit themselves together leisurely in his mind. Art McTally. If Fergal had recognized Flynn's voice that night, all of them had known him too: McTally had known where to come, to see, to try—He had always wanted Nessa—and not just for herself, but to possess a lady, he humbler bred—oh, yes— and now, to pay out Fergal O'Breslin for what he'd fancied was snobbish downlooking of a servant-man. He had boasted of all he could give her, but he'd not come to ask—he'd meant to take her willing or no. Fergal could, that queer timeless space, have told accurately what had passed between them here, the feeling and the events and the words spoken.

McTally had startled her, she dropping the new gown she was making of the stuff Shevaun gave her. All crumpled on the floor, and only the one needle she had, such a little precious thing to keep care of, a steel needle cost eight or ten shillings now. When she was home, she'd be wanting to finish the gown. He went over and picked it up, found the needle, and carefully fastened it firmer through the cloth, and folded the gown and laid it on the table. It was only cutout pieces of cloth, really, as yet, and had never covered her body, but finished or not it was Nessa's gown, an intimate part of Nessa; and he smoothed it out neatly all folded together—she was like himself, she liked things orderly.

He said to the child, and did not recognize his own voice at all, "That was clever, Sean, to remember to tell me—two pistols —a good boy you are." He said to Liam, "So he is away—with her—towards Longford town, northeast by road or field—am I right?"

"I think—yes, northeast, I heard the horse—down across the field toward the road. Yes—O'Breslin, we'd never—afoot—"

"Why, no," said Fergal, "and not *we*. I will go after them. That, there in the sack, it's winter-seed, cabbage and leeks—I owe Mulcahy ninepence for it, if I'm unable you'll pay him or return it. You will stay here with the child, Liam, and if I'm not here with Nessa by tomorrow dusk, you will take Sean to his mother—and—tell the factor you will take over tenancy—if you wish to do that." He turned to the door, and as he moved, suddenly time started forward on its track again, for him, urgent, desperate, imperative. He stayed just a second, to snap, "How far ahead is he?"

"Five minutes—seven—" gasped Liam. Eternity, thirty seconds, how long?—he was still breathless, and the boy still chattering about the two fine pistols.

Fergal ran out and veered right across the garden, damn the path, across the wet loamy field—ran the wrong way, best speed he could make, for the big stone house where the bailiff lived— where the bailiff's stables were—half a mile away. Time was a hound-pack at his heels, now: the breath drew harsh and hard in his throat, across the boggy loam and onto the undug land under trees, up a little slope, and the stream murmuring tranquilly to itself in the dark—two strides across it, and his legs wet to the knee, sudden ice-cold shock of the water scarce noticed—and out of the trees down another little slope, there was the house, big stone bulk looming dark, outbuildings—no light, somewhere within maybe Horder taking fierce pleasure forcing himself on a helpless woman— There were the stables.

And all the way, one deep small compartment of his mind, quite apart from time, telling him the blind, Christ-damned fool he had been.

Art McTally, like as if he pulled aside a curtain to let Fergal O'Breslin look at the truth.

Nessa, Nessa, Nessa.

The stables, and damn any groom on the premises to guard—

26

She had said to him, Don't you know what it feels like, Fergal
—loving someone?

Settle respectable to a wife, he had said. However it came
about. Reasonable. Romantic feeling damn' bad basis for marriage.

Wrong term. Not romantic feeling. A thing immeasurably deeper
and stronger and more primal.

Nessa.

He felt strong enough, strong as God, to rip the door open,
was it locked; but there was only a bolt, and the good warm pun-
gence of Horse breathing out at him. No groom, no guard about.
Twenty stalls, and just the one horse, the factor's horse, of all the
doubtless highbred Irish hunters this stable had once held. Never
mind that. Thank God for Jason Horder's need to show himself the
all-powerful little king, need extending to the horse he rode. Ramping big English hunting-horse, seventeen hands high, the long
driving hocks and deep roomy chest. The horse, in a stall halfway
along the aisle, startled to snorting and stamping—gear hung tidy
on nails outside. Damn' complicated English saddle-cinch, mouth-
spoiling English bit with double rein. Automatic, he murmured
soothing meaningless words to the horse, as he fumbled frantic at
the halter-buckle, cinch-buckle.

She whispered to him there in the dark, More to marriage . . .
than the body, the eager warm body . . . oh, yes. She said to him,
sadly, Maybe in time you understanding.

"Easy, boy, easy now." Out the wide stable door, and damn
the noise or the factor—how long ahead now? fifteen, twenty min-

utes! He was in the saddle, he dug heels to flank, sent the horse down to the road in a startled loud gallop.

His mother said to him from a great distance off, *If you'll but open your heart*— But he had, it was—long before—only he such a Christ-damned fool, not to know consciously in himself—

The anger a quite separate emotion from that, and less for McTally—as low-bred thief, upstart groom, plain woman-stealer —McTally as an individual—than for human agency taking her away from him.

There was a half-wasted moon just out from clouds, the night clearing, and the road showed white before him; he drove the horse merciless at breakneck pace. McTally wouldn't have as big or as good a horse, he must be gaining on McTally—but would McTally stay on the road? Wouldn't expect pursuit so soon—quickest, safest way to take—was he making for the town? God, God, the white road straight and empty ahead—powerful big horse moving smooth under him, must have put two, three miles behind already—and ahead, nothing! Then, round a gentle bend, little dark quiet village, Ballyhinch village, three or four buildings, a dozen scattered houses. Through it in ten seconds, and folk waking for the loud scatter of galloping horse, likely—of course, sure to God, McTally going round the village, wouldn't he, out of canny habit? Maybe time made up on him—

Road rising a little now, going inland from the river bogland, and more trees either side; dear God, if he was to sight the quarry at all, he should by now, by the next mile—

Wed to her a year of time, knowing her body, and only now knowing all the rest, about the loving that was more, that was all —the body but another means to tell each other about the loving. Nessa, Nessa.

The road here ran straight as an arrow for a mile, and halfway along, ahead, where trees made a dark smudge on the left, rode a single horseman.

Fergal ground spurless heels into the lean flank and bent along the smooth-stretched neck. He felt the stride extend under him, responding—and saw the horse ahead lift from a trot to a gallop, as the rider heard hooves behind. But, not so good a horse, and he was coming up fast—fifty yards, forty, twenty behind, and abruptly they were both in deep shadow of trees. He heard the horse ahead reined roughly aside, off the road, crashing through bracken. Damn' fool, like to break the nag's leg, in wood in the dark at that speed!

"McTally, you whelp of a mongrel bitch!" he shouted. "Stop where you are, I've a gun on you!" Time to think, bastard would know that for a lie, even had he a gun he'd not chance firing when McTally had the woman with him. But in the moment's startlement— "One minute I'll give you, Art!" He pulled the big hunter to a frothy-mouthed stand, jerked him ruthless down and over a deep ditch into undergrowth and the wood.

A handgun spat at him sharp, out of the dark ahead. Telling him the direction—and not far ahead, either—he lay flat along the horse's back, walking him cautious through the thick wood. The gun spoke again, both wide shots, by damn if he had a pistol he'd aim straighter, McTally with no benefit of experience shooting at enemy, never out of the stables at Lough Eask all through the war! And then he heard the other horse, taken too fast through rough growth, stumble and fall—and he knew it was his game now.

He left the saddle in one leap, taking the rein with him to drop to ground—old habit, to keep trained troop-horse standing without tethering—but the hunter wasn't cavalry-schooled, and started away, snorting. Hell with the horse, now. He lunged forward, shouting, "Nessa, hold his gun-hand if you can, I'm coming—" He tripped on an upthrust root and sprawled headlong across the fallen thrashing horse and a man leg-pinned under it, by his writhing and sobbing breath.

He groped for the man's throat, he panted, "Bastard, son of— Nessa! Where—"

"Here," came her faint voice behind him somewhere, "I'm here, I'm all right, Fergal—oh, Fergal—"

And so then that anger rose hot over everything else in him, he drove fist into McTally's face, he called him every obscene name he knew—confused struggle there in the dark, and the horse heaving up over them suddenly, thudding off in panic, McTally's whimpering hard-drawn breath in his face, McTally wrestling against him cursing too. McTally rearing up under him, desperate effort, hitting him with something hard—stunning blow on his cheekbone, colored lights of pain before his eyes one moment. The pistol—he grasped frantic for McTally's gun-hand, he got the wrist and twisted it savage, and McTally let out a sharp high yelp of pain.

"God's sake—O'Breslin—let up! All right, I—" He went limp, he gasped, "Enough, O'Breslin—"

Fergal held him as he was; they breathed panting, harsh, close there, like lovers. "Art McTally, you misbegotten—son of Satan—something other you'll call me—aside from name! Say it to me, Art McTally—*chief!*— Your chief, you reckoning—betray chief and chief's lady! Let me hear it from you, McTally, Christ damn you—"

"Chief, my chief," gasped McTally, "my chief you are— O'Breslin—and I acknowledge betrayal—"

"Chief's man," said Fergal lovingly, "you low-bred serving-man to clan-chief, McTally, damn you—you will give me information before I kill you, so you will. Tell me where I will find Kevin McCann! Tell me—"

"Christ, let up, O'Breslin—" McTally's voice rose as the savage pressure on his wrist twisted cartilage and threatened bone.

"Tell me! Where—where? You'll be out o' pain quicker you say—"

"Longford—town-house o'—bailiff for the—Challoners' Guild, rooms he has—"

"Death-warrant for you both," said Fergal, relaxing his hold— just a fractional second, to shift hand to throat, but McTally knew life was at stake, and he lunged up sudden and strong, and struck viciously with the reversed handgun. It caught Fergal square on the temple, a solid lucky blow—and he felt McTally heaving him off, scrambling up, and then he felt nothing.

His mind came back to him slowly, to bring him her voice and her arms. "Fergal, my darling—my darling—" To tell him he was lying held against her, his head on her breast, her arms warm, her hand on his face. To his inexpressible comfort, close to Nessa. After an unknown time he turned to press closer to her, and she gave a little gasp against his cheek. "Fergal, Fergal, all right you are? Oh, my dearest, I thought he'd killed you—"

Everything came back to him, but it was no longer important, right here in this minute of time. All that was important was that

they were here together, and safe—and all important, that at last
he knew the one thing, about loving. About loving Nessa.

He turned wholly to her and got his arms tight round her,
lovely warmth and softness against him, he pulled her down to
him. "My darling heart, Nessa my own heart's dear, I love you—
I love you—I can't say how I love you—" Not enough, not close
enough, no way at all to say it. He said it desperate, incoherent,
he raised himself to get her somehow closer, hard against him, and
her little startled gasp she buried willing and eager on his mouth.
"Nessa, my darling, darling—love you so—forgive me, dearest
heart, all the foolish things I said that time—not knowing—heart's
vein, heart's life, love you—"

She strained up to him, as incoherent, and just as suddenly he
began to laugh, breathless, against her warm mouth, her cheek.
"My darling, my darling—isn't it senseless then, love, heart's
love—dead o' night in a strange wood, look, in a bog o' wet leaves
we are, no bed for a beautiful lady—chief's lady!—oh, God, Nessa,
no way to say it to you—"

"Fergal, Fergal"—between laughter and tears—"try to say it
to me, we can try—say it to each other—"

And it was like the first time for them, God, no, better than
that, damn the place or time or the cold and the wet leaves, no
matter— They lay at peace, like as no heaven could ever give, at
last, warm together and close, close, and he laughed on her breast,
"No fear, darling dear—this time—no broken skull I have—to say
I don't know what I feel, Nessa my dearest heart, my own . . ."

"So it was only when someone else wanted me that you decided
maybe I am a reasonably good wife. Dog with a bone is all."

"Was not indeed. Other way. Damn, I said to myself, low fellow
like McTally wanting her, maybe she's not all so well-bred and
ladylike as I thought—but nonetheless she's one o' my belongings,
so better fetch her back."

"That's what I say, dog with a bone! And I'm a very great fool
not to have kept still and gone on with Art. He's *far* more substance
than you, he said so and I believe it—gowns he promised, and
aught else I wanted. Truly, I'm sorry I didn't—"

"Well, now, a chance you had."

"It was the moment's startlement, I'd no time to think. I *am* sorry now," said Nessa, settling herself more comfortably against him. "Another thing, for all he's a bold outlaw-man, he's soft as butter underneath, he'd be a deal easier for a woman to manage. No barking orders at her, no complaints that she's untidy in the house— Yes, you do so, Fergal, only the other day—"

"I will say, you're a trifle more orderly than most females, but you could do better at it."

"How I *hate* tidy-minded men," breathed Nessa in his ear. "Just as I say, now with Art I could scatter my clothes all about, and never bother to fold the blankets just so on the pallet, and leave the plates on the table all the while, and never a word he'd say—but there, what am I talking about? If I'd gone with him I'd have no such menial work to do at all, doubtless he's so well-off from his robbing, he'd give me half a dozen maidservants. I am a fool."

"So you are," said Fergal, kissing her. He laughed. "Damn, we're both fools, girl—lying out wet and cold so, be taking our deaths o' cold and dying of lung-congestion—here, come up—" Reluctant, body protesting, he moved and got up, pulling her with him.

"Ooh, it *is* cold—"

"Damn, where are we?" He stumbled through trees in the dark, the moon gone now. "And come to think, what happened to the horse? I ought to—"

"I *think*," said Nessa, pressed close as they felt their way through underbrush, "Art took the one you—I mean, his own went off like a mad thing, didn't it—not to stop this side of Derry by the noise—and I was so frighted when he hit you, and you—but I did hear the other horse, and I think he caught it—"

"Well, by God, so Horder's lost his fine hunter! Oh, damn," as he blundered into a tree.

"Oh, was it? I never thought where you— How f-far are we from home, Fergal?"

"I couldn't say, I wasn't counting paces, I was just bent on claiming back stolen property—not that I'd miss it overmuch, it was the principle of the thing, see you—"

"I'll call you one of those terrible names you put on him!"

"Didn't I say, not so genteel a lady! My Christ, no good trying find our way in the dark, I've lost all sense of direction, and we

must be a good five miles from home anyway—we'll have to wait
for light. Here, we'll find some good thick bracken to keep us
warm—" As he burrowed a nest for them, gathering bracken on
each side, he remembered that night he'd come off the Arans, and
fought his way up that cliff to lie shivering in heaped bracken.
Better here, holding her close, their bodies gradually making the
little hollow a place of warm comfort . . . "All right, love?"

"Mmh, lovely," she murmured drowsily. "But—soon as we
can—should get back, Fergal, Liam will be worried—maybe tell
Shevaun."

"Yes. We will, soon's it's light enough to see. Nessa, darling
love . . ."

He woke to a late dawn, and smiled at her flushed sweet sleeping, kissed her gentle to waking. But now there was another urgency in him, apart from her—apart from McTally. He'd have
killed McTally, in the hot moment, but now, let him go, he was
not important. It was Kevin McCann was important, the score
between them to settle once for all, if he died in settling it. He
did not want to die and leave Nessa, this new wonderful thing they
shared; but the unfinished business of McCann was somehow bound
up with his honor as a man.

Kevin McCann, over in Longford, snug and soft-living on callous robbery and underhand dealing with the English. Life or
death, by God, he would pay Kevin McCann what he owed him,
and with interest!

But he knew what she would say to him—sensible woman,
thinking logical. Let it go, why seek out more deadly danger for
that? Leave it as it had ended seven months back, only a fool taking
vengeance at cost of his own life maybe . . . Well and good, but
every time he changed his shirt the little knotted white scar on his
side reminding— Debt owed, betrayal made on him! Woman not
knowing how a man felt for such a thing.

Take her home, now, and come on back, this road, for Longford.
Damn, and he underestimated himself, sure—get into town in the
dark, do the job and slide out easy, secret: not much danger!

He said nothing to her of that, as they started back; some
thought he'd given to safety here, but furious as Horder would be
at the theft of his horse, his first thought—and probably his last

—would be outlaws, and the hunter breaking away as they left, to account for the noise outlaws would normally avoid. It was safe enough, if they got back soon—and safe.

They hid once from a patrol, and went around Ballyhinch village not to be seen on the road. It was on for midmorning, both of them tired and famished, that they came at last across the field below the cottage, having left the road to come shorter way. Both gave little involuntary sighs of relief as the cottage came in sight up the gentle rise.

"Oh, I'm starving," said Nessa. "The last hour, nothing in my head but the rest of that fine ham left—"

"I'll share it half and half," he said, an arm round her, "and then be on my way. . . . Back, girl, over to Longford—to settle my score with Kevin McCann."

And she said all he'd expected, quick, sharp, exasperated, tearful. "*Senseless!* Men forever so stupid about their d-damned honor! Fergal, no—you alone, not even a pistol—he'll kill you for sure this time, you *can't* be so stupid—"

"Now, look, woman," he said. "I'm not off to give you argument or listen to it. That is how it is, is all. We both know everything we'd say to each other, arguing here half the day—waste of time."

"Fergal, you *damned* fool, you must see how senseless—"

They had stopped there where the path to the cabin came down, and absorbed in the quarrel did not hear the door flung open—both started at Liam's anxious, thankful call. "O'Breslin—Nessa—oh, God be thanked you're both safe—" He came running down to them, the boy pattering after excitedly. "And, Christ, I've not known what to do for the best—O'Breslin, up at the house—shots, just now, ten minutes gone—regular fusillade o' shots, pistol I think—"

"What? Horder—oh, my God, *Horder*," said Fergal quietly for the thought sharp in his mind.

"Yes, yes, that's what I—that man he killed before—I didn't like leave the boy alone, nor take him—didn't know—and it might not have been Horder, O'Breslin, Carmody was here then, just come—he's gone up to the house now—he said round an hour back, a stranger stopped him in the village, an Irishman but a-horse he was, and asked for you—or for—Shevaun Donlevy—" Liam took a breath. "And he told him about Shevaun—"

"Asking for me, who the hell—but shots at the house—God, a man like Horder, no telling! I'll go up—no, Nessa, stay here, no argument!" Fergal turned and ran. Horder, a man shot in the back, first on Jason Horder's tally of murdered natives, not damn' likely!—and a military judge ruling, no crime, native Irish not human people by English law.

"O'Breslin, but you've not heard what else Carmody—must tell you, I think it was—what he said about this man, it sounded—" Liam running after, calling incoherently.

"Go back, stay with the woman and boy!" Fergal shouted at him. He saw Liam drop behind reluctant, obedient, as he turned into the road at a tearing run. Long way by road, he wasn't thinking straight—he veered off to the fields, running the way he had last night, a nightmare repeated, through wet loam, over the icy little stream, and down to the big stone house. But this time he swerved left to the house-front. Couple of hundred years back when the house had been built, maybe for a clan-chief, there'd been a walled courtyard all round, but the wall stood only in front now, knocked down halfway along the side of the house for easier access to outbuildings. He ran round the wall and into the front grounds—bare turf mostly, patches of grass, a few dispirited laburnum trees—to the high windowless front, the shallow steps up to the great iron-hinged door.

There was a horse at the tethering-post by the steps, a handsome big bay. The door was wide open, and a little crowd of people huddled together half in, half out—four women, two middle-aged men, the house-servants; they looked frightened, but more pleasurably excited, and Fergal felt an upsurge of relief for their expressions. Friendly, Shevaun said, liking her, and they wouldn't be looking so if Horder— "What is it, what's happened here for God's sake?" And Carmody was coming round the house the other way, his look brightening a little on Fergal.

"Ah, O'Breslin, reckon it's good you come—I didn't like for to go in, can't get no sense out o' these folk, see?—but I do seem to make out it's somewhat to do with your poor sister, and by the noise, up somewhere there in the east wing, see—I do think—"

The older man stepped forward. "O'Breslin you are? Pardon, O'Breslin, daresay we are all a bit upset—" Upper servant-man, not just since the settlement-act, you could read it in his automatic

dignified deference, the subtly sincere respect in his tone (that he
would never have used to the English factor) for one he knew as
a clan-chief. "I don't know, I'm sure, O'Breslin, what it's about—
in he marched calm as an English officer—but the fine black Irish
curses on his tongue—and your lady-sister, somewhat to do with
her it is, for sure—Horder was out at one of the home-farms, he
came in just before all the shooting started—"

He went on talking, but Fergal did not hear; the fear for Shevaun seized him again, for that, and he brushed by the man, ran
into the vaulted stone-floored entry-hall dark and gloomy for being
north-faced; he saw the narrow spiral stone stair to one side, and
raced up it, and he cried as he ran, "Shevaun! Shevaun, answer
me—if you're here—I'm coming—"

It wasn't Sheevaun at the top of the stair, but Hugh; he caught
at Fergal's arm, and he said in a queerly soft, awed voice, "Oh,
Fergal—Fergal, thanks to God, a miracle it is, maybe blasphemous
to say, but I can't help to think it! Fergal, he says security and
shelter and a good life to come, if once we reach Galway safe—all
right it is, Fergal, we're all right, all safe here. I could not help to
think it, maybe God's wrath on us because—but it's not, I know
it now sure, God is with us, God will deliver us— Fergal, he says
fine land and freedom—"

And Maire there too, holding his other arm, talking but he
could not stop, he scarce heard what they said, he heard Shevaun's
voice down the corridor, and ran past them toward that place.
He brought up short against the doorpost, he looked into the
chamber, and his mind said to him dazedly, All a dream—a dream:
running that way after the horse, and catching up to the wife-
stealer, and all the beautiful new thing between him and Nessa,
Nessa darling—likely he had died last night, Horder or McTally
had killed him, and he'd never known it until this minute—all the
rest just a dream in death.

For it was Roy Donlevy there, Roy who was dead and lost—
Roy, same as ever in life, big solid bulk of man, heavy-shouldered,
crest of flame-red hair, not a day older he looked, of course, of
course— And Shevaun pressed close against him, head buried on
his shoulder, he holding her tight, and pistol still in his right hand.

Fergal leaned on the doorpost to keep himself upright, and
with the last breath in him he whispered, "Roy. Roy."

Donlevy turned his head. A bit more sun-browned he was, now Fergal saw clearer, and new small wrinkles about his steady blue eyes. "Well, Fergal, boy," he said pleasedly, his same deep calm voice. "Not too good you're looking, I understand you've not been having the easiest time in the world. Never mind, it's done with now—once we're out of the country safe." He patted Shevaun's back. "Now, woman, give over, you'll drown us all, go on like that."

"Roy. Roy—the letter said—dead in Spain, of wounds—"

"An exaggeration, boy, or another man's name taken for mine. Another Donlevy there was in that regiment sent to Spain, sure. Mistakes will be made, with the best intentions all round. I've just made one myself, and damn, I'm sorry—I am."

"No—" Shevaun lifted her head a little way, mopping at her eyes. "*Glad* you—he'll never hurt anyone ever again—he—"

Horder, sprawled there across the room, half on a chair, half on the floor, bloody shirt, pistol fallen from his hand, powder-bag scattering grains in a little trail. Horder, indubitably and soundly dead.

Fergal came a step into the room, almost staggering; and then a little strength came back in him, and his mind began working right again, if slow, and he said, "Oh, God, thank God, Roy," and went to embrace the two of them there together. "Roy, man, thinking I'd never see your ugly face again in this life, and not one damn' bit improved in looks you are but I'm damn' glad to see it for all that—"

"A deal you have to complain of, leading me the hell of a chase as you've done! Rid half over Connacht I have, dodging these damned English patrols, wasn't until I got hold o' Justin Desmond over the border there I had any notion where you'd gone. A friendly, decent sort of fellow he is, isn't he?" said Roy placidly.

Fergal laughed, and felt the ridiculous hot tears in his eyes for the very placidness, damn, wasn't it indeed Roy, same old Roy, never excited about anything? "Why for Christ's sake—call *that* a mistake, man?"

Donlevy looked over Shevaun's shoulder at the corpse of the factor. "Well, now," he said soberly, and his eyes were cold, "there are injuries enemies make which call for sudden death, sure to God there are. And other injuries, death only little vengeance.

No, I never meant to kill the man, I did not. I came in here to take back my wife, and well I knew I'd need to be fixing that man down here, some way, tied up secure in a closet, say, lest he come after us—all of us—before we were well away. I thought it might be a good notion, see you, to tie him up and gag him and set him up on the roof-coping, maybe, with a sign pinned on his front in both tongues—say, like, *Ireland's champion womanizer*—" Roy smiled very slowly. "Wounds from gun and knife not so deep as those taken from just laughter, folk laughing that way at a man. Not so? But he was light-cocked as a Spanish pistol, go off if you looked crooked at him, wasn't he? And a damn' bad shot, do you want to know. I didn't count, but he must've had a dozen tries at me, all up and down this corridor—never came within ten feet. No choice I had, a pity—when I managed get clear range on him, I had to drop him—and at that, I aimed for his pistol-hand, but he moved at the last minute and took it in the chest. Sorry I am, it was too good a death."

"It was that," said Fergal. "Roy, man—I don't believe this now—how come you here, where've you—what was it Hugh was babbling about out there?—remember he said—"

"Oh, we've a deal to talk over," said Roy, "yes. But right now, I do figure we'd best put first things first, and make arrangements to get away clear. I wonder, for example, if the shooting'll have been heard by any military, and they coming to investigate? Indeed, best get out we had—Shevaun, pull yourself together now, that's my good girl, come along—"

She came, stumbling after him as he moved to the door, still clinging to him. "But I'm *glad* you killed him, I'm glad, Roy—*not* a mistake!"

27

MUCH AS IT had last night, time stopping and then starting forward again. Yes, God, if any English had heard the shots, be a patrol up here double pace—have to run they would now, bridges burned with a vengeance behind them, for murder of an Englishman— and yet, stupidly, all that came to Fergal's tongue to say, as they went down to the stair, was, "Where'd you have the horse, Roy?"

"Borrowed from military stables outside Galway town. I came over last night, below Carrick, though I do understand they're not troubling much about the border these days. But small talk we'll exchange later—now, look—hell of a time I had getting back to Ireland, and some coin it cost me, and be damned if I'll let chance ill luck stop us getting out safe! Listen, Fergal. Whole story I'll tell you later, but I've a deed to land, a great piece o' good land, abroad—a safe place for us all—like as I was just telling—"

Hugh breaking in eager at his side, "You said—free, no law about religion, any can live there free and unmolested—Catholic or Protestant, Christain or Jew—"

"You and Maire McCann welcome to come," said Roy, and his gaze briefly speculative on the pair of them, "enough for all, and Shevaun saying she'd have you come."

"Oh, yes, Roy, please—"

"Four hundred acres, Fergal, good land. It's to get out of Ireland safe, now—and in time. I've arrangement with a Spanish ship-captain, he's to make Galway harbor the first week in November, he'll take us to the Continent—that gives us bare two weeks, get over to Galway from here. I didn't know I'd be awhile finding you!

Damn' lucky we're this near the border, wilder land to hide in over in Connacht—once there, we'll have a bit o' breathing space, any luck. Thing is, right now, we need to hurry, get clear off before the military get wind of this business, take me?"

"Yes," said Fergal—time rushing past now as urgent as last night, as a few minutes ago. "Yes, get out quick, away from this district anyway— God, Roy, that much land! Where—? A place to live safe, until maybe the King— Yes, get away now—" He stopped: they were down the stair, in the entry-hall; the house-servants still there inside the open door.

Roy placed the senior of them, one look: the dignified older man, Brady that would be. "Any sign of English coming?" he snapped.

That man looked back at him with interest, but spoke to the man he knew as gentry-chief. Courteously he said, "You're meaning to leave, O'Breslin? On the run from them—then the factor is dead?"

"The factor is dead," said Fergal. "There will be another, but Horder is dead."

"Reception-meeting in hell," said the manservant calmly. "No English heard the shooting, O'Breslin. It is twenty minutes, longer, and they'd have been up from the garrison by now if they'd heard, or any road-patrol going by. I sent Seumas to watch up the road. They won't be knowing now until they're told. We can give you time." He looked round at the other servants. "We can delay reporting this, until you are well away—and give false description when we report. Oh, yes, folk on farms about will have heard, but none of them will go volunteering information to English."

"Sure you are, they've had time to be on us, did they hear?" exclaimed Roy. "Good, that's good. A little time in hand—not much. You can't delay long, man, for your own safety—they'll know how long a man's been dead, hour or two either way—"

"Easy tricked, English," said the man softly, still to Fergal, "for that they always underestimate us, don't they? We'll say we were terrible frighted, and ran off—frighted to go to the garrison and tell, see you. They thinking us all feckless, stupid folk, way they do, not twice they'll think—say, crowd of silly natives, that's all. I do reckon we could give you four-five hours, O'Breslin, no danger to ourselves here."

"That's good," repeated Roy, "good. Time in hand—and, by God, loot to take from this house, factor's house, coin there'll be — Fergal—"

"Roy," said Fergal, "Roy, man, time or no, if I'm to leave Ireland, for a day or for life-span, I've a debt to pay before I go. You will take the others on to Galway, I'll meet you there later if I live—but before I go, I must settle my score with Kevin McCann—over in Longford town. A bullet I owe Kevin McCann, and life uncertain as it is—the debt I'll pay off before leaving the country, by God and all His archangels—settle the score—"

Hugh put a hand on his arm. "Fergal, leave the vengeance to God," he said strongly. "We are safe—I know it—upheld in His hand we are. Let God take His own vengeance on the evildoer, late it may be, but sure. A woman you have to think of, Fergal, and others bearing regard for you. Come now, come away, put the vengeance out of mind! Once I said to him, his soul on a short-term lease to the devil, and the mortgage due soon—soon, by this means or that. Come with us."

Fergal raised his eyes to meet Roy's, though he returned the pressure of Hugh's hand. "Not so good a Christian," he said, deadly quiet, "and not so much common sense maybe. It's a score I must settle, all I can say for the feeling in me—a reckoning I must make. I will go to make it, Roy, and God willing I'll meet you in Galway a week today."

"So," said Roy ruminatively, "a bullet you owe McCann? Well, I have news to catch up on here, as well as tales of my own to tell. Later will do for details. Longford town, is it?—how far, nine miles at most, the wrong direction. But times, longest way round is shortest way home. All right, man, we'll both go." He turned on Hugh, who was launching fresh protest. "Can we trust you to get the women safe over the border? Upwards of thirty miles to Justin Desmond's place, you can wait there safe. Every chance Fergal and I can pick up horses, even an English coach or cart, in the city—to get us all to Galway easier, in time. If you—"

Fergal took a breath, and saw how it would go; initiative and energy returned to him. "By God, yes, that's the way! You—" He caught the servant's shoulder. "You know where Horder kept his ammunition, maybe an extra pistol? Good, go and fetch it, all there is—rest o' you, look through the house for coin and value we can carry. But mind, Hugh, don't take it all, or they'll accuse the servants of looting the place—"

"Very well," and Hugh stepped back. "I see you mean to go —and that is so, about the horses. God keep you both safe. A way to take value from here and protect the servants from charge, I know where the inventory papers are, and I'll destroy those and the accounts. In any case, the military will put down the theft to us—to me, likely—when they know we have gone. I'll see to all, Fergal. An hour to collect everything and be off, with luck we'll all be across the border five hours from now."

"Good man—" Fergal saw Carmody peering in the door interestedly, and beckoned him. "Go an errand for me, Carmody, run down to my place and tell Nessa—they're to pack up everything, we're leaving here quick—say, Hugh and the others will be joining them inside the hour, to explain—and my thanks for all you've done, I'll not see you again—tell Nessa, aught we can't carry you're to have—luck with you, man!"

And Shevaun suddenly cried out, as if the sense of it just reached her, "Roy, no—don't leave me again, Roy, I won't let you—"

The manservant came back down the stair and handed Fergal two pistols, a leather pouch of powder and another filled with balls. Roy took Shevaun by the shoulders and held her away, to face him straight. "Don't you go weak on us at the very last, my girl, after all the brave spirit you've showed! Two days, less maybe, together again and all safe. You'll do this one last thing for me, Shevaun— understand?"

" Try—Roy, all right, yes, I'll try be brave—"

Roy reached inside his tunic, brought out a flat leather case. "This is the deed to the land, and you'll guard it with your life. Here," and he gave into her other hand a fat pouch, "is twenty pounds equivalent, Spanish and French coin. Just in the case of ill luck—no tears, now!—but full share we've had o' that, no more to come! You'll go with the rest over the border to Desmond's place, and Fergal and I will join you there in two days, about."

"Yes, Roy—yes."

Hugh had turned into the little room off the hall, and came back now holding out a cloth bag. "You may need money in the town, to buy horses if you can't steal. If we're to have the accusation, might as well have full profit—there's forty pounds here."

His eyes were calm and steady now on Fergal. "If you are God's instrument of vengeance on McCann, no choice you have but to go. God go with you both, and keep you safe. We will meet you at Desmond's—as and when you come."

"God go with you, Hugh, to bring you all there safe." And then they were out and down the steps, and he mounted pillion behind Roy.

"This road, northeast?"

"Right. Oh, God send they make it there without harm—but this thing I must do for my honor—tell you about it, Roy, he—"

"Don't fret yourself, boy," said Donlevy, lifting the horse to a trot. "I just said it—so much ill luck, bound to have good we are now!"

Fergal stared at Roy across the little inn-table, and he said soft, abstracted, "Drunken you'll have me, even atop of a meal— I've not tasted whiskey in half a year. . . . Brother, you're lunatic. Only word. I thought when you said *land*, France or Spain—bad enough! But, colony in America! Wild land settled by these fanatic Puritans! And the most English, and nominally under English law—"

"Not this settlement," said Donlevy. They talked low in the corner of this dim tavern: hours to kill, both of them too experienced to plan attack in light. This place was three streets off that where the bailiff of the Challoners' Guild let rooms to Kevin McCann; and they had marked down a stables not far from here, to investigate for horses later. Old and callous he was growing maybe, Fergal thought: the horses they'd get as likely belonging to Irishmen here as English, but he wasn't feeling so nice for distinctions now. . . . Longford, like as Carmody said, as full of Irish residents as before the Act, only not their own masters now, as shopkeeper, tradesman, merchant, clerk—same like the miller, carpenter, cobbler in village, profit-earners for English owners, was all.

But he wasn't thinking of the settlement-act, for once. The last seven hours seemed fantasy, one sense, and for all their long talk, on the way and secluded here—this murky crowded place, no notice paid to strangers—he felt again incredulity for Roy sitting there opposite, flesh and blood. They had told one another the tales they had to tell; he was still trying to take in Roy's, a jumble of unfamiliar backgrounds. "Damn, Roy," he said, "if it wasn't you telling me, no imagination you ever had for lies, I'd say it couldn't be so, things don't happen so easy." . . . The man from this wild place across the sea, Bradford his name, coming as representative to petition the Parliament for official colony-charter—and falling in trouble, consequent on this incredible thing Roy kept insisting, that those settlers there would have no laws in a charter as to religion, but grant right of landholding, franchise, and all legal privilege to any man, Protestant, Catholic, Hebrew or any, no fear or favor. Those folk banished from other colonies for religious views, and bound to have none such intolerance in laws they made for their own. A man named Roger Williams founding the settlement near twenty years back—well, a Welsh name that was, not a notion an Englishman would ever have— And this agent Bradford having to flee England, Cromwell's Puritans charging him with heresy, and Roy coming to know him in France. A good man, Roy said, if he was an Englishman, London-born but going out to the colonies as a young man, and driven from house and land there for his toleration of all sects. So he was sympathetic to those who suffered such persecution, and also—

"Well, he liked me," Roy had said, smiling, "and I him, you know. On garrison duty I was then, with some leisure, and he was ailing, with little money, and I used try to cheer him a bit—listen to him talk, let him win a chess game or two, you know how one does. No family he had of his own, and he knew he'd not long to live—he wanted me to have his holding. Didn't believe it at first, when he showed me his will—four hundred acres— And my enlistment wouldn't be up till March, but, the commandant let me take early discharge, seeing how it was about the legacy—"

But, in a land settled mostly by English, all roundabout this new colony—and— "It's the hell of a long way off," said Fergal, looking at his whiskey. "What's the heathenish name again?"

"The Rhodes' Island and Providence Plantations. I believe all he said about it, Fergal—and it's writ in the deed, no discrimination on any human soul for reasons of faith. And he said, good land, rich for pasturage or wheat."

"So it is good land," said Fergal. "But not Irish land. Not my Donegal land. Half across the world— Would we ever get home again, Roy, ever at all?—If the King's restored, and reverses the Act to make restoration to all of us— That's not a voyage a man

makes without thought—or money! America . . . Hell of a way.
And if restoration is made, next year or ten years away, men with
claim to have land restored ought be in reach to lay that claim
soon, or maybe get overlooked." He finished his whiskey, and
turned the empty cup on the scarred table. "I don't know, Roy."

"I said all that to myself, boy," said Donlevy soberly. "And I
went on to say to myself, So maybe Charles Stuart will one day
gain back his throne—not an Englishman he is, but not an Irishman
either. And officially he's committed to the Anglican church. Is he
indeed going to remember back to the Irish Federation Army, that
fought for him against Parliament—and he knowing well that every
Irishman in it, from O'Neill on down, gave not one damn who
ruled England, save for how it might affect Ireland? I don't know
either, Fergal," and he spread his hands, shrugged. "What I ended
up saying to myself, shortsighted sometimes sensible—me, I'll take
the cash and forgo the interest on the debt."

"And you're likely right," said Fergal heavily. "Yes. Saddled
horse safer than twin foals hoped for year after next. Not ungrateful
I am, Roy, you know that—you with no call to share. It's only—
Connacht not my place, nor Roscommon, nor Longford, but damn
what bad things happened to me those places—Irish land, and I'm
an Irishman. . . . Yes, we'll go across the world to have a look at
your fine inheritance—but—a senseless feeling, maybe, what weapon
do I or any Irishman hold here, now?—but it's a bit like as if—I
saw a soldier making rape on a virgin, and turned my back, and
said, *No business o' mine.* . . ."

And Roy reached a hand to press his arm in somber understanding silence.

Oh, yes, callous he grew—there was a time he'd have arranged
to come here, face to face with Kevin McCann, to do it all honorable; but that he didn't care about now. Come down to it, had
McCann given honorable warning, he putting three bullets in Fergal that time, cool as be damned? And honor be damned too,
thought Fergal, it wasn't, exact, to do with honor—a man expected
an acknowledged enemy to attack, different thing was friend turned
sudden traitor. . . . But think deeper, O'Breslin, past the personal
. . he'd said, seeing rape and passing by uninterfering: but McCann
the robber of his own countrymen, the dealer with English for

private profit, he was the one procured the virgin for raping, you might put it—or helped hold her down for another to take first chance at her.

Very careful Fergal cocked the second handgun, and motioned Roy back, one savage gesture. Whatever vital part presented itself in range, he'd aim at with no warning delivered—hell with honor—count even, three bullets he owed Kevin McCann, but he'd be satisfied with one repaid, so it found the heart.

"Take care," breathed Roy.

Fergal motioned him back again, to guard the rear, and started up the stair. Damn' careless Kevin grew, leaving an outside door unbolted, and the clerk in the shop at the front premises so casually ready to give information!—*McCann? right down side walk, he do have rooms on second floor o' house at back.* . . . Unless it was a trap: would Art have confessed he gave out the direction to Fergal O'Breslin? Have to chance it.

He went up the stair quick and quiet, a narrow stone stair leading straight up, and all dark—foolhardy maybe, having to feel his way each step. He should have—vindictive, cynical, even sorrowful—been remembering long-ago time, himself and his dead brother Aidan, Roy, boyhood games and friendship with Kevin McCann. He did not: all in his mind was that minute seven months back, when McCann, wide-smiling in a mirthless grin, had sent three bullets into him—and the last two while he lay helpless with the first draining his life's blood.

And to his life's end he could have told the number of steps to that stair—fifteen cautious silent steps he took, and came to a shut door on a little landing at the top, and paused there for a breath. He had a pistol in each hand, primed and cocked. He stopped there and slid the left-hand gun careful through his belt, and ran a hand over the door to find the latch-handle. He heard voices in the room beyond. Ailsa's giggle, and a drawl that was McCann, and a heavier voice that was Dermot Flynn. Hell!—two men—and no telling how placed beyond the door. Chance it— He eased down the latch and discovered that the door opened outward: and no light filled the narrow opening. He pulled it wider and slid through, and surveying the scene he reflected that McCann grew careless indeed—but he'd have been used to feeling safe here, his own place, center of the town.

Just the middle of the room lit, where a table and chairs stood: dim outline of high English bedstead in one corner, other furniture. Half a dozen candles on the table, making a little pool of light, and all about that golden circle, deep shadows. Dermot Flynn lounging there in a chair, profiled to Fergal, and Ailsa leaning on the table above him—girl indefinably grown more coarse, the man heavier for better living . . . McCann only a shape out of the light, other side of the room.

"Not so impatient, Dermot, let me fetch the whiskey and we'll discuss in civilized fashion over a drink." Cupboard-door opened there, chink of bottle from the shadows.

"Civilized, hell," said Flynn. The girl was teasing at him, whispering in his ear, plumping down on his knee uninvited; he shoved her away impatiently. "We'll talk straight, you doing the most of it, Kevin! Some questions I want answered, see—"

"Why, sure, boy," said McCann easily. "Partners we are, all open between us—why else did I bring you up here private?"

"It did cross my mind to wonder," said Flynn, and he laid his right hand casual on the pistol in his belt, to draw it half loose. He was that side on to Fergal, and ten feet away only, and Fergal saw that the gun was cocked. "I never believed your tale about Dan Kindellan—jealous o' me over a girl!—mindless hulk, not his own idea it was, try to knife me in the back! Your creature, likely you primed him with some lie about me—should've known I'd be too quick for Dan!"

"Uncharitable," drawled McCann. "The poor fellow was never strong in the head."

"For God's sake bring the whiskey and come and look me in the eye, Kevin! Afore we come on to certain private dealings you've made here and there, and fair shares held out on me, what of Art McTally? Gone off two days—on what crooked errand for you?"

McCann laughed. "Now that's really comic. His own damn' fool errand Art's on, and serve him good if he gets himself killed. . . . Yes, I'd reckoned maybe—you were holding suspicion, that sort, on me. Well, I can explain it, boy—"

Fergal drew in a silent breath of relief. Art not back, at least to see McCann. Lying low licking his wounds somewhere. Not a trap—for Fergal O'Breslin. He began to think, a trap for another man. Oh, sure to God, McCann not able to keep a straight bargain even with fellow-thieves over thievery! He smiled tightly to himself: McCann, the lone-running wolf, playing double game on Flynn and the rest too—but only just so long; in the end they knew him for what he was. And, damn, would he never come into the light, a decent target?

Flynn said, to echo that thought, "You're the hell of a time fetching that whiskey—"

And McCann laughed again. "Something else, Dermot." A little quiet snick from the shadow—hammer drawn back on a gun—and Flynn moved like lightning. Too late, the girl had been slyly reaching round to the pistol in his belt—likely on prior orders—he felt her hand and heard that ominous click at once, and he seized her in his left arm, dragged her round to cover his own body, and his own cocked gun was up toward the place McCann stood out of the light.

The two guns spoke almost simultaneous, Flynn's gesture so swift McCann had no chance to hold his fire. His ball hit the girl in the breast, true aim—she was likely dead as her weight staggered Flynn back. Flynn's shot had gone wild, smack into the wall. He whirled to take two strides out of the circle of light, gain five seconds there to recharge his gun—but cold-cautious McCann had had two pistols primed to hand, and his second shot took Flynn square between the shoulders.

Fergal raised his right-hand pistol and waited for the acrid haze of gunsmoke to clear. In a moment McCann emerged into the light, walking delicate as a big cat across the room, pistols still dangling loose from either hand. He stood over the prone, motionless Flynn, and he said, smiling, "Now that was helpful in you, my friend. That woman was coming to be a little nuisance—a relief to be rid of her."

And Fergal found at this last minute that he could not do it quite like that. Warning, no, in the sense of giving fair chance—but he wanted McCann to know whose hand sent him to his reckoning with the devil. He said in an even voice, "Not rid of either for long, Kevin—you'll be meeting next minute in hell!"

McCann jerked round, involuntary, to present easy target. Just time for vicious recognition to show in his eyes, before both bullets struck him, straight to the heart at that range.

Fergal did not wait to see him fall across Flynn; he was out the

door and down the stair in ten seconds, colliding with Roy halfway.
"What the hell, Fergal—all right are you?—an army up there? It
sounded—"

"Get out, God's sake—half the street here in a minute!"

"Well, I wouldn't say you're wrong, a bit o' noise outside already," said Roy placidly. They came out to hear running steps up
the path toward them, calling voices. They turned aside, groped
through shrubbery to a low wall, scrambled over, ran across someone's garden to a rickety wooden fence, and past that over another
patch of bare ground to another higher wall, and over. Pausing to
listen and breathe in the dark, they heard some beast whuffle low
and start at the noise.

"God grant that's not a bull," said Roy. "Now where the
hell have we got to? Here's a building of some sort, I can feel a
door—"

"Get round it, a chance it fronts on some street, and we can—
Jesus, it *is* a bull!" Long angry snorts and stampings nearby, and
sudden thunder of a short preliminary charge on the invaders. In
one prompt move they were both inside the door, and five seconds
later something large and heavy crashed against the stout wood
wall. A prolonged outraged snuffling followed.

Stable this was, by the warm odor and subdued rustlings of
horses in stall, all about. And a moving light coming this way—
they moved by instinct aside, expecting to encounter a stall-door,
but the aisle widened out at its head, apparently, to an open
space— Some dark tall object looming, and they took cover,
crouching in its shadow.

The light was a pierced iron lantern swung in the hand of an
old man who came plodding up the stable-aisle. He muttered aloud
to himself in exasperation as he came: "Now what's gone with that
daft bull? Seeing shadows again! And me alone here—damn that
feckless boy, just out to see his wench if truth told, dozen fine
excuses to beg off work—I do swear, be rid o' the lazy lout I
will—" Door opened a crack: "Here, you vexatious beast! Quiet
down now!" He waited a minute: outside, the bull gave a last loud
snort and moved away.

The old man shuffled back down the aisle. By what the fitful
lantern-light showed, this was a big stable: public city stable, stall-
space for hire, maybe forty stalls. They heard the old fellow's steps,

after the light vanished, and then nothing: his little quarters at the stable-front would be out of earshot here if they talked low.

And in the minute before they moved, suddenly the waning moon sailed out of a cloud-bank and shot a broad stream of light into this place through a little window high in the wall. They were in what had been a great store-barn attached to the stables, good sixty feet square; but it held no piles of grain now. It was, evidently, hired-out space for coaches—for the few high-gentry English here, army officers, important bailiffs, who would keep such for prestige. Six or eight carriages, and the biggest the one they crouched beside, a tall four-horse traveling coach with a crest on the door-panel.

Fergal and Roy looked at each other in the moonlight. Roy whispered, "Boy, what did I say?—and that renegade monk o' yours, too? God's hand over us, safe enough!"

No need for longer words. The means to hand, the way opened as if by miracle. Stableman alone, easy overpowered and bound—and an important-looking coach to carry the women, extra horses to take for the men—no difficulty crossing past the garrison at Carrick, and no challenge or suspicion, in such a vehicle, all the way over to Galway—good time made, any pursuit sent after would have no hope of catching up.

"You've had the most action tonight," said Roy amusedly. "I'll go and take the old fellow, and careful not to hurt him, sure, we just want him out o' the way six-eight hours! Is either of us clever enough to unravel the mysteries of English carriage-harness?"

Fergal laughed. "God helping us thus far, even that He'll reveal to us!"

Roy pressed his arm and went off silent down the aisle. Fergal waited there, and he thought, First step toward a new piece of life ... this piece done with. Wild land, half across the world—and what to come? Not a journey a man made frequent or easy—the odds were, ten days or so from now, leaving his own land not to set foot here again.

The house at Lough Eask, sun shimmering on blue water (and a precious manuscript-book hid under the hearthstone, record of this race)—his mother's eyes trying to smile as she gave him farewell, he riding out to war—

He leaned on the English coach, as the moon drifted somber

through another cloud-bank, and he thought desolately, No weapon in our hands now to defend, no. He had admitted the sense of it: bird in the hand, so the English proverb said.

But there was another proverb, for Irishmen to remember. *Who waits, and gathers stones, will find a time to throw them.*

At the back of his mind, brief and vague, that English captain: *bad seed we sow.*

He heard Roy coming back, running light up the aisle: "All right, Fergal! We can get on—"

And Nessa, his darling, if God was good, waiting over there for him. Ireland, wilds of America, anywhere in the world, a deal of life still to be lived—sure to God there was! And he thought, I can tell Hugh, Maire is free, to be wed to him and make the babe legal-born.

He took a breath, and straightened, and went to meet Roy.

Epilogue

Providence Plantation
March 1662

FERGAL HAD JUST come in from the barn that midmorning, to complain bitterly of his eldest son's defection. "Old enough for some responsibility, all I say, and he knows he should help me clear the stalls, I've mentioned it often enough. Aidan!—oh, I daresay he's off to school by now."

"Mercy to God, we did forget to tell you," said Nessa, "Hugh asked him to come early to school today, to help with the younger ones—he says Aidan is quite good with them, you know he's always patient with Rory. Out of my way, *if* you please, Fergal—" She was wielding the broom vigorously, and he told her to take care or she'd be miscarrying. "Don't be silly, I am quite all right—and Aidan is learning responsibility by that, as well as he'd be else, which you can't deny. Hugh says he's very clever for not quite seven—" She uttered a little scream of vexation as the kitchen door was flung open to let in a gust of wind and scatter her sweepings. "Really, Sean!—oh, mercy, is it your mother gone into labor? I'll come at once—"

"No, Mother's fine— Uncle, Hugh says you're to come right away, to the docks—I was in town on an errand for Father, and Hugh was just coming—he sent me to tell you—you're to hurry! It's somewhat to do with a ship just in—he was that excited, so it must be important—"

Fergal acknowledged it; Hugh was seldom excited; but a damn' nuisance, have to ride into town. He dodged Nessa's broom again and went out to saddle a horse. "Uncle, can I take the colt? Careful I'll be, really I will—"

"All right, but see you are, I don't want his mouth ruined."

"Hugh said to hurry—"

When they rode into Providence settlement a mile down the road, Fergal found a little interested crowd at the dock. Out in the bay were the masts of a good-sized bark, and he could hear Hugh somewhere in the crowd arguing at someone. "You will have the money, though it's extortion and an un-Christian thing—" And murmurs of agreement from the townsfolk. He pushed through.

"What's this about, now?" Big unshaven lout of a fellow with a grip on the arm of another man—Hugh turned to him in relief, but Fergal's gaze was widening on that man. Thin and ragged, unshaved for a month, and looking to be starved and exhausted, still— "By God, is it, can it be—*Justin Desmond*?"

Desmond smiled faint and accepted his hand; his own felt only bone, and he leaned on the arm Fergal put round him. "God's love, man, you're a walking skeleton—talk later we'll make, come and sit down, I'll get you some food—"

"Five pound," growled the big fellow. "Extra trouble I took, never meant come s' far north, him sayin' there was folk here he knowed, t' pay passage for him—and many a man'd have laughed in his face, chance a wild tale like that, him a castaway without a whole shirt—"

"For God's sake, all right, you'll have your five pounds! Hugh—have you got the coin convenient?—any o' you—I'll pay back—" And he added, "Sure to God, wouldn't you know a Virginia man'd expect pay to do charity!" The big man talked Virginia; he flushed angrily at that jibe, but kept a hand on Desmond while Hugh and old John Mawling and the D'Anjou brothers made up the sum among them.

"Right I had, my master, if he couldn't pay passage, indenture him to work it out—"

"Oh, yes, we all know you keep slaves in Virginia colony," said Mawling, and spat deliberately between the ship-captain's feet. Fergal took Desmond's weight as the Virginian let him go.

"Come on, boy, just a bit of way—Hugh, help me with him—take him up to your place, nearest—Desmond, I can't credit it—"

* * *

With a solid meal in him, looking already a little stronger, Desmond told them his story. "Nought unusual," he prefaced it with a grimace—the bare bones of it soon told. Wife and two children dead of a plague, last year; he'd been taken by revenue-patrol last November, and shipped for slave-sale to Jamaica. But a dozen men of that shipment had got away, the ship anchoring to take water at the isle of Bahama; and they stole a native craft, hoping to reach the mainland of the Floridas where there were Spanish Catholics to ask aid of.

"No seamen amongst us—I don't know if any of the rest lived —we were caught in a storm, and I was carried overboard—hell of a great wave, I thought I was done. But I got to an island—" And the Virginian bark taking him off. "A long chance, I'd no notion if you'd ever reached here—and no idea the land was so big! And eight years, a deal can happen in that time. I'd not be a burden to you—"

"Don't talk soft, man, you'll not be. Time past, you've made me a few favors. Heart up, Justin—better times to come, thank God you got free of them! We'll feed you up to yourself again"— Fergal clapped him on the shoulder—"and you'll take up land here—" He thought but did not say, perhaps find another wife to breed you good sons for that land.

"Land—I've no money to—"

"You don't need it, boy, free for the plowing. We're always glad of new settlers here, small community as we are."

"Free?" said Desmond, incredulous. "Free? I—do you tell me that? And—I remember you said it—no legal proscription—for religious faith—I can't believe that—"

"Not in this settlement. You're all right now, Justin, the bad time past. . . . So they are still collecting the superfluous Irish natives for slave-revenue. We'd wondered—we don't hear much news here, you know—"

Desmond rested his head in his hands, "Captain o' the slave-ship—he jested about it, yes. Said the market might be getting glutted—he reckoned, upwards of two hundred thousand Irish sold to slave-dealers this past nine years. At the port of Tangier, all the Mediterranean ports, Jamaica and the West Indies isles. Yes, they're still at it, but the profit's slackened off, some. But you—you all look to be doing well here, then? You've prospered, land as you hoped and all?"

"Well, we've done, yes." He told Desmond how it had gone. Himself and Roy with good fields, fine pasture, cattle and horses. Liam Fagan, and a good man he turned out to be, wed to the eldest Sullivan girl; Roy had known Sullivan in France, one of the few Irishmen who had managed to smuggle out wife and family to him, and they had come to take up land here four years back. One of the priests here had come with them from France, an Irishman too, a couple from the Spanish settlements to the south, and a church being built now. Other Irish had come from the Continent where they had lived precariously, hearing of this haven, and doubtless more would be coming. Hugh welcomed here as school-master, he and Maire with their own house by the school, settled and happy with two sons and a daughter, handsome clever children. Shevaun with three more of her own, another to come any day, and he and Nessa hoping for a daughter now, in June, after the two sons.

And as he talked, it came to him (the days going by easy and ordinary, and the important insidious changes the years wrought scarce noticed for the little days obscuring them)—it came to him how deeply changed they all were, what inevitable (and violent or subtle) changes had come, for a handful of Englishmen drawing up new law—a hundred years back, sixty, forty, twenty years back: for men's ideas about God getting intertwined with politics—for the lust of power over other men, in the name of God or the devil.

Briefly, a little wonderingly, he thought of himself—the clan-chieftain: God, eleven years ago this month, he and Roy shivering naked on Atlantic shore, escaping off the Arans. And the women, learning and living new kinds of lives—the gentry-women out of the big stone houses with dozens of servants. Nessa sweeping her kitchen floor . . . Maire McFadden proud of her five rooms of little wood-frame house, her fine kitchen-garden. Hugh, birthed violent out of backwater into life—and the better, stronger man for it.

"It's good to hear—you prosper," said Desmond dully; and Fergal laid a hand on his shoulder.

"Thoughtless I am, you ought be in bed. Come up, man, I'll help you."

* * *

But a night's rest and more food gave Desmond strength to talk more, next day. . . . Fergal was unwontedly silent as he bolted the doors, Nessa banking down the hearthfire meanwhile, and they prepared for bed.

"Did I tell you, Fergal, that cat Shena has got herself with another litter of kits—imagine. We did think those last summer must be the last, she's quite old. . . . Fergal, I was just thinking about Margaret Christy—you know. You think—?"

He grunted, folding away his shirt and doublet neat in the bed-chest. "For Justin? Women—always matchmaking! Give the man time to catch his breath!"

"Oh, I didn't mean to go flinging her at him right away. . . . You're brooding on all he told."

"Would I not be," he said heavily, and turned to look at her. "Not you?"

"I don't know," she said, low. She was sitting up in the bed, rebraiding her loosened brushed hair; she dropped her hands and made a little gesture. "It's—like as if—another life."

"Yes," he said. For quite a long while, he remembered—the voyage to the Low Countries, and the longer, harder voyage all across that world of Atlantic sea, and the first seasons here—they had used to talk hopeful for it, one day going home again. Their own land, the ways and tongue and folk they knew. This was shelter and a good living, but— They had said, if and when the King should take back the throne he would surely repeal the Act of Settlement and the Penal Laws as well. But in time, with all there was to do here, not so often had they talked of it. The children coming, and new ways to learn for seeding and harvesting, new ways to plan as the stock-herds grew.

They had heard the news of the iron general's death four years back—after he had tyrannized over Englishmen too, and earned much deserved hatred. They had heard the news of the King's restoration two years ago, and they had wondered eagerly then—but, as he told Desmond, they had little news from abroad, half across the world. Well, now they knew; from Desmond they heard the outcome of it.

"How would Charles Stuart dare reverse the Act of Settlement, or the Penal Laws?" Desmond had asked bitterly. "He's had enough of living hand-to-mouth in exile—he's not off to do one thing that would rouse all those Parliament supporters against him, maybe to start civil war all over again. Oh, yes, a cautious way he'll go in England, to favor men who lost land and money through siding with the Royalists—the Penal Laws are all but forgot in England, no notice paid to them—and why not? There isn't a handful of Catholics left there now, they've all fled or changed allegiances. But Ireland, that's a different business altogether. Reverse that Act, rescind the Penal Laws, he'd bring down on him the wrath of fifty thousand of his most influential subjects, for taking away the fortunes they own in Ireland, their profit off Irish land. He couldn't risk it—and he's fond of money himself, and the Crown holds a deal of that land, to add to his own income. But some legal notice had to be taken all the same, and an excuse trumped up to keep the Act in force some way. How? Why, boys, the canniest politicians in England drew up that bill, to present all solemn to Parliament. If you're off to tell a lie, any politician knows, don't go halfway at it—the bigger you make it, the more plausible it sounds—to those who want to believe it."

New Act for the Settlement of Ireland, without doubt soon to pass Parliament and become official law of the land. Relating a marvelous piece of fiction indeed: how rebellious Irish subjects, every native in Ireland, had deliberately fomented revolution and treason against honest English law. But they had been peacefully pacified by loyal Protestant citizens, who punished the bloodthirsty lawless rebels only righteously as became upright Christians, only by enforcing already existing law, no killing or imprisonment but the utmost Christian charity showed them. And the same upright citizens subsequently, most righteous, restored His Gracious Majesty to his rightful throne, to swear fealty to him. And loath as His Majesty was to penalize the very few of his Irish subjects who had not joined rebellion, his royal honor was incumbent upon him to obey those same laws passed by the Parliament in the reign of his grandsire James Stuart near sixty years ago, to confirm the tenancy of loyal English subjects to all the land in Ireland, in accordance with that law denying all citizens' rights and landownership to Papists.

"It's a delayed jest on both sides," Desmond had said cynically.

"This, it just continues the Act in force, under the Crown instead of Parliament. And they've added provisions to the Penal Laws, to oppress us even further. But their settlement scheme has failed, and that they've had to admit, and that's our jest on them. They meant to destroy us as a people, to empty the land and populate it with English. But you know how that went—the English won't come to occupy, all they want is the profit off the land, so they need us to work the land and earn the profit for them. They stopped trying to keep the Connacht border guarded years back, and they've had to forget that one of the Penal Laws about not renting to Irish tenants—there's none other they can rent to. They're now busy taking back all of Connacht, rescinding all those little land-grants they handed out, and granting all the province to new English owners. What were the figures, as near as anybody could guess? —two and a half million of us they killed, between '48 and '51, and how many starved to death since, and maybe another quarter million sold into slavery abroad. Well, the population's building up again, slow but regular, in spite of everything, the herds growing, the land under plow. For every Englishman living in Ireland on the stolen land, there are five thousand Irish still alive and still breeding. What they've accomplished, where up to fifty, sixty, seventy years back they held all the ports and controlled all trade, now they have it all—all of Ireland—it all belongs to them by their law, down to the tenants on the stolen land. No native Irishman has any legal rights, we are not regarded as human beings by law. They've destroyed the whole structure of our people, the only class of Irish now is lowest tenant-farmer, and that below the lowest-bred English soldier patrolling to protect the English bailiffs and land-agents. Laws in to keep us that way, no gap in the hedge to crawl through now. Hanging offense to try to leave the country, for any native—men no longer let to take service as foreign mercenaries—they need us to work the land for them. And we must pay tithes to the Church of England. Hanging offense to educate our children, to live in towns, to enter trades or professions, be aught but tenant-farmers thankful to earn just enough to pay for a roof of sorts over our heads and just enough food to live on. Churchmen all still renegades, hanged where they catch them. But they've concocted a new law for us too. The only Irish who have any legal rights at all, who are free of the Penal Laws, are those who turn officially Anglophile as they term it, to renounce the Catholic Church and swear fealty to the Church of England. And aside from any matter of religious conscience, what man with any pride of race in him, any love of country, will do that—to oblige the enemy? Slaves! They don't put fetters on us at home, but they might as well." Desmond put hand to brow in defeated gesture.

And Fergal said slowly, "I wouldn't say owning the tenants whole, Justin. No. No, I wouldn't say that at all. Talk of organized rebellion?"

"Man, half a million tenant-farmers living near the bone on just enough to keep body and soul together? On what the English landlords let them keep? And every house searched regular for weapons? Talk! But I can't see any chance of joined action, not for a long time to come."

"But it will come," said Fergal. "As Irishmen, we both know it will come. Soon or late."

Now he finished putting his clothes away, and went to make sure the window was shut. He snuffed the candle and got into bed beside her. He said, abstractedly echoing her words, "Another life . . ." So it was done, the last die cast, and for certain they all knew now.

Or did they? Did they?

This was good land; they had a good living here, and they were free. But it was not home, it would never be home.

And perhaps it was a strange thought he had, that followed on that thought. Any Irishman knew, there would come rebellion against the slave-masters. Likely many rebellions—over how long a time? All the time it would take. But if those at home could not win back freedom—at whatever effort— How long might it last, the oppression and the slavery? With England's military strength, it might be generations. But any Irishman knew, not forever.

This would never wholly be home, for any of the Irish who had, this way or that way, escaped from the oppression and slavery, because they had left something unfinished at home. Their own nation, so long a proud and free nation, under the heel of the foreign tyrant. Whether any of them here and now could ever go home again, their sons, the succeeding generations, would remember the story and the race duty. To the end of the world, and whatever should come to the world. That at whatever end, at whatever cost and at whatever time, that nation should somehow again be free and whole.

He drew her close, pulling the blanket warm about them, and he thought of how many of his countrymen were lying hungered and cold—at home—tonight. He laid his hand on the warm roundness that was the child in her body, and he said into the darkness, "Another life." But it meant something different as he said it that time.

For, he thought, to the end of the world, wherever in this world Irishmen found themselves, whatever else they would do, whatever else other men should ever say of them, those keeping honor and honesty would forever be passionately concerned for the religious and political freedom of all men—from their own stark knowledge of the lack of it.

For, please God, the line would breed true.

Author's Note

THE PENAL LAWS remained in legal force in Ireland until 1838. Not until after the 1916–1921 War of Independence were three of the provinces liberated and the independent Republic of Ireland established in 1922.

CRITIC'S CHOICE
Captivating historical romances

CRITIC'S CHOICE

Espionage and Suspense Thrillers

THE ADVERSARY A. M. Kabal	$3.50
THE CITY OF FADING LIGHT Jon Cleary	$3.95
THE CHINESE FIRE DRILL Michael Wolfe	$3.50
DECISION IN BERLIN Robert Dege	$3.95
THE DEVIL'S VOYAGE Jack L. Chalker	$3.95
THE FACTORY Jack Lynn	$3.95
FATAL MEMORY Bruce Forrester	$3.95
THE FORTRESS AT ONE DALLAS CENTER R. Lawrence	$3.50
FREEZE William Raynor & Myles Wilder	$3.95
THE HOUR OF THE LILY John Kruse	$3.95
KENYA John Halkin	$3.95
THE LAST PRESIDENT Michael Kurland & S.W. Bart	$3.95
THE PALACE OF ENCHANTMENTS Hurd & Lamport	$3.95
THE TERRORIST KILLERS Geoffrey Metcalf	$3.95
THE TWO-TEN CONSPIRACY Leon LeGrand	$3.95
THE VON KESSEL DOSSIER Leon LeGrand	$3.95